THE ISLAND OF THE WOMEN
AND OTHER STORIES

George Mackay Brown (1921–96) was one of the twentieth century's most distinguished and original writers. His lifelong inspiration and birthplace, Stromness in Orkney, moulded his view of the world, though he studied in Edinburgh at Newbattle Abbey College, where he met Edwin Muir, and later at Moray House College of Education. In 1941 he was diagnosed with pulmonary tuberculosis and lived an increasingly reclusive life in Stromness, but he produced, in spite of his poor health, a regular stream of publications from 1954 onwards. These included *Loaves and Fishes* (1959), *A Calendar of Love* (1967), *A Time to Keep* (1969), *Greenvoe* (1972), *Hawkfall* (1974), *Time in a Red Coat* (1984) and, notably, the novel *Beside the Ocean of Time* (1994), which was shortlisted for the Booker Prize and won the Saltire Book of the Year.

His work is permeated by the layers of history in Scotland's past, by quirks of human nature and religious belief, and by a fascination with the world beyond the horizons of the known. He was honoured by the Open University and by Dundee and Glasgow Universities. The enduringly successful St Magnus Festival of poetry, prose, music and drama, held annually in Orkney, is his lasting memorial.

D1459467

GEORGE MACKAY BROWN

*The Island of the Women
and Other Stories*

Polygon

This edition first published in Great Britain in 2006 by
Polygon, an imprint of Birlinn Ltd
West Newington House
10 Newington Road
Edinburgh
EH9 1QS

www.polygonbooks.co.uk

9 8 7 6 5 4 3

ISBN: 978 1 904598 90 9

First published by John Murray (Publishers) Ltd in 1998

Copyright © the estate of George Mackay Brown

All rights reserved. No part of this publication may
be reproduced, stored, or transmitted in any form, or
by any means electronic, mechanical or photocopying,
recording or otherwise, without the express written
permission of the publisher.

The moral right of the author has been asserted

British Library Cataloguing-in-Publication Data
A catalogue record for this book is available on request
from the British Library

Typeset by Hewer Text (UK) Ltd, Edinburgh
Printed and bound by Clays Ltd, St Ives plc

Contents

The Island of the Women

The horizon, as far as the eyes of the girl could span, quivered. Between the horizon and the furthest spur of rock, the sea was a gray herd moving towards the shore. On the spur of rock wave after wave was wounded, gash and arch and scatter of silver spray: they dragged shorewards, one after the other, and died there, among the sand and pebbles, with long sighings and susurrations. All day, until the wind-driven trek of ocean from the west stilled towards sundown, the waves would perish on the shore with monotonous regularity. Yet it seemed to the girl that the sea, after the gale, had a happy sound along the coast. It was not so much death as consummation, the end of a long journey, the handing-over of a multitude of sweet secret messages.

What was that? – a flagon bobbing among the rocks, a sudden gleam and wallow? (The skippers did send messages of half-hopeless human urgency that way sometimes, a fragment of writing pushed into an empty wine flagon, and sealed, and flung overboard. That there was a sick man – so-and-so – on board; that there was a fine school of whales just under the horizon, ripe and drowsy for the harpooning; that there seemed to be a new island to the north, among drifts of sea-haar – let word of that be brought soon to the king; or simply, 'I love thee well, my sweetheart, Brenda, I will be home soon and in thy arms' . . .)

The dark gleam rose, between two surges, and was a bull-seal, a magnificent animal with immense eyes and silver-gray pelt. Then, off the skerry, the water was thronged with seals. They drifted slowly here and there, their faces set towards the sudden sun-glittering heave of ocean. The bull remained apart, in his ring of water. He looked up at her. The girl pursed her lips, whistled. The wind took the brief shrill music out of her mouth and blew it inland, scattered, towards the mountains. She laughed; she loved the unknowable seals almost as much as her horse and her hawk.

Then, as she walked on along the goat path, the sun dazzled directly on the sea where the seals swam; it cancelled them in gold intolerable rinsings of light. The herd was still there; the girl's ear could detect the selkie-noise among the many sounds of the sea.

She whistled again, long and thin, into the sea wind and the net of light.

It was time for her to turn, to be getting home. The first of the suitors was expected today, from Brittany, about noon. There might be more than one; so many were coming.

The waves died, monotonous and seemingly fulfilled, among sand and pebbles and rockpool; the broken water was drawn back again into the blue immensity: ocean acknowledges no death.

The girl sat down on a stone at the side of the goat path. She would rest for a hundred wave-falls; then she must turn and go back to her father's Hall, and the new life. This was the last day of her freedom.

She would of course obey her father's wishes to the last detail. That was her duty and her fate and her desire. Yet she resented the unknown trappings and ceremonies of the estate that she was about to enter. She sometimes thought she could never endure it; her heart would break, she would go out of her mind, if she had to live far from this corner of Norway, with a man perhaps that she would not like, for the long remainder of her life. But that was what it was to be a woman, the only daughter and heir of a rich merchant. It was always possible that the chosen husband would be a good kind man, and that she would grow to love him in time. But the resentment still moved in her, a little vinegar in the veins; it curdled, but dissolved soon in the warm expectant blood of late girlhood.

She whistled into a lull of wind. The sun-dissolved seals stirred and eddied. She laughed. The rage against fate, against what society ordained, never lasted long. Marriage would be a perilous venture, fraught with miracles, or loss, or mere boredom.

She yawned. She had been up since before sunrise, sewing the small pearls into the bodice of the white wedding-gown, candlesplashed among old Maria and the girls.

Another long wave gathered, curled, hung, died in dazzling joyous ruin: and out of the ruin, flung high, a dark-green flagon lay streaming on the sand! A message out of the sea! The girl rose. She scaled the shallow cliff, going quickly down with skilled feet and hands, until she stood among crackles of dry seaweed. She turned. A young bright-fleshed stranger was standing between her and the sounding sighing verge! – a castaway or a pirate.

Before she could gather her wits, the stranger said, 'I know you, girl. I have known you for a long time. We've been watching you since you were a child. We've come to love you. You should not do this thing that's being forced on you. You'll be unhappy for ever. We love you. There's nothing we won't do for you. Come now, quickly, I am a king in the west' . . .

What the man said was strange and astounding, and the mode of its delivery was marvellous too; his mouth when he spoke was like a struck sea-harp.

Near his feet, along a rock, lay an empty seal-pelt. The sun, dazzling again suddenly out of a rockpool, confused the girl still more.

The stranger took a step towards her. His naked feet left no prints in the sand. She put out her hand between him and herself. That frail defence was scattered. The stranger entangled her, arms and knee and mouth. Her mouth struggled, fluttered, failed, was a tight flower, opening flower, scattered flower. There was blood on her arm from the quick blue scratch on his face. She kissed him on the wound, then on his mouth. His arms relaxed. She turned, she broke free. Her feet scurried in the sand, crashed among dry seaweed, left the shore. She flew up the cliff as quick as a bird (or so it seemed to her, telling it all to the old woman later, beside the fire). As she hung, breathless, against the goatherd's stone, she heard the enchanting voice again, 'It *will* happen. You can't escape this. Be miserable in your rich prison for a while. My name is Imravoe, King of Suleskerry. I will come for you in the end' . . .

She was sitting quietly on the stone, her eyes blinking against another sunburst. The dream was broken. It was a matter for wonderment, and slow laughter. She had sat too long last night among the candles, over the love-gown. She had in truth never moved from this stone. It was a dream begotten of sun and resentment and sea-dazzle. She kneaded her eyes. The little beach below was empty; there was neither a spread of selkie-skin nor the message-bearing bottle. The seals had moved out of their sun-prison and were splurging and eddying further out, all about the squat powerful head of the bull. Neither he nor any of his tribe seemed to be in the least concerned with her existence.

The girl said, in the small correct voice she used to the chaplain and her tutor and the guests from ship or distant castle, 'I have fallen asleep. I had a dream. My father is rich and influential. There are a dozen young men coming to make offers for my hand in marriage, from all over Scandinavia and far beyond. My father is good and considerate. He won't force me to marry any suitor that I don't like – I know that. So Imravoe, handsome dream-king in the west, I must take another road. I must go in at another door, and be at last a wife and a mother.

But I think I won't forget the beautiful harp of your mouth, Imravoe, though it was only a dream-song, and dream-kisses.'

She got to her feet. She waved farewell to the indifferent seal-dance below. But, before she turned, the bull-seal, alone of the tumultuous congregation, turned his full dark melting eyes on her.

Her mouth was a cold shell. Her cheek was salt-crusted. There were five petals of blood on her wrist.

When the girl came round the corner of the last crag she saw three strange ships anchored in the bay below her father's Hall. She hoped devoutly that they were merchants from France or England; or envoys from the king in Bergen; or new ships that her father had bought for his timber and walrus trade.

When she arrived in the courtyard her old nurse Maria met her and told her what her heart now most dreaded to hear: the first three suitors had arrived.

She met them at the long table in the Hall during supper. They were all, in their different ways, impressive young men. Tryg was a Swede from Gothenburg, fair-bearded, a soldier, one of the king's bodyguard in the east. His bravery and chivalry had been spoken of long before she set eyes on him. He threw back his head and laughed often, and then looked eagerly from face to face at the table, as if life was a business of huge enjoyment and he could not have enough of it (because all too soon, especially for soldiers, the well is drained and dry).

A slender dark youth sat beside Tryg. His name was Oswald and he came from Jutland. He was a famous skald among the great houses of that land. It was said that some rich and beautiful ladies in the south were in love with him for his talents. Very occasionally Oswald put his dark melting eyes on the girl and then looked away, half offended, from the cold blue look she gave him in return. After supper Oswald sang two new songs on a harp, one heroic, one about love; and all the people in the Hall applauded his skill. But when the poet looked at her for whom the songs had been especially composed, she had not, in the midst of all the clapping audience, put one hand to another.

The third suitor was a German princeling. He was not as handsome and gay as Tryg the soldier, nor so talented as the skald Oswald, but his wealth put them both to shame. On his arm he had a ring of pure gold, and some master craftsman had carved the intricate dragon design on it. A great silver-smith had made the brooch at his throat, set with pearls and opals. The stuff of the blouse he wore was silk brought by caravans and camels from the furthest east, and his shoes were made of dark subtle Spanish leather. The young prince Wilhelm spoke little. There was no need to speak. His clothes and his jewellery proclaimed to all the world his wealth and status. This girl would live in splendour and ease all her life if she married him. She would drink out of emerald cups.

The Norwegian merchant, the father, smiled and nodded among this brave company, and frequently raised his wine-cup. Powerful and famous men had come in quest of his daughter: his house and lineage were securely established for many more generations, after he himself was dead.

But when, near midnight, he looked for the girl, he saw her sitting alone in a far corner of the main hall. 'Well, of course,' he said to himself, 'it is no easy matter, it is in fact a very serious business, for a young girl to choose the man she must live with for the rest of her life. It must be bewildering for her, so many different accomplishments. She is thinking how painful it will be to leave her home and horse and hawk – all she is familiar with. But I would like to know, all the same, what is in her mind and heart' . . .

Dancers shuttled between him and his lonely daughter. When the music stopped and the dance was a still loom at last, he looked again and saw that his daughter was no longer in the great chamber. She had, perhaps, gone to bed.

Tryg was laughing louder than ever beside the fire. Oswald was in the middle of a group of girls, turning his black melting eyes from one to another. The German princeling glittered, magnificently alone.

But she was not in her room.

They found her, near midnight, down at the shore, looking seaward across a dark heave of water.

In her chamber she stayed for seven days afterwards, until the three suitors had gone home. She would not so much as say goodbye to any of them. In vain her father beat with his fists on her door, and sometimes murmured gently through the panels, and sometimes shouted in a loud hectoring voice. She would not take the bar off for him or for anyone.

Only old Maria was allowed in, with water for her hands and face in the morning, and with a tray of fish or fowl at noon, and in the evening to unlace her and comb out her long bright hair.

On the seventh evening she told the old woman about Imravoe.

Oswald's sail, the third and the last, disappeared among the islands. The girl came out of her chamber then. Her father turned away from her. Her behaviour had deeply wounded him. She went at once down to the rocks. The shore was empty. But on the western horizon stood a strange sail, red as a butterfly. The sail quivered in the summer wind. She wandered for miles along the coast. Not one sleek seal-head broke the sea-surface. She wept for a while among the shells and stones, when she thought of how she had hurt her father. She wept for her own foolishness. Imravoe the seal-prince had surely been a dream. Even if it was not a dream, how could a girl with warm blood ever marry a cold sea-creature! She wept because the dream, though beautiful, had been false.

When she neared the Hall, going back by cliffs that the sea had gnawed here and there into caves, she saw the ship with the scarlet sail anchored out in the bay. There, coming to meet her from the main door of the Hall, were her father and the most handsome man she had ever seen. Her father said to her, half sternly and half kindly, 'My daughter, here is the lord Odivere from Iceland. He has come to see us on a certain matter of business. I hope that you will give him a fairer hearing than you gave to certain others who were here recently.'

The man was young. His beard was a golden fleece from nostril to throat. He put a grave steady look on her. Then he smiled, tilting back his head and narrowing his eyes a little. He even laughed, as though he was glad to be out of all the sea dangers between Iceland and Norway; but mostly, it seemed, for joy at finding such beauty on the far shore. His laughter was not like the wild extravagant death-defying laughter of Tryg the Swedish soldier. He laughed like a man who has come home after a long voyage. The girl smiled. She took both his hands in hers.

'I am pleased to see you, Odivere,' she said.

Her father looked anxiously from one face to the other.

This fourth suitor was wealthy too. He had three good well-carved rings on his fingers, that he wore modestly; not flashing his splendour in the eyes of the world like that arrogant German princeling.

'I hope you will bide with us for some time,' she said to Odivere.

Her father smiled from face to face as they passed from the sunlight into the Hall. He called for a cup of wine for the traveller – no, three cups – to celebrate his safe and welcome and much-hoped-for arrival, around the fire.

And then, over the wine, the young man began to describe his voyage to them; how a south-easterly gale had driven his ship half-way to Greenland; how they had sailed among a great school of whales to the north of Faroe; how they had heard strange singing in the waters between Shetland and Orkney, and the helmsman had shouted excitedly that he had seen a mermaid (but it could only have been the glitter of the moon which is so intense that ear is enchanted as well as eye, and imagines ineffable harp-strokes); how, further east, they had been gently besieged by a great herd of seals . . . The young lord Odivere had a vivid tongue, and she thought his descriptions far superior to the stylised bombast that the poet Oswald chanted above his harp.

'My friend,' she said. 'You have travelled a long distance. You must be tired. I have greatly enjoyed listening to the story of your voyage – especially the herd of seals that came about your ship. Now I think you should go to bed. I will get Suena and Broda, my girls, to make up a bed for you. Have a good sleep. I look forward very much to see you again in the morning.'

Her father set down his cup; he came between them and threw his arms round both their necks, and put their faces together.

Suena and Broda were summoned from the kitchen to make a bed for the lord Odivere.

They went on speaking pleasantly for a short while, until Broda called from the south bed-chamber that the blankets were spread now. The traveller bade his hosts goodnight gravely. He raised the girl's hand to his mouth. The girl inclined her head.

The father's face dimpled and flashed with joy.

When Odivere disappeared at last through the door of his bed-chamber, the girl said to her father, 'I think I love this man. I am sorry for grieving you this past week. This man I will take for my husband, if he asks me.'

'He has asked *me*,' said the merchant. 'I have given my consent.'

Later, when the cups had been cleared away and the fire

banked down, she went to see if their visitor was comfortable. What she heard on the threshold of his chamber made her pause and listen again: scufflings, whispers, the sounds made by dark hot lips, Broda's silly giggles.

The girl returned on tiptoe, trembling, to her own chamber.

She did not sleep for a long time, because her room was full of sea-glitter and sea noises. (It was getting on for mid-summer.)

When she rose next morning her father was making arrangements already for the marriage and the marriage feast; so many sheep and pigs would have to be slaughtered, so many loaves and cakes baked, so many hogsheads of ale brewed. And it wouldn't be the chaplain in the Hall either, old Father Paul, who would perform the ceremony – a horse-man was already on his way to the bishop at Nidaros.

The Icelander greeted the girl kindly and lovingly next morning. She suffered him to put a kiss on her hand. Her face trembled when she looked at him. It was impossible, surely, what she thought she had heard beyond the curtain last night. It had been another false dream. Broda and Suena passed from kitchen to table with the breakfast plates, looking prim and cold as always. When they were alone she suffered him to put a kiss on her cheek.

Her father took Odivere aside after the meal to discuss the question of dowry.

After the splendid marriage in Norway the lord Odivere took his bride west to Orkney, where a large farm had been prepared for him in one of the islands. This estate he had purchased with the dowry.

There the young couple settled down. Odivere oversaw the work of the farm and opened trading connections with Ireland and Denmark. He had plenty to do, dealing with skippers and farm-workers and foreign merchants.

The lady Odivere organised the household. This she learned to do well after a winter or two. She had brought from Norway her old nurse Maria, and under Maria's tactful instruction she learned how to deal with servants, and all the work of spinning-wheels and butter-churns and the baking of bread that women servants have to carry out under the supervision of the mistress of the house. The lady Odivere herself saw to it that the Hall where they lived was beautifully furnished, and clean, and full of fragrant smells whenever a stir of wind blew the curtains apart.

In time – after a little initial resentment and suspicion on the part of the islanders, who always turned away from anything new – the lady Odivere came to be liked by everyone on the estate. Even the tinkers who passed through uttered her name with a nod of the head. She was generous and considerate to everyone, as a great lady should be. In the end she was loved from end to end of the Orkneys.

For Odivere it was not quite the same. He was respected, not only for his position, but because he understood well the skills of farming and trading. But the men he had dealings with held aloof from him. There was a coldness about the man. Merchants signed his bonds and put bags of silver in his hand and went away. His farm servants did mindlessly the work that he told them to do, with horse and scythe and flail. Sometimes when the work was ill or carelessly done, they quailed before his sudden violent rages. Fires burned brightly in the great chamber on a winter day, and the ale cups went round, and stories were told; but there was never such fellowship in the men's quarters. The islanders could not bring themselves to love that cold efficient stranger who was their master.

Some people disliked Odivere very much, and took no pains to hide it; for example, old Maria. She did not curtsy or smile when Odivere came in from hunting with a brace of grouse or a long stiff hare and laid these trophies at his wife's feet. He would throw back his head and laugh. Then the lord and lady would kiss each other beside the loom where a tapestry was growing. But when they turned again with happy faces, there the old woman was standing by the window, frowning as if two tramps had somehow strayed in and were filthying the place.

'Maria, why do you dislike Odivere so much?' said the lady Odivere one day when the old woman was combing out her hair.

'I try not to think about him at all.'

'No, but you put on that vinegar look whenever he is here.'

'I have heard things on the roads.'

But what kind of rumours she had heard about Odivere she would not say; no, not for any bribing or cajolery.

'There are evil tongues everywhere in the world,' said the lady Odivere. 'Why won't you tell me what these stories are?'

'I do not want you, my sweeting,' said old Maria, 'to die of grief.' And she would not say another word as she drew the comb through the long glittering crackling hair.

One morning the lady Odivere found a servant girl, Sig, the daughter of one of the ploughmen on the estate, weeping as she cleaned a great trout at the side of the burn. 'What's wrong, Sig?' said the lady Odivere kindly.

But Sig would not say what ailed her. Her shoulders shook. Her face throbbed with grief.

'Has the cook beaten you for neglecting your work?'

No: the cook had not laid a finger on her. She begged the lady for pity's sake not to ask any more questions.

But the lady Odivere persisted. Sig *must* tell her. She was ill, perhaps?

'My lady, I beg you – I am not ill. I am in my usual health.'

The lady Odivere had had enough of the girl's peasant stubbornness. She became quite severe. 'Sig, unless you tell me at once why you are crying I will send you back this very day to your father's hut. You will work no more for me in the Hall.'

The knife and the trout glittered beside each other in the

sunlight. The girl turned her smeared glittering face up to her mistress.

'Please, dear lady, ask me no more. I can't endure it.'

'Then you will pack your box and leave the Hall at once. I won't have such stubborn people working for me.'

At that point Sig broke into uncontrollable sobs. Her small body shook with grief above the stones and the rushing water. The lady Odivere was sorry at once for having added a new hurt to the girl's sum of anguish. She sat down beside her on the grass and put an arm round her.

And then, while the gulls wrangled on the shore over the entrails of the great fish, the lady Odivere heard all that Sig would ever tell her – a few broken words among sobs and sniffs – but she gathered that some man in the island who had no right to do so had taken Sig in his arms and forced unwelcome kisses on her; and worse.

A coldness came upon the lady Odivere then that would not have troubled her if the brutish wooer had been some plough-boy, or the man who looked after the falcons.

She kissed Sig gently, and told her she was not to worry; and she told her how much she liked her; so much indeed that she was going to take her away from the kitchen – where there was always a certain amount of horseplay and loose talk which was hurtful often to young innocent girls – and she was going to make Sig one of her own personal servants. From that very day Sig would work in the lady Odivere's chamber, at embroidery most of the time, but also at dress-making and weaving. Nobody would harm her there.

Sig turned on her mistress then a face of such love and gratitude – though it was all messed with her late sorrow – that the lady Odivere had to smile back, even through the gathering lourd of her own heart.

That evening, as old Maria was preparing her for bed, the lady Odivere said, 'Maria, you do not like my husband. I think I know the reason now. My dear Maria, my husband cannot help his nature. He has been endowed with an over-abundance of sensuality. I do not hold it against him. I understand. I love him in spite of the way he behaves sometimes when he thinks I am not there.'

Maria shook her head. She was just an ignorant old peasant woman, she said. She did not understand such subtle high-flown talk.

'I mean,' said the lady Odivere, 'that he has little wayward outbreaks of love, now and then, for this girl and that.'

'He kisses women,' said old Maria. 'Everybody knows he does that. That's nothing.' Then she gave such a violent tug to her mistress's hair with the comb that the lady cried out.

'There'll be kissings in dark places till the end of time,' said old Maria. 'That's nothing. I would laugh if it was only that.'

They heard the sound of a foot on the threshold. Maria put her wise withered mouth to the cheek of her mistress and went out by another door before the lord Odivere should enter . . .

There came a disquiet on Odivere that winter, a growing restlessness. He took no pains to hide from his young wife what ailed him; he had the wanderlust, he wanted to be abroad for a year or two. This hunger for new lands and seas was no new thing in the countries of the north; it was precisely that that had lured the Norsemen out of their poor mountains and sea-coasts towards Iceland, and Greenland, and Vinland (that men later called America) and France and Sicily and Byzantium. Once at least in every Norseman's life a rage and a hunger possessed him; he would wither and die if he could not break that gray circle of the horizon. Even Sund the old ploughman, who did nothing but sit at the Hall fire all winter long, had been to Ulster with Guthorm and Arnor the poet; that four-month-long excursion had kept him in stories (which were, it was said, lies mostly) for fifty years. An adventure into the sun once a lifetime, was due to every man who lived on the fringes of the Arctic Circle. Their women expected it. They did not complain; though sea travel in those days was a hazardous matter, and the chances were one in seven that husband or son or father might not return. Not without cause they called the sea 'the old gray widow-maker' . . .

It was a priest from Lindisfarne in England who breathed first on the smoulders.

This man, who had come to visit the shrine of Saint Magnus, sat in Odivere's hall one night in spring and described with many vivid tongue-strokes the crusade to the Holy Land that had just ended. He had been there, in the army of Baldwin of Flanders, a chaplain, and he had seen the ladders against the broken walls of Acre, and he had heard the heroism and sorrow and triumph of Christ sung in the oases of the infidels. He showed them where a Saracen spear had entered his neck; he would carry the silver scar to his grave. The Orkneymen listened beside the fire while the grave voice went on and on, until about midnight Odivere got to his feet and told them that there was work to be done in the morning: ploughing, and peat-cutting, and caulking the ling boats. Then they all went to bed. But Odivere and the priest from the Holy Island sat over the fire, talking earnestly till the sun got up . . .

It was the next day, after the priest had ridden on to Birsay where the relics of Saint Magnus were, that Odivere broached the subject of sea travel to his wife. She raised this objection and that: who would look after the estate? Who but Odivere knew how to bargain with the foreign skippers when they came with cargoes? Who was going to tell the sowers when to sow and the reapers when to reap? The great farm would decay, surely, if the master was gone for a long time. But Odivere brushed these objections aside. Thomas would be there always, the most trustworthy grieve any man could have. Thomas would be in complete control. If anything, Thomas would run the estate better than Odivere himself . . . She raised the most serious objection of all, with trembling lips: he might never come home again. He might die of an arrow in Galilee. The sun in the east bred terrible plagues – hundreds of crusaders were buried under bright Palestinian stones.

'My dear love,' he said to her seriously, 'I'm sorry to leave you, I assure you. But my soul is in great danger. I *must* go on this holy voyage before I die.'

She did not ask him how his soul was in more danger than that of any other sinful man; the solemn look he gave her warned her not to enquire too closely. She asked, in a still voice, how soon he intended to set out.

'Within a month,' he said. The English priest had told him about the new crusade that was about to be launched. The armies were gathering from all the dukedoms and principalities of Europe; they were streaming down, in companies of a hundred or a score, or singly, towards Marseilles and Genoa; and the priest had described the marvel of an endless ragged horde of peasant-soldier-pilgrims – normally coarse and foul-mouthed – singing devout hymns as they wended their way, on every road of Europe, to the ships. He himself, Odivere, would go, a solitary rider out of the north, to join that great hushed host . . .

And so, at the end of the plough-month, he went; not alone, but squired by a dozen young men from the estate. His wife had spent the interim weaving a white pennant with a blue cross on it, for him to carry on his lance.

Before he left he gave her the golden chain that he wore always round his neck. There was no need for such an ostentatious thing in the austerities that were before him now. The chain, he said, would be a pledge of their unending trust in each other. The precious links lay cold on her neck and bosom.

They kissed each other farewell for the last time in the door of the great Hall.

The lady Odivere stood on the clifftop till the longship dwindled and disappeared beyond Hoy. Then she turned and went back to the Hall, where everything seemed to be going on as usual. Maria was calling the girl who kept the fires a lazy little slut – what was she thinking of, letting the pot boil dry! And Thomas the grieve was telling a group of menservants that he intended to sow barley in the quarry field this year . . . Little Sig came up and said her ladyship was not to mourn – the lord Odivere would be back before winter with the heads of half-a-dozen infidels hanging from his saddle.

But the lord Odivere did not come back that winter, nor the following winter, nor the winter after that.

The business of the estate went on – it even prospered a little, because Thomas the grieve was honest and hard-working and a first-rate organiser. An old man died in a croft on the hillside. A man from the north end of the island married a girl from the offshore holm. A child was born in a fisherman's bothy, tremulous precious breath, and the priest arrived within the hour with sacred water-drops. And, again, an old woman breathed her last in the first snow of winter.

The carnival of life and death went on in the island but the lady in the great Hall had no part in it; or rather, as the months stretched into years, she felt more and more sure that Odivere was under the bright stones of the east, and that she must resign herself to the slow withering of widowhood. For surely, if he was alive and well, he would have contrived before this to send her some kind of message.

Anxiously she questioned every skipper who came to the Hall to bargain with Thomas about ivory or wool or wine. No, they had no word of Odivere. And then one day Albrecht, a skipper from Antwerp, told her that the crusade was over, as far as he could judge – at least, northern Europe was full of disbanded sun-blackened soldiers, going home with their wounds and their pock-marks – and a right rabble they were too, said Albrecht indignantly, and all they seemed to have learned in the Holy Land was thieving and battery; they would never do any good any more in such settled occupations as farmwork or building or weaving; that southern sun had made dangerous vagabonds of nearly all of them . . .

But the lady Odivere listened with growing hope to the Dutch skipper's lugubrious recital. For the war was over, and now, after three years, her husband might be on his way home.

The weeks and months passed, and still there was no sign of Odivere. Every tramp and vagrant who touched the island was brought up to the Hall and given food and drink, and asked if he had been at the latest crusade; and if so, did he know anything at all about a lord called Odivere? . . . But most of those poor wandering folk had been on the roads all their lives, and they knew nothing about wars and soldiers – all their knowledge was of the sources and roots that kept the breath in them for another day. They went the longest way possible round any battle trumpet, being themselves as peaceable as fish or stars. They could not help the lady. But they hoped that the lady's husband would soon come safely home. War, they said, was a terrible thing. They hoped all the four limbs and five senses of him would be gathered soundly home to her some fine day soon. Yes, and his red kissing mouth too. And they thanked the lady kindly for the meat and drink and the small silver coin she put into their hands . . .

One or two of those vagrants turned out to be disbanded crusaders indeed, but they had never heard of Odivere, except for one man, a half-crazed Spaniard. The grieve Thomas brought the man to her door one morning. It seemed he was on his way to Saint Tredwell's loch in Papay island: the goal of many a poor sick creature. He could speak no Norse, that much was obvious after she had put the first question to him. But when she uttered the name Odivere, he looked at her closely, then he turned his face away and spat on the stones. *Odivere* – he looked at her again and a wolfish lascivious grin split his face. She pressed him. It was obvious that the name meant something to him. Again, *Odivere*. First he narrowed his eyes and made kissing noises with his mouth – it was horrible to see the miming of the half-insane creature – he gave lewd lonely kisses to the wind. And then his face darkened, and he made with his hand a swift gesture of disgust, and again spat among the stones.

Nothing more could be gleaned from the man. The sun had poached his brain. 'Odivere,' she said once more, half afraid now. But he only shook his head. He turned away with blank eyes. Thomas the grieve told her, later that night, that the mad crusader was out of the island. He had got a passage in a fishing boat to the island of Papay, where the saint's loch was.

The very next morning the lady Odivere woke to the sound of argument at the door of the Hall. She recognised the voice of Thomas the grieve, but the other voice was remote and strange. She could not hear what was being said. It seemed to her, as she listened, that the new voice had a sea quality in it; now secret, now surging, now thundering, now lulling. And Thomas was the great rock holding the flood back.

'You can't see her ladyship now,' Thomas was saying firmly. 'Perhaps later. Her ladyship is asleep.'

'I *must* see her,' said the stranger. 'I have news for her. I have come from the Holy Land. I have spoken to the lord Odivere.'

As soon as the name was uttered all the doors of the Hall were opened. Servants ran here and there. Old Maria appeared at her door, peering everywhere, putting her hand up to her deaf ear. The lady threw on some clothes and went on bare swift feet to the great chamber. A strange knight was standing beside the fire, sipping and appraising a cup of wine that Thomas had poured for him. He turned to the mistress of the house. His face and hands were darkened with the sun, but there was a kind of distant familiarity in his look, as of a person that one remembers out of childhood, remotely yet vividly. On his breastplate an Atlantic seal was graven. He bent towards her and put a cold kiss on her hand; and the formal kiss too roused a sensation from the past that she could not put in its proper context; her fingers smelt of brine; a sweet lonely joy moved in her heart.

The knight said, without waiting for her to speak, or for any further courtesies, 'I have news of your husband. I have lately come from the city of Constantinople. It was there, at a certain place – and it wasn't church or market-place either, I assure you – I met the lord Odivere. I was on my way home from Jerusalem, with the wound I got in a siege there' . . . He opened the side of his kirtle and bared a four-inch ragged furrow across his ribs. 'The lord Odivere however was not at that siege, or at any other battle or skirmish that I heard of. It seems, from what I could gather, that your husband got no further than Byzantium. He was caught in Byzantium like a wasp in a pot of honey. I assure you, lady, that in Byzantium there are many places and persons to allure a certain kind of man, if he feels so inclined. There are the silks and the roses and the wine – all much more pleasant than arrows and scimitars in the desert, I assure you . . . Well, my lady, your lord did not seem over-pleased to see me, once he understood that I too hailed from the same northern regions as himself. I did not meet him – as I said – face to face in a street, but in a room where there were low-burning candles and music and phials of perfume – a labyrinth of sensual delights . . . My lady, I have come here because I have heard that you are anxious about your husband's safety. Let me reassure you. He is as well as any man can be who loves the good things of life. He was, when I saw him, more than contented. He was so taken with Byzantium, in fact, that he may have some difficulty in breaking away. Alas, one's money runs out like sand in such a gay city. The lord Odivere may not be home for a year or two yet, but in the end I think poverty will send him back to you . . .'

Everything the stranger had said was meant to wound her. She was well aware of it. He was saying, with more than insinuation, that the lord Odivere was a coward and a sensualist – an avoider of the battlefield, a frequenter of brothels and stews. Why then did the happiness increase in her with every bitter word the stranger uttered? The years fell away. She saw a lonely girl among the rocks of the North Sea.

There was a seal on the stranger's kirtle too, sewn on the fabric in thick silver-gray wool. There was a seal stitched in leather on his cordiner shoe.

She thought, as the voice went on and on, that she might faint away between the fire and the bench. She was aware of Thomas filling up the seal-knight's wine-cup. Little Sig came and put slippers on her cold feet, one after the other. The stranger scattered the dregs of his wine into the fire: the flames hissed. He turned away. He had had enough of her and her husband. She said, her voice trembling, 'My friend, I have many things to ask you. It is good of you to come. It would please me greatly if you would consent to stay for a while yet. You are most welcome. If you stay with us we will look after you well.'

The stranger turned at the door. He said, 'There are many more things I have to say to you, if you want to hear them. What I have said about the lord Odivere is the merest outline.' The cold salt bite was still in his voice.

'Thomas,' she said, 'this knight and myself do not wish to be disturbed. There's too much noise and chatter here in this Hall. We will speak together in my chamber. Maria, send Sig in with a jar of the Irish wine.'

The stranger and the lady passed through the curtain with the hunting scene woven on it. They were closeted together all day. Those in the great chamber heard, till sunset, the ceaseless murmuring of their voices, that occasionally flashed with anger or pity or delight, and seemed like music then. Once the listeners heard their mistress weeping.

Old Maria was intrigued, when she brought in the candles, to see their heads close together. She spread the bed wide enough for two. She said to Sig, as she laid the empty wine jar on the board, 'Fill that up again. They'll need it before morning. She didn't look like this on her wedding night at all. I don't think they knew I was in the room just now – fancy that . . .' And old Maria went back to her station outside the curtain.

Candles were quenched, fires covered, one after another, all through the great building at midnight.

The two voices still drifted from the lady Odivere's chamber, slow, hushed, fragmented, with gaps between the utterances. Then a single voice murmured on and on into sleep. Then there was utter silence; and at last the old woman could leave the curtain and shuffle away to her own bed.

But Maria did not sleep at all that night.

Before dawn she heard the gate creaking open and a clatter of hooves over the cobbled courtyard, and she knew (turning to sleep at last with a sigh) that her mistress's brief night of ecstasy was over.

The seal-knight had come to the Hall in spring, in the month of ox and plough.

The island folk had never seen their mistress happier, as the light lengthened out towards summer. She was always visiting cottages, and especially she went to the doors where there were cradles and young children. But then, for a day or two, a graver mood would come on her, and she would wander most of the day along the cliffs and down to where rocks and sea fought their everlasting wars: an endless advance, endless retreat that, after a lifetime, leaves the western coast very much as it had been.

Children and seals: these had in their different ways a fascination for her that summer. If Sig should happen to remark at dinner-time that a great cluster of seals had come to Ramna

Skerry, or to the caves of Fallado, she would push her plate away
and pull her cloak about her and go off at once to the shore (and
she dared anyone to follow her). She lived in the sun and wind
all summer, the happiest creature in the island . . . But at
harvest time she shut herself indoors. As the year darkened she
was seen less and less among the looms and the cooking pots,
even. At the beginning of Advent she kept to her own chamber,
and only Maria and Sig had free access to her. The women were
of course all curious; but they got no satisfaction from either the
old one or the girl; their queries and wonderments were met by
a frown and a forefinger set to the mouth. They were to mind
their own business. They were to remember their station. Was
there no work for them to do in kitchen or milking shed? Let
them see to that.

But one day near Christmas the inhabitants of the Hall heard
sounds that made them tremble and blanch: screams, beseech-
ings, muted moans, gasps, flutterings, a last anguished cry. Only
old Maria was with the afflicted lady that day. When all was
silence once again, Maria drew the curtain aside and asked the
girls what all the white faces were about? They would all know
that kind of sickness before they were much older. Back to the
butter-making with them, back to the wash-house and the egg-
collecting. Her ladyship was a lot better now. The worst was
over. There was nothing to fear.

The work of the great Hall revolved for a day or two about the
hushed mysterious chamber.

At the end of that same week the island women heard a piece
of news that astonished them. A young wife, Gerda of the croft
of Faa, a year married, had given birth to a girl child in mid-
week. Nord the father had shown the wailing bundle to everyone who knocked at the door with a little gift. But now, what
was this? It seemed that Gerda of Faa had not brought forth a
single child at all, but *twins*. There he lay in his cradle, the
second one, breathing sweetly and innocently. What if he did

not look like his twin sister, or like his mother and father, but had altogether finer and purer features? This sometimes happens – it is to be accepted – nothing is to be gained by asking questions. All the same, this small boy, coming into the world three days after his sister, caused a great amount of speculation and head-shaking and wonderment in the island.

Another year, and another, passed. There was no word of Odivere.

Love, Birth, Death – that trio – paced out a grave measured circling dance from end to end of the island.

What had that old Saba seen now? Saba went about among the crofts saying that she had seen the strangest thing down on the shore.

Saba was a half-crazed old woman who lived in a stone and turf hut between the two hills. She had witnessed this marvel in the early morning when she was getting whelks from the rockpools. A great bull-seal had come out of the west and swum ashore a good stone-cast from the pools where Saba was rummaging. Once it made land, the creature stood up and it was as tall and bright as any man. It left the shore and walked through the fields. Saba had hidden behind a rock. After a time she got on with her whelk-gathering. An hour later the seal came back. Saba hid herself again. The seal was carrying a child on his shoulder – a little boy three years old maybe. The child's neck glittered in the morning light. The seal-man walked straight into the sea with the boy, and swam into the west. A host of seals came about them. She watched, she said, till they were lost in the sunrise.

Nobody believed the old creature. She was always seeing things. It was that same Saba who had seen the longship sailing on dry land, and she had seen the firebird making a nest of ice; and a hundred other crazy things besides. There was no child missing in all the island . . .

A sad thing had however happened during that same week. One of the twins in the croft of Faa died – the little boy. There was nothing to prepare the islanders for it – no sickness, no decline. One day they saw him running among the sheep, wind-and-sun-smitten; the next morning he simply ceased to be. And Nord dug a hole for the innocent one and buried him before anyone was aware. The parish priest had been very angry when word was brought to him of this unhallowed burial. Nord and Gerda were severely censured next Sunday before Mass; they stood with drooped heads under the arch . . .

Saba came at last to the door of the Hall with her story of the seal and the boy with the burnished throat. Maria spoke roughly to her – she was a nuisance to the whole island with her rubbishy talk! She should put less ale in her porridge, then she would see ordinary commonsense things like other folk! . . .

But the lady Odivere, when she heard the raised writhen voices in the courtyard, went out and invited the poor old troll-ridden smelly creature into her chamber. And she asked her about what she had seen the previous week, and prodded the old one's memory. How had it been with the child – did he seem to be frightened in the selkie's arms? Had he screamed when the cold sea rose about him? And the seal itself – did it seem to be fond of the child it had stolen? Did any words – well, scarcely words – were there any sounds in the beast's mouth as it entered the water?

The old woman was now very vague and confused about it all. She repeated the same things over and over – seal, bairn, brightness – child, burnish, selkie – glitter, sea-beast, boy . . . But yes, now she remembered. There had been singing in the sea. It seemed like a herd of harps drifting westwards.

The lady Odivere sent old Saba away with a pot of honey and a segment of cheese and a crock of ale.

Odivere came back to his island at the end of the next winter. The first they knew about it was when Brecht appeared at the door of the Hall one morning. Brecht was one of the farm-boys that Odivere had taken with him six years before. They did not recognise him to begin with. He had a beard, and he had almost forgotten how to speak the island tongue: he took Thomas the grieve by the hand and spoke a kind of patchwork language made up of French, Spanish, German, Turkish, Slav words . . . It was a good thing that Thomas had a memory for faces – he recognised, under the suntan and the reckless mouth, the lad who used to spread dung and seaweed in the fields.

He led the young crusader to the part of the great chamber where the looms were; and there the lady Odivere heard that at last her husband was well on the way home. (Brecht had been sent on before to prepare the household.)

She accepted the news calmly. She was far less excited than the erstwhile farm-lad who stood before her, laughing and gesturing and gabbling a strange speech – of which the key-words however were unmistakable – 'Odivere' . . . 'tomorrow' . . . 'ship'.

The lord of the island came, the very next day, as had been promised. He landed from his longship on the beach where Saba had seen the seal and the child and the mysterious brightness, and had heard the harp herd. The assembled islanders saw a lean laughing gypsy-coloured man walking up the sand to meet them; but they recognised him well enough under the exotic mask that the East had forged on him. Odivere looked around eagerly. Where was his wife? He thrust through the smiles and hand-clasps and the shy welcoming words. And there at last he saw his lady. She was standing on the sea-bank above, wrapped in her fur cloak. Time had put a mask on her face too: webs and traceries and desiccations: but gently incised, so that she appeared even more beautiful than she had done in her first youth.

She turned a dutiful cheek to his first eager kiss.

All the islanders clapped their hands and shouted their joy

then. Someone had brought a bagpipe. There was music and dancing. But after a time it dawned on them that not all the young men had come back with Odivere. Jon was missing. Solmund was not there, nor Thord. A few of the old folk turned and went home to mourn in secret. Paul the falconer had died of plague in Corunna, on the way home.

Norna who had waited for Paul for six years screamed on the shore. They led the distracted girl across the shoulder of the hill to her widowed hut . . .

After the bereaved ones had gone home, there was a little more music and dancing, but it was muted. The crusaders showed the island girls Byzantine coins, and bits of amber, and rolls of Spanish leather. Their teeth flashed in their beards. They gestured wildly. Their once-hewn speech was liquid with vowels. One of them began to play a guitar – an instrument the islanders had never seen before – and there was more dancing . . . In the midst of the celebration, the eager lord and his silent lady returned to the Hall.

And Thomas was waiting in the doorway to give an account of his stewardship.

Odivere could see at once that the estate had not suffered through his absence. On the contrary, there were more pigs and cattle and sheep now. And when he looked into the mill the sacks of barley reached to the rafters. And the millstones turned slow and fruitful and ponderous with the rains of winter. The miller and the miller's son recognised their master through his sun-mask; they greeted him happily from a floor of thundering stones.

'Thomas, you have done well,' said Odivere to his grieve. 'You have been faithful and provident. It seems to me that I could do no better than let you run my estate in future. For the truth is, Thomas, this crusading has upset the old rhythms of my life. Perhaps in a year or two I will settle down once more to farming and trading. But it will take time . . .'

None of Odivere's eastern retinue had kept the taste for farming either. The sun and magic and spices seemed to have stolen some of their wits away. 'They'll come back to the plough,' said the old ones. 'They'll *have* to. They can't hang about here like parasites. It takes us all our time to feed ourselves' . . .

But as the weeks went past and spring came, neither Odivere nor his island-easterners showed any keenness to take part in the rituals of agriculture. Instead they hung about inside the Hall at all hours of the day and night, throwing dice, getting drunk, plucking out on their guitars a strange languorous music. They were continually in the way of the weavers. They lounged about the fire after everyone else was in bed and asleep, telling their adventures, over and over, sometimes quarrelling. They stood about in the stables between horsemen and the horses. The island girls shrank from their half-courteous half-shameless advances. Sig broke in on her mistress one morning sobbing from the crudity and unnatural desires of one of the easterners (whom she had known six years before as Thrip, a shy boy from the croft of Smoor who used to blush whenever a girl so much as looked at him).

Odivere himself was hardly better. He lay for days at a time in bed, saying that it was too cold for him to get up. And he wished aloud that a fleet of great ships would come and cast grappling irons on this island of his and drag it south for a thousand miles into the sun.

Meantime the faces of the adventurers lost their sun-colour, and their extravagant speech returned gradually to the old laconic rhythms of the north. But still they showed no inclination to fish or cut peats or gather seaweed. Their whole attitude seemed to suggest that they had broken out of the ring of servitude – they had tasted freedom and now they were free men for ever.

It could not last. Odivere realised as well as anyone that the situation could not go on. His estate was not rich enough to support so many drones. He did not relish the mildly reproachful looks put on him and the lesser crusaders by Thomas and the farm-workers. Most wounding of all was the reserve of his wife. He had looked for a rich sensuous time-enhanced welcome. Instead his lady, though she behaved as a wife should whose husband has been absent about some business or other, had this steady coolness towards him. She kept him at arm's length. That had not been in her nature before. Could it be that she thought poorly of all the luxury and laziness he had brought from the east?

'Get up, hounds! Holiday time is over! Rouse yourselves! The wind's blowing! There's an otter in the burn, a fish-eater. A day's hunting, lads, then it's back to the old drudgery for us all' . . . Odivere strode about the chamber, kicking this sleeping man and that. The early sun came dazzling through the door. 'A silver florin to the best hunter!' The easterners shuddered awake, they flung reluctant blankets from them. They recognised the old resolute voice. The long adventure, it seemed, was over. They drank their morning ale and went out into the sun and wind.

All morning the cliffs and caves in the west of the island rang with shouts, challenges, laughter.

The farm-workers went about their tasks. The black oxen dragged harrows over the seeded earth. Sig and her girls sewed busily at an altar-cloth for the monastery. Old Maria scolded the women in the kitchen.

The lady Odivere sat alone in her chamber.

There was a silence in the west. The otter-hunt had moved into a new secret place. They had cornered their quarry; they were stalking it. And then another outcry – a shout of triumph and wonderment from the hidden end of the island.

The oxen were unyoked.

Odivere came up from the beach, alone. It was now late afternoon. He carried a dead seal in his arms. Odivere strode over the fields to his Hall. The earth-workers had never seen such a white trance on any face. They fell back from him. He strode on over the buried seeds.

'Lay it down on the grass,' said old Maria who was sweeping the flagstones with a broom. 'Strom will skin it after dinner.'

He kicked the broom away. He shouted in at the door like a herald.

'Woman! Wife! I want a word with you.'

The girls dropped threads and needles. The women gaped at him from the rattling pans and the luscious tangled smells of hare and haddock in the kitchen.

'Woman!' he shouted again. 'Come here!'

Woman: he had never addressed the lady Odivere in such a coarse peasant way before; nor with such passion; nor in such public circumstances.

The summoned one lifted the curtain and let it fall behind her. She came quietly through the great chamber, and smiled at the agitated embroiderers beside the fire, and gestured to the kitchen women to get back to their pots; and stood at last gravely in the doorway.

The body of the young seal lay on the swept stones. Blood seeped out of its throat. Its eyes were open, and lustrous still, though the frost of death was in them. It was a young lithe animal, with a pelt like mixed silver-and-ashes.

But it was not the beast that Odivere was asking his lady to look at. He held up a golden chain to her face.

'Woman,' he said quietly. 'I would like you to explain this to me.'

She was down beside the animal, kneeling, lifting its trenched head, kissing the dead eyes and the dappled cold flank, crying, cradling it to her. Her hands were red. She wailed like any

bereaved country girl, one stifled cry of grief after another. Her
arms and her mouth were dabbled red.

'Woman, tell me about this,' said Odivere. 'Tell me how the
love-pledge that I gave you before I sailed to Palestine happened
to be about the neck of this beast.'

She kissed the dead animal again, and rose to her feet, and
faced him.

The gold glinted between the man and the woman.

'You have killed my son,' she said.

He shouted with pain. His face darkened. The gold shook in
his hand. He turned away from her. He was possessed with utter
disgust.

Old Maria herded the sewing girls and the kitchen girls into a
cold room at the back of the Hall where they could hear
nothing. (But still they heard fragments of the terrible dialogue.) And the croftwomen were standing in their doors here
and there, all round the Hall.

'You have killed my son,' she said. 'My dear child. You have
murdered my son.'

He quelled the disgust and horror rising through him. 'You
must tell me,' he said. 'There is something I should know,
woman. Some dark business was brewing here the time I was
fighting for our holy faith in the east. A beast for a son! I sowed
no beast-seed in you before I went away.'

'Your seed was as barren as ashes,' she said. 'The great lover
Odivere! But out of the fires came only dust and dross.'

'Oh woman,' he said, 'I did not think it was possible for the
wall between beast and human to be breached. You have done a
thing too horrible and too hideous to be thought on. My love
for you was as pure and rich as this gold here in my fingers.'

'Hell rot you,' she said, 'for a liar. Do you think no stories
came out of the east about the famous Odivere? A hero, indeed!
The only battlefields Odivere saw were the beds and boudoirs of
women. You are a liar and a coward. How many corrupt beds

did you lie on? Fine stories were brought to Orkney about the
great lord Odivere and his whores and his rusty sword.'

Several darkling figures had come up from the beach – the
otter-hunters, who had only succeeded that day in killing one
small seal. They lingered now in a group at the corner of the
stable.

'I am a sensual man,' Odivere said. 'I did kiss a girl or two in
Alexandria and Constantinople. I will not deny it. You knew I
was that kind of man before you married me. It is part of my
nature. I cannot help it. But *this*!' . . . And he pointed to the
dead animal that was growing ugly and sodden in death, like an
old sack. He vented another cry of horror. 'To have lain with a
sea-beast! To have had a fish for a lover! They say that witches
do these things. I have heard that they kiss the stinking arse of a
goat.'

'Do they miss you, I wonder, the little painted eastern
whores?'

'That was natural. This here was foul and hellish and unnatural.'

'This young creature will be missed in the sea caves tonight.
His father the King will miss him.'

'Unnatural. Foul and hellish. Witch-work.'

'Odivere,' she said, 'before you throw that word at me again –
"unnatural" – I must tell you a thing that I have learned about
you. Why did you not go home to Iceland with me after the
marriage in Norway?'

'Witch-work. My own wife, that I loved dearly. A witch!'

'You could not go back to Iceland. That's the truth. They did
not want you back in Iceland. The bishop had put a ban on your
return. And why? Because young Odivere, the swashbuckler,
had gone beyond quarrelling and wenching. He was frequenting
the Black Masses. He was praying to the devil. He was in league
with the angels of Hell.'

He dropped his head again, and a long time passed before he

raised his eyes from the cobblestones. He whispered, 'There is a certain punishment for women of your kind! . . . Igor, Brecht, come here at once! I want you.'

'The young rake, Odivere, had spent his father's money in Iceland. Girls and dicing and drink. There was no inheritance. The fields and the farm-stock were all in pawn. Then word was brought east, from Norway, about a young rich heiress. Plenty of gold there, if Odivere could get his hands on it. The father was anxious to have her married, now that he was old and she would soon be out of her girlhood. But what way could a prodigal and a bankrupt like Odivere win the lady when wealthy noble famous young men from all over Scandinavia were riding to the castle on the clifftop? Impossible. Not all his charm and his good looks could unlock that door. It was just possible, if a certain terrible thing were to be done. One midnight Odivere knelt in a black cave where a black candle was burning. The crucifix hung upside down, like a bat. A perverted priest began to recite the Paternoster backwards . . .'

'Punishment for witchcraft, the fire,' said Odivere. 'A nest of flames.'

Brecht and Igor were lingering uncertainly in the courtyard. 'Men, seize this woman!' Odivere shouted. 'Lock her in the tower. I want her feet chained.'

The men hesitated still.

'Igor,' said Odivere, 'Brecht, pretend she is some old hag that you've picked up for a penny. She's gone through your pockets while you were sleeping. Handle her the way you would handle such a one. Chain her wrists too.'

The sun had set. The blood of the seal was a dark stain on the cobbles, and its body was a shadow among many shadows in the courtyard.

'Satan was pleased to grant the prayer of the lord Odivere that night,' said the woman. 'Odivere sailed to Norway the very next morning. And there he found a young girl whose heart melted like wax in his hell-kindlings.'

She knelt and kissed the humped shadow. The Odivere's men took her by the arms and led her up to the tower. It rose up, a keep and an armoury, at one corner of the courtyard.

Odivere flung the yellow chain on the dunghill.

The islanders heard in the first darkness the rasp of a key. They saw, later, a candle-glim high in the tower. They saw, later still, two shadows leaving the studded door.

That same night, when one of Odivere's men went to lift the dead selkie from the courtyard, only the pelt came away in his hands. On the stones lay a stiff naked boy!. . .

The lady whispered a prayer for all the creatures that God had made – stars, animals, grains of dust, corn, suns, fire, men and women and children, the whole joyous web of creation. Her hands clanked as she held them, dove-wise, in front of her cold unmothered face.

Sorcery: the lady Odivere was to be tried for sorcery – for unnatural actions which men blanched to hear and to utter – for putting enchantment, no less, on the limbs and members of a beast out of the sea.

For days the wildest of rumours out of the island had gone as far as Shetland and Caithness: such as, that Odivere had murdered a farm-boy for stealing a trout out of his net. It was said too that some kind of black spell had fallen on the island – all work on field and net had come to a stop – there was said to be drink and dancing day and night, and the Hall had become a small scented eastern harem – Odivere had brought the sun back with him from the east, and it had driven the island mad. A hoard of gold (it was whispered) had been discovered in the sand, buried between the high and low water marks. It was rumoured that the lady Odivere had drowned herself in the sea; also that she had retired into chastity, silence, and contemplation in a little cell she had made for herself in the cliff face; and her only speech was with fish and sea birds. It was even said that a burning creature, half sun-beast and half man, had rampaged one evening across the island, felling everyone in its path with red whirling hooves, and leaving scorch-marks here and there in cornfield and peat-bog.

But when the earl in Birsay opened the sealed letter that Odivere despatched to him, all these gross stories vanished like smoke. The truth was sufficiently terrible. The lady Odivere, while her lord was fighting for the Christian faith in the east, had taken for her lover a sea-man and had borne him a son, a weird dimorphous creature, half boy and half beast. And this hideous perversion of nature could only have come about through the lady's study and practice of witch-craft.

The earl and the bishop consulted together over this letter of Odivere's. They decided that the accused woman would have to be judged by an assembly of the leading farmers and merchants of Orkney. A few priests and monks would have to be brought in, since it was considered that the crime had powerful supernatural elements. Indeed the bishop was of opinion to begin with that the lady ought to have been tried by a church court only, witchcraft being utterly outwith the province of laymen; but in this the earl overruled him. It was a matter that closely touched both estates, since Odivere was one of the leading men of the earldom.

It came together, this solemn assembly, to the island at the beginning of May, and Odivere made over the great chamber of his Hall to them.

The lady Odivere was brought down, still chained, from the tower; and some of her judges were moved by her white suffering face; but then they called to mind the terrible things she was charged with, and murmurs of 'whore' and 'witch' and 'hell-seed' went along the bench.

The lady Odivere, asked if she had any defence against the accusations, merely shook her head.

The earl and the bishop looked at each other. They had expected a spirited passionate defence. The trial was over almost as soon as it had begun, for the guilt, it seemed, had been tacitly acknowledged. The earl whispered to the bishop. The bishop nodded. A few of the farmers and merchants made 'horns' of their thumbs and forefingers, to keep themselves clear of her witchcraft. The monks from Eynhallow and the priests from St Olaf's in Kirkwall kept crossing themselves.

Then judgment was swiftly given: death by fire. The lady Odivere would be given seven days, a full week, to make her peace with God. On the seventh morning she would be taken out and tied to a stake, with her feet among peat and driftwood. The executioner would put a torch to this kindling. There, in her own courtyard, she would drink the flames and die.

'Amen,' said the bishop.

The lady Odivere bowed her head, acknowledging (it seemed) the justice of the sentence. Then Brecht and Igor took her out of the great chamber. The key of the tower glittered in Brecht's hand . . .

Odivere himself had not attended the court; he sat all morning in the brewing-shed with his men, drinking and playing cards. He was available if by chance the court should summon him to testify. The drinking in the shed had been going on since breakfast-time.

From the brewing-shed Odivere and his men could hear the formal judicial voices (though they could not distinguish words). There was heard the coarse rasp of the earl; then silence; then the querulousness of the bishop – silence again – then a murmur like a shaken hive.

Odivere threw a diamond and a queen on the board.

A black voice from the Hall spoke solemn phrases. Then there was silence again; scattered coughs and clearings of the throat; a single heavy clank; a shuffle of feet, dispersed open-air voices, the earl's gravelly voice in the porch.

The trial was over. Sven said that perhaps they should go to the door of the great chamber and hear what the verdict and judgment had been.

Odivere swilled the ale round in his goblet. He said there was no point in doing that. He was enjoying this game of cards. The ale was passable. There could be only one judgment, anyhow.

Sven laid on the board a card with a cluster of hearts on it. The other players sat studying the fan of cards in their hands. Amund filled up the pitcher from the barrel.

Soon the card-players heard many feet in the island, going down towards the small boats drawn up on the beach. The rocks echoed and rasped. Then oars rose and fell through pellucid singing circles.

Anders said that Odivere should perhaps be saying farewell to the jurymen. At least he should see the earl and the bishop safely and ceremonially from his island.

Odivere's cheeks were two patches of red. He set a card with a single black dagger on the scatter of swart cards in the centre of the board. A barrel of ale had been drunk since morning.

Odivere said that the earl and the bishop would manage to get off the island without him, surely. If they could come they could go. He thought that from now on there should be a chain round the waist of the witch too. He didn't see why he should bother his arse about people who had after all merely done their duty that day. Even if they were earl and bishop. There was a girl in a croft of Upgrind – he would like it if Brecht and Igor brought her to the Hall that same night. He thought her name was Vetra. Would someone please pour him more ale?

Sven, suddenly cinder-faced, set his cards down carefully on the table. Then he got up and lurched through the door. A second later they heard a retch and a splurge outside.

'What a waste of good drink,' said Odivere. 'Anders, you take Sven's hand of cards.'

*   *   *

The earl said to the bishop, as they were being rowed across the firth to Hrossey island, 'That poor Odivere, I am deeply sorry for him. He had shut himself away, obviously. I am glad he didn't have to testify – it would have broken him. He could not even come to say goodbye to us.'

The bishop said, 'I'll send Serenus to the woman. Serenus is a kindly confessor. If anyone can reconcile her, it's Serenus. Serenus will melt her heart.'

'Yet,' said the earl, 'you would have thought that Odivere, stricken by this terrible thing, as he must be, would have arranged some refreshments for the court – a keg of wine, for example. You would think that Thomas his steward would have thought of doing that.'

'Her women were weeping for her,' said the bishop. 'Did you see them? I did not think there would be tears like that for a sorceress. The smell of evil was very thick in that island. I am glad to be out of it.'

'That poor Odivere,' said the earl. Still shaking his head, he stepped ashore on Hrossey.

The lady Odivere, in the days remaining before her execution, was allowed three visitors in her prison.

Serenus, the young monk from Eynhallow, said, 'In this mid-terrain betwixt Heaven and Hell, so perilously poised, it is not only that invisible spirits, black angels and white angels, wrestle for our souls (and believe this, lady, the soul of one single human being is worth more in the proving hands of God than the hoarded wealth of the world, Indian diamonds with the pearls of Atlantis) but – though we cannot tell what ecstasies Heaven or Hell will hold for us, in the way of bliss or torment – men love to enact what they consider to be the ceremonies of these immortal residences, with incense and with faggots. So, as you have been adjudged, lady, to be a hell-trothed witch, for you they have assembled kindling and in that fire you are to spend your last brief time on earth. I saw men hammering the stake into the courtyard as I passed through an hour ago. But you are not to be afraid because of that.'

'It is Odivere, not I, who should be made to stand in the flames,' said the lady.

'No, do not harden your heart. Let all wrangling and recrimination have an end now in you. For if you remain in that temper, daughter, you can have no part in the vision that I shall put before you now. I have shown you – and you have heard me meekly and well – how men imitate the eternal ardencies of Hell with the little fire where you will stand tomorrow at noon. But thanks be to God, if temporal justice can make a mime of Hell, that other justice which I represent can bring down a little of the heavenly bliss; the merest shadow and hint of that ecstasy, but sufficient. I cannot say whether you are guilty of this dreadful crime or no, for as yet you have not opened your heart to me in holy confession – but, my dear, God has made everything sweet and easy for the troubled soul in its pilgrimage betwixt birth and death. I cannot do anything about the fire. Burn, it seems, you must. But you have only to whisper a few brief syllables to me, under the seal of confession; show to me (that is, to the Church) the sorrows and troubles of your heart, for that fire out there in the courtyard to be no longer the doorway into Hell, but rather the welcoming flames of Purgatory, where for a certain season you must abide, with mingled pain and hope. Then, when the last dross is refined out of your soul, for you then will be the endless bliss of Paradise' . . .

Sig said, 'So then when I suddenly looked into the kitchen, there was this little gray mouse nibbling at the cake. A sweet mouse, as bonny and harmless as ever I did see. It had a crumb in its whiskers. I could have taken it home. And then Hanna, that old cook. Such yells out of her. 'The cat! Bring the cat here! Bring

Ard the tomcat quickly!' Up on the high stool she jumped, and teetered and squealed rafter-high. This little mouse, it licked the crumb off its whiskers, and looked up at old red-face so sweet and innocent. By the time the cat was roused up from the hearth, the little thing was back in his hole under the cupboard somewhere, safe and warm' . . .

'Sig, dear, it does me good to have you here.'

'O never fear, lady, I won't let the likes of them go rough-shod over me. "Sig," says this Igor to me last night, "you're a pretty girl. I like you," he says. "Sig," says he, "I have a ring that I got in Byzantium. I would like you to have it" . . . "Before you go any further," says I, "I don't like you. I used to like you. I don't like you now or any of that Palestine crew. That crusade ruined you," I said. "Maybe," I said, "if you were to do some hard work, you might learn to be proper men again, not butterflies with poisonous stings." "Tonight," says he . . . "Not tonight or any night," says I. "For your information I'm betrothed to Finn. Finn's only a ploughman and he has no gold rings and he's never been out of Orkney. I'm seeing him tonight. So there," says I.'

'What you must wear,' said old Maria, 'is your wedding-dress. I have it laid out. No, they'll take the chains off you in the morning. First I'll bathe you, lady. There's still some of that lavender water that the skipper Pierre brought from France. We'll empty that bottle. Then I'll put the wedding-gown on you. I've looked out the Spanish slippers. But bare feet might be the best. Yes, I think so. And no jewellery at all. And your hair down free over your shoulders. That way you'll stand white and innocent among the flames. If that doesn't pierce the scoundrel with guilt to his heart, I'm a stupid old woman' . . .

'O Maria, I'm terrified even to think on it' . . .

'Tut-tut, it'll be nothing. Don't think of it. Look at me. A poor old living corpse. The fire has been at me for thirty years past and more. I have burnings in my haunch-bone night and day – I get no rest. Burnings in my stomach too – it's no pleasure for old Maria to eat any more, her that used to love her porridge and puddings and ale. Burnings, burnings. Burnings at the heart, too, on a Mass-morning, for wicked things done. My dear, you do well to get your fire over with early. Could you live another forty years, night after night, in the same room with that stinking ox? You do well. Only a quick bright passing pain. I think you should take off the marriage ring. That'll stab him, when he sees that – it will, when he sees your naked innocent ringless hands among the first flames.'

There was no more talk among the crusaders, after the trial and verdict, of a resumption of work on the estate. They didn't return, chastened, to the rituals of the quartered sun. Shoulders were not put to wheels. They moved no purposeful stones. Nothing was done in the way of preparing the barns for the hoarded heavy broken sun-wealth of summer.

Instead, the card-playing and drinking were intensified. A kind of madness took possession of Odivere and his men. They coursed hares on the links and rode home shouting through the sunset cornfields; then it was drink and song and wenching till morning in the Hall . . . There was a great fecund white bull in the island, a magnificent beast. One morning they attacked him. Triumph (that was the name of Odivere's bull) was browsing peaceably in the meadow when Brecht appeared between the rocks. He pranced up to Triumph and waved his saffron shirt, and shouted. Triumph looked at the half-drink man placidly, then returned to his tufts of grass. Suddenly there were men all round him, screaming, waving, and the flat of a sword lashed his haunch. The beast turned troubled eyes on mask after clownish mask; and then a knife fell quivering into his neck. He saw the red spatter, his widening nostrils took the reek and smell of blood, and he bent his head against his tormentors.

They fell back in front of him. Sven tripped on a grass-hummock and fell. Triumph stood over the whimpering man, shaking his wounded head. Another dagger flashed into his haunch from behind. He turned to quell the sting, and an axe sliced into hide and flesh and broke open a new fountain of blood. Triumph turned tormented eyes on his master Odivere, who had fed him out of his hand and cherished him when he was a small bull-calf. Now his great hulk was laced through and through with pain. Odivere stood in front of him with a sword. There was a flash in the sunlight. Triumph, the famous bull, sire of hundreds, died of that skull-wound.

They would turn up at a croft – especially a croft where there were women and girls – and announce to the crofter that they intended to stay the night, and they hoped that he had a good brew of ale in his kirn. They always arrived so suddenly that it was too late to send the womenfolk away.

And (as I said) they made a road of any ripening field.

The women in the ale-shed had received orders from Odivere to brew huge quantities of strong ale, for, said he, on the eve of the execution, they intended to make a feast that Orkney would remember for many a long day to come. He had invited the earl to come; but the earl had sent a curt cold refusal (Odivere didn't know why: wouldn't the earldom be well rid of a witch? . . .)

Odivere's men broke the bounds of night and day. They slept anywhere and anytime; Valt the fisherman found Igor sleeping at noon in his yawl. He didn't waken the debauched easterner; he went back fishless to his house; he didn't want a knife in his ribs.

So the days passed between the trial and the execution.

The executioner arrived in the island the day before the burning. (No man in the island, by threat or promise, could be prevailed on to do the job. Odivere had had to send to Caithness.) The ruffian with the red beard got a great welcome when he arrived. The easterners hugged him and smote him heartily on the shoulder. Odivere sent for a keg of ale and flagons of wine. They all stood about the newly-erected stake and toasted the man who, at noon next day, was to thrust a torch among the peat and tar and grease and driftwood. Serenus and his penitent heard that shout from the dark tower.

That same afternoon Odivere sent for the young monk. He wanted news of his wife. Was she in despair? Did she suffer much in her mind? Did she still hope that the man she had wronged so hideously might relent at the last hour, and set her free to go home to her father in Norway? For that (said Odivere) is the most exquisite torment of all, when in the closing circle of doom the seeds of hope still quiver and throb. Did she weep much?

Serenus answered that it promised well for the lady. She had travelled far, in the last day or two, beyond any such mirages of hope. She waited on the certainty of death with a sweetness and tranquillity of spirit that it was touching to observe.

At that the lord Odivere broke out into a rage. He wanted to hear no more! To Hell with her (he shouted). No, she would not have the chains taken from her. That old hag Maria was not to be given access to her, no, nor Sig either, little show-off and parasite that she was. Let Brecht and Igor see to that. He assured Serenus of this, it would be no easy fire for the witch in the morning – he had given orders to the executioner to make it a slow languorous burning. The witch would stand, sack-clad and chained, among flames that would be in no hurry, and in fact might not be out before sunset. There would be a bucket of water to damp the fire down if it should show signs of over-eagerness. There would be a flask of oil to induce sudden flowerings. There would be subtle variations in pace and tempo. This burning would be a work of art.

'God pity you,' said Serenus mildly, and turned away.

Sven arrived breathless at that moment to announce to

Odivere that a large school of whales had been sighted to the west of the island, two miles offshore. They were headed, among sea-quakes, snortings, and falling fountains, from the North Sea into the Atlantic.

'Whales! Whales!' Men came running into the courtyard with harpoons from all over the island, and the one word was in every mouth. A whale-slaughter meant that there would be a fat merry winter in the island for even the poorest dung-spreader.

'Make the boats ready,' shouted Odivere. 'Take the first boats you find!' The easterners pushed the empty ale cups from them. They got to their feet. This day, the eve of the execution, would be the bloodiest day of all.

There were shouts all along the shore. Dogs barked. Gulls screamed and circled. They could hear the distant plunging and wallowing in the west. Every man in the island was down at the shore now. Old Trigg had hobbled out of his croft with a sickle. A small boy danced with excitement among the rockpools, and pleaded to be taken into a boat.

Soon the sea to the west of the island was littered with bobbing boats and flashing blades. The whale-hunters rowed strenuously into the reddening sun. Even Serenus the monk held the tiller of a yawl. The executioner sat in the bow of another boat, sharpening a blade on a stone.

The whale-hunt turned out to be worse than a failure – it was all unmitigated disaster. A first broken squall came out of the north-east and scattered the advancing wedge of boats; the frailest craft sought the lee shore. The whales blundered on at the horizon that was now suddenly bleak and gray: the whales were frail fountains, deep distant bell sounds. The wind freshened as the sun set – all crimson and jet wellings – over the sunken coasts of Atlantis. Squall followed squall, they massed into a salt-flung settled gale in the spectral twilight.

'I think,' said Anders at the tiller of Odivere's boat, 'we

should turn now. The night's getting worse. The whales have escaped anyway.'

'Keep going,' said Odivere. 'We'll feed the island with whale-steaks all winter.'

Odivere's yawl rode the sea like a spirited horse; it quelled wave after rising wave.

Now there was more jet than red or yellow in the west. The whale music was lost in the many voices of the sea.

Oars struck light spindrift – oars wallowed deep in the heart of a wave – the rowers flung their blades at the tilting bottle-green surge till their shoulder-knots cracked. Odivere shouted from the bow. Oars were shipped. Darkling hands rigged a small square sail. The yawl steadied, plunged, snorted foam, champed.

Once Odivere looked round. There were only two other boat shapes behind him now – he guessed these faithful ones were Brecht and Igor. A boy's voice sounded out of one of the boats in a lull, thin and frightened. It was answered by an ancient cracked voice – the old rheumaticky man who had been hauled aboard at the last minute with his sickle: Trigg. Then the wind scattered all voices and boat-sounds. The sea was a harp of tumultuous dark strings; the gale plucked and smote. Some-times Odivere, standing in the bow, was half blinded with rinsing after rinsing of spindrift.

'We're alone now,' cried Anders from the helm. 'The others have turned.'

'Keep going!' shouted the skipper. At that moment a bird flew at him with wide wings out of the sea and wrapped his neck and beard. Odivere tore it off. It was a rag of saturated sail. He turned. There were indeed no boats behind the yawl now; the sea was empty. He heard, between wave-cry and wind-cry, one thin human cry. Then wind and waves alone spoke to one another.

Gray shaded darker on gray; gray would soon be utter

blackness. There was no distinction of land or sea or sky. The faintest luminosity showed, between surges, where west was. Once momentarily, the sky tore itself apart and showed a single star; then closed again.

Why was there nobody in the yawl now, out of six men, but Anders and himself? It was very strange. Sometimes Odivere felt that he was participating in a dream of loss, in which everything and everyone he knew and loved was being taken from him, one by one. A salt hive broke against the bow, his head was deluged with stinging singing drops.

Anders sang, 'I'm going now. Goodbye, Odivere. Time for home.'

Odivere fell across a thwart, struggling to get to Anders and wrench the tiller from this last of the faithless ones. He rose. He reeled from the blow of a loose sail-rope. The steering-oar, when he got to the stern, swung loose and free. Anders too had vanished; and no blind face looked at him from the sloping side of the next wave.

Odivere said, 'I'm alone then, at last. The boat can take me wherever it wants.' The steering-oar, untended, fluctuated madly.

Fatalism more than sleep settled about him where he sprawled in the stern. He abandoned himself to the night and the storm.

Odivere woke in the gray of morning. He found himself (as he knew he would be) alone in the boat, in the open Atlantic. The storm had moderated a little. The ocean was fretted with torn lacings of spindrift. He stood up in the stern and scanned the sea around. Far off, to westward, he thought he saw an upturned boat. On the slope of a wave he saw a sodden hump that could have been a man or a sack.

Odivere struck out with his oars for the nearest island; he recognised the hills of Rousay. As he got nearer he saw that there were no storm watchers on the beach. Men were working in a field at the shore, but none volunteered to help the exhausted man to beach his boat. (It was as if for them Odivere did not exist.) He asked the labourers if their master was at home. Not one of them so much as raised his head. Odivere left the churls and dragged himself half-a-mile to the Rousay laird's house beside the burn. The laird, whom of course Odivere knew, gave him a distant welcome, as if he was a stranger and not a particularly winsome or welcome one. He invited Odivere inside, and set him down at his board, and summoned meat and drink from the kitchen. And later – Odivere being so weary now that words could hardly crawl through the cage of his teeth – the host had a bed made for him on the floor beside the dying fire. The man was courteous throughout, but still there was that cold reserve in his manner that is not usual as between laird and neighbour laird.

Odivere dreamed. His dream was an exact repetition of the events of yesterday's whale-hunt in every harrowing detail; with one or two additions. The monk Serenus was safe also; in his dream Odivere saw him standing among the monks of Papay island, under an arch . . . Then the dream shifted to this very island of Rousay. Odivere saw, with a pang at the heart, the cold white body of the lad who had pleaded on the shore at the very last minute to be allowed to come – the body was caught in a rock-cleft.

The image was so startling that it woke Odivere, and he knew immediately that it was stark truth, no dream.

He rose from his bed. Scullions were astir in the kitchen; otherwise the great house slept. Outside, a few labourers moved here and there between the fields and the shore. Odivere approached a man he took to be the grieve, and told him about the boy in a rock-cleft: did he know where in Rousay such a rock-cleft might be, and if so would he and his fellows help to get the body ashore? The man ignored him. The Rousay islanders seemed to move in another world, beyond the cares and concerns of Odivere. He turned from them. He walked alone along the coast, looking closely into every rock fissure and cave. And there indeed – but caught in so fantastic a tangle of rock that no solitary man could dislodge it – was the naked body. Ropes, leverage, a dozen hands would be needed.

At noon Odivere returned to the Hall. He asked the laird for help in retrieving the body from that fierce stone grip.

The laird looked puzzled. He said that his people were vigilant, especially in a storm. Such a thing would have been reported to him – and action taken – as soon as it was known. He suggested that perhaps Odivere had dreamt all this. And Odivere, with a start, agreed that indeed it had been a vivid dream; but now he had proved it with his wakeful eyes.

'I'm sorry,' said the Rousay laird. 'I can't spare any of my men simply because you have been troubled by a dream and a sunlight illusion. All hands are needed today in the hayfield' . . .

To make quite sure, Odivere walked along the cliff again at sunset. There indeed was the body of the boy wavering and gleaming through water, fronded with seaweed, for now the tide had risen and covered cleft and corpse.

The storm continued for another night. Sea and sky were one cold smoking tangle.

Odivere received from the laird of Rousay correct but unenthusiastic hospitality. It was very strange; his host did not seem to know him. Surely the name Odivere was at that particular time in everyone's mouth, on account of the sensational trial. The Rousay laired seemed not to have heard of it.

Patiently, once more, Odivere told his host the story of the seal-man and the adulteress.

'In which island did this terrible thing take place?' said the Rousay laird.

'In my island,' said Odivere. 'In the island that you can see to the west – it lies along the horizon like a recumbent giantess. Why, man, you were there the other day! You must remember! I saw you standing in my courtyard. You were one of the jurors at the trial.'

'That can't be,' said the laird. 'I have not been out of Rousay since Easter.'

'But Odivere – Odivere – surely you have heard of *Odivere*. I was six years at the crusade. There have been ballads made about me.'

The Rousay laird shook his head.

'No,' he said, 'I have never heard of Odivere. It is a strange pathetic legend you have told me, about the woman and the seal and the child. (By the way, there is no drowned boy at the Westness shore – my men searched all this morning.) Very strange and very sad. And according to your story the woman – who was your wife – was burnt for sorcery.'

'It is truth, no story,' said Odivere. 'The burning has not taken place yet. But she will burn, subtly and terribly, that whore, as soon as I get back to my island. She will burn. Her bones will crack and bubble. You will be able to see the flames from Rousay.'

'I welcome visitors to this island,' said the laird. 'Rousay has always been famed for hospitality. But I do not like the end of your story, stranger. The end was vicious and evil, and uttered with a damnable relish. I know of course that you are a liar. I have had so-called "crusaders" here before today, and I enjoyed their stories (though I knew that the little bits of truth at the heart of them were lavishly ornamented, in the eastern style). But you, Odivere, or whatever your name is, have a wicked mind and a black tongue. The storm has nearly blown itself out. You will leave Rousay in the morning. I will not be sorry to see the last of you.'

'I'll go now,' said Odivere. 'I won't stay in a house where I am not welcome. I am late for the burning as it is. I will sleep in my own boat on the beach. And I will take the body of the boy back to my island in the west – I won't have him buried in friendless earth. I will lift him from the sea with my own hands.'

So Odivere left the laird's Hall in Rousay, before midnight. He went down to his boat and covered himself with canvas.

The Rousay laird said to his wife, when they were alone together, 'That man and his island! But the strange thing is that there was an island out there that sometimes broke the horizon. I've never seen it myself. The old men used to speak about it. But always when they rowed towards the island, it melted like a dream. They called it The Island of the Women . . .'

He snuffed the midnight candles one by one.

Odivere awoke lying on the wet bottom-boards of his yawl. It was a cold clear morning. He walked round the coast for a mile. He was shocked to discover, sprawled face down on the beach, the body of Brecht, the young islander who had been to the crusade with him, whom he liked more than any of the others. He pressed the wild eyes shut. Brecht also he would take back with him for burial.

It seemed he would have a fair passage with his freight of death. He would manage alone; he was a good seaman.

But when Odivere looked across the shimmering waters towards the horizon, his island was no longer there.

EPILOGUE

When Serenus, the abbot of Eynhallow, was an old man – in fact, the winter before his death – he wrote in his journal this entry:

Who of all people came to our austere island yesterday but a wandering skald, one of those merry rogues who live by uttering all manner of lies and fantasy? I chided the man for the vanities he dealt in, and he has had the impudence to reply, 'O Lord, Father, but we tell such marvellous lies that they turn out to be far better than truth – I mean, Serenus,

not better than the holy truths you meditate on in this
monastery, but better than the tawdry kind of truth by which
other men live – the little proverbs and adages that light them
from the cradle to the grave. I might go so far as to say,
Father Serenus, that we vagrant singers show those 'light-of-
common-day' folk that their lives are truly a web of wonderment from birth to death, if only they could see themselves
with our eyes' . . . Thus the vagabond, leaning there against
the arch with his harp across his breast. He even had the
effrontery to wink at me two or three times as he sought to
justify his trade. Brother Timothy was for sending the man
packing at once. Brother Timothy told him quite sharply – he
is really the mildest of men, Brother Timothy – that there
were no ale-wives or randy ploughmen in this island, it was
inhabited by monks only, he was likely to get small pickings
here, let him be gone as soon as possible to Egilsay, Rousay,
Gairsay, or Wyre . . .

Of course in the end we let the ballad-singer bide over-
night in the island. The brothers, after the austerities of Lent
and the raptures of Easter, were a trifle jaded. I had a few
words with Brother Timothy. He agreed, with some reluc-
tance. Before supper the community gathered round the fire
in a circle and the ballad-man (whose name is Jocelyn)
recited to us a long poem entitled The Lay of the Lady
Odivere . . . Such extravagance and wild imaginings! It was
about a woman, the wife of a crusader, who had taken in his
absence a seal for a lover, and had had a child by him, and
then upon her crime being discovered (by means of a love-
token, a golden chain, that is cunningly worked into the
ballad) she is sentenced to death by burning; from which
woeful end she is saved, however, by a conspiracy of whales
and seals, and out of an empty island her seal-lover takes her
to Suleskerry, that rock in the far Atlantic . . . But yet I must
confess that the ballad was performed with such style and

artistry, with such cunning rhythm and regular peals of rhyme, that at the end the brothers sat rapt round the fire, and it was five minutes or more before a word was said. Jocelyn broke the spell by winking at me. Then Brother Timothy said, 'That's that, then. There's straw in the barn, my good man. You are to sleep there. Go in peace. Now vespers' . . .

That night I could not get to sleep in my cell. It was the strange ballad that kept sieving through my skull like sand, every grain of which was hued like a rainbow (as in cold actuality sand is, when viewed carefully through a prism; such is the wonder of God's creation, that lies beyond the normal reach of the senses). The ballad roused memories and scenes in my mind that I had completely forgotten; one in especial of a croft-wife who had been accused by her husband of concubinage with seals. I was a young monk at that time. The abbot asked me to go to the island where those folk lived and look into the matter. I questioned the man first. He had come home from the market in Kirkwall (somewhat drunk – he admitted this when I pressed him) to discover his wife nursing in her arms a young seal. She had found it, she told him, on the rocks, abandoned by its mother, and so she had taken it home and was feeding it with goat's milk out of a bottle; for if she hadn't done that, she said, the creature would have died of loneliness and hunger on the shore.

In the mind of a certain kind of man any weird or foolish notion can take root; and this crofter, whether his wife was cold towards him (as some women are, by nature, and cannot help it) or for some other reason, I do not know, conceived the idea that his wife had for long been a lover of seals, and that this young selkie was out of her womb. He had had a merry day among the ale-booths of Kirkwall, and – such things happen – had kissed one or two lasses after his ox had been sold in the market ring. (He confessed as much to me.) Altogether he had had a successful day – and now, to come home to this! He called her the filthiest names he could put his tongue to. His wife ran from the hut, frightened. The young seal was sleeping beside the fire. He killed it with a knife – cut its throat. The wife crept back, hoping that the rage would have died in him. When she saw the seal covered in blood she took it in her arms and wept heart-brokenly: a strange touching 'pièta'. But her grief over the creature only made more vivid his suspicion. He would do this and that terrible thing to her. And after he had beaten her black-and-blue, he would lock her in the cottage and set fire to it: that was the worst threat he made to the stricken uncomprehending girl. In fact what he did was to go to the island priest and lay a charge of witchcraft against her.

The man told me with great frankness the whole sequence of events, as they appeared to him. I could see that, deep under the fantasies, he truly loved his wife; and that intensified his anguish.

Next, in privacy, I spoke to the woman. She was a shy strange pathetic creature. It seemed indeed that the procreative fire that is implanted by God in every human being burned low in her. But the blackbird that stood in her door – the cats that curled her milk round their small swift tongues – the pet lamb and the pet kid at the end of her house: all testified to a simple passionate love of all creation.

They had been married five years. And the cradle that the man had made with his own hands in the first winter of their marriage stood in the corner empty.

I was able to reconcile the man and his wife. By the end of that day I was able to join their hands. The tenderness, the self-reproaching, the joy! – it was as if each looked deeply into a mirror and found the image each was seeking. I left them then with a benediction. I found my boat at the shore and glanced back. They stood against the sunset, hand in hand.

Ballad and event bore a marked resemblance the one to the other. But – and Jocelyn was right about this – the actual occurrence, homely and affecting, has in the work of art been rigged out with all manner of exotic trappings. The croft-woman is a rich lady. The crofter is a laird with a Hall and a fertile island and ships. His little merry jaunt to the ox-market in Kirkwall has become a splendid six-years-long adventure. And the blunt cold seal-cub with his gruntings and his liquid eyes is transformed to the issue of a splendid amorous knight from the sea . . . Also the characters, when they speak, utter memorable resounding things; never the feeble hesitancies and little broken half-understood phrases by which human beings endeavour to show their minds and hearts to one another.

It is as if men, at the times when they are free of the yoke and can relax over the fire with an ale-jar, love to remind themselves of some dimly-remembered ancestral splendour, perhaps the primal innocence before the angel of Eden thrust them forth into time with his flaming sword. They retain memories of that primal state when they were the unsullied sons and daughters of God; and also of their fall, after which they were still heroic and magnificent, even though in misery; and that memory is the fountain-head of tragedy, with its pity and purging and purple splendours. All the most wretched and comical little pieces of snobbery that one hears on the street – such as old Tib saying in a loud whisper that in fact she is true daughter to the Thane of Ross, that potentate having stepped by her mother's door to request a cup of water the time he was out hunting wild-cats – all that grotesquerie by which folk gull themselves into believing that they are not what they seem, and but for some mistake or hitch they would be other than dung-spreaders or fish-gutters

– that too can be referred to memories of some splendid beginning, some heroic flaw, in even the meanest of people.

And so Jocelyn in the ale-houses – wherever in Scandinavia or Scotland he goes – makes these poor folk feel themselves for a brief spell to be great, beautiful, tragic . . . It is all a dream and a crumbled pageant, once the tale is told. Yet I think that a skald like Jocelyn helps men to endure wretched vain lives; and indeed Heaven must have ordained the trades of musician and artist and poet for this very work . . .

But (as I said) even at the best art is only the shadow of a consolation. Priest looks, beyond poet, to a time when the mask and the motley must be off, and the flesh; and the bone itself is dissolved, at last, in light. The consolation he offers is this: to remind men and women that though in this world they eat dangerous difficult bread, they are heirs also to another kingdom where all the citizens are of noble unsullied birth – are indeed dwellers there already, for the splendours of that lost kingdom are all about them in the sacraments, and especially in 'the blessed sacrament', which takes their few offered cornstalks and makes of it immortal Bread. By right action, in the ruts and warpings of history, they obey the laws of that other kingdom; and, so doing, old Meg making her butter is a lady of great wealth and power, and Jock hauling creels from the floor of the firth has finer hands and more exquisite hungers than any prince.

I am of the opinion – not shared, alas, by such as Brother Timothy and his lordship the bishop, who want our kirks and chapels kept austere – that we ought to enrol all these arts as handmaidens of holy religion; so that our church interiors resound with sweet music, and glow with harmonious patterns of colour, and are broken into beautiful spaces with hewn stone and wrought iron, and echo with the uttered poetry of a continuing revelation which (by the breath of the Holy Spirit) has divers modes as men live in turreted cities, or in rich river-fed valleys, or beside the sea. (Here the poetry would have a cold bare beauty.)

Jocelyn will have a trout for his breakfast before he leaves in the morning.

Nor could I help but reflect, lying sleepless in my bed, how shrewdly the ballad delineated the role, under Heaven, of Man and Woman. (There are foolish mouths always to whisper, and even say openly, that there is small enough difference. Why should not women navigate ships, and take swords into battle, and even officiate at our altars?) In so far as women weep the same tears, and make word-webs, and see images in mirrors, they are one flesh with men. Yet it has always seemed to me that men and women are nourished with different essences. The flavours and aromas which (all unconsciously) male and female give forth in their daily living are utterly distinct. The hoarder of seed, until such time as the sack smoulders in the barn and the sun is outside; the passionate receiver of the seed, the furrow, the enfolding, the earth-smithy where, out of ordered tumults of flame and darkness, a new stalk or a new child is moulded – they are as remote, and yet as necessary to one another, as light and darkness. Man is the red Adam, a creature of the sun. All his proper business is enacted in the light – his ploughing, fishing, trafficking, battles. Towards the source of the sun Odivere went, therefore, and lived under the sun for seven years, and came home burned and branded with the sun. (He had taken too great a draught of it, more than his northern flesh could endure – and, like Icarus, the wax melted.) Odivere, like all men, followed such sun-begotten abstractions as heroism, courage, destiny; in a distant country he proposed to weave those high eternal truths into a life that would be otherwise unremarkable. Posterity should hear and applaud his adventure! In this Odivere plays the part of Everyman. Men from the beginning to the end of time feast on such high hopes and visions ('I will be a great adventurer,' . . . 'a mighty builder of churches,' . . . 'the wisest of astrologers' . . .) Indeed these lures may take them far in the end. They will sift the atoms of creation through their fingers. They will end by building temples on the stars.

For woman heroism, courage, endurance, faith are utterly different: to be enacted in simple daily tasks, in the washing of shirts at the burn, at butter-kirn and loom and baking-board, in the drawing of a comb through a child's bright hair. The small field round about her croft is her whole life; its fertility is the same thing as the fertility of her body. She is a far more earthy creature; she looks at her limited world far more penetratingly; and understands the actuality of seals and grass and stones (not like men, in some abstract or symbolical sense; but sensuously, and simply, and intuitively) – that is to say, with a dark mysterious wisdom that belongs to the subtle changing moon rather than to the sun.

The darkness is her true time, when she gathers strength in sleep and silence for the things that have to be done and endured. Occasionally she may take in at the earth-fissure a passionate sun-burst, for her womb is the seed-jar of the future; there must be children to till the loved acres after she and her sun-mate are dust.

In just such a way, I think, is this ballad of Odivere to be understood. There is shrewd observation under the masquerade and the fantasy. We are not to suppose, for example, that a woman would, or ever could, take a beast for lover – no earth-beast either, but a cold passionless sea-creature. That is not to be thought of. The darkness of a woman yearns for the sun and the seeds of the sun, not for the barren otherness of salt. A woman bereft of natural love goes either of two roads

– into sourness and withering (and indeed there are one or two crones on the hills that would have done well in their apple-blossom time to have kissed the boy that mucks out the byre); or into a region where love broadens to include all God-created things, the cornstalk and the seal as well as men and women and children. In that ripeness and wisdom she falls at last, the keeper of the hearth and the loom, into the hand of God.

This is perhaps how we are to think of the lady Odivere and of her seven years of waiting.

There came to my cell once a stranger. This was in my youth, in the very same year I think that I mediated between the crofter and the wife that took the orphaned selkie from the rock. We have been trained to make a swift shrewd sounding of any man who comes among us, and this stranger I judged at first glance to be one of those gay prodigals who leave home with gold sewn into silk linings, and for a year or two are seen only on distant shores by travellers; these generally wend home at last, with tattered shoes, and enter into their inheritance, none the worse for the sunburn and the pock-marks on them; and they become good husbands and farmers and merchants. It had been otherwise – I realised soon – with the man who stood before me now. He had travelled; he had got experience; and his eyes were pools of darkness and suffering.

'I have come to you, Father,' he said, 'in the hope that you can help me, but I fear I am beyond hope or help' . . . *He had the markings of eighty years on his young face. I told him that no man, while he drew breath, however wicked he had been, stood outside the circle of grace, unless pride kept him there. I encouraged him, as well as I could, to tell me his story. He stood silently before me for a while. Then he shook his head, and sighed, and said that it was impossible; I would*

never believe the thing that he had done; he ought not to have come to me at all. I told him that men were capable of very great evil – I had heard one or two black confessions in my time – but yet the Church had power to remove any burden, however onerous.

'Never this burden,' said the man. 'It is impossible. I live in such a world of shadows and whispers that I do not know whether I truly exist. I am – or I was – a man. I remember a childhood, in another place. I grew up between ice and a burning mountain, I caught butterflies and tadpoles, I fought and laughed with other boys, I learned to sail and to take eggs from the crag face. I sang in the church choir. These are mirages now in an endless hot circling desert. I try to hold the good images in my mind – they quiver, they dissolve. I am alone again in my world of dust, whispers, shadows.'

At some moment – he could not exactly say when – a finger had touched his spirit, and from that day his life had begun to rot.

I begged the stranger to tell me something about his life.

'No one,' he said, 'could have had a happier childhood. No one could have had a more forward-looking and eager youth' . . . Everything he undertook prospered. He seemed to be one of Fortune's darlings; and this was seen most strikingly in the matter of a business he had set his heart on particularly. He ventured far and boldly for it, and at last the undertaking was crowned with success. He found himself suddenly rich (and with the youth and health still to enjoy his good fortune). He had not known that life could hold such happiness . . . But then, after a year, the first shadow entered his life. It grieved him very much. The spring, the pure source of generation, the life-bearing stream that courses on, in spite of skulls and epitaphs, through many generations into the future – that was choked in him. The

stone could never be lifted. His name would perish from the land.

The man spoke only in hints and generalities, as if indeed he was an articulate shadow; nothing solid, definite, specific, issued from his suffering mouth.

I was a busy young monk at that time, going here and there throughout Scotland and the islands on errands for the Order; and with even the most burdened of penitents I spared no longer than a quarter of an hour. But I realised that this man, even though he had not yet declared himself a penitent, was a rare bird to have dropped down into our cloister; and that day, though I had letters to write, I heard him out with fascination and bafflement.

So then, he went on – speaking more to himself than to me – there was that cold shadow on his life. But who in the world doesn't carry a shadow of one kind or another, at some time? So the man had reasoned with himself. There were other round succulent fruits on the tree of life that might be reached for; for example, fame. If not by generation, by exploit he would blazon his name on history. He sought for fame where in those years fame was to be found – he ransacked time and space for fame – he came home with a few first gray hairs and the taste of ashes in his mouth.

To what? To what did he come home? He came home to an inheritance that was infested with shadows. The daily round of toil, that he had abandoned in order to shake the tree of life, that was now an empty ritual, a whisper, a tastelessness. Once he had relished overseeing the work of plough-time, seed-time, harvest. Black powerful shadows trampled now in the glebe, a cunning shadow stumbled behind, a beautiful penetrating shadow wavered between . . . He pulled lithe shining shadows out of burn and loch and sea.

The 'gay eastern phantasmagoria' – these were his words –

lingered with him for a while; then it quickly faded in the cold light of the north. He might have known. Shadow meshed with shadow: a net was being woven for his life.

He could have endured it all. What are men after all, he argued, but shadows drifting between birth and death? He could still eat and sleep and slake his lust; the shadow that was him could still flush between fadings. All the shadows surrounding him were in a sense 'natural' – a part of every life. So he consoled himself. A man could grit his teeth and endure.

But then . . . He could not go on, there in the chapel. He shook his head fiercely. His mouth twisted and locked.

I touched his arm. I encouraged him. A name, some hard fact, might lead me to the source of his anguish.

O no, he had not bargained for what happened then! Never. He had not known that such things could be. It was terrible. It was too hideous and horrible for belief! It could not be borne. Never.

I told him about 'the dark night of the soul' that has tormented many good and holy men.

O no, he answered. This was no night, no sharer in time with sunrise, noon, sunset; no bringer of stars and dews. This that he had experienced was the total darkness than could not be dispelled. It was real. It was more real than any reality he had ever experienced; childhood, love, death. This horror was the essence and the concentration and final hardening of all shadows into a stone, a black immortal jewel that had usurped the place where once a blithe heart had been. Nor could any priest or bishop, not even the Pope himself, remove it from the centre of his life.

I reasoned with the man for another hour. I told him that the omnipotence of Christ could in an instant melt the black jewel that smouldered where his red heart used to pulse.

'Ah, Father,' he said wistfully, 'the sweet earth, cornfields, the sun and the wind and the waters – they have become

beautiful shadows only – and I in the centre, a black immortal shadow.'

The thought had occurred to me, quite early in our dialogue, that perhaps it was a ghost, no man, that came and drifted around me that day in our chapel. Had he not said some mysterious words about 'tasting death's reality'?

He suddenly cried out, 'Don't you remember me? You were there, at the planting of the stake! You were there – I saw you – when the boats were launched against the whales. The storm took us, it gathered and drowned us. You and I, we are the only survivors – the others were lost. Only say you recognise me, and there may still be a germ of hope for me!'

I did not recognise him. I replied, somewhat lamely, that I see so many faces in the course of a year that they all blur into one face – the precious suffering face of Everyman. Perhaps I had seen him, I said – I could not honestly remember. As for such sensational ongoings as burning and whale-hunt – they had always lain outside the quiet round of my experience. The only enterprise that concerned me was the gathering together of all the tumults of human action and suffering into the one enterprise that mattered, the pilgrimage of Everyman from Eden to Paradise.

Shadow-and-whisper, he suddenly turned his back on me.

The monks gave him a meal before he left Eynhallow. He ate the fish and bread, and drank the ale, without relish. Soon afterwards he took his leave. I did not see him again. I never learned who he was, or where he came from, or what his end might be. (I think no man could carry inside him for long such a freight of negation. The 'black jewel' would soon wear out the strongest life.)

A vast circling magnificence, endless surge and gleam, frets always about the shores of time, and throws up now and again – it may be after a westerly storm – a cask of apples, a salt-eaten log, a skull. Sometimes a wanderer by the shore, beset and bemused with the difficulties of his own life, comes on a sealed bottle half buried in sand. He opens it; inside is a parchment scrawled over with beautiful antique script. What does it say? Is it the last urgent message from a ship in distress (now long since drowned)? Is it a sailor's love letter, given to the sea so that the sea's enchantment might enter it? A merchant's bill of lading, two dry columns of profit and loss? . . . The parchment, being indecipherable, means nothing, and has endless possibilities of meaning. Some hand, some- where, wrote it, for some eye, somewhere, to read. Since we are all part of the great web of creation the message in the bottle – whatever it is – has something to say to that wanderer on the shore (who is you, and me, and Everyman); but what, we will never know. There is only the beautiful antique script, fading fast now in the wind and sun, to pause and wonder over. The seals, with gentle plashings, clamber on to the skerry; they turn innocent eyes shorewards.

Seeking correspondences, we wonder, and try to connect, and lose our sleep.

Jocelyn, merry old ragbag, you have a lot to answer for.

The Fortress

JANDRECK

Jandreck, he kept this fortress.

Jandreck, his eye watched the sea.

He knew the balance of stones, and their heaviness, and how they make dust of bones. (A bone is like the moon, a fleeting thing, and it has not the steadfast sun strength of a stone.)

And Jandreck had a horn that he blew. At the call of Jandreck's horn the people came together burdened with every valuable thing, from the pasture and the shore and the fertile field. They stooped in at the narrow door of the fortress. A stone and a stone and a stone were drawn across. The fortress was locked and bolted, so.

Then Jandreck stood on the tower, his eye on the sea.

The second most beautiful of the girls was given to Jandreck. The chief of the people had, the summer before, numbered the girls in order of fullness and fairness, and he kept the most beautiful one to be his wife. But she had a sharp tongue often, the chief's woman, Vrem.

In the time of Jandreck, the chief was called Fley, and he was two suns younger than Jandreck. Fley was strong and prudent. He had gray eyes.

The name of Fley's wife was Vrem. The name of Jandreck's wife was Eort.

The people had gone all together, but for old ones and children and one who had broken his leg, to the other side of the hill to catch three wild horses. They heard, far off in the blue wind, the honk of the horn.

Fley and Vrem and Eort turned in the blue wind about the track of the spirits of the wind, the horses.

All the people returned, horseless and half afraid and stealthy as shadows, to the ridge above the fortress.

Jandreck (they saw) crouched on the shore, above a fire, roasting a fish. The horn was in his belt.

Fley said, 'We were drawing a strong circle about the confused narrowing circle of the wild horses when the horn blew. But the sea is empty.'

JEALOUSY

Eort was spinning in the doorway of Jandreck's house. A yellow wind blew; it was harvest time. Vrem came up the path from the shore carrying fish. The three boats had come back from the far side of Rousay. All the women were gathered about the silver-layered gull-tormented boats. Vrem, the chief's wife, got her share of the fish first, the fattest and the best. No one complained about that.

Vrem stopped beside the spinning-wheel.

She asked Eort why she wasn't down at the boats for her share of fish.

Eort said that the guardian, the strong one, protector of the people, did not like fish. He ate only creatures that had red blood, he ate strong roots, he ate barley that was rooted deep in the earth but sent up its hoard to be ripened by the bountiful sun.

Vrem said that last time she had seen Jandreck he had fish-bones in his beard and his hands stank of fish. That was the day he had given the false call on his horn.

Eort stood up beside her spinning-wheel. She said it was a shame that a great warrior like Jandreck should be squinnied at by any slut or hussy. She cried, 'It's a hard thing, the best of the catch goes to people who have plenty and to spare, while the keeper of the tribe has to make do with the trash of the sea . . .' She said furthermore that if Vrem could cook the fish properly, it would be a good thing, but she ruined every pot of fish she set on the fire. No wonder that Fley had belly pains from time to time in the night.

Eort shouted so strongly that all the people heard her. The women left their disputes about the sharing-out of the fish and trooped up the path to gape at the two stretched faces on either side of the spinning-wheel.

A child ran in terror to the hill.

Vrem stretched out her hand to Eort's hair that was long and yellow as wind-taken corn, and her hand hovered there like a bird.

'Let them fight!' said the old man with no teeth and little breath. 'Scratch her eyes out!'

Eort said the people were a laughing-stock among the other peoples and islands, because the chief had chosen an ugly graceless slut for his wife. 'There's a cast in your eye! Your breath is rotten!'

Vrem sprang at Eort. She dragged Eort by the hair so violently that the spinning-wheel toppled over. Eort fell among the wool. Vrem wound Eort's hair round her fist and dragged and pulled. Eort screamed once and then was silent.

Vrem breathed harshly above Eort, 'Jandreck . . . he should have been mine . . . my man!'

Some of the watchers lifted their hands to the sky. Others shouted and laughed. The wicked old man whispered, 'Kill her! Kick her teeth in!'

They heard, very loud and near, the blort of the horn.

They turned. Jandreck was leaning on the door-post of the tanner's house, looking idly at the scene. The echoes of the horn went still from wall to wall of the village.

Vrem let go of Eort's hair, but a few bright strands were tangled still in her fingers.

Eort got to her feet. She turned towards Jandreck. She bowed her head. A tear fell from her face onto the hot dust.

Men who had been working in the harvest field came running to the village under the fortress, breathless, carrying sheaves and sickles. One panted out, 'We heard an outcry. Are they coming, Jandreck, the men from the sea?'

Jandreck said, 'The sea-robbers are nothing to the two she-cats over there.'

Vrem muttered, 'I will tell all that's been said and done to the chief when he gets back.' (Fley was in Egilsay that day, making terms for a barter of shellfish and peats.)

Jandreck said, 'No one believes an angry woman, not even Fley.'

Vrem screamed at him suddenly, 'Fley will be told what you've said! Fley, believe me, is getting tired of you, Jandreck. You blow the horn, and blow the horn, and nothing happens. Nothing, except that men and women drop whatever they're doing – good useful tasks – and run to the tower as fast as they can with all their belongings. For nothing. The chief says, "Some day that man will blow his horn and the people will ignore him. The ships will come, the fortress will fall, the people will be butchered. I wish (said Fley) we had a more reliable guardian than Jandreck."'

The child that had fled to the hill in terror returned to say that the chief was sailing home. His boat was in the Sound.

'I will speak to Fley before sunset,' said Jandreck mildly. 'But I know that Fley loves me and trusts me.'

The harvesters returned to the half-cut field. The fishwives all chattering, went down to the fish-count again. Vrem, her face blue and shrunken, turned her back on Jandreck and went into her own house. Her three fat fish lay scattered in the dust outside.

'Oh, Jandreck,' wheezed the old man, 'why did you stop such a good fight!'

Children forget quickly. The young ones ran together to the headland to see the chief's boat coming in.

Jandreck knotted the horn to his belt. He walked slowly across to Eort and tilted her drained face up into the sun.

He kissed her.

He said, 'I am glad the chief chose Vrem and not you, Eort. There are secrets of the heart, not to be shouted out in a public place. You know, Eort, that I love you alone among women, and always will.'

There was a thin clear sea-borne cry. The chief, from the bow, was greeting his people.

Only Vrem his wife did not hear, she was making such a clatter and clang in her house with pot and griddle and basin. In between times, she berated her child.

Eort gathered up her sullied wool.

The old man nodded on his doorstep in the sun. 'Women!' he muttered. 'It was always said in olden times, "A woman will bring death to this people."'

THE SIEGE

There was trouble in winter between the men of Egilsay and the men of Gurness.

The men of Egilsay said that Fley of Gurness had not kept his word about the harvest-time bargain. The shellfish from Egilsay had been delivered on time at the foreshore of Gurness. It was true, the Gurness men had rowed peat in four boats to the beach at Egilsay; but the Egilsay men claimed that the peats were of the poorest quality; they crumbled into red ash almost as soon as they were lit.

Messengers went back and fore between the two peoples, as the days got shorter and stormier. Fley was very patient with the red-faced shouting men that came to see him from Egilsay.

At last the messengers from Egilsay ceased coming. 'It means,' said Fley, 'either that they are satisfied, or that they're planning a mischief.'

Jandreck said nothing. He spent most of the daylight hours down at the shore. He seemed to get enjoyment simply from picking up stones and shells that intrigued him, either by their shape or colour or the encrusted intricacies that the sea had put on them, or holes that the sea had worn in them.

It was just after sunset one evening, about the time of the first threshing and winnowing, that Jandreck, letting sand sieve and whisper between his fingers, head another sound than the sound the sea makes when there is a moderate north-north-easterly wind on it, and the tide at mid-flood. Jandreck heard, in the fast-encroaching twilight, a muted stealthy rhythm. Out there, unseen still, was a cluster of boats, and it was as if the blades of the oars were wrapped in hides or blankets. This very faint music – most men would have heard nothing – was coming closer. Once Jandreck heard a sea whisper, echoed and uttered again, urgent and secret. An order was being passed from boat to boat.

It was the dark of the moon. Three stars appeared, one after the other. A bone among seaweed gives more light, but now Jandreck's eye saw to the north little white cleavings of water, made by the on-surge of bows.

Jandreck took the horn from his belt. He set it to his mouth. He filled the shell with air. The horn cried to the people. 'Look out!' . . . 'Come to the fortress!' . . . 'An enemy is near!'

In ones and twos the people came, burdened, to the fortress. Some had been eating – the marrow juice shone along their jaws. Some had been asleep, they carried their blankets. Some had been listening to Gruth, the old man, telling his stories. They glared at Jandreck as they passed the links on the way to the fortress – it was not the first time that Jandreck had interrupted a good story. Burdened with pot and spade and oars, they went into the fortress.

Eort went into the fortress alone.

Fley and Vrem and their child came out of the big house: Fley's servant staggered under the weight of Fley's goods. The chief urged his wife and son on to the fortress. He turned aside at the links and said to Jandreck, 'Man, you choose the queerest time to make those huge belches on your horn!'

Jandreck beckoned Fley to come to him. He pointed north across the water. 'We are to have guests soon. I do not think you sent out any invitations.'

The chief bored with his eyes into the black weave of night. Then, after a time, he saw three separate wedges of bow-foam, three boats to each wedge, nine darkling shapes in all. 'Get that old thing into the fortress!' Fley shouted. (For the old man – not the story-teller but the mischief-maker – was approaching the fortress, led by two neighbours, and he was complaining bitterly about being dragged yet once more from his fireside. 'All for nothing! For nothing!') His two companions prodded him on.

A latecomer appeared from the hill – a shepherd – he nodded abruptly to Fley and Jandreck, then stooped in at the low door.

Last of all Jandreck and Fley went into the fortress. And stone by stone by stone the bolts were shot.

One would still have sworn that there was nothing offshore, other than wind on sea and rock. But even inside the double-beehive-shaped fortress Jandreck kept his hand to his tilted ear. He could hear the measured muted rhythms of oars, and the too-gentle rhythmic bow-smashings of sea. And, seven stars later, he heard, minute as cracking eggshells, the noise of keel after keel on the stones. And, again, a veiled whisper spun from mouth to mouth.

The Egilsay men found, in the centre of the web of darkness, a deserted stripped village (for every man and woman and child had carried the wealth of the people into the fortress. They had put out their hearth-flames, and left no kindling. And they had scattered their animals among the furthest pastures.)

Now a dog heard what Jandreck had heard a while back, and it began to howl. Dogs far and near joined in.

Jandreck had climbed up the winding stair that held the two concentric walls of the fortress together. At the top he leaned over. He called down reasonably and quietly to the Egilsay men. 'Here at Gurness,' he said, 'we are always pleased to have visitors, on a dark night especially. But mostly our visitors have a sign of peace in their hands – a honeycomb, say, or a cheese. What are you Egilsay men doing with daggers and axes on a dark night, when all peaceable folk should be indoors?'

Arkin the Egilsay chief looked up and he saw the head and shoulders of Jandreck framed with stars.

'We couldn't get warm in Egilsay tonight on account of the rotten peats you sent us. So we crossed the Sound to see if we could get better peats.'

'If you find some,' said Jandreck, 'you're welcome to them.' (Jandreck knew, and so did the Egilsay men, that all the Gurness peats were safe inside the fortress.)

'We will starve you out!' cried Arkin. (Well Arkin knew that inside the fortress were meat and fish, ale and cheese and honey and meal, and a well of sweet water.)

'There speaks a hero!' said Jandreck. And he threw back his head and laughed so loud that it seemed the very stars rang. Inside the fortress there was a storm of laughter. The fortress was a bubbling pot of mockery. Even the wicked old man wheezed and watered at the eyes. The children clapped hands, they danced from foot to foot.

'Arkin, I am sorry for you,' shouted Jandreck. 'Such a well-made plan! It deserved to succeed. We in Gurness should all have been red-throated corpses now. Why, Arkin man, did you whisper the plan to that woman of yours, Greve? She couldn't keep her mouth shut, the she-mountain. She babbled and she hinted. She was never done pointing over to Gurness and making the sign of the cut throat with her hand. Arkin, we keep a clever spy or two in Egilsay. Oh, Arkin, it was such a beautiful plan!'

Greve, Arkin's woman, yelled in her huge voice from the darkness below. 'Jandreck, you're a liar!'. . . And in a low agitated voice she said to Arkin, 'No, there was no hint – not a ghost of a whisper from me, Arkin. You know me better than that . . .'

There was a seething in the darkness at the base of the fortress. The men of Egilsay were angry. Possibly some of them were inclined to believe Jandreck.

'We will take your village and fortress apart, stone from stone!' cried an Egilsay man near the door of the fortress. It was a rather unfortunate last word to utter, for at that point Jandreck let drop a heavy stone from above. The man's skull cracked like a huge nut.

The Egilsay men ran back then from the fortress – a torn confused rush.

Another stone swooped down and caved in the ribs of a frantic boy. He fell. His mouth was a froth of blood.

Jandreck said sweetly, 'Last time I counted there were a thousand good-sized stones up here. But we have gathered a few heavier ones since then . . .'

A wise attacker would have gone home at once from a hopeless situation. But Arkin had been bitterly hurt by the failure of his infallible plan. What could have gone wrong? Disappointment is the father of obstinacy. Arkin decided that the people of Gurness would suffer, if not death, then a great deal of discomfort. It is not pleasant in a fortress after the third day, when the smell of dung and sweat and festering fish begins to intensify. Even rats, if herded into a narrow place, will turn and savage each other.

The men of Egilsay sheltered that night in the cold houses of Gurness, without fire or blankets.

All night Jandreck led chorus after chorus: all the thirty-eight victory songs of the people. The Egilsay men, in addition to no warmth or comfort, had no peace.

The next day the Egilsay men, gray in the face, stood about the village, axes in fists, just out of stone-range. The smell of the roasting mutton brimmed out over the high wall of the fortress. The bellies of the Egilsay men grumbled with hunger. From time to time one or other of them hurled a threat or an insult at the fortress. Arkin and Greve still kept to the chief's house.

The Egilsay men chewed bits of seaweed along the shore. One or two of them tried to fish from a rock, but the sea was empty. An Egilsay man suggested to Arkin that they cross the hill and take what they wanted from the Hundland settlement beyond. But Arkin said they had enough on their hands with-out making more enemies.

An Egilsay man spat after Greve as she went down to the cave at the shore, but only because he knew the enormous woman couldn't see him. But Arkin saw him from the corner of his eye – he thrashed the man with a long tangle. The man, squirming on the turf, yelled. Jandreck, from the top of the fortress, nodded. From inside the fortress came a torrent of mockery. The thrashed man staggered away, his face small as a fist with pain and shame. 'That one at least will be warm,' cried Jandreck from the fortress.

Just before dark there was the smell of stewing hare from the fortress. While the hares stewed in Fley's huge pot, the people sang.

'We are just going to eat a very good stew!' said Jandreck to the Egilsay men below. 'What a pity there isn't enough for you too. We do have plenty of ale, though, enough for a month. Take some with our compliments.' Then Jandreck poured out a bucket of rather sour ale from the top of the fortress. It made a mighty splash on the flagstones below. A single drop touched the dry lip of Arkin. Arkin licked it with his tongue, then spat it out.

'Plenty more ale!' cried Jandreck. 'We have plenty more.'

Inside the fortress the Gurness people ate as noisily as they could, and loud splashing noises were made as the ale was poured. Never along that coast had there been such heroic belching.

About the time of the hundredth star the Egilsay men crept miserably into the cold houses. Arkin and Greve went into the chief's bare house. The man Arkin had beaten lay all night face down under the stars.

The second morning of the siege broke – cold, with scatters of rain.

Arkin and Greve must have been discussing the situation during the night. Arkin came and stood under the fortress, but outside the range of Jandreck's stones. Jandreck was there, as always, at the tower.

'Tell Fley, that coward, that I would like a word with him,' shouted Arkin.

Jandreck said, 'Fley has other things to do than talk to the likes of you. Fley is busy. We are like a happy beehive in here. Fley is organising everything well. At the moment Fley is discussing with the cooks our breakfast. I think we are to have slices of bacon grilled, and barley bread, and of course the ale of which there are ten hogsheads here. A pity, though, there isn't enough bacon to send out to you.'

'I will be glad to settle this affair honourably,' shouted Arkin. 'I can't stay here for ever, waiting for a chief that never shows his face. We have made no preparations for the winter fire-feast in Egilsay. Listen, Jandreck, we have here a champion. Tell Fley that. I'm proposing that our champion fights the best man among you. We will accept the verdict of the outcome. The champions can fight with any weapons they like, axes or knives, or with their bare hands. When the fight is over, we will go home peaceably. If our champion wins Fley must promise to send four boat-loads of good peat to Egilsay.'

'There are some very strong men in Gurness,' said Jandreck. 'The shepherd can break a stone with one blow of his fist. One of our fishermen broke the jaw of a small whale earlier this year. We have a few men in here who love nothing better than a fight. Let's see this famous champion, Arkin.'

Arkin turned. 'Come now,' he said.

Greve, Arkin's woman, emerged from the chief's house. She was so huge she had to ease herself out sideways. She walked over, grinning, and stood beside Arkin in the square.

Now Jandreck was not alone at the top of the fortress. A score of the Gurness folk stood with him, including Eort and Vrem. The cruel old man had come up to see the fight, if there was to be one; he held on to the wall and wheezed as if he was at his last gasp. Fley was not there – he had chosen to humiliate Arkin by ignoring him utterly. The shepherd who could break stones with his fist was there. The fisherman who had wrenched the whale's jaw was there.

'Here is our champion, Greve,' said Arkin. 'Send out your best man. Send him out, or be shamed in the islands for ever! Be known far and wide for your bad faith and your rotten peats!'

Greve, still grinning, began to prepare for the fight. She stamped her feet and the ground seemed to shake. She spread her legs wide. She changed her fat fingers into ferocious claws. Never had the men of Gurness seen such an enormous woman. Her shoulders were massive and swarthy as an ox. She raised one clenched fist against the fortress – it was like a granite boulder. She took her two black braids of hair and knotted them at the top of her head.

'I have always wanted to be in the arms of a Gurness man,' said Greve. 'To be in his arms, and to put my arms about him. I will put more passion on him than he's ever had before. He will

say, *I did not think there was such strong passion in the world.*
Then I will begin to hug him properly.'

Jandreck looked earnestly down at the open palm of his hand.
This, he knew, was the kind of performance that would, before
winter was over, go sounding from end to end of Orkney. What
Gurness man could stand up to that shemonster? There wasn't
one. But if Gurness did not accept the challenge it would be a
very shameful and cowardly thing. The tribes in Hoy and in
Sandwick and in Deerness would laugh about it for generations.

The stone-splitting shepherd, standing beside Jandreck, began to sweat. 'Somebody must fight her,' he whispered. 'I'm the
strongest man in the fortress. It must be me. Tell Arkin you
have a champion. Tell Arkin the champion is coming out now
to fight Greve.'

'Shut your mouth,' said Jandreck to the shepherd. 'Be quiet.
You must be here to deliver the lambs in the snow.'

Then Jandreck raised his voice. 'Listen, Arkin. Are you
listening? I'll tell you why our chief, Fley, is out of sight. It
is simply that he does not recognise you or your cut-throats. He
made an honourable bargain with you last harvest: an exchange
of shellfish for peat. We dug the very best peat out of the Evie
hills and we sent the rich black heavy squares to you in four
boats. And you told a lie about us all over the islands: *From
Gurness we got a load of sulphur and roots and ash: no peats.* I tell
you what a liar is, Arkin. He has added a shadow to the
brightness of his flesh. He has eaten darkness. He is not a
friend of the sun. The black foot of death is inside the door of a
known liar. He has sowed a winter seed in his field. We in
Gurness are still a people of the sun. What good will it do Fley to
speak with a winter chief, a lord of shadows? (And that gross
shameless mountain of a woman, she is a shadow too, if she
shares in your lies.) All the same, Arkin, we will send out a
champion against the queen of night in the square below. He is
the brightest man among us.'

A hush fell over the fortress and village.

After as long as it takes a wave to gather and break, the single narrow door in the fortress was eased open. There was a stirring in the interior darkness. Out into the cold square came a little boy of about four summers. He stood blinking in the light, smiling, quite unafraid: even when he tilted up his small white face into the flaming astonishment of Greve's face.

For a second the huge mouth of Greve gaped at the infant. Then she put her fists to her sides and threw back her head and bellowed with mirth. The child laughed too, a little tinkling burn under a peal of thunder. Then Greve bent and took the boy in her arms and lifted him up to her red merry cheek. She kissed him resoundingly. She set him down again.

She turned to Arkin. She said, 'That's it, then. I'm beaten. So are you, Arkin. So are all our people. We should have left the men of Gurness alone. Why, Arkin, could you not be content with Egilsay? No, for two years now you've nagged at us night after night: *What I want now, what I truly want is the well-made keep at Gurness. If only we possessed that, our people would be safe for ever* . . . You tried, man. It was no good. We are well and truly beaten.'

Greve took her sheepskin jacket about her, and fastened the thongs.

One by one, gray starved shadows, the men of Egilsay began to drift out of the village and down to their boats at the shore. Arkin went last, alone.

'Goodbye, Arkin,' said the child. 'Come again.'

Before she followed the troop of shadows down to the shore Greve shouted up to the people in the tower. 'The peat you traded with us last harvest was good black peat. I have said it. Now may the black shadow of that lie be lifted from the mouth of Arkin.'

'Go in peace,' said Jandreck.

And the little boy said, 'Go in peace.'

Greve turned and walked down to the shore. At every step the earth quaked.

The four-year-old child of Fley and Vrem stood on the sea-bank and watched the departure, one after another, of the nine Egilsay boats.

THE WINTER FEAST

Days shortened. The pale sun moved through an ever-narrowing segment of sky.

One day there was a little white flurry. Jandreck stood on the sea-bank with snow in his beard.

A week before the solstice there was a storm that lasted for three days. No boats put out. The stone houses shuddered. Rousay and Egilsay and Wyre could not be seen for spindrift and low cloud.

On the shortest day the feast began in the great barn. The floor had been swept by the women the day before. The large barn kept still the fragrance of corn.

At midday the two oldest people, a man and a woman, went secretly into the barn. Everyone kept indoors – it was known to be bad luck to see the old ones going in at the barn door.

The old ones closed the door behind them.

When they knew for sure that the old man and the old woman were inside the barn, the folk came out of their houses and they drifted towards the barn door. Soon everyone in the village and fields around was standing at the barn door, except Jandreck and the chief. All were silent; even the children had been told to be quiet.

A girl, Peig, unmarried still, knocked on the barn door three times.

There was no reply. They could hear, very faintly, a murmur of voices inside. The oldest pair, as always, had begun the ceremony on their own. No one in Gurness knew what words had been uttered already. The beginning must be always a mystery.

Peig called: 'It's cold out here for me and the child that isn't born yet. We are cold and hungry. Let us in.'

Peig opened the door cautiously. The people followed her, family by family. They heard the old soft voices, but no distinct words yet. And to begin with they could not see the oldest man and the oldest woman. It was cold and dark inside the barn.

The people sat down here and there about the floor. A child picked up a barley husk and rubbed it clumsily between his fingers: a golden shadow.

When the stir died down a little, they could hear the words. When their eyes were washed with darkness, they could see, against the far wall, the thin white shaking beard and the withered mouth under the shawl.

The voices replied to one another, as if the elements were conversing across a great gulf: the land and the sea, root and star, the bone and the seed.

THE WINTER SONG

. . . That indeed was the happy time, when I saw the first green shoot in the ploughed field. And I sat on the shore, and spoke to the fish in the sea. I said: The boat is tight now. The net is ready. Tomorrow is the tryst . . .

'Darkness and snow. But that day the sun was brighter than it had ever been. There was an answering fire in the earth, a ripener. Now, always, darkness and cold.'

A young man stands rich in the door of summer. The sun is his, and the sea. He stands with five fish at the door of summer. The field is all greenness now. The girl is standing at the end of the field. She waits.

'Darkness now, darkness and ice. I turned the corn wheel under the sun, I made bread. I turned the wool wheel, I made shirt and coat and shroud. I turned the milk wheel, for butter and cheese. Now there is only the frozen pole of night.'

Sickles flashed under the red sun. Sickles glimmered in starlight and dew. This was the death of corn, but that death was life to the people. A long table was set in the great house. Bread and ale and cheese and lobster were brought to the table. I sat at the harvest table beside a smiling girl.

'Night now, always, and winter. The cradle stood in the corner of the house opposite the bed. I filled the lamps with fish oil, oil of the moon. I lit a fire. A bucket of water stood in the niche. Soon a hungry man would come in from the field. No more. Night now, and winter, and death.'

Days shortened. The sun was pale. Earth and sea were barren. But we had the sun in our cupboard: we were not afraid in the first snow. In our cupboard we kept a loaf and a bottle. The woman going between the fire and the well was ripe.

'Death without end. Once there was a song of birth and death under the thatch, a weaving of dark and bright threads. Yes, the earth then wore a green coat, and the sea was a blue coat sewn all over with fish. Now, and for ever, the world will wear armour of ice. The sun is dying. The hour of the sun's death is come. When the sun is dead, the children of the sun must die: people, beasts, fish, roots, stars.'

The bone on the beach, the bone under the furrow. There is no hope for us now. We must die. We are marked with the ashes of death. We used to comfort ourselves, 'There is a seed under the snow.' For us there is no seed under the snow. We go in at the door of night, winter, death . . .

The old mouths fell silent. There was a long silence in the barn. Then the child with the barley husk suddenly wailed and clung to its mother.

There was one loud knock at the barn door.

The old man and the old woman said together: *Night. Winter. Death.*

The door opened. The leader of the people entered. He was holding a lighted lamp in his hand. On his arm he carried the youngest child of the people, a week-old baby. Fley carried the baby into the barn and set him in the midst of the people. The lamp shone on the faces of the people, a new light.

The two old ones left their corner. Helping each other, hobbling, half blind, they crossed the barn floor and sat smiling among the people.

The old ones said: *New light. The new light.*

Then the people rose up, laughing. Led by the chief bearing lamp and child, they moved in a procession to the chief's house. Winter's gray circle had reached the full. Now it was on the wane: the green and the blue had begun to encroach.

The chief's table was spread with a feast richer far than midsummer or harvest – as if the whole fruitful year had been preparing for this one night: lobsters, hares, honey, bread, flagon after flagon of the oldest ale.

At the wall a dozen torches burned redly.

The midwinter procession, as it entered the chief's house, was greeted with harp-strokes.

All the people were present soon, except for Jandreck. Jandreck stood at the rock on the shore. Summoned to story-telling or ceremony, Jandreck twisted his mouth and turned his back. The cold eye of Jandreck was on the sea, always, summer and winter.

The empty barn waited for seed-time. Against the walls of the barn leaned the sun symbols: plough, seed-bag, harrows, scythe, flail, quernstones, vat.

THE PLOT

There was a young man called Swathe and he was the best cragsman among the people. Swathe brought home many wild birds to be smoked and salted; each spring thousands of eggs from the cliff edges.

Swathe was not a popular man among the people. It was said that he thought too highly of himself. It was considered that he spoke too much at the meetings about things of which he knew nothing.

But one or two of the younger men followed Swathe everywhere. Some of the girls kept their best smiles for him.

One quiet morning at the end of winter Swathe came to Jandreck at his station above the shore.

'Jandreck,' said Swathe. 'Some of us are going to hold a meeting tonight at the cave – a few chosen ones. We want you to be present.'

'What is the meeting about?' said Jandreck.

'It is a secret matter, not to be spoken about in daylight.'

'Everything should be uttered in daylight, except love and crime. I don't think I want to go to your meeting, Swathe. Indeed I can't go. I am here to watch the horizon.'

'You may be sorry some day that you didn't come to the meeting,' said Swathe. 'It is secret, but it concerns everyone.'

The very next day Swathe and two other young men approached Jandreck on the links.

'Jandreck,' said Swathe, 'we have a gift for you. Here. Take it.'

Swathe then put into Jandreck's hand a piece of carved walrus ivory. It was a beautiful piece of work. On the ivory disc was carved a sun, and a whale, and an island with a farm and people, and under the waves a swarm of fish.

'Brae here carved the walrus-bone last night, at home, after the meeting,' said Swathe. 'A good carving. It is a sign of the prosperous time that is to come to this people. It is more than a sign, Jandreck, it's a summons. When I saw the carving, I said, "This must be given to Jandreck. Without Jandreck our task will be much more difficult." They all said after me, "Yes, the carving will be a gift to Jandreck."'

The young man called Brae said, 'It's the best carving I have ever done. It's yours, Jandreck.'

'It's well done,' said Jandreck. 'Brae, I congratulate you. But I don't want it.'

'It's valuable,' said Swathe. 'The shepherd has just seen it. The shepherd said, "I'll give Brae my first three spring lambs for this carving." We are giving it to you for nothing, Jandreck.'

'I told you,' said Jandreck, 'I don't want it. I have a hearth-stone and a wife and my station here at the shore. If I were to think about precious things, and begin to desire them, my eye would grow dim. Take the carving. Sell it to the shepherd. Give it to Vrem: her house is stuffed with fine objects.'

Swathe went so far as to push the carving inside Jandreck's jacket. Jandreck pulled it out and threw it away. It stuttered among the round stones of the beach, and went reeling this way and that, and lay silent on the sand at last.

Brae picked up the walrus carving. Without a word, without looking back, he walked along the shore and the other young men followed him.

Jandreck and Swathe were left alone.

Swathe said, 'An important thing was decided at the secret meeting in the cave. We are all sorry indeed, Jandreck, that you were not there.'

Jandreck said nothing.

It was the darkest night of the month, with no moon or stars. The little crests of the waves could be seen off Eynhallow. A dead fish glowed like a lantern on the shore.

Jandreck said, 'I know there's someone there in the darkness at my back. Who is it?' But he did not turn his head.

(Once or twice in the past Jandreck had had night visitors – honied whispers, breaths of allurement, inarticulate sighs and adorings . . . Jandreck said always, on these occasions, without turning his head, 'Woman, whoever you are, go into the sea.

Cool your fires there' . . . Then, always, he was alone with night and silence.)

The darkness rustled. The darkness whispered. A masked voice said, 'What is to become of this people? Answer me.'

Jandreck said, 'The god has always looked after the people.'

The masked voice said, 'This triangle of land and shore and sky is too small for the people. The people are growing in numbers year by year. The young men are strong. The girls are fertile. There are many children. There is not enough land for the hungers of the people. This has been discussed at the assembly of the people for three years past. The chief ends all discussion by saying, *We are the people. This is our land. The god, if we behave honourably and charitably among ourselves, and to the other peoples round about, will see that we lack for nothing* . . . But already there are too many mouths and too few fish and cornstalks. Jandreck, what is to become of this people? Answer me.'

'The chief speaks for the people,' said Jandreck. 'I think those must be dolphins in the sea out there.'

'The other peoples,' said the masked voice. 'With the other peoples – with some of the other tribes – matters are very different. Three men from Hundland came and stood at the boundary stone last harvest. *It goes badly with us. There are too few ploughmen in Hundland. Most of our girls have no husbands. Help us, you strong men of Gurness.* From Costa two men came and stood near the other boundary stone. They said, *Our chief is old and sick. He has no sons. When the chief dies in Costa, five young strong beasts will rage together on our hillside. Protect us, you cunning men of Gurness.* Mention was made of these matters in the assembly. At last the chief stood up. Fley said, *The people of Hundland and the people of Costa have their gods. A god looks after his people in a troubled time. We will not meddle with the people of Hundland or with the people of Costa, nor their gods. I will not take these tribes over and be their chief . . .* That is what our chief said. That is how our chief refused the rule and the gifts. This is the kind of chief we have. What is to become of our tumult and overspill of people, Jandreck? Answer me.'

'Fley always speaks with wisdom,' said Jandreck. 'I think it must be nearly midnight. That dead fish is shining brightly.'

'We could possess the lands of Hundland and Costa and Gorseness before next harvest,' said the masked voice. 'If we had the lands of Hundland and Costa and Gorseness we would be a strong people. No other tribe in Orkney could stand against us. The island of Gairsay and the island of Wyre would come soon and ask for our protection. We would be as strong as the people of Birsay, stronger even. There would never again be such nonsense as last winter, when Arkin of Egilsay told the lie about us and then set siege to us for three days. But Fley will do nothing. What is to become of this people? Jandreck, answer quickly.'

'To do nothing is sometimes to do a great deal,' said Jandreck. 'There, listen. The end of the ebb! In a short while you will begin to hear the song of the flood.'

There was silence on the land and in the sea. Then, after a pause, the masked voice resumed. 'There is a natural ordering of things. Nothing can prevent it. Human societies grow from small to great. In this way, a cast of luck, such as our victory against the men of Egilsay last winter, is a sign to be taken advantage of at once. Small grows to great, for the man who can read such matters and is resolute to profit by the signs, while the great ones hesitate and shake their heads. The strong young well-governed tribe takes over, for their own good, weak and decayed tribes. That cannot be prevented. Can you prevent the tide from ebbing and flowing? You can stay the sand in the hour-glass, but not the flux of time.

'In the end it will come to this – the thirty tribes of Orkney, in their scattered valleys and islands, will be a single people with a single chief. Here in Gurness we have never had so many young strong thrusting men. They need more land. They are hungry for more land, more sheep, more boats. But our chief is weak. Fley sits at the hearth-flame and plays with his young son. Fley is useless. But there is in Gurness a strong one. He will know how to act when the time comes. Jandreck, do not stand in the way of the young and the strong. The best of the story of this people is now to be told. Jandreck, what will the story say about you? Answer me.'

'I will not answer you now,' said Jandreck. 'There are a few hours of darkness left. I will think about what you have said. There is trouble of some kind in the cliff over there. The birds are quarrelling.'

Soon Jandreck had the night to himself.

After dawn next morning the body of Swathe the cragsman was found dead on the shore, two miles from the village. It was thought at first that Swathe must have fallen from the crag face. But it was soon known that he had no bruises or broken bones: there was not a mark on him. A young powerful man, there he lay dead among the seaweed.

A few girls wept for him.

Next day they burned his body near where it had been found. The chief said, as the flames grew and clustered, 'There will be fewer eggs for our pots and jars next summer. There will be fewer puffins to hang in the smoke. For never in the memory of the men of Gurness has there been a cragsman like Swathe, so brave and so lucky. Opinions differ as to the best time to die. But it may be that youth is the best time to turn one's back on the light: before the evil days come.'

'Oh, yes, oh yes,' sighed the wicked old man, brineless tears on his face.

Jandreck did not go near the fire and the funeral. He watched the sea.

He did not hear any more about cave-meetings or conquests.

No one offered him a precious gift again. He hears no more the masked voice at midnight.

STORIES

Gruth was the name of an old man and he had long been the keeper of the stories. When some of the people gathered in Gruth's house after sunset, and heard the stories from his mouth, each felt that he was not just an individual who had been born and must die sometime: he was part of a larger pattern. Gruth put depth and meaning into their days, beyond the immediate necessities of food and drink and love and sleep.

Here are some of the stories that Gruth chanted in the firelight. Set out in cold script, they seem ordinary enough. But the mouth of the story-teller uttered enchantments. It had power and range and subtlety (though, some of the older folk said, Gruth was not so good as some of the old story-tellers). Gruth would repeat words and phrases over and over again, sometimes whispering, sometimes shrieking, sometimes singing. He might take up two stones and dash them together at a certain part of, say, a war chant. If the story concerned the sea, he might lift a scallop shell to his mouth and murmur into it. Always his hands moved, weaving the story. Eort once said that she could have followed the events of the story from watching the old man's hands, even if she had been stone deaf.

Very rarely, Gruth would go into a trance, or some spirit would enter into him, and then he told of things that had not yet happened but would of necessity come to pass.

The older people would never forget the time, thirty winters before, that Gruth had prophesied the death of a former chief. It was utterly unexpected: the chief, Fley's grandfather, was a young man in excellent health. Gruth that evening was telling 'the love story' of the musician and the gray-eyed girl, the last of the original dispossessed Gurness tribe – that is, how a remote man of the people had, in a time of famine, bound the old and the new together with a love song, and so brought back fullness to furrow and folk . . . Half-way through the story – just at the part where Orfeo the musician wakes from his dream on the hillside and sees the gray-eyed girl in a gap of the hills – at that beautiful part of the story Gruth had fallen silent, as if his mouth was locked and he might never speak again. Also his eyes were shut fast. And his eloquent fingers were laced together tight. The silence lasted a long while. The listeners stirred uneasily and looked at each other. One or two rose up and left the house. There was no sound in the story-teller's house but only the whisper of burning peat on the hearth. Then Gruth unclasped his hands, and held them, palms out, to the people. He said in a very sweet pure voice like a boy: 'Now Antrin has scattered the herd of swine' . . . The listeners were astonished. Antrin was the name of their chief at the time; Antrin and a herd of swine did not follow at all from the half-told love story that was so familiar to them. Gruth's eyes were still closed, but he was seeing vivid images. After another silence, he chanted, 'The great pig, the boar, has covered the tracks of the herd. The boar turns. The boar looks at the young chief . . . Antrin offers his spear point to the boar. A hawk hangs, remote, high, uncaring. Antrin makes a seeking circle with his spear. The beast breaks through the rim of the broken circle, the beast makes an upthrust with his tusk at the belly of the hunter, the arc of that circle goes red through belly and thigh, and again through breast and shoulder, a red arc, and again through throat, a red swift rending circle. The snout is at the three wounds. The beast screams. Then, red-snouted, the animal crosses the hill to where the herd is' . . . Here the mouth of the story-teller smiled, as if an inevitable treaty had been sealed as between man and animal. The listeners looked at him with blanched faces. A voice said in the darkness, 'Gruth has drunk too much of that new ale!' A voice said, 'It is terrible!' Another voice said, 'It is good – the words are well-ordered.' Another voice said, 'It is nonsense! Antrin the chief is sitting beside me near the door . . .' And Antrin said, 'I will take care not to have any dealings with wild pigs in time to come' . . . Then the house was filled with laughter. The only one who did not laugh that night was Gruth. He sat, grave and apart, his eyes closed. When the house was quiet again, suddenly Gruth shook his head and opened his eyes. 'Well,' he said in his ordinary voice, 'that's the end of the love story. I hate to boast, but, friends, I think I have never told the love story better than I told it just now.'

The listeners thanked him. They got to their feet. One by one they went out through the door. None told Gruth that they had heard only half the love story: the second part had been a vision of death.

It was the next spring that Antrin was found dead in the heather, with wounds in throat and breast and belly, and a broken spear in his hand. The chief had gone out that day alone with his hawk.

Here are some of the stories that Gruth told the people winter after winter: but in this cold script the music and the magic are out of them.

The hundred stories of Gruth of Gurness: they may appear to be the stuff of imagination rather than of history. The modern mind tends to reject whatever seems to be fanciful and contrary to established fact. Are we to take it seriously, for example, that a snow eagle became a girl? We know that such things are against nature and impossible.

Yet, as the poets have insisted over and over, there is a truth of the imagination as well as the truth represented by accumulations of fact. Fable, myth, fairy-tale distil the essence of a nation's documented fact, so much being lost, or unknown, or given different weight and emphasis according to the bias of the historian, who is forever imposing false patterns.

Here, by way of preface to the Gruth-narrative, is a kind of background. Thus and thus it might have been, the thrust of certain tribes into the west – the tribes being of a single origin, as their root-language seems to indicate.

So, in India, there are words and syllables little different from the utterances of a Barraman or a Donegalman.

How far must we go back to find the beginnings of the people?

Very far back memory must venture, gathering legends and fables – so far back that even the legends and fables falter and are silent at last.

The imagination dares a step or two beyond the most ancient memory, and what it sees is a solitary figure against the sunrise, somewhat like a man, yet not a true man, for the skull is set thickly on the shoulders and the arms hang down almost into the dust, and the hairy fingers pluck an insect or a berry out of the scrub.

Imagination covers her eyes. She cannot bear to look on such a savage creature, half man and half beast.

Turn round, imagination, face the terrain which memory explores over and over in dreams and myths; and behold, it is an altogether kindlier scene that meets the eye. There, under a tree, stands a creature that is undoubtedly a man; he hunts; he has a vibrant bow in his capable delicate hands; his arrow trembles in the throat of a young deer. A woman comes from a shelter deep in the woodland, a house of green branches; she has gathered twigs and now she blows the twigs into flames on a broad flat stone. The man skins the dead animal where it has fallen.

Presently the woman hears a cry from the green tent that is their shelter. She goes in search of it. She returns, carrying a child.

The first man has set the carcase on trestles over the fire.

They stand together, the man and woman and child, under the tree that is heavy with fruit.

Should they not stay here, in this pastoral innocence, before there is any knowledge of time or destiny?

No, because even as they eat the tender flesh of the creature, they know that what nourishes them is the fruit of death, and that they themselves must perish if they stay in one set round of existence like the other creatures; no, they must be faring on out of this green place of mortality into ever-widening circles. And whither travel? As sun and moon and stars travel, westwards. Their blood drives them and lures them the only way, into the unknown west. Not this good year, when fruit and animals are plentiful. But some winter perhaps, when the apple-trees are bare and the steppe empty of prey, then their children's children must obey their blood and follow the constellations into the promised land, the glories beyond the sunset, a deathless bourne.

And as the tribes of children's children moved west, from place to place, driven by hunger, lured by curiosity and the promise, there were dissensions and disputes, so that from time to time – generally after a long period of settlement – a group would suddenly, one dawn, leave the valley and head off west on their own, without so much as a farewell to the chief and elders of the folk. And those forerunners were generally the best of the young men, and they took women with them, for there had been careful secret plottings under the stars all the previous winter. Also many of the best sheep were missing.

It fared variously with those bands of rebels, hivers-off, breakers of the bonds of kin, explorers, westerlings, over the generations.

For in the villages of the settled people, among the rich grasslands, life grew richer and easier for most of the in-habitants, by virtue of fortunate discoveries and intuitions – spinning, weaving, brewing, the smelting of ore, bee-culture, taming and bridling of horses, the careful selection of the seeds of wild corn and their sowing in furrows, sinking of wells for pure unpolluted water.

Then, after three or four generations of prosperity, unquiet rumours were brought from the east. A kindred tribe – but long unknown to them, except that they shared certain words and legends – was on the move under the horizon, they had ridden into a famous city with swords and torches, and left it in ruins. 'Ah,' said the shepherds of the distant flocks, 'have we not seen the flames by night? Have we not given water and bread to the fugitives? Have they not told us, their eyes wide with terror and wonderment, that those murderers, a mighty host, are by no means content with what they have taken, but on their charts they have marked your little city for destruction also?'

Thus the shepherds, hunters, falconers, reported to the chief and elders assembled. Thereupon a great dispute ensued. Some were for forging spears and swords in the smithies, and turning shepherds and artisans and ploughmen into soldiers, and building a high strong wall around the town. And orders were given, thus. Others in the place of assembly shook their heads over the pale prosperity-ruined unpreparedness of the people. But nevertheless the forges blazed and a wall of strong bricks began to be built about the town. And the lithe young hunters burdened themselves with bronze spears.

The wave of ruin fell on them with great fury and suddenness. In the darkness before dawn, the streets rang from end to end with bronze axes and the cries of the defeated. The town was clothed in rags of flame. The savage kinsmen from the east beat down door after door, looking for the treasury. A young woman cried against the invaders from the temple steps . . .

A few of the city dwellers – a remnant – came together before morning, and they gathered scatterings of the flock from the hillside, and – the blood-tide at last wakened in the young men by adversity – they prepared for a trek into valleys far in the west, where they might be able to settle again for a while, and ply the wonderful skills that the gods had given them.

And so it was, while the conquerors lay about the charred streets drunk with wine and blood and silver, that this remnant of the people set out with burdened mules: a sorrowful remnant, yet full of hope. After many days, the little flock of sheep cried with the smell of new succulent grasses blown to them on a wind from the west.

You understand, friends, it is not of this people of Gurness in particular that I speak.

The folk of Gurness and their kindred tribes had moved into the west long before. Yes, they had moved out of another doomed city, further back, six generations before, irked by internal dominations and rivalries and constrictions and the rule of old men; or touched to foreknowledge perhaps by the prophecies and wisdom graven on old stones.

I speak of the general movement of the tribes – a pattern that is repeated over and over, so that one settlement I have just been describing becomes a motif in an ever-unfolding pattern.

How lost is the little thread of the Gurness folk in this huge world-weave!

We locate them, at last, somewhere in northern Europe – Latvia, perhaps – at the time of one of the ebbings of the Ice Age.

Before and around them are kindred tribes, with whom they sometimes make alliances or have confrontations of blood and broken skulls; but in the end they always speak uneasy peace to one another; for there is the dark folk-memory of a greater danger in the east, not too far under the dawn.

One day there was a total eclipse of the sun. The men covered their mouths. The women had tranquil faces. The animals hid themselves in the ashen twilight.

Next morning a man who had gone east to the then bound of their biding, to seek out a lost ewe, came back breathless, to announce that he had heard the beat of urgent strange hooves under the horizon. An unknown tribe was on the move.

The falconer came back without his hawk. There were horn calls to the south also, and agitation among the birds, and a cloud of dust, and flames from the villages of their immediate neighbours.

They moved then westwards and northwards. The mountains were bare and wore on their summits the everlasting star of snow.

They struck their tents. On they journeyed.

Something further should be said of this sun-wandering and moon-wandering and star-wandering.

In the hard light, between dawn and sunset, men come and go; but a young man now and then, here and there, at large intervals of time and place, will sit in the desert and make signs and calculations on the sand with a pointed stick. On a certain day, there will be a cry *eureka* on the edge of the tents, the young man will blunder into the set-apart place where the elders are deliberating and he will set before them, bright-eyed and eager, a new wonderful thing: wheel, perhaps, or spindle, or lamp, or yoke, or loom.

The elders, affronted, will reject the invention; perhaps banish the young inventor beyond the bounds, as a stealer of forbidden knowledge; but mostly they will point the finger and laugh him to scorn, as a dreamer and a scion of dreamers.

It may only be, when that young discoverer is dust, that the invention passes into general use, and is wondered at for a while, but at last is taken for granted.

Wheel, spindle, lamp, yoke, kiln, loom: they pass also into the imagination of the people, and enrich the language and the ceremonies.

So out of the sun's light and fires have come those blessings that strengthen the tribe in the times of danger and tribulation.

Who, generations after the discovery of wheel-and-kiln, rises up from the rock spring with the brimming pitcher, and sets it on her shoulder?

Who draws the hard thin line of wool from the spindle?

Who fills the lamp with oil after sunset and sets it, mildly glowing, in the niche?

Who takes one by one from the reddened hearth the small loaves, and sets them on a stone to cool?

Always, when we try to picture the final end of a sun-discovery, the closing of the circle, it is a woman old or young that is there.

Without her the important discovery that has become a life-giving symbol would have no meaning at all.

Men calculate, invent, cry *eureka* at last. But a deeper mysterious power has impelled them to lure these things into the light.

It might be said indeed, that without the mysterious hidden moon-wisdom of the feminine element, the inquisitive restless sun-inventiveness would never have roused itself from brutishness. The creature against the sunrise, with skull set thickly on shoulders and arms hanging down to the dust, would not have made a first shambling step into the west.

Therefore, in the legends, the story-teller Gruth of Gurness gives honour, again and again, to girl and mother and widow; wherever, moon-like, she wanders among the fixed stars of fate, she sheds wonderment and beauty.

A new day breaks. Men go out with adzes and with arrows, the sun on their brows, in the little settlement that they have established, and have lived in for so many generations that it seems to be almost everlasting.

Now let Gruth the story-teller of Gurness take up the epic.

I

They woke. Great towers of ice stood all about them.

Many died in the shadow of the ice fortresses.

The invisible ice-giants struck them down with axes made of light and coldness, eager biting edges. Then were great feasting times for wolf and eagle.

They were not men, but giants, the dwellers in the towers of ice.

The fire in the heart of the sun-chief, our ancestor, it was all but quenched by the breath of the ice-giants.

The people called then on the sun to help them in those ice battles.

Their hearts filled with the last sun-fires, the young men rose at dawn to march against the ramparts of ice.

The ice towers melted before them. The ice-giants fled before them, howling, into the north.

The rocks were theirs, and the first green herbs growing among the rocks. A small blue rose opened in the sward.

There by a lake on a rock sat an eagle. The eagle held a fish in its talons.

This was the first time our people had seen a lake and fish.

As they looked, the eagle became a girl, and still as they watched the last pinions fell from her, and the furled wings opened and were lissom arms in the light, and the talon unlocked from the sturgeon, and was an offering hand.

Then the girl gave them the fish, and she went with that sun-people into the west. The ice-maiden dwelt in the tent of the sun-king. And the strength of eagles entered the blood of our ancestors.

But a few stayed among the ice mountains and the fjords.

II

The people woke in their tents and the trees of a forest stood all about them.

Fear fell on the tribe because of the green presences all about them, never known before.

But the sun came scattering through the foliage and cheered them.

A tree said, 'We are friends to this people, friends of the sun, we too are children of the sun. Welcome.'

A tree said, 'Look, I am giving you arrows and strong pliant singing bows.'

A tree said, 'I give you my wood for fires in the cold nights of winter. And that you may broil and bake your meats, not gnaw at blood and raw guts like the wolves.'

A tree said, 'Friends, you will have little huts to shelter you, and a hall where the people may come together in harmony and peace.'

A tree said, 'How shall the young men and women come together without dancing? Hidden in me is a harp and a pipe that will make you sweeter music than the stretched skins of goat and bullock. Also the old ones will comfort their age with music, and the circling song will seem like the pattern of their days, the labour and the sorrow made beautiful.'

So the ancestors had at last great friendship and love of the forest.

There, in the forest, with the animals and birds, in their villages, they lived for as long as a hundred years. They honoured their dead with fire.

Also the animals and birds consented to yield them their strength and innocence by way of arrows and cooking fires and scattered bones.

A young hunter that hunted on the mountain, in a high place where no trees could grow and the snow began, came back after a month with a wolf over his shoulders, and he said to the chief: 'From the high place where I stood I looked eastward and I saw the biggest fires and I heard, very far away, the songs of a powerful people. Also their horses reared towards the west' . . .

Fear fell on our tribe.

Then the oak tree spoke: 'Look, friends of the sun, I am giving myself to you. There is no long continuance under a static sun, for hawk or serpent or man. You are not far from the sea. Sometimes, at sunset, you can hear the ocean music coming through the branches. You must leave this bourne and must give yourselves to the sea in ships. How shall you make ships, who have never seen sea or ship? Necessity, once you come to the shore, will put cunning on the hands of the woodmen, they will study on the shore, on the first brimmings of ocean, the birds that float and fly there. The freedom of wings will come on them, and the joy of winds and waters. Cut me down, wood-men, drag me after you to the shore.'

Sorrowfully our people began to prepare for the trek to the ocean.

And some would stay.

To them the chief said, 'To linger overlong in one place is to grow rank and rotten. The strong eastern tribes will smash you under their hooves.'

And many wept.

On the night before the trek, a strange girl glanced at them from behind a tree. The twigs were growing still from her shoulders and fingers, and a leaf drifted down slowly from her mouth.

'I am to go with you,' said the girl, 'so that the friendship of the forest will be with you always.'

The girl that was half a tree went with the people when the people came out of the forest into the full light of the sun, driving their flocks, and heard, far off in the west, the sea and the summons.

And they dragged with them the great oak, that had been so full of promises.

And the tree-girl married the chief of the people.

III

Seven generations the people lived wretchedly on the coast, eating seaweeds and crabs and the tough oily cormorant.

The great oak that their fathers had dragged from the forest lay in a cave, half forgotten.

And there were disputes at the assembly, and some turned and set their faces east, to the old friendship and ease of the forest.

And three came back from the trees after many years, wretched and bleak, and said how the forest was possessed by the mighty tribes moving ever towards the west.

The tribes made a great clearance in the forest, said the returning fugitives. They had made from certain trees ploughs and yokes, and ploughmen and oxen wounded the earth with those curved ploughs, but afterwards from the wounds at the end of summer grew long nourishing grasses that gave them sun-food and sun-drink, more delightful in the mouth than pig-meat or broiled pigeon, and more strengthening, for it seemed that that nourishment kept a purer sun-essence.

Into those intensities of fire the deserters had blundered, seeking backward to the peace of the trees, and those faithless ones had shrivelled, or they were made wretched slaves, hewers of wood and drawers of water. And these few miserable remnants had escaped, children of slaves, and were now returned to the true people, bringing the secrets of plough and bread.

'Forever wretched are those,' said the chief of our folk, 'who turn their faces against the wheel of time and fate. Here we live a thin life, on a bitter coast, compared to the happy fruits and foliage we knew. But the sun is our lord still, the sun will unlock to us the secrets of the sea and voyaging.'

The next morning, the young man who had all that summer looked at the waves, and at the comings and goings of sea birds, and had made silent arcs and curves and circles on the sand with the pointed end of a stick, so that the busy people, the scavengers and riflers of rockpools said, 'That boy does nothing for his keep, he is an idler and a dreamer, he is a burden to us' – this young man, the watcher of birds and the maker of curves on the sand, came at evening when the folk were sitting round the fire, and he said, 'I know now how to make a boat, and I have made a boat in the cave where the mighty oak has lain for so long, and oars likewise I have taken from the oak, and I have stitched a sail, and tomorrow I will launch this hollow oak bird into the sea, and I ask the elders of the people to come and stand on the sea-banks and observe this wonder, for I would not have it wasted upon the ignorant chewers of crab-bones.'

The chief, a young man himself, made a place for the dreamer beside him.

And there was silence in the gathering.

And the young boatwright said, 'I am a clever man, as you know, I am a friend of birds and waves, but it would have been no good to me, that friendship, but that I had a visitor last month when the moon was near its full, a stranger, a young woman. Her mouth was full of syllables and secrets, and she kissed me, and when I awoke at dawn in the cave I saw the image of a boat in my mind, true and exact and lovely, so purely planned in its dovetailings and fitments that all I had to do in the cave of the oak tree was to carve and cut the planks, and secure them with twine, and lock all together with wooden pins, and this I have done when those seaweed chewers were heaping on me all kinds of insult, even threatening me with exile and starvation and death. Such creatures are not worthy to look on the miracle of the first boat.'

The chief saw next morning the boat dancing on the sea.

That was in winter. By the solstice of the next summer there were a dozen boats going between horizon and shore, and the new fishermen sounded for drifting shoals of fish, herring and cod, and brought them back to the pots and the cooking fires, sometimes many, sometimes only a few.

So that generation passed, and the ship-dreamer was one skull among many, but now the craftsmen in the caves knew the way to build boats.

And that generation, and the one following, flourished beside the sea. They grew cunning at making of nets and hooks.

And the people – though a few of the young men drowned each winter – would gladly have stayed in their sea villages, now that the sea was their friend and mother.

But the chief said, 'Lingering in one place is nonsense and worse than nonsense. We know this in our bones. I have heard, far inland, the urgent beating of hammers on anvils, nights-long. The easterners drove our fathers from the forest, now they will drive us from our sea villages with their horses and long bronze lances. They too are children of the sun, and they are more powerful in every way than us, but we are the first chosen children, and our fate is to make a golden everlasting settlement in the west.'

Women began to weep in the doors, at the thought of leaving the villages and fruitful shores and the graves of their dead: mounds of burnt ash above the sea-banks.

'You boatbuilders are to turn your minds,' said the chief, 'to the building of one great ship. It will carry us all to the last bourne in the west. There, there will be no more hardship, sorrow, withering or death. But first, the shipbuilding, the star chart, the long voyage.'

At the time of the setting out they had seven large ships.

IV

Then it was, our fathers had long acquaintance with the bitterness and the bounty of the salt ocean.

Westward the ships sailed, with a headland to starboard and a headland to port.

Through that channel they sailed. Headland by headland on each side, widening, gave welcome and farewell.

The bows of the ships snorted foam. The ships threw water from them, this way and that.

The ships strode across fields of sea, valleys and hills of ocean, many days and many nights.

The nets drew bounties of fish from the green deeps.

The gates of the land opened so wide they could see nothing but ocean to the west.

'We will yet sail west,' said the skippers.

The first ship turned north and the others followed and soon there lay land on either side once more, blue in the distance.

The moon grew from a finger-nail to a silver apple and shrank again to a cinder. The casks of sweet water were empty.

There stood on a shore in Ireland an old man. The sailors threatened him with knives, to show them where a well was. The old man laughed at the knives. He said it mattered nothing to him whether or not they killed him. He said that the women on the ship were such wretched salt-crusted shrunken trulls, a mouthful or two of good water would make them blossom again.

So the old man led them to a well above the shore, and they filled fifty barrels. A young man said they should now kill the ancient on account of the insults he had put on the women of the voyage. But the chief thanked the ancient and gave him fish and let him go.

The women drank. If they had indeed seemed wretched on account of the voyage, now with this Irish water a loveliness and lissomness came upon them, and they sang like girls on the shore.

So the ships drove north, until the gate of land swung towards the open sea westward, but yet there lay islands and hills and straths on the starboard quarter.

Thereabout they encountered the sea-monster Jascoyne. It fell in great wrath upon a ship in the rear and broke it in two and all the sailors were drowned. When the monster saw that there were no girls in the sea it was enraged even more and it reared up to break them, ship after ship.

Then the chief took his own daughter and bound her and threw her into the sea. Circles of brightness and fragrance rose from the place of her drowning.

And Jascoyne followed them no more.

Sailors came to the chief in the first ship and they said, 'Our stomachs are sick with eating monk-fish and cormorants, and we see a flock of sheep on that hill.'

The young sailors swam ashore, and they asked the shepherds to let them have seven of their fattest sheep.

The shepherds said nothing.

The young shipmen drew knives from their belts and held the knives against the throats of the shepherds.

The shepherds said nothing.

Then the youngest shepherd took a bone pipe from his belt and set it to his mouth and his cheeks grew round as apples and his fingers went hither and thither upon the stops.

The sailors stopped their ears against the music and each man seized a ewe from the flock and blundered down to the shore, and so came burdened and struggling to the ships, carrying the sheep.

But one stayed behind. He danced on the shore to the music. As long as the music lasted, his dance went on, and the music did not stop and the moon got up.

Next morning it was noticed that that young man had not returned.

'That was very beautiful music that the shepherd played,' said the chief.

The sheep-rievers said they had stopped their ears against the music.

'These are enchanted islands we have come among,' said the chief. 'We have not done well to linger here. We should take up the anchor now and sail west.'

It was noticed that none of the young men who swam ashore to bargain with the shepherds was ever afterwards of much account on the voyage. Age came on them quickly, ash in their black curling beards and a stringiness in their throats, and all they were good for was weaving nets and baiting the hooks, and mumbling foolish old matters over and over, till at last they died.

One of the nets was brought up next morning and in it lay tangled the body of the dancer. They had not seen him so beautiful, lying on the deck with sun-bright water streaming out of his mouth and hair.

Before they sank him in a sail weighed with stones, his mouth opened and spoke: *I have been given the gift of poetry by the shepherds of Alba.*

A girl said she heard him singing for a great while afterwards, under the sea. So sweet the songs, she could not but weep.

The ships sailed between islands to the left and mountains and black forests to starboard.

Night came down with no moon. The ships in the rear heard a rending and a crash and many cries, and the ships anchored at once. At sunrise they saw that the chief's ship was a wreck on a skerry. The shore beyond was strewn with bodies. The chief himself had gotten to land, and some others. They stood on the shore with their hands over their streaming mouths.

On ship and on shore the women set up a disordered chorus of grief.

There came out of a hut like a beehive a very old man that walked gravely down to the shore.

The old man said to the chief, 'You were bidden to sail into the west after the sun; in the west is the isle of the ever-young, where the treasure abides that does not wither, and those who have behaved well in this round of bitterness and sorrow inherit that paradise. But you have chosen to follow the old ways of trouble and greed, wrath and pride and murder, and therefore you will be beset with monsters and storms wheresoever you turn.'

Then the old man walked into the sea until he came to the wreck. On one side of the prow he cut a crescent moon and on the other a sun. On the stern he cut seven stars.

No sooner had he cut the sun on the broken wood than the ship healed itself, it came together again, the splintered strakes made whole and wholesome curves, and the shattered mast rose up tall and clothed itself in its sail, and the ship fell from the reef as a seal takes to the water and the ship danced blithely on the bright waves.

And the chief and the people went on board ship.

And the chief thanked the old magician.

Who said: 'Is it possible a whole nation can come to that blessed shore in the west? It is not possible by any means. This happens, here and there, now and then, all over the earth, there is a man or woman or child of such beauty and simplicity of life that he sets out alone on the voyage to Tir-Nan-Og, and he is greeted there with glad shouts, and with apple-blossom and harp songs. It may be that the others will come there too at the last, through storms of fire and wind, and be brought ashore by the young hands after long suffering. No more than that can I see now, for my vision is limited. Glad I would be of the certain knowledge that somewhere, sometime, a whole entire people sailed into that harbour in the west – no, not one people only, but all the races and nations who have ever inhabited the globe. That will not be possible until men have the innocence of the animals and the wisdom of angels.'

Then the chief thanked the old wise man and asked if the ships would come to a good enough shore as far as the things of time go.

The old man answered: 'You will come to a shore good enough, but others dwell there already, a gray-eyed folk, kinsmen of your own from far back, precursors, and they have lived so long and with such reverence there that the blessing of the place has entered into them. There will, after you come, be little peace about those hills and fishing-grounds. You will give and take blood and sorrow to the end. Let a faithful man watch from the headland, an eye that sees into the past and into the future . . . As for true peace, let each man meditate that in the sanctuary of his heart. It may be, at last one perfect man will redeem the whole earth.'

Then the old man went back to his cell, and an otter followed him with a fish in its mouth. There was a fire outside the old man's door and a pot over it, and the old man took the fish from the otter and cleaned it and put it in the pot.

The ships sailed on north.

This story of the voyage takes a short time to tell, but many years and generations had passed since they left that fishing shore in Western Europe.

At this time there were disputes between the skippers of the seven ships, nor could the young chief hold them together, having less authority than the old chief his father who had died when his son was a child.

One skipper said they ought to hold west still, in accordance with the old promise and the old injunction. Another said they should return to Ireland with the green hills. Another, that they were sailing towards the bergs and the whales. Another, that the black forests of Alba were dense with wolves and deer, and they would never starve if they settled by a sea loch. Another, that in the west the last torrents would sweep their ships over the edge of the earth.

But still the little fleet held together, sailing on north.

Beyond Cape Wrath a great sea fog wrapped the ships for many days.

While the ships lay blind and fearful in a sea loch, a girl swam out from the shore and was drawn into the chief's ship, and she spoke words that our people could not understand.

Then this girl kissed the young chief, and then after the kiss he understood everything she said.

The chief asked the girl if there was land to the north-east.

'Yes,' she said, the mild islands of the whale, Orkney.

The other skippers called her a witch. Was she not pointing them against the way they ought to be going, following the sun wheel and the star wheel? Were not the blind fogs all about them, because they were sailing north and east? The girl let a pigeon fly from her hand, and it flew north and east.

'We will follow the bird,' said the chief.

The seven ships followed the bird.

The mists melted before the flight of the bird, the doors of the sea-haar opened, and there were the islands with the sun on them, like emeralds in the water.

Then the skippers separated. They chose each one the island that seemed to him the best and greenest: Rackwick and Skaill and Birsay and Rousay and Ronaldsay and Westray.

But the young chief followed the flight of the bird. The bird rising and falling led them between Birsay and Rousay to a green fertile headland called Gurness.

There in Gurness a mild company was waiting on the shore. An old man stepped forward to greet the ship and the seafarers.

The bird fell on the crag and when they looked again it was not a dove but a black raven.

The raven screamed.

So the people ended their voyage.

But the different branches of the people were scattered throughout the islands. There they subdued the peoples that farmed and fished there, and took over their houses and fishing boats and fields.

Many died on those shores. The remnants of the people who were uprooted from their nesses and bays gathered a few needful things and fled into the barrenness of the hills.

The young chief and the girl from Caithness stood in the prow off Gurness and made signs of peace with their hands to the old man on the shore. He returned their greeting. There would be enough land for the voyagers, if the hill behind were drained and dug and seeded. There was abundance of fish in the sea for all, said the old man.

Then an arrow flew from the ship and struck the old man in the throat. He fell there, with the word of peace half spoken.

More arrows flew from the ship. Bows sang. The arrows hung in the air and fell and struck many of the people on the shore.

Then the people of Gurness turned and in their flight gathered some gear and beasts together, this man a goat and that man a spade and the women spinning-wheels and pots and querns.

The villagers disappeared in a gap of the hills.

But a young girl with gray eyes remained after the others had fled. She bent over the old dead peace-maker and she took his head on her knee and kissed him many times, weeping.

The young sailors gathered about the girl and there were disputes as to who should have her.

She was very beautiful, with gray eyes, that girl.

The raven screamed thrice from the headland.

There was a harpist on the ship and he said that the Gurness girl should stay with the voyagers, so that the blessing of the land should not be lost utterly.

Then the young men about the girl grew still as stones.

The girl put a last kiss on the forehead of the old man and she rose and walked through the group of invaders towards the hills into which her people had fled.

The sailors would have thrown the bodies of the Gurness men over the crag but the chief said they must be honourably burned.

They wrapped the old man in flames but his body was not consumed: it shone like silver in the fire.

In the morning, after the funeral pyres were out, the skeleton of the old man was not there. But a dove complained here and there about the cold ashes.

The chief appointed a young man to watch always from the headland, to give warning of the approach of strange ships.

It was known for a certainty that the powerful Celtic tribes out of Europe were migrant still, in ships greater than their own. Also those warriors had spears, welded and ringing with the magic of iron.

'We will build a tower on the headland,' said the chief.

They could see, in Rousay and Egilsay, the fires of their fellow-voyagers who had sought other shores.

The young watcher of the sea reported that he had seen a fleet of ships out in the ocean. That fleet had sailed on to Thule in the north.

The harpist tried thrice to follow the path the beautiful gray-eyed girl had taken but he lost his way thrice among the hilltracks and bogs and after three days came back to Gurness.

'I saw fires among the hills,' he said, 'and once a stone sang past my ear, and I saw a savage face that seemed to be carved out of stone. The stone face glimmered under the stars.'

So the district of Gurness was captured by the ancestors, and settled, and the fishing boats and ploughs taken over, and work begun.

But often a man – a shepherd or a hunter – would be found dead in the wetlands beyond.

Sometimes a woman would dream in the night. She had seen the ghost of a dead householder trying the latch or raking among the embers, or looking deep into the stone jar in the niche.

V

The people lived on the land they had taken, and they fished and tilled the soil.

The chief appointed a man to keep watch always, for sometimes after sunset they would see some of the gray-eyed men they had driven from the land into the hills: shadows.

In a summer fog, the hillmen seemed to loom on the edge of the cultivated land, with huge menacing gestures. Often, a few goats or sheep or swine were missing.

On a clear morning, early, they would see a young woman in the gap of the hills. This woman was seen, generation after generation, looking down on the settlement and lingering. Then she would turn and go among the hills.

Sometimes a ship would pass on northwards, and linger awhile on the horizon looking for lands to settle. All the lands being taken, the ship would sail on north.

One morning in winter the village woke to find that the gate of the sheepfold had been broken and the entire flock driven away. The people of the hills had done that reft, silently, at midnight.

The watchman said, 'I do not have eyes in the back of my head. I put the light of my eyes always on the heave of the ocean westward and on the rapid outpourings of the Eynhallow waters this way and that . . .'

So next spring they bargained for ewes and a ram with the people in Rousay, their cousins.

One day when men were ploughing with oxen the watchman came from the headland and said, 'There is a ship in the west, sailing from south. The ship slackened sail, she lingered and dipped, now she has turned and is sailing with the tide through Eynhallow Sound, towards this shore. There are many well-armed men on the ship.'

The chief looked for a while at the ship. Then he ordered the sheep and oxen and swine to be driven inland, with as many baskets and spindles and querns as the women could carry.

The men followed.

The watcher was left on the headland to parley with the shipmen.

The chief, looking back, could see men swarming out of the ship and swimming to land and going here and there among the houses. Of the watchman there was no sign.

For seven nights the people lived wretchedly beside the loch, with no shelter from rain or wind.

A spy was sent out to see how it was with their village. The spy came back in the morning to say that the village was like a hive of savage bees. The men from the sea were feasting by torchlight on the dried fish and the cheeses the people had thought to be safely hidden and stored away.

From the hills came echoes of mocking laughter from the gray-eyed folk at the twilights of dawn and sunset.

'Now,' said the chief, 'we will go and parley with the men from the sea. Either that, or we will perish of hunger here beside the loch. The shipmen after all are of our race and kin, sun-seekers.'

When the men paused on the ridge above the village, they saw the ship on the horizon, sailing on north. The village was empty and silent. They entered the village and saw that many of their furnishings and artefacts of wood and straw had been broken up to make fires.

As the chief stood in his own door, he felt a coldness at his hand and a flurry of wind at his shoulder, and a strength like the living earth thrust itself between his arms and his side. He looked, and it was a young horse. And a filly stood, with lifted hoof, in the square of the village.

The men from the sea had paid for their lodging with two horses. 'They are fair-minded men, in their way,' said the chief.

The chief heard a footstep.

It was the watchman.

'I had thought the sailors had killed you,' said the chief.

'There's a good cave for hiding in,' said the watcher. 'What we need here is a strong wall to guard ourselves against such raiders.'

And they built a strong wall, time after time, against the invaders from the sea. But always the shipmen came this way and that round the wall into the village, and took what they wanted, and stayed awhile, and lit fires and gorged themselves, and sailed on north or west.

This happened over many generations.

And some of the best young men died in these assaults on the sea wall, time after time.

And the gray-eyed men from the hills would come down at moon-dark or in a dense fog and drive off sheep and swine.

The watchman watched from the wall.

The horses went like the wind round their fields. The young men rode on them, shouting. The horses were not too proud to bear the yoke and to bring in peat in straw baskets.

VI

There was this young boy called Dedal and he was poorly regarded, being useless with sling and arrow and a danger to fishermen, blundering about the fishing boat trying uselessly to pull in a line.

The young women laughed at him, pointing fingers.

Dedal lit a fire in the cave one day and worked with wet clay and that evening he brought two pots to the chief's house. The chief said the pots would do well enough for holding grain or milk.

Dedal made a pot for the comeliest of the young women, six or seven.

Still the girls turned their faces from him.

Dedal was considered to be ugly as well as a burden on the community.

'A good urn for the ashes of the dead,' said the old people. 'Let Dedal make that. Our burnt bones would be at peace in a fine jar.'

One day in summer Dedal sat long on the beach, drawing with a pointed stick on the sand. He drew a circle, then concentric circles, then he drew what seemed like the outline of a round hive. Dedal considered the sand-scratchings for some time, making changes now and again.

Dedal went up from the shore to the quarry where a dozen men that day were dressing stones to make a house for the chief and his new wife.

Dedal said to the quarrymen, 'Carry all the stones you have quarried to the headland, then come back for more. A thousand stones will be needed at the headland soon.'

The quarrymen made ugly twistings of the face against Dedal, and contemptuous gestures, and spoke ugly abusive words, and some of them spat.

'Carry all the stones to the headland,' said the chief. 'Do what Dedal says. Then come here and quarry more until there are a thousand well-dressed stones.'

All that summer men laboured in the quarry and at the headland. They dug a deep foundation, with an ever-springing well of sweet water at the centre, and upon the strong foundation they built the fortress, course laid on course, a powerful stone keep, reaching to the sun. And Dedal went here and there, directing the work.

The watchman sneered, sucking the juice of summer grasses on the sea-bank below the tower.

The tower grew tall, two concentric walls one inside the other, bound together by a stone spiral stair that wound up to the outlook wall at the top, as a hawk rises, circling. As a hawk pauses in its flight, to look down on the teeming earth, so the wall bent inwards somewhat and then resumed its sunward circling soar.

The wall of the keep was entirely blank but for one low narrow entrance at the base and that could be securely locked from inside.

Inside this broch the well kept a sweet bright brimming, with many water songs.

The chief had words with the watchman, then with the young men, then with the mocking women. The chief asked Dedal to sit at his table, on his right side, at the midwinter feast that year.

The watchman watched from the top of the tower.

The watchman called from the tower one day in late spring, 'A ship!'

The chief climbed the spiral to the look-out and there off Scabra Head in Rousay stood a ship, that drove north, then seemed to hesitate, and then turned in through the tumultuous door of water flooding in between Costa and Eynhallow. As they looked they could see the armed men in the ship.

Then the low narrow door in the base of the tower was opened and all the people went in, carrying food and jars and blankets. And the large food-store in the village was hidden in a secret place where it would not easily be found. The horses and sheep, goats and swine and oxen were driven to the lochside of Swannay by the herdsman and his boys.

The ship anchored out in the bay and the shipmen swam and waded ashore and they were armed and they swarmed through the houses of the village, searching for food and gear and girls, but they found nothing.

The shipmen came and stood about the tower, looking up. The watchman whispered and a shower of heavy stones fell on the shipmen, so that a few were killed and many grievously injured, and some got nothing worse than bruises and broken toes.

The shipmen withdrew somewhat, to be out of range of the heavy stones.

The shipmen took counsel together, considering how the tower might be attacked.

But there was no way into the broch but the one little door in the base.

One shipman ran at the door with his axe, and an arrow hurtled down on him and quivered through him like the strike of a falcon. He fell three footsteps from the entrance.

The skipper called, 'We came here to bargain with you peaceably for meat and fish and butter and honeycombs. I have a purse of gold coins.'

Then an arrow sang from the top of the tower and took the purse from his fist and coins bright as the sun spattered and rang among the shore stones.

The shipmen withdrew somewhat further, to be out of range of the arrows.

The shipmen sat all that night on the cold shore, considering which way to capture the fortress. In the morning their hands and mouths were blue with hunger.

Then they trooped down to the shore, to put to sea again.

They saw a man in the ebb, who seemed to be conversing with an otter.

They killed the man.

Then they swam out to the ship and weighed anchor, and sailed out to the open ocean between Rousay and Egilsay, bearing north.

The people came out of the fortress, laughing. 'Now we are safe for ever,' they said, 'because of the fortress.'

'We are safe for ever,' they said, 'except for the hill people and the ghosts of the hill people killed by our people on that first day, and by the gray-eyed girl who is always watching our comings and goings – the witch.'

They sang a song of victory in the village square.

Later that day fishermen found the body of Dedal in the ebb. From the eyes of the otter rolled two tears into the sea.

VII

What it was, I tell thee, the sorrows, the grief of women unending!

A storm; boats overset, fishermen with salt stiff mouths. Lamentation of women along the shore, many nights and days.

Worm in oats, mildew in barley, thin hands in winter. The wailing: *How should we deserve such hunger, whose men have laboured hard in the light with plough and seed-bag and harrows?*

Yea, but six sorrowful harvests, one treading clothed in rot upon the bone heel of the former harvest. That was past enduring.

Yea, and but a few endured. And they ate cold seaweed in the ebb, in snow and darkness.

The word of wisdom: 'For that our fathers, the first comers, took this land by stealth and by cunning and by treachery, and scattered the dwellers in this land among the hills, and have made no peace with them for nine generations, but our shepherds and hunters have mocked their wretchedness, up there among the bogs and mosses, for that reason we must endure drowning and blight. For the land and the sea are true to those who have struck a lasting bond and seal between themselves and the blood-and-dust of men. But we have broken that treaty and land and sea will deal with us always as strangers, and as thieves and as a guilty red-handed folk.'

A fifth thin harvest mocked their labour.

No rain fell on the sixth summer, but the wheel of the wind going this way and that swung always back into the east and their crop was scorched by that bitter wind.

And some said, 'We did wrong to settle here in Gurness. The promise was that we should sail west to the golden shores and the immortal fruitage.'

VIII

In the time of the seventh spring, at ploughtime, there were no young men to put a yoke on the ox and to blow cobwebs from the ploughs that had slept in the barn all winter.

There was a young lazy fellow in the village called Orfeo and the carpenter came from his bench and put a new plough into the hands of Orfeo.

Orfeo said, 'I know nothing about ploughing.'

The women stood all about him, bitter mouths. 'Plough,' said the women.

Orfeo said, 'It is foolishness to plough barren dust.'

The women said, 'Plough, man, and afterwards scatter seed.'

Orfeo said, 'I am broken with grief, the girl I loved died at the end of winter. I can't plough.'

The women raged all about Orfeo. 'Plough,' they cried, 'or we are all lost.'

Still Orfeo stood with the new plough in his hands.

And one girl with golden hair tore her hair and gave the strands of gold to the wind.

One woman took up a stone and threw it at Orfeo and it struck the plough and the ploughshare broke until only a curved frame was left in the hands of Orfeo.

And Orfeo plucked the strands of hair from the wind and he set them across the wooden frame and his hand smote the strings and the plough-harp cried in the new wind of spring.

The women fell on Orfeo and would have torn him with their nails and teeth, but Orfeo took the plough-harp and fled from them among the hills.

Ox and mattocks and women then, delving the barren field towards the seventh famine.

IX

Orfeo said: I wandered among the hills all night. I carried the harp on my shoulder. I wished to die among the hills.

I wandered here and there among the hills. There was neither moon nor stars. I sat down on a rock. I was tired. I wished to die. Then I would be one with the dust and silence of the dead girl.

There in the mirk before dawn I saw a man standing before me. The man said, 'What are you seeking here, stranger?'

I meant to say, 'Death'. Why then did I say, 'Love'? I said, 'I am looking for a girl who has gone from me among the shadows' . . .

The man touched the rock and a door in the rock swung open and the man bade me follow him through that door.

At the end of a long passage was a circular chamber. Men stood here and there against the wall.

A mask was carved on the stone wall, shaped like a skull and painted green and blue and yellow.

The keeper of the rock-gate said to the mask, 'Here is the musician. He has come at last.'

The mask was silent.

The man turned to me. 'The god says, *Let him play on his harp.*'

I struck the harp-strings but no sound came. (How should music come from a broken plough and a few torn hairs?)

The painted stone glared out at nothing.

The keeper of the gate said, 'Your music has pleased the god. The god says you are to sit down among us and eat and drink.'

I knew that if a man eats and drinks with the dwellers under the hill, he belongs to them for ever. I did not care. I wished to die.

A very old woman with gray eyes and a whiskery mouth brought me a cup. The drink tasted of heather flowers. My senses swooned.

The cakes she offered tasted of heather honey.

The keeper of the gate said, 'The god wishes to know why you have come here from the evil village?'

I said, 'I am looking for a lost girl.'

The old woman took away the empty cup and plate.

The stone mask seemed to twist in the light and smoke of torches.

The keeper of the gate said, 'The god says, *Let us see if his music will bring the girl.*'

I said, 'This is a broken ploughshare. I can't play on such a thing. Let it see to its own songs' . . . (For now the drink and the desire for death had made me reckless.)

I set the plough-harp on the floor between the mask and myself. It began to chirp with great sweetness. The harp sang on and on, like lark-raptures over a cornfield.

I said, 'Now, harp, be silent.'

The harp trembled and was still.

The keeper of the rock said, 'The god is considering what should be done with a spy.'

I waited a long time in that place. The stone mask stared out at nothing. The gray-eyed men stood at the wall.

The keeper of the rock said, 'Man from the evil village, the god has spoken the word.'

I saw, uncaring, that the gray-eyed men had taken flint knives from their belts. They held the knives in front of their faces. As if they had heard an order I couldn't hear, they took one step forward. I was encircled with sharp flints.

I did not turn from them.

From the floor, the harp began to sing. Softly at first, and slowly, it uttered notes that were words, an intertwining of music and speech, in a language I did not know. The words seemed old, very ancient, from the beginning of time. The song seemed to describe a simple green place, a man and woman and child under a tree, peaceful animals all around, and a bird on a branch and burdens of ripe fruit.

The harp trembled and was silent.

Then the harp began to shriek! Could ever be such pain and desolation? The harp lamented like the earth's last woman over the burnt stones and the murdered men of her house. There was nothing left alive in the world but herself: the tree was rotten from branch to root, the skull of the ox lay in a barren furrow, the shore was littered with dead fish.

The harp was silent again, in a silence more terrible than the death song.

The keeper of the gate said, 'The harp has told the story of this people, how it fared with them in Gurness the year before you seafarers came, and again the year after you came. The harp has told the story of all battles from the beginning to the end of time.'

I opened my eyes again. The gray-eyed men stood all about me in a closer circle. I knelt at the centre of a dozen edges, held out by the hilt at full stretch of the arm, all pointed at my throat.

The keeper of the gate said, 'This is the end for you, son of evil.'

What is the end to a man who longs for an end, what better could he ask than darkness after a slow and beautiful dance of daggers?

I closed my eyes.

The end seemed like a small beading of dew on my throat.

I opened dead eyes, and saw a gray-eyed girl kneeling in front of me. The face was the face of the old woman but new-fashioned in sweet flesh and the lingering fragrances of meadowsweet and clover.

She raised her lips from my throat to my mouth.

She offered me the brimming cup once more.

At once the harp sang its first song: the lark sang and sang, an unending tissue of sweetness, promise, fruitfulness, reconciliation . . . Touching the strings I fell asleep.

I woke from that dream on the hillside. The wonder of the dream lingered. Soon that too would go, and I would be poor Orfeo still, the useless one, the burden on his people, outcast, the man with the broken plough. The death-farer.

I turned to the gap in the hills. A shawled figure stood there. I walked towards her. It was the gray-eyed girl. She took me by the elbow. We turned our faces to the village.

Half-way there, I struck the harp. It was not the crude music of the day before yesterday. My harp had learned the songs of the Underworld.

At sunset the gray-eyed girl and I came to the flock of sheep, and then to the blighted cornfield. I played the song of ripeness that the harp had uttered in the chamber under the hill.

Soon a cloud broke on the hills and the fields all about Gurness shone with rain. Every blade wore its shining drop.

I thought I had been gone for one night only. But my mother said I had been out of the village for seven years.

What is dream, and what is truth? I think often of the stone mask that listened and spoke, and yet was a dumb carving on a rock face. I think of the harp that sang by itself the music of innocence and death and ripeness but is only in truth a frame of wood and strings; a lark or a crow according as the player brings initiated or uncouth fingers to his tryst with silence.

That summer, late, there was a great surging golden harvest in Gurness.

The ghosts of the first people troubled the village no more . . .

Orfeo died at the beginning of winter. He had been delicate from his childhood. Not many tears were shed for Orfeo. The women of Gurness dealt more harshly with him after he led the gray-eyed girl home.

But next spring the chief married the gray-eyed girl, and it is from them that all the chiefs of Gurness are descended.

*　　*　　*

Those are some of the stories that Gruth told in the house of the story-teller winter after winter. There are more than a hundred other tales that Gruth told, but if I were to relate them all, this overall story of the fortress would lose all proportion and meaning. The hero after all is Jandreck, the guardian, and Jandreck said that the tales of Gruth were nonsense.

Winter and summer, Jandreck watched the sea. The elders would say, 'There's no point in Jandreck watching the sea any more. The Picts still come, but they are no longer a danger. They come as settlers and traders, not as pirates.' Jandreck paid no attention to them or their words.

One night of snow and a blunt bright moon, more than a score of people from the village and the fields beyond came to sit in Gruth's house and listen to a story. Towards midnight Gruth began to tell 'the love story' – Orfeo and the gray-eyed girl, the dispossessed one, the lost one, the bringer of new life. Gruth had just reached the part of the story where Orfeo wakes on the hillside from his dream and sees a shawled figure in a gap in the hills at sunrise . . . At this point Gruth fell silent. His eyelids drooped. He sat rigid, he clasped his hands tightly together, a shudder went through him. Still he said nothing. A few of the listeners looked uneasily at each other. The mouth of the story-teller was locked, it seemed. One man, yawning, got this feet – he said he would have to be up and out early in the morning if he was going to catch haddocks. A light-hearted voice said, 'Well, Gruth, and when is Orfeo going to kiss his sweetheart, eh? Why do you keep us waiting? Love is swift as a bird.' A few listeners laughed, but uneasily. 'I think Gruth is going to speak now,' said a woman.

Gruth spoke. His words became a chant: not at all like his usual story-vesture, a rough homespun. Gruth shrieked: 'Jandreck the faithful one is broken! Jandreck is no more than a drained fly in a web! She has taken hot irons to the eyes of the watchman. She has put a stone into the mouth of the horn that

saved the people many times. The darkling keel of a dragon-
ship, the uncurling death-bringing waves. The strangers! the
bright-haired strangers! the sea-cold eyes. The horn is dumb in
the night. They are in every house now, the berg-men, gloved in
blood to the elbows. They are in and out of the fortress like
savage bees in a hive. The web of stone is broken that was to
stand for ever! In Jandreck's hut above the shore an eastern axe
smashes the lock. They drain the last blood out of the strong
keeper of the people. A stone is put in at the mouth of the horn.
This is the death of the people. One girl only of this people will
grow old. She stumbles along the dark shore into the dawn.'

Gruth was silent again; his face clenched tight as a fist. The
listeners looked at one another. Eort cried out, 'That old man
is a liar! Jandreck is a true husband to me! Jandreck has never
looked with longing at another woman!' Vrem said, 'Gruth
has had these visions before – they always turn out to be true.
A pity that he did not tell us the name of Jandreck's
sweetheart.'

Eort left the house of the story-teller in a flood of tears.

Fley said, 'It may be that Gruth spoke figuratively. Sooner or
later age and illness overtake us all, and then, as the old ones
used to say, we lie down beside the dark maiden of death, and all
the brightness of our strength goes from us and we are dry
bones. We are a part of the great story then. This is the kind of
wooing and destruction that Gruth was speaking of.'

Some of the people in the house of legend nodded: Gruth was
indeed speaking in the language of poetry. Others shook their
heads.

Gruth opened his eyes and smiled. 'Well then,' he said, 'thank
you for coming to my house this cold night. I am always glad
when you come. I must have told the ancient love story of Orfeo
and the gray-eyed woman a thousand times, but only once, I
think, have I told it with such joy and freshness. It is well to tell
that story over and over. The music of Orfeo was the beginning

of our prosperity. Afterwards the spirit of the place was at peace with us. We were the true people of Gurness then.'

Just then, through the still winter night, they heard the savage blort of the horn, thrice repeated.

'This is too much!' said the shepherd. 'Just when we're going home to our beds! We have to drag everything through the snow to the broch! Jandreck has never sounded the horn at midnight before.'

Fley said, 'We will obey the horn all the same. Jandreck is true. Jandreck knows what he is about.'

Soon the fortress was thronged with men and women and children, and stacked with bags of corn and farm implements and nets and oars and clusters of dried fish and jars of honey and salt.

But no sword or axe or fire came against the broch that night. In the morning the people went back into their houses, hollow-eyed.

Vrem said aloud, as she passed the open door of Eort, 'Men – you can never trust them. Even gray-beards like a pretty girl now and then.'

TIME

Years passed in the large island. The many people lived peaceably beside each other. Sometimes a harvest was good, sometimes it was bad, mostly it was sufficient. No more pirates came from the sea lochs of Scotland. In the lands of the south it was known that, in the Orkneys and Shetlands, there was no room for more settlers, also that the islanders knew how to defend themselves and govern themselves.

Time walked through the island in a green coat.

The ships that came, from Lewis and Arran, were peaceful traders.

There was no need for a man to watch the sea, but Jandreck stayed at his post.

The years passed. One year Fley the gray-eyed chief took a fever and he died. On the shoulders of his gray-eyed son the blue coat was hung.

Vrem stayed mostly at the fire after that, an old bitter toothless woman; she tried to make mischief between family and family, but few paid heed to her.

The years passed. Eort was growing old too. She had no children or grandchildren around her as she turned the spinning-wheel: sitting at her door in summer in the sun, and, bewintered, at the peatfire. All the villagers smiled, thinking or speaking of Eort, who had a quick temper but a generous heart.

The men of Gorseness came one day and stood at the boundary stone. They said to the son of Fley, 'Be our chief. Our chief is old and childless. We would be glad to mingle our blood with yours' . . . The next year the elders of Costa came to the boundary stone on the other side. They said, 'The men of Rousay have rifled our lobster-creels every morning this past summer. Our chief is a child. We would be glad if your chief would be our protector' . . . And the year after that the men of Hundland came. They did not stop at the boundary stone but they drifted, a few old men, into the village and they knocked at the chief's door. 'Chief,' they cried in their small high voices, 'we are old people and the young people have gone to be sailors and the heather and rushes are invading our green fields. Chief, send some of your young people to plough and reap for us. When we die, the land will be theirs' . . .

The years passed. The people grew and flourished. The boundary stones were set further and further from the fortress and the village.

Time passed, in a green coat, dancing to the ancient music.

People died and were a few burnt bones in a jar. A young man and a girl looked at each other, and the dove would fall between them. A brightness here and there was brought forth and laid in shadowy earth-arms.

The tongue of Gruth was silent for ever. Fire ate the tongue and lips of the story-teller. Gruth was a few cinders in a jar.

The wicked old man died among his lies and schemings. Fire cleaned his bones. The ashes lay in a crude clay jar. A child, a granddaughter, wept for him.

Flecks of gray touched the dark beard of Jandreck. There came a fine intricate network about his eyes. One winter he got gnawing pains in his shoulder and his haunch-bone.

'Jandreck,' said the young chief, 'there is no need for you to sit night after night at the headland. That danger is long past. Some morning you'll be found dead in the snow, with one open eye still on the sea.'

Jandreck smiled. He said, 'Perhaps I am too old to sit outdoors in rain and wind and snow. But I've grown so used to the station at the headland that I'd be lost if I couldn't go there' . . . Before the next winter Jandreck built a hut of stone on the headland, with a little hearth where a peat-fire could be set. He would keep watch from that shelter.

Jandreck went to his house in the village to wash and eat, and to speak kind familiar things to Eort his wife. But always, at night, he returned to the headland and the hut.

Once children going past the open door of the watch-hut heard words inside. They peeked in. Jandreck was nodding and smiling and talking to himself, half asleep in a corner. On a hook at the wall hung the great rallying horn. The children could not make out what Jandreck was saying. They cried like birds at the open door, till Jandreck opened one eye: then they ran away laughing.

Immense and dark the broch brooded over the village. One summer night, in a gale, three stones were shaken from the tower. Nobody bothered to replace them, any more than a stone or two would be set back in the cliff after a wave had struck it. The fortress was to the people now a natural thing, like cliff or hill; let the tides of time work on it.

Once Jandreck sat over the supper that Eort had prepared for him. Afterwards he nodded asleep beside the fire. He began to speak, 'Jandreck, Jandreck, old foolish man, what does it mean?' . . . 'Jandreck, you are going to die. Jandreck, you will be burnt bones in a jar' . . . 'Jandreck, it is lonely for you now. You are bound to a barren wife. You and she, Jandreck, will go lonely into the darkness, one after the other' . . . At this point Eort took him by the hand and murmured to him. He cried out angrily, 'I have been the slave of that fortress! Because of the broch I have never known the love of a girl! The people delighted in stories – to me they were foolish drifts of words. Men praised ale and music – water was good enough for me, and sea-sounds. I go to my grave a robbed and a cheated man' . . . Then he woke up beside the fire, and saw Eort bent anxiously over him. He smiled, and rose to his feet, and lit the lantern. The sea moved out there, too long unwatched.

A girl stood in a dark opening between two houses and watched the old strong lantern-splashed man going between house and hut.

The night passed. In the morning Jandreck stood in the threshold of his hut and saw a girl moving among the pools below the cliffs. He had seen her with a cold eye, a hundred times, in the village, on the hill, at the shore. He turned his face from that common enough sight. He shook his head. She was the granddaughter of the wicked mischief-making dead old man.

Two nights later, as they sat at supper, Jandreck would not look at Eort. He spoke the usual things, but he would not look at her. Yet his eyes glittered as if he had a fever; on his old cheeks two embers glowed and faded and glowed.

He did not speak again to Eort, but after he had nodded asleep beside the fire, he said suddenly in a young pure strong voice, 'She's beautiful, isn't she, Jandreck, down there at the rockpool putting whelks into her basket?' . . .

ANOTHER LOVE STORY

She *is* beautiful, is she not, Jandreck? There she is again at the
rockpools below you putting whelks into her basket. Why did
you not notice her comeliness before, Jandreck? Ten days ago
she was an ordinary plain-looking girl. Suddenly she is a young
woman. How sweetly her little burdened fist goes from pool to
basket! You have a fire in your hut, Jandreck; all at once you
would like her to warm her blue cold hands at your peat-flames.
What is there so special about her? It could be her sea-coloured
eyes that make you catch your breath this morning; but the
shape of her new bosom under the shawl melts your heart even
more, and that red eager restless mouth of hers. No, Jandreck, it
is no single part of her that draws you – everything about her,
even her one defect, the large mole on her chin, is caught up
into a harmony that cannot be described. And, Jandreck, she
pays no more attention to you than a wave or a gull. She is so
taken up with getting a basketful of whelks for her mother.
Jandreck, you who have spoken many brave urgent resounding
words among the people, why can you say nothing to this thing
of a girl on the shore?

An ordinary girl – that is, ordinary to everyone but to you,
Jandreck – and she seems utterly unaware of the great guardian
of the people, who stands there in the open door of his hut
observing her now morning after morning. And every morning
your great strong heart melts inside you like a jellyfish. One
morning she gathers seaweed to boil in a pot at home for her
grandmother's asthma. One morning she just walks along the
sand; how prettily she scampers back wherever a wave breaks
and sends a swirl of froth-fringed sea higher than usual; how
daringly she follows the spent wave back to its bourne, only to
come rushing and shrieking back from the next unfolding wave,
her skirts held high to show her tender sharpely knees. Then,
again, it is whelk-gathering for her mother's fish soup. Never by

the least look or sign does she acknowledge your presence. Yet you are there, morning after morning, always at your door-post; and sometimes the pain of looking is so great that you have to close your eyes – even one morning, go inside and shut the door. Jandreck, you do not know what you would reply if she were to call up to you suddenly: some flat and heavy answer, to be sure, something quite different from the poems that are stirring in your stone heart, with delight and pain and foolishness; and would break out in blossom; but from childhood you have used only necessary and practical words, like stones for setting in a wall.

One morning you say, 'Jandreck, you are a fool! You have a good kind wife who loves you. You will look no more at a silly idle creature who comes down to the shore every morning about this or that, and goes away again (but all the same her coming and going are more like a dance to unheard harps than plain walking). Jandreck, this foolishness is a sign that you are growing old. You will forget about her. You will look at her no more. What is she, after all? Her grandfather was that evil-tongued old man that caused so much mischief for years in the village. Wasn't her uncle the one who stole the crabs one summer out of your creels? – you broke his nose over that business. But why does this girl come every morning to the shore, alone? This is strange. She must know that I am there always. I will not allow myself to be tormented any more by such a young cold compassionless creature. I will look no more' . . . And that morning, Jandreck, you kept inside your hut until you knew that all the villagers were indoors having their midday food. Then you opened the door. The beach was empty. How empty, cold, ashen the remainder of that day was for you! At sunset you longed for her to come down to the shore, just for a little while, before it grew too dark. She did not come. Jandreck, you woke up from a dream of North Sea pirates that night – half ship, half dragon – a nightmare of fire and blood – the village in ruins – to find that you were whispering her name in the darkness over and over . . .

Next morning, Jandreck, you were at your station again in the open door. And the girl came, regular as a gull on the incoming flood. She looked or pretended to look for little shells. Her earnest sweet face was bent over stones and sea-tangles and tidal pools. For the first time she turned and put a single look on you; a cold look, as if you were a heap of stones or a scarecrow; then back to her probing she went. And, Jandreck, your heart thundered like a hammer for an hour or more.

It went on, morning after morning: the cold slow dance of the girl along the shore before the brooding burning tormented eyes of the guardian, whelk-gathering, wave-daring, or only an empty exquisite drifting . . . Soon enough it was summer and bright warm mornings; and with the full moon great floods and ebbs that covered the highest rocks and, six hours later, left wide pools among the red blossoming sea-gardens. The sun flashed one morning out of the deepest rockpool.

She came that morning rather earlier than usual. She was there before you had the door of the guard-hut open, Jandreck. It was a series of shrill cries and splashes that brought you from your table and out into the sunlight. At first you could not see her; there was only that commotion in the deep pool left by the ebbing tide, as if a dog or a seal were playing there. What rose through the torn water was the enchantress. Again and again she immersed herself, went completely under, and rose laughing from the wave and the mirror. She turned round, scooping water from her eyes. Did she see you, standing breathless and beauty-struck at your threshold, a stricken man? Did the sea-girl see you and raise her hand in greeting? No, she raised her hand to squeeze water out of her black hair, a surge and a gush that put a new brightness on her shoulders. Then she turned again, and stood looking out to sea – as if she saw something that you could not see, Jandreck. (What sea-borne thing could you have ever seen that morning, man, but the one dazzling vision among the rocks?) She bent her knees, she sank into the pool till only her head was above the surface. A large fabulous dark bird, her head brooded upon the wide isle-broken horizon ring.

Jandreck, great guardian, you could stand it no more. You groaned and covered your eyes. And lurched into your hut like a man drunk or wounded. And your beard was damp with sweat. Your hands were trembling. You had not dreamed an old man could know such pain.

There came the first whispers of a sickle in the oatfield.

That was the morning, Jandreck, that there came a small knock at your door. And you took your fists from your temples and went heavily to the door and opened it. The girl was standing there, her face and hair still wet from the rock-pool. She was holding in one fist a little loaded skin bag. She held it out to you, Jandreck: a gift, a boiling of whelks.

She smiled.

Jandreck, you asked her (your deep voice trembling) to come in.

The Lairds' Story

1 THOMAS: THE NEW LEDGER

In the reign of Mary Queen of Scots, one of her many illegitimate half-brothers, Robert Stewart, was made Earl of Orkney. The new earl brought north with him into the islands many of his retainers and their families. One of those Scottish servants was a man called Thomas Somerville, who had been a forester in East Lothian. Somerville was young and good-looking; he quickly took the eye of the earl, who had an eye for the handsome and well-made in art and in humanity. Earl Robert made Thomas Somerville a tax-collector, after having him taught the rudiments of arithmetic and accountancy. Tax-collecting was in those days a full-time job, Earl Robert having opened up a wealth of new revenue sources. Ten years after he came to Orkney, Thomas Somerville was laird of the island of Njalsay; he had married the only legitimate child of the old white laird who had Norse eyes and the Norn tongue. (But in his youth the laird had, it was said, loved in Kristiansand a poor travelling fairground girl.)

He planted a sycamore tree on the sheltered side of the Hall.

Thomas and Isabella had five children. This was carved for Thomas the winter after his death:

> ANE GOOD AND GODLIE MAN,
> KIND SPOUS AND FATHER, IN HIS
> TIME HE OVERSAW NINE GREEN
> HARVESTS IN THIS PAROCH.

But, it's said, the tinkers danced all night round a bonfire in the quarry the day Thomas Somerville died.

2 ANDREW: THE WEATHER VANE

The eldest son of Thomas Somerville was Andrew Somerville. He was a young man of eighteen when he sat at the high place of the Hall table. He was a serious man, much given to scripture study, and to the to-fro locked struggles of episcopacy and presbyterianism, that went on for a generation and more. All around him the lairds of Orkney came out in favour of the episcopacy. In the farms and crofts the islanders had no say in the matter; many of them still had their crucifixes hidden under flagstones, and in times of sickness or bad fortune they would go to the crumbling papish chapels to pray, leaving a small coin or a fish or a cake behind them.

Andrew Somerville died aged thirty-one, leaving behind him Margaret his widow, daughter of a merchant in Kirkwall. They had no children. Andrew was buried according to Presbyterian rites, that party being then in the ascendancy. The carving on the chapel wall:

SOUGHT HE EVER THOROUGH LIFE
THE LIGHT OF TRUTH IN MIDST
OF MIRKEST STORMS.

And in the ale-house these words: *A poor gormless cratur he was . . . Yet we speak no ill of the dead . . . Yes, and the mouth of him gaping here and there, a dribble and a drabble and no clear word . . . Men cold in death deserve a good silence . . . Yes, and the long neck with the wobble of Adam's-apple in it, a scunnerful thing . . . That he and all should rest now in peace . . .*

3 GILBERT

The younger brother of Andrew, Gilbert, now became laird: as good a bishop's man as any, and a stout defender of the king (with his tongue at least). After King Charles was martyred, Gilbert sent out some of the young island men with muskets to follow Montrose into defeat and death in the Highlands of Scotland, but he said he must stay at home himself, to see to the good governance of his island. When Cromwell stood clear victor, and sent garrison troops into the Orkneys, Gilbert's tongue only wagged to give passable advice to ploughmen and fishermen. He had many winter-begotten children in Njalsay, and three were born to him by his wife Marion, daughter of a lieutenant-colonel of the Lord Protector; an English woman. Gilbert, it is said, died of an inflammation gotten from travelling between one winter bed and another, accompanied by a ladder and a dog. The good-wife Marion sent words on a paper to the tomb-maker in Kirkwall. Back came the stone:

> ENRICHED HE THE GLEBE
> WINTERED THE ISL
> HIS BOUNTEOU

(for the stone is broken diagonally across and the lower half lost).

The old woman of Garth said, *I was at the kisting of three up there in the Hall, among the candles, but never to this one who sent out my boy Thord into a place of dust where are no candles and decent coffining, no but only Scottish wounds for matters he kent nothing of, and a Scotch ditch to hap him for a grave.*

4 CHARLES AND 5 OLIVER

Two sons Gilbert and Marion Somerville had, Charles and Oliver. Charles was nineteen years old when he stood under the heraldic stone bird of the great Hall, sole laird. It was the sails venturing out or homing in on the curved horizon that Charles had always been interested in from a child, merchant ships going between Scandinavia and Scotland, and increasingly now to the rich American plantations. Flax and seaweed and barrels of butter and feathers Charles Somerville took with him to Kirkwall in person to be put in a meagre dark corner of some Leith-bound hold; but once the young laird, on an impulse, got him a passage eastward to Germany. The ship *Elderflower* never came into the port of Hamburg. Charles, and every sailor aboard, and the narrow-eyed merchant with his ledger, drank gray water and disappeared . . . Still, for sixty years Oliver, his serious-minded fair-curled brother, conducted the affairs of hall and island in Charles's name, nor would take a penny of harvest profit for himself, nor himself attribute a halfpenny to patch kirk or mill. So the island, like an uncompass'd ship, drifted and withered. Till his last day, it's said, at the age of ninety-one, Oliver Somerville sat at his desk in the Hall, or rode on horseback through the fields, or stood on the banks above the shore watching the catch of the island fishing boats being landed; and all he did was remotely and matter-of-factly done, as if he acted for another – as if, some fine morning, a very ancient briny man were to hobble, crutch-swung, up the long Hall drive and sing in a sea-voice: 'I'm back, Oliver man, I'm a bit late but I'm home again. Have you been seeing well to my estate? Have you applied yourself diligently to my ledgers and my ploughlands? Oliver man, I hardly knew ye, with that hook to your shoulder and that squinny in your old eye. Where's the fine golden beard that you used to have, Ollie? – all gone into smoke and ash . . . Well well, man, you can rest you now, for the laird is home again, that over-wandered the seas' . . . That salt ghost never spoke to Oliver. Yet he felt it might, and so Charles's engravure was made only a month or two before Oliver's own. It read (the former):

A BRIEF WANDERING THIS LIFE UPON AN UNCERTAIN SEA*
HAPPY HE THAT MAKETH FAIR PORT.

The tinker said to the limpet shell, 'Njalsay's dead this long while. He isn't even six feet of Njalsay dirt, he's in the guts of a thousand fish, he's sea slime, nothing. Me now, I don't even have a name, I was littered in a Norway ditch. I eat roots, I'm worm-eaten, windblown. The terns are here again. Time to be up and off' . . .

And the second tombstone read:

OLIVER SOMERVILLE, 1653–1744
SERO SED SERIO

The voices at the well.

Minnie: *The peerie nippit nose of him, and the white rime in his eye.*

Mergit: *He gave me a shilling the day my Sam'l drowned, twenty Aprils since.*

Maribel: *Yea, and the bit o' whine in his throat, like winter sough in a lum, the times he was displeased, at the shore maybe or in the harvest field.*

Molly: *The poor old cratur, he's in God's hand now, and a mercy on him.*

6 ANDREW THE SECOND: SOLDIER OF THE KING

Andrew Somerville the second son to Oliver was fifty-three, and laird of Njalsay for only a twelvemonth, when Charles Edward Stuart raised the rebel standard in the west. The news took some time to get to Orkney; at first there were only rumours from the mouth of packman or sailor. But at last the treason was nailed to the door of St Magnus in Kirkwall. Before that, however, Andrew Somerville had gone his rounds of the island gentry, eager to stir those Jacobites into action. In their high houses they expressed surprise, joy, resolution; but that was as far as any of them would go. Andrew returned to Njalsay. 'Scum and cowards!' he said again and again. 'They'll fight this war with their pledged silver cups. Not a gold guinea for the true king, not a gun, not an orra-man to be a soldier. Woman, where's my gun?' . . . The laird's musket was found in the rafters, with webs about it. Andrew Somerville dressed himself next morning in lace, his silver buckles and buttons, his scented wig and feathered bonnet; and he set out for the wars, alone. He was ferried to the Caithness shore. He hired a nag from a Thurso ostler, and rode south in cold spring weather. He met sometimes a cotter, or a shepherd, or a tramp, and questioned them, but not one had heard about a patriotic war or knew even the name of Charles Edward the prince. 'Of course,' said the chevalier from Orkney, 'how could they ever know of such grand stirring matters?' His anxiety was all to get to Inverness, and there, if possible, take a coach south. His idea of heaven upon earth was to reach London just as King James entered his capital in triumph from France; for it seemed to him now that he would be too late to take any part in the fighting. (This was sorrow to him – he longed to lie on his death-bed, an old man, with a silver scar or two on him from a just war.)

It came on to rain, sleet mixed with heavy thunder-drops. The old nag cast a shoe and could go no further: Andrew set it free among the gorse. By now he was in poorish shape himself: chilled to the bone, hungry three days, quite worn out. 'But soon I'll be in Inverness, and all will be well. What's a little wet and hunger? Nothing. The true king is back on the throne' . . . In his silk coat the laird had had his goodwife sew, severally, twenty guineas. He limped on, on foot, to Inverness. On the side of a hill, with a throb of relief, he saw a little cabin – a poor place, surely, but there he might get a cup of broth with whisky, and some news on the war perhaps. The rain sloped down, heavy relentless pewter. Andrew Somerville stumped through the thick heather.

The door of the hut was barred from the inside. He knocked and called. No one answered. Then, putting his ear to the panels, he heard low groans, and now and then a high eerie whimpering, and fierce whispers. 'God save Prince Charles!' he shouted through the panels. At that, cannily, a bolt was drawn, the door was opened an inch or two, and the face of a young woman peered out at him. In his fingers Andrew Somerville held, like a key, a gold guinea. The girl shook her head. She opened the door wider. Inside all was silence and darkness; but a half-minute later the stanched music of sorrow and pain broke out again. Andrew Somerville found himself peering into what might have been a cell of Inferno; and an unendurable stench rose about him and made him retch.

'What are these poor creatures?' he asked the girl at last.

'They are the last soldiers of Prince Charlie,' she said to him in a beautiful melancholy voice. Then, after a while, she told him about the battle on the moor that had been fought three days before; and how the guns of the German upstart had blown the remnants of the loyal host to pieces.

Andrew Somerville put the guinea on a shelf. Then he turned and went out into the sweet rain.

Orkney never saw him again. He lived for twenty-five more years, in France and Holland, a genteel beggar. He contrived, now and then, to get a letter smuggled to his wife Annabel.

King George's men came to Orkney when the war was over, to settle accounts. The lily-livered Jacobite lairds flocked with their silver cups to a cave, and spent wretched months there, until a pardon of sorts was issued. There was to be no pardon for Andrew Somerville, esquire, who had actually ridden to the wars with a musket. Annabel and her four children were herded into the factor's house nearby: then the great Hall of Njalsay was reduced to a ruin. The roof was torn off; windows were taken out; doors were broken. A fire was lit inside. At the end of that day the building looked like a gaunt skull. Andrew's only son,

James, an 'innocent' of twenty-three, clapped hands with joy as the hot stones came in a cascade from the roof; and wild rooted tongues of fire flung about in the skull of the great house.

Andrew died in a little Dutch village. At the end of the bed hung the remnants of his silk suit, with its silver buttons. He had prepared, months previously, a farewell letter to his family. By long slow devious ways the letter found its way to the Hall (which was now restored by an Edinburgh architect, in the classical style, and was considered to be much more handsome than before).

The new laird, James Somerville, was too feeble-minded to be able to read the last words of his father, far less to make out their gist. But his mother and three sisters read, and James smiled to see how the paper with the black lines and loops on it was on a sudden all shining and smudged.

'Why do women always look so nice when they cry?' he asked.

The stonemason came over from Kirkwall. There was a spirit of reconciliation in the air after those bitter civil wars. New wars and victories against France and Spain had fused Scotland and England into one belligerent nation, Great Britain.

The carver cut slow elegant letters on the limestone:

ANDREW SOMERVILLE, EVER LOYAL
AND SINCERE TO HIS CONVICTIONS,
DIED IN THE LOW COUNTRIES,
AN EXILE AND A GENTLEMAN.

In the ale-house at the crossroads:

Sigurd: *Prince Charlie! What did Prince Charlie care about him? Prince Charlie wouldn't have wiped his boots on the thing.*

Svenn: *Ay, but mind you, he was true to his kind and his creed*

Rob: *Mind that old Andrew. Such a temper! A face on him like a Hallowe'en lantern. I was a boy when he left.*

Dod: It was me rowed him that morning across to Caithness. A
         fine sight, in silks and silver, sitting in the bow of my dirty
         old yole. Off Stroma, he put a guinea in my hand. I was
         never so rich, before or since. I think I never saw a man so
         happy as old Andrew that day. And none of us ever saw
         him again.

Rob: An old idiot. He should have bidden at home and sired a
         son sound in the head. Too late now.

7 JAMES: THE STONE BIRD

He was a loop of light in the tree in the morning.

He was the first leaf and the last leaf.

He was the bird flying, the furled bird, the hidden bird.

Also he was the stone heraldic bird over the main door.

He was not himself. He had one high bare remote room in
the house. He was afraid among those shadows.

He was his mother and three sisters.

He was the story of his father.

He was the spider and the candle-flame.

'Sarah, when will you read to me again out of the book?' . . .

He was the whirls of snow, the hanks of snow between the
boughs, the dead sheep under the snow.

He was the tramp that stood all day at the gate with open
palm.

He was the tall black bending man of words, the minister.

He was Annabel and the young fisherman clinging beside the
tree, under first stars, with their mouths together.

He was the fire in the roof and in the windows and in the
door. He was the roar and crunching and black smoke. He was
that merry dance of flames.

'Mother, take me for a walk again beside the sea' . . .

But the first pain in his head was not him. There was a bird in
his head stirring, trying to get out.

He was Charlotte and Sarah in the burn-pool, white and glittering and shrieking, with heavy breast-globes and red-brown wet strands of hair like seaweed stuck on white shoulders. (And Charlotte saw him, and shrieked out against him.)

Their picnic was not him. His flight up to the Hall was not him, a wild horse was dragging him back among the shadows.

The music was him, his mother and the harpsichord sweetly speaking together, in the big room with two candles.

'Charlotte, the men in the quarry say Father is a wicked man. He'll be hanged if ever he comes home' . . .

A man came. He came again. He blushed when Sarah was in the room. He spoke strange words. He came and stayed many days. The man was quiet and smiling and dangerous in the house. There was a deal of noise and laughter in the house, music and dark wine, high voices, many people known and unknown, comings and goings. Sarah and the apple-faced man stood in the new chapel together and Sarah wore a long white dress. Quiet words were spoken. Mr Gaunt the clergyman from Kirkwall read a solemn thing out of a book to Sarah and the man in black. The laird went out by himself and walked around under the tree. He was one leaf in the many thousands between April and October.

The bird in his head was there now always. It was often quiet as a folded dove. One morning the pan was a hawk. He tried to tear his eyes out from inside his head. The dove was not him. The hawk was not him. The bird that was neither pigeon nor kestrel flew out and away! He opened blank eyes. He was lying on a bed. The gardener and the kind boatman and the man who always had rabbit snares in his pocket were holding him down. His body was thin as a cage. His mother stood in the doorway, her back turned, shoulders hunched, shaking.

After the flight of the bird, he lay in bed many suns and many moons, an empty cage, exhausted.

'Why is Sarah not here, mother? When will that man let

Sarah come home again? I am tired. The bird in my head was always quiet when Sarah was here. Close the windows. The bird has gone now.'

He was the first drifting snowflake. He was the first star.

He walked like an empty cage beside the sea. Peg knelt at a rockpool, shelling limpets. Peg turned her face to him. He put his mouth against Peg's mouth the way he had seen the fisherman and Annabel doing it under the tree. Why had Peg sudden terrible eyes? The limpet shells fell like heavy drops of rain into the pool. His face was all aflame, from cheek to chin. His fingers were tipped with red, warm runnels. 'Peg, what's happening?' . . . Peg was not there. There was a crunching of beach stones, swift skirt-drawn susurration of sand along the beach, far off; silence. He was alone.

The bird had leapt at him out of Peg the shore girl. It had torn him. The bird was trying to get back into him.

He was Annabel his sweet dear sister. He was Sarah, the lost one. He was Charlotte sewing on a frame in the new high bower of the Hall. He was his mother with the ashen streaks in her hair and her sad singing fingers. He was the story of his dead father, traitor and hero.

The bird was always somewhere there now. It was seeking him out. The shadow of the bird was everywhere about the new Hall. He stumbled once on the wide balustrade going down into the garden, and fell. The bird leapt out of three steps and swiftly stroked him with hooks, knee and cheek and palm, and was off again, a hoverer lost in the ivied eaves.

There was the great summer storm. He stood at the shore. He was the sea leaping against the crag. He was the one salt stinging drop on his lip. He was the red cliff. He was the rocks that the sea gnawed, clattering from the cliff. The storm passed over. He walked along the tranced beach next morning early. He was the single grain lured unseen from the cliff on that still sweet summer morning. He laughed.

The bird lived in the stone heraldic shield. The bird hung and glided and brooded in the huge cage of stars. The bird sat furled down among the black roots of the island. The bird came softly, muffled in snow, rustling the new-fallen snow with dark webs.

The locked cage of his flesh. That was where the bird would drop down at last, and enter, and stay always. Then he would be the bird and the bird would be him. And all the Hall clocks would stop.

Always the women along the shore, lighting fires of dry tangles, bowed to him as he went past. The women in the fields bowed over hoe or harrow as he dandled by, aimless as thistle-down. He was thistle-down. He was the sulphur and burning peat of the sun, through his thick clothes. He was the bent women with their masks of patience and poverty. The men in the quarry did not bow. They tilted their faces as on he went down the road, they blanked the lower part of their faces behind furtive hands to see the fool fluttering past. The fishermen turned backs on him, hauling up their boats on the noust. The tall black column of words bent above; the minister put a few kind words upon him. The children swept round him once like tall wild lupins in a gale, laughing, plucking at his long gray coat; one put dew of spittle on him. He laughed among the children. Then the black bird flew up out of the cluster of children and flashed at him, hand and face. The flung stone fell from his forehead into the grass. Drops of blood fell onto the stone and the grass. The children were away on the wind, taking the terrible bird with them.

The laird sat under the tree. He wept. The tree whispered peace to him. But the bird that he must become and that was slowly becoming him furled, invisible shadow, among the ancient leaves.

'Bird, come soon, or fly far away' . . .

Annabel was a blank in the house. Annabel was fading smells of salt and dew. Annabel was in Edinburgh, learning accomplishments, 'studying to be a proper lady' . . .

Sarah was a shadow and the memory of a shadow: faded fragrances.

He was filthy with the dirts and sweats of a summer. Charlotte took him then by the hand to the pool in the burn and knelt beside him and washed him thoroughly. He cried with the sweet pain of the water. Charlotte's wet bright fingers went over his face. He smiled. Charlotte took the globe of his head and bent it down till it broke the circle of the pool. His long hair drifted like weed on the surface. The sun was warm on the thin cage of his body. Charlotte squeezed his hair till his hair wept rushets and droplets. 'Come James, you must go into the pool now, head to toe' . . .

He stepped down and squatted on the mud floor of the pool. He rose. He hung with his foot on a stone. He loved his glittering crystal coat. He laughed up into Charlotte's laughter. Then the crystal bird that had been in the water all the time dragged him down in its web and covered his face and put cold claws into his nostril and throat. They threshed the water together, bird and man . . . He was lying in the grass, choking and cold. Charlotte was blowing breath into his cinder of a mouth. The gardener chafed his fingers and knuckles. His mother stood far off, under the tree, her face turned away, shoulders small and hunched and shaking. The boatman came up from the shore. He covered James with the long gray laird-coat.

He was the first sheaf in the harvest field. The shadow of the bird went over the corn. An old woman who was following a scytheman bowed to him. The scytheman strode on under the sun, flashed, strode, flashed, strode.

'Mother, Father spoke to me this morning. He has come back. He is in the tree.'

What the bird wanted was to tear the last flesh from him and then to have his bones for its cage. What James wanted was to be the gathered beautiful changeless curves of the bird and to brood always in the perches of the lintel. Then there would be peace. All the crazy clocks in the Hall would stop.

He walked here and there through the island. He shouted, 'I am going to meet the bird soon! I must leave you! Come and eat in the kitchen up at the Hall. Charlotte is going away soon – a man was here – he is coming back – he will take Charlotte away for ever. My mother is old. Don't worry about my mother. But come up and eat in the Hall. My mother eats as little as a mouse. She had long fingers once, they made sounds like dropping water. They are silent now as old flowers. Come tonight, if you can, or next week. You're all welcome' . . . The men, as soon as his crazy back was turned, spat. The women shook sad heads. The children came up to him with feathers and bits of eggshell, and stuck them on his gray coat. 'Be a bird,' they cried. 'Be the bird now.'

The tramp came into the kitchen and was given a cold chicken to eat.

He prepared, in solitude, to become the bird.

On the Wednesday night, late, while the great house slept (all but poachers on hill and at trout-burn) James Somerville of Njalsay, esquire, left his bed and climbed the ladder into the attic and opened a turret window. The light of the full moon blinded him. He trembled in his night-shirt. He stood on the ledge, smiling and shivering.

He chirped, 'Come, bird. It's time.'

The man leapt wings-wide clear of the turret to enfold the bird. The bird tried to thresh into the man. The man tried to drag the bird, flaming, into him. Beak and claw unlocked the cage. The bird shrieked with the man's sweet kiss. Bird and man dabbled in blood. The bird began to feast on the heart. The man shrieked through the feathered throat and beak of the bird.

The man-bird fell. Stone feathers broke on the sundial below.

The clocks stopped beating.

A lantern in the garden – running shadows – cries at the gate

and among the bushes. A white glimmer passed through the
hallway; it fluttered, moth-soft, down the steps to where the
laird lay. Charlotte bent over her brother. She kissed his cold
clawed cheek. The lantern swung above. The gardener said, 'Get
him up to his room, quickly!' The boatman said, 'I think the
mother should be wakened. There may be urgent things to
settle.' (But the mother lay on till dawn, a little mute faded
flower on her dark bed laid, fingers folded and mute, uncaring
always now.)

The gardener and the boatman and two poachers carried
James up the garden steps and up the dark wide curving oak
staircase, lantern-splashed.

The gardener gathered up light pens of arms and folded them
on the bird-thin breast.

Over the lintel of the great door, the heraldic eye of the bird
and the paling eye of the moon looked at each other. The stone,
when the sun rose, had crumbled by a single grain.

Charlotte put her face against the ditch-and-smoke-smelling
face of the wandering tramp, and wept there.

JAMES CHARLES SOMERVILLE

Madge: *The poor cratur, and poor cratur he was, he is well
relieved; I was heart-sore for him, as sorry as if he was
my own boy. Innocent as a bird he was.*
Ezekiel: *God, and that the likes of that should be set in authority
over the man that works in the fields and kens flesh from
fowl. There are changes coming. There will be a change
soon.*

8 THOMAS THE SECOND:
THE MERRY GUNS OF INDEPENDENCE

The hundred and fourteen boxes of Irish linen safe in the hold,
the bill of lading and the bill of exchange given and sealed and

taken, *Loyalty* up-anchored from the road-stead of Belfast at ten in the morning of Saturday. She shook out sail in a fresh south-westerly and entered the North Channel. All aboard were in good heart, and in hope of a safe arrival in Hamnavoe by the middle of the following week, except for Barnabas Gray who had put too much of the gray Irish barley-spirit into him, and lay in misery in his hammock. Galloway reared up, blue out of the faint haar. The wind shifted into the south. *Loyalty* had never trampled ocean so high and proud. Spindrift sang over broken hives.

The merchant laird, Mr Guthrie-Somerville, sat in his cabin over accounts, or walked the deck, a douce stout fair-dealing man. The sailors thought it no hindrance to have him on board. Nor did he interfere with skipper or mate, as to the vessel's ordering.

Alfred the boy brought food into his cabin thrice a day, salt half-stewed dollops, but he did not complain; he said (smiling) the wine tasted better for the honest coarseness of the fare.

'God send,' said Thorfinn Spence the skipper, 'the haar keeps inland, and coats the hills, and doesn't come creeping out upon the sea. Or it might be the end of next week before we see Orkney' . . .

Now Barnabas Gray was out of his hammock of ashes, and able to wind a rope.

Ghosts of giants, the long coast of Scotland lay to starboard. The wind swung, a withershin arc, to south-east; *Loyalty* put her head down, a proud cleave and curve, and drove on.

Night came down. Alfred brought two candles to Mr Guthrie-Somerville's table; and afterwards a bottle of claret. 'The gentleman,' said Alfred later, 'has given me another sixpence!' . . .

We stood well out on the Atlantic, sailing all night to profit by the favourable wind. 'We could be home by Tuesday,' said Thorfinn Spence, 'and sitting about the fire in *The Arctic Whaler*' . . .

The wheel of the wind circled still, withershins. The dawn – a red ball in the fog between two distant ghostly mountains – sent us a sluggish north-easter.

And now what Skipper Spence feared happened; the haar spread, in flying shrouds and tatters, and small cold incessant rain, about us. *Loyalty* was a ghost in a firmament of ghosts.

Atkinson, super-cargo, about this time began to thumb through his bible, and to squinny at this text and that: never the best of signs.

We saw Mr Guthrie-Somerville only once that blind day, walking for an hour about the deck, his thick cloak about him and his wide brim pulled low about his brows . . . Alfred brought him his gristle and grog; then, at evening, his wine.

The skipper thought, if things changed for the better, landfall might be Thursday. Once, towards sunset, Simison screamed, 'Rocks!' But they turned out to be those harmless sharks that drift about the ocean, and rise and fall, and disappear.

We could not tell, with any exactitude, where we were.

Night came, and folded *Loyalty* and all her people in a second black shroud. That the fog still lay on the ocean we knew by the wetness of our beards and breeches. A single lantern glowed spectral in the stern. With night the contrary wind had packed and gone. We dabbled in a sea that was all black idle singing: with, now and again, bell-notes of wonderment when a slow heave hit the starboard hull.

That watch, Skipper Spence went round with a new-opened rum bottle. All drank, except Atkinson who refused with a prim pursing of the mouth – and Barnabas Gray, who was bypassed (the bottle was handed over his head) – and of course Mr Guthrie-Somerville, who was sound asleep (the good man) in his bunk. Soon, one by one, the rum-warmed sailors sought their hammocks.

Morning brought a cheerful sight to our eyes. The sun rose, hard and bright as a diamond: the haar had vanished as silently

as it had fallen. Also the wind, though slight, had backed south-
east, and set *Loyalty*'s canvas creaking. Nor, we saw with joy,
were we lying among dangerous Hebridean reefs. We stood far
west on the open Atlantic. Scotland lay, a long uneven saw-edge
of mountains, along the eastern horizon.

Slowly the wind stirred and freshened. *Loyalty*, the dandler,
was soon up and about her business. The sail swelled. Atkinson
put his bible back into his sea-chest. Mr Guthrie-Somerville
came on deck to take the morning air. He opened his little
ebony box, he snuffed fiery grains. Thorfinn Spence cried like a
trumpet, 'Hoy Sound Friday morning!' *Loyalty* smashed
through the fresh wind-fretted sea.

We had been companied since dawn, distantly, by a large
handsome brig, bound north also. None of us thought it
curious at first that this ship, that flew no flag, could easily
have outsailed us and, in the rising wind, put the round of
the northern horizon between us. Instead, she seemed to sail
at exactly our speed, hour after hour. Indeed, Spence reported – his long glass on her – that she was slowly closing
with us.

Memories of the press-gang, that in earlier wars had taken so
many men by force out of peaceful ships, and set them in the
fire-and-thunder of men-of-war, made a cheek blanch here and
there. Yet the ship did not look like a war vessel of His Britannic
Majesty, with her clean-cut mercantile lines and dove-breasted
rigging. We saw towards noon that she carried guns; but that
was a commonplace in the vessels of wealthy shippers: dangerous times had been on the oceans, and might be again.

John Atkinson had taken the precaution of retrieving once
more the sacred volume from his sea-chest. He turned his thin
back on us, and read, and leafed.

Alfred said, 'They won't touch us with an important man like
Mr Guthrie-Somerville on board.'

Thorfinn Spence stilled the brazen of his voice. 'It could be,' he said, 'that there is some kind of trouble on board, and they're seeking our help' . . . But no signal flew from her mast.

The two vessels drew slowly together, as if drawn upon two threads by one distant invisible star.

Spence levelled his glass again. 'Not sickness,' he said. 'I see a dozen weather-tanned faces along the rail.'

He passed the glass to Mr Guthrie-Somerville, who turned it here and there blindly, and twisted it, and levelled it west again, and saw nothing. He handed it back, smiling, to the skipper.

Spence remarked, 'It may be one of the revenue ships, though again she doesn't look like one' . . . Then, for the first and the last time, I saw the important man who had chartered *Loyalty* three months ago look agitated. He checked his step, he turned, he paced quickly back and fore, back and fore. He stuck an enormous charge of snuff into his nostril. (There was, I expect, more than a gross boxes of Irish linen on board, destined for Sweden. Hidden deep in the hold – and cargoed long before we joined the ship – sat hogsheads of French and Spanish wines and brandies, and as much tobacco, in tarred and resinous coils of thin rope, as would smoke-cure Leviathan.)

The vessels were now so close we could have read the name of our casual wayfarer with the naked eye, if there had been a name at the prow to read; but there was not. A Scottish voice hailed across the dwindling sea space – 'Where bound, friends – Iceland or the Republic of America?'

Thorfinn Spence, guileless man, brazened back: 'The Orkneys, for Gothenburg, freight of Irish linen!'

Immediately two things happened together. A flag went up and fluttered high on the main-mast. It was a flag I had never seen before, with red and blue level bands and a cluster of white stars at one corner. At the same time two guns opened fire. The side of the nameless ship blazed and smoked.

In fifteen minutes *Loyalty* was smashed beyond recovery. I witnessed the sudden death of a ship. It shuddered, crashed, broke up. There seemed to be a storm of wood. I saw Alfred the boy lying at my feet, blood oozing from a splinter in his neck. Thorfinn Spence, his fists in the rigging, crimson-faced, sent curses and blasphemies against the treacherous hull that was now half lost in its own dreadful smoke and stench of powder. Through the smoke a single star blazed and faded: the American was firing again, to give poor *Loyalty* (it seemed) superfluous death. What I remember distinctly was an acre of shapeless white linen afloat on the sea; and as I watched (it seemed for a long time) a dark stain spread over it. (I think now, twenty years after, a breached wine barrel must have soiled it.) I remember thinking: *The swan's death*. When I came to my senses again, I was lying in the commodious cabin of a ship in the port of Boston, USA, as comfortable as a man can be who has newly lost a leg and a hand.

In this free and fair broad land I have lived ever since, a trusted scrivener in an import house in New York.

Manse of Njalsay, 1810

NOTE on Thomas Guthrie-Somerville, late laird in Njalsay Isle, Orkney.

Born Thomas Guthrie, in the city of Edinburgh, son of Thomas Guthrie, W.S., lawyer, he commenced clerk in a shipping office in the port of Leith, and entered into partnership with Weddermain, Salter and MacIntosh, merchant shippers, with the proceeds of his paternal inheritance. Being young, eager, intelligent, adventurous, he regularly sailed to the Baltic markets, and proved himself early to be a prudent and fortunate trader. In the town of Kirkwall, Orkney, he met Miss Sarah Somerville, elder daughter of Andrew Somerville, laird of the island of Njalsay: he married her within the year. They begot seven children, four sons and three daughters, of whom only one son and one daughter survived infancy. Upon the deaths, within three twelvemonths, of two sequent lairds (the said Andrew Somerville and his only son James Somerville) the lands and fortunes of the Hall of Njalsay fell to Sarah Somerville and to her spouse Thomas Guthrie. He, as the new laird of Njalsay, took the name of Guthrie-Somerville. The interests of his business necessitated his continuing residence in Edinburgh. The Njalsay estates were overseen by a factor of proven integrity and efficiency. (But the Guthrie-Somervilles visited Orkney often, and resided at the Hall whenever opportunity offered.) The firm of Weddermain, Salter and MacIntosh continued to prosper, despite the French wars and constant menaces and perils on the high sea. Mr Guthrie-Somerville, wishing in the late summer of 1779 to enquire into certain irregularities in his Orkney estate, travelled to Belfast in Ireland and boarded the chartered vessel *Loyalty*, bound presently for Gothenburg, Sweden, by way of Hamnavoe, Orkney, where fresh water and supplies were to be taken on, and certain other undisclosed business done. The *Loyalty* carried a considerable cargo of best Irish linen. Six miles west of Lewis Isle the *Loyalty* was sunk by cannon fire from a rebel American ship under the command of John Paul Jones. Mr Guthrie-Somerville was taken from the sea by the American sailors and brought to the port of Boston, Mass. There he was fairly dealt with, upon promise of adequate ransom, until the treaty of peace was signed. He returned to Scotland, resigned (being then elderly) his merchant shipping interests, and ended his days in the Hall of Njalsay, revered and respected by all. He died (as scripture saith) full of years, after last harvest: to be survived by a sorrowing widow, his son Jeremiah, and his daughter Wilma (Lady Daven). Unfortunately, the circumstances

connected with the *Loyalty* have much reduced the estate
in wealth: the Hall, from being a fine handsome building
completely rebuilt after the fire of 1747, has suffered
structural damage of recent years due to neglect and
inadequate means. It seemed as if the wealth of Njalsay
had flowed out through the broken hull of *Loyalty*.

Old Maddie: *Bad befall them. My peedie boy Alfie was in the
ship that sunk. Nobody saved him. Nobody stirs to
save the poor. They tell me – and it's true – that
boat was crammed to the gunnels with whisky and
silks and tobacco snuff. So the King's men sunk
her. And poor peedie Alfie went down with her.
Poor peedie Alfie, he didn't live to be old and
brought to his grave at last in an oak box with eight
silver handles, at scythe-time. Alfie was poor, so he
died young. I warned him well – 'Alfie,' I said, 'you
bide at home on the hill with Maddie thi gran-
damm. There's worse things (I said) than a few
sheep and a rig of tatties and a winter fire' . . . But
no, off to sea with him soon as rumour came there
was a ship in Hamnavoe harbour. And that was
the last I saw him.*

9 JEREMIAH: THE ROSE GARDEN

He made a rose blossom in the desert (something like that,
the minister said). But indeed on this savage bare island he
had put a coat of green and gold, a fair coat where (before)
were only a rag and a patch here and there. The creatures of
the savage earth, they whispered black against him behind
their hands at kirk door and ale-house. They starved half the
winter, their backs were curved early to the curve of the hard
earth, they lived and grew old in misery. Yet that existence

they clung to, against all that he strove to accomplish for their welfare.

Their little sharp sticks scratching the earth, in narrow rigs scattered here and there. Their thin hoof-rotted sheep, out there beyond the encircling dyke. Their hovels full of smoke and vermin.

Look at this – look here at the comeliness of the Hall, lying so broad and fair there on the crest of the brae (though, it's true, most of the great house is shuttered and silent). Look at the wide garden, the tree, the pool in the midst of the rushing burn. They looked, they shook their heads dumbly, like oxen.

What he meant to do was to give to each and every one of the crofters just such proportion and comeliness, both in their patterns of work and in their habitations: not large, it's true, but trim and decent and becoming to man's dignity. They wanted none of it.

He built with his careful money that little school at the crossroads, he brought from Aberdeen and lodged at his own expense John Nimmo the dominie. 'Look, men – please listen to me – bairns will read and write from now on, they will understand writings, numbers, how to measure one thing against another. They will learn about the distant places of the earth, and the things that happened in distant times. With such knowledge their days will have meaning. They will drink from fountains sweet and good. Tom Sweyn, take your brutish face away from the ale-lamp! I am sick of you and the stubbornness of you all. Though you are dumb poor creatures yourselves, will you stand in the way of your children and your children's children? Will you stand between them and the sun?' . . . Some of them stood between him and the ale-house door, and looked as they would have done him a mischief with their trembling clenched earth-coloured hands. But resolutely he passed among them, and took his way through their miserable green patches of oat and bere, up to the Hall and the fire and his Virgil and the decanters, and to his thorn of a lady.

'Look, men – it will profit all of us, you and your families as well as me. The rents I get from you – the sour butter and salt fish – are an offence. Mr Sheldon here, my good factor, has shown you how simply it might be done. He has led you, a dumb flock, round the home farm: the drained enclosed fertile compact rotated fields. His reverence, at my urging, has taken you to see what he has accomplished at his own farm, the Glebe. A little patience, a little tolerance, a little understanding, and you – every man of you – would have a neat little farm of his own, with a sure yield harvest after harvest. Let me tell you once more. Now, listen!'

They looked at him with their untrusting eyes. They shuffled their feet. They cast their faces here and there.

He broke, therefore, the dyke. He gathered the wintry patches and rags in one heap, and he bestowed on this crofter and that a single holding, one single sufficient green coat of land (whether the man liked it or not). And again the factor went round, from door to door, patiently urging and demonstrating, his hand full of seed, the sun at his shoulder.

Some young men, rather than listen, went to the whaling ships in Hamnavoe harbour, when the brown sails came in April. One man took to the roads with wife and bairns; they drifted hungry from ditch to ditch, a burden on the countryside. Some walked to the agent in the town, and enquired about Alberta and New South Wales. But most studied with enforced patience at last the new pattern that was being forced upon them. (Here and there a violent man would fall upon his neighbour on account of some patch of bog that previously he had considered his by ancient right, but was now alienated from him, and gathered into the new economy; there were wounds, threats, laird's soothings, factor's outspread chart, interviews in lawyers' offices . . .)

In three years they were eating better bread and drinking sweeter milk. The summer hillside wore larger patches of green and yellow. They handled with amazement, for the first time, shillings and half-sovereigns. They sent one or other of their boys to the school at the crossroads whenever they could spare them from herding, peat-cutting, dyke-building. They quarried stones to build wider higher walls. Twice a year they paid the rent with coins. Every family lived among its own sun-blessed fields.

Margaret Anne, girl at the school, seemed suddenly like a rose to the horseman on the banks above: the covered curves of breast and the curved mouth, coming up from the rockpools with her basket of dulse and whelks. That summer, early, she blossomed. The horseman's long fingers stroked his chin.

Seenie, among the peat-banks, she was in bud: leaning on a long spade under the sun at noon, shadowed by kestrels. On the dark glimmering loch below, the man looked up from his trout line. Seenie's white leg, bare to the knee, drove the tusker in again. The angler looked. It was long before he offered again the fly to the fish.

Andrina that attended the minister's wife at the manse, and scoured tall windows and mirrors: one month she was a thin cold girl. The next moon changed her. 'Andrina, my wife, Mrs Guthrie-Somerville, the lady up at the Hall, she has heard about you. She wants you in the kitchen and the garden. No, I will speak to the minister. I will speak to your mother. You are to start Monday morning' . . . Andrina, new-opened rose, hung her head; she dared not speak; and the horseman turned and rode on.

And Liza, that was to be married to Jock Coolag after Christmas – that such a sudden softness and dewiness and fragrance should be wasted on a coarse ignorant poor fellow! 'Now, Jock, there is no point our arguing about this any more. It must be so. Updyke is too small, it is not viable. I intend to merge Updyke with Quoysmithers. No, man, you will not be the poorer. I know you have spoken about New Zealand, more than once. New Zealand is a good place for a young man like you. Men grow rich these days in New Zealand. Jock, your passage is paid, I have seen to that, the boat leaves Leith before Martinmas. Jock, I am giving you fifty sovereigns in your hand the morning you set out. Liza? Liza will follow – it is too late now to see about her immediate passage. Jock, I assure you, you are doing the right thing' . . . Seven salt oceans from her lover, Liza withered in a cold magistral hand.

A few petals fallen, a few dry and lustreless, yet Miriam stood beautiful in grief at the door of Sneuk as the plain deal coffin was carried out and about and slowly down to the kirkyard at the shore by six neighbour-men, the minister following, shawled heads watching from this gable-end and that. Miriam turned and covered her face. Then, purposeful woman (for life, however cruel, goes on), she gathered up the funeral cups from the table and hung them on their hooks at the dresser, and the half-empty whisky bottle she corked and set in the cupboard. And she stabbed the peats into flame, for soon the gray shawls would be coming from the crofts around to comfort her, a young widow among unploughed fields. It was the horseman who came first. 'Mistress Thorfinson, you are not to concern yourself. It is not my wish that any of my people should go hungry. Rest assured, you will not be put out on the roads. Miriam – if I may call you that, I have known you long enough, since you were a small girl – Miriam, what I'm proposing to do is this. Sam Thomson of Pennybrae, your neighbour, is to work the fields of Sneuk. He has two tall sons and a daughter that will help him. Well, then, you yourself are to bide here in the cottage, unmolested, until such time as you find another place. There is no hurry, Miriam. You are young still, and there is a long summer left to you, a good blossoming time. Miriam, you are to consider yourself under my protection. Miriam, don't cry. Yes, do, for the tears on your face, the dew shining between your fingers, make you more comely than ever. I will see you in the winter, Miriam – comfort yourself – your grief will be the less by then' . . .

By reason that he had put a new pattern and rhythm and purpose on the formerly wretched agriculture of the island, the laird of Njalsay restored in some measure the fortunes of the Hall. Tradesmen came from Caithness and put a gray light slate roof where heavy flagstones had been. A craftsman from Edinburgh arrived and removed the high tall plain window from the first stair and put in its place a glory of stained glass: a huge red rose at the centre, at one side a maiden (beautiful but in rags), on the other side a field ripe with barley, and three harvesters, with scythes at different angles.

The laird built a little chapel for the occasional visits of the episcopal priest from Kirkwall.

The years passed, prosperously.

Neighbouring lairds and their ladies were well entertained, with port wine and whist and music by candle-light, and fishing and grouse shooting in season. And always the welcoming word to the visiting lairds' growing daughters: 'My dear, you are grown as beautiful, I swear, as any rose' . . . But the lady of the Hall, Mistress Guthrie-Somerville, was not to be seen. In her room, alone, she read her novels, and put the lace handkerchief to her nose at the sad parts; or she sat at her embroidery frame, her thin fingers choosing carefully this coloured wool or that.

One summer morning her finger drew a black thread from the basket.

JEREMIAH GUTHRIE-SOMERVILLE: HE CLAD THE ISLE
OF NJALSAY IN A GREEN COAT: AND UPON THE COAT
HIS LOYAL WIFE CHARLOTTE JANE STITCHED A ROSE
OF UNFADING BEAUTY. BOTH HERE LIE, GATHERED TO
THEIR REST WITHIN ONE MONTH IN THE HARSH
WINTER OF 1863.

Seenie at the shore, among the other women, waiting for the fishing boats.

Dead is he? – is that a fact? – and was a kind good man in his way, though there were them that gave him out to be a monster of cruelty, putting them out of their yards and rigs. Be that as it may, he was no grand haughty lord when it came to kissing. Oh no, his red mouth it was for every lass, high and low. There was I, up at the peats one day alone, so innocent I didn't know love from lollipops, when there he stood between the peat-banks with a long bending trout rod in his hand. I got such a fright I gave a screech. 'No no, Seenie (says he) none of that Seenie (he says) you're as fair a rose as ever bloomed in Njalsay' (says he). And with that he bent down and put his tobacco-stinking mouth on my cheek, and (says he), 'Thy petals of lips, Seenie, give me the two petals of thy mouth.' And faith, he near smothered me with his smootchings. I thought, will I hit him with the long tusker in my hand? . . . Then I thought to myself, 'The laird is the laird, what the laird does is right and good' . . . So, with wondering what to do, run or bide, I never knew a thing before he unbuttoned me and his fingers were at the bud of my new breast, and he was whispering, 'Secret of April, oh Seenie, and in my garden thy tree shall open in oneness to the sun' . . . Seeing him so sweet-mouthed and foolish and kind – and faith, there were worse men in the world – I took his shaking gray head between my two hands and I kissed him, I surely did, over and over. My dad lived rent-free in Scar till the day he died, and never lacked for a dram whenever it was winter and he couldn't work and he was shaken with winter coughs.

10 TOBY JUG

Who was then laird of Njalsay, after the epitaph on that tomb? The lady of the Hall, Charlotte Jane, had rocked no cradles. Who then was the new laird? Was it Allie the beach-comber, whose mother had been Margaret Anne? There were scatterings of rose leaves all over the island. Was the new master to be Davie, son to Seenie of the peat-banks, him that lounged day-long at the shop at the pier, smoking his clay pipe and some-times delivering an errand for Smellie the merchant? It was not to be thought on that a boatman like Gavin would be taken from his salt and tar to stand under the heraldic lintel; even though he was a hard-working well-liked ferryman. Yet Gavin Forss had the hooky nose and hawk-bright eye of Jeremiah Guthrie-Somerville, and his mother was Andrina who had in her youth scoured the windows and mirrors in the big house. And little Liza of the hill, whose lover had gone to New Zealand and never come home again, and had not let on by the scrape of a pen whether he was alive or dead, or wealthy or destitute – Liza died giving birth to a fatherless boy called George. A well-doing farmer's wife, Peterina Bruce of Kirkvalt, who had ten children already, took the infant into her keeping, and reared him well (better, it was said, than her own). George, when he was seven, went to the dominie and learned to read and write and to manipulate numbers, a thing that none of the other Bruces had been suffered to do. When George was fourteen he was taken into a lawyer's office in Kirkwall, and set at a high desk there. There he sat till he was gray and creaky in the joints, copying day after day, year after year, ornate scripts – wills and deeds and pleas and conveyances. He read in the *Orkney Herald*, with a stir of interest, that Mr Jeremiah Guthrie-Somerville of Njalsay had died (for things had been whispered into his ear). Indeed he asked for the day off, in order to cross over to Njalsay and attend the funeral; which he had no right to do, because he had not been invited, and he looked odd in his gray ink-spattered office suit among all the blackcloth-coated funeral-banded gentry of Orkney. After he had seen his true father laid in genteel earth, George went to the kirkyard down at the shore and stood for a while above a little weathered sandstone tomb that said simply: LIZA SMITH OF THE HILL 1822–1854 . . . George

Bruce, lawyer's clerk, he was not sent for either to assume a more august calling.

Would the new laird be William Garth, tenant of the twin farms of Pennybrae and Sneuk, whose mother still stirred briskly about the byre and well and hen-house, a fine-looking woman still with fadeless roses in her cheeks? It was not to be William either, though Miriam Garth his mother had fought for the boy tooth and nail, both up at the Hall and in solicitors' offices in Kirkwall. She had made no secret of the boy's paternity, indeed she threatened openly at one stage to call him William Jeremiah Guthrie-Somerville; and in the end the formidable croftwoman had wrung concessions from the Hall. The boy was to be paid fifty pounds a year until he was eighteen. Then, if Sam Thomson of Pennybrae was still hale and alive, notice was to be served on the said Sam Thomson that he was to quit and vacate the said farms of Pennybrae and Sneuk of which he was tenant, and sell or otherwise dispose of his stock and removables to William Garth – father unknown (yet known), mother, Miriam Garth of Sneuk – who would take over the said farms as his own absolute property – a gift of the Hall, signed and witnessed and sealed. This had happened – Sam Thomson was not thrown into absolute penury, he and his wife and daughter; he was adequately compensated, in open and secret ways, both by Jeremiah Guthrie-Somerville, esquire, and by William Garth, the new young farmer with the light of progress in his eye. Indeed the usurpation produced no bitterness. Providence designed that young William Garth looked favourably on Winifred, Sam Thomson's stay-at-home daughter. They were married the next winter (much, to begin with, against the wishes of Mistress Miriam Garth, who considered her son too good for 'the likes o' a bit o' a ferm lass'). And, to clinch the strange bit of business satisfactorily to all concerned, wasn't the croft of Sneuk now warm and empty, and a haven for the evicted Thomsons to move into? In Pennybrae there were hard words often between the mother and the daughter-in-law. But the new farmer planned intelligently and worked hard. There was a new cradle-load year after year. Old Miriam became gray and bible-reading; the strings of the generations gave out at last a kind of acceptable harmony to the folk who lived in Penny-brae farm . . . But when the will was read out, on the late afternoon of the laird's funeral, in the long drawing-room of the Hall, William Garth, farmer in Pennybrae, received no mention . . .

Instead, Gavin ferried across on the *Gannet* one afternoon in March a little bright-eyed smiling man. At last, half-way across the Sound, Gavin asked out of curiosity and amiability what business the stranger had in Njalsay, for he did not look like a seedsman or a minister . . . The blue eyes twinkled behind the round spectacles; the cheeks dimpled; he spoke in such a strange English chant that Gavin could hardly follow the gist. What the stranger said was, 'I am the new squire of this island, dear me, my name is Tobias Ponsonby, and would you be so kind as to tell me, please, is that red pile on the hillside the house I must live in? It looks like an over-blown rose. I ask myself, is it wise of me, at my time of life, to come from teaching Latin and Greek in a boys' school to the yoking of a stubborn peasantry? The die is cast. I leave a world of marvellous solidity and harmony to live out my life among sea-slime and dung' . . .

So Tobias Ponsonby, only grandson of Mrs Annabel Ponsonby (born Annabel Guthrie-Somerville) came into his inheritance.

TOBIAS: EXTRACTS FROM THE JOURNAL
OF THE LAST LAIRD

They laugh at me. They do well to laugh at me. I am an irrelevance. I serve no purpose in this island. I gather in the rents twice a year: which they pay over with dark unsmiling eyes. Of their work and of their lives I know nothing: except that both share some of the brutishness of the ox. Does that sound proud and arrogant? It is not meant that way. The ox serves an obvious purpose, the earth's dark power has nourished him, the brightness of the sun is between his horns. Earth and water, animal and sun nurture between them the food that we put into our mouths. From that sacred cycle of labour I am excluded, except that twice in the year I gather in guineas from farm and croft – their sun-sweat. I sit in the cold library in the Hall and read my Virgil and Horace. I console myself: here is beauty and harmony too fine and rare for them. Only a few can relish those sweet grape-treadings . . . But without the sweat and thew of peasants there would be no *Georgics*, no *Odes*. It is matter for wonder.

When I came here, being poor (not so poor as Mansie the crofter and Sam the fisherman, but poor nevertheless according to the lairds' scale), I had to dismiss almost everyone – factor, gardener, ghillie, cook, the six girls who kept the windows and mirrors shining with their restless dusters. Only one woman I kept, and that because she simply refused to go. Three times I gave her notice, each time more abruptly than the last: only to find her on the Monday morning at the kitchen fire, kindling peat, or coming in with buckets of water from the well. Lizzie Scar's mother and grandmother and great-grandmother before her worked at the Hall. She seems to think she has more right here than I do; and of course, in a way, she is right. With the utmost regularity and docility and stubbornness she cooks meals for me, washes my linen, fights a losing battle against the encroachments of rot and web and dust. I can just manage to pay Lizzie, out of the rents I gather twice a year, in May and November. But last month I read in *The Times* that there are motions before Parliament to secure the crofter against his superior, by strictly limiting rents and revoking the laird's power to evict; and worst of all perhaps by forcing the laird to compensate out-going tenants for any improvements they have effected in their cottages and fields. All that, if it comes into law, will bear hard on me.

They laugh at me, or they turn indifferent faces when I pass by on the road walking. (There is no horse for the laird any more; the stables have been padlocked sicne my first harvest here.) They have much to laugh at, no doubt. I have a round bespectacled empty amiable face, and a plump torso, rather like Mr Pickwick. As far as they are concerned, I do nothing, I am as idle as a butterfly day after day. I seem to serve no function under the sun, except to gather in their sun-sweat, the twice-yearly rents. They cannot understand my precise high-pitched English speech, any more than I can take but a word or two of their Norse-Scots. The things that interest the men – ale, women, smuggled tobacco, religion – I have no relish for. I move among them, an utter stranger, and a parasite to boot.

Not but what there are many kindly good folk on the farms. The third winter I was here, going for my afternoon walk to the shore and back, I was caught in a sudden blizzard, a white-and-gray whirl. All sense of direction was lost. I stumbled into ditches, was thrown against fences, I tried standing still, my back to the onset. If anything, the flakes flew thicker past my face. Most of the time, on account of my glasses, I was blind. I remember saying distinctly, 'Isle of Njalsay, soon you will have a snowman for laird,' and I laughed aloud at the thought. I turned, and encountered diffused silver-gray light. The cloud shredded and thinned, and showed a patch of blue. Then, as if veil after veil were withdrawn, Njalsay shone in a new immaculate white coat, with farms and steadings and stacks sewn on it, a fertile embroidery. There, across a thick-quilted field, stood the croft of Sneuk (Sam Thomson, tenant).

It was Sam Thomson and his goodwife who urged warmth back into me, sitting in the high straw chair beside a leaping peat-fire. 'The poor sowl, the poor sowl!' Edie Thomson said over and over again, chafing my hands and cheeks with a rough towel. And Sam put the cup of hot toddy into my hands; soon enough the fire in my umbles melted the last ice along my veins, and there were three happy faces round the hearth of Sneuk. I ate a dinner with them. Rising to go, before night came, I tried to press a half-sovereign on them. They refused, austerely. The fellowship we had shared was beyond price.

When I walked between the withering tree and the frozen burn, there in the door of the Hall stood Lizzie Scar wringing her hands. She uttered all kinds of blessings on me for being a living man and not a winter ghost yet.

Out of such tough black primal rootedness – as Virgil knew – impossible fragrancies can spring. The poet makes these fragrancies as hard as cuttings in stone. For us more ordinary creatures the beauty comes, and exists for a short while, and vanishes; and leaves a dull wonderment. The ecstasy and the heartbreak are in the stone.

That snow lasted for three weeks, blossoming and shrinking, hard as iron, soft as down. One afternoon in the last of the thaw, as I was returning from my afternoon walk – all slush and cold puddles – I saw on the table in the entrance lobby three fine fresh-caught haddocks on a dish. Lizzie Scar came shuffling out of the kitchen. 'Rob Stronsay was here an hour ago – the fisherman, you know – he left them fish for you' . . .

It was old Gavin Forss who came one day to the gate of the Hall, gasping and speechless. I was in the garden, trimming a rose-bush. He took me by the elbow, he pointed with his free hand out to sea. (It was that morning I saw what a vivid resemblance Gavin had, with his Duke of Wellington nose and fowler's eye, to the line of portraits in the long corridor of the Hall, my ancestors.) I followed with my eye Gavin's shaky indication. On the horizon, fallen east, was a plume of gray smoke, as if a ship was on fire. But the fire on this vessel was under measured control. She moved through the calm Atlantic as fast as most ships in a moderate wind. She did carry a kind of rudimentary sail, but it was the controlled fire in her belly that drove her on so swiftly through the breathless summer swell.

Old Gavin looked at me, and shook his head.

'You are looking, Gavin, at the future,' I said. 'These ships are called steamers. I have read about them. The engineers they carry are more important than the skippers. Fold your sails, old boatman. The first wave of the future is about your feet seething.'

Gavin began to wheeze with laughter. He looked at me, and shook his head, and put the back of his hand to his merry brimming eyes. Still laughing, he left me, going down to the shore and his boat with the furled sail.

It is true: the future is flooding in fast, even into the remote places of the world. It will alter the patterns of life in an island like this, no one can guess how. The old hierarchy has fallen: laird, minister, tenant, fisherman, beggar. Society operates in a new way – the characters have not yet found their true places. The merchant, Edward Sinclair, in the new hamlet above the landing stage, is now the wealthiest man in Njalsay (and the possessor of money becomes increasingly the arbiter of taste, the pillar of worth). Where there used to be one minister, there are now two: Mr Timothy Bain of the established Presbyterian church, a hearty man who likes his glass of brandy and his game of whist, and Revd Macaulay, the young dark intense sin-fraught Free Kirk minister; they divide between them, acrimoniously, the little spiritual kingdom of Njalsay. The poor earth-and-dung conservative tenant has of recent years become the forward-looking farmer, moderately prosperous, his own man (because increasingly I have had to sell the farms to my former tenants, in order to keep the Hall in tolerable repair). The powerless laird – myself – resembles no one in the island so much as Jock the wandering beggar-man; both are irrelevant; both are parasitic, though one is posh and the other patched; both are occasions of mirth in the island . . . There is also a new power in the land, the schoolmaster.

A school was built fifteen years ago at the crossroads. A school-master, a young man with a russet beard and radical opinions, took up residence with his pretty wife in the new adjacent schoolhouse. All the island children between the ages of six and twelve were compelled by law to be educated in the subjects considered necessary for full community participation in the late nineteenth century: reading and writing, arithmetic, scripture, geography and history, music; for the brighter pupils a little Latin and French and geometry . . . For half-a-generation now the schoolmaster, Mr Smellie, has been thrashing knowledge into those shy beautiful children for nine months in the year. The natural freedom that they knew of old is confined to potato-picking, harvest time, New Year, the Lammas market in Kirkwall. I see them trudging miserably to school through winter rain and summer light with a book under one arm and a peat under the other.

Will this enforced schooling make them better men and women? Will it open to them the tranquil springs of Greece and Rome? Goodness, truth, and beauty are universal timeless founts; ideally, all men ought to taste of them; for, properly relished, they are the elixir of immortality. One passes, pilgrim-like, from knowledge into the pure serene of wisdom.

Smellie will have none of that nonsense. He is a man of facts, information, numbers. He seems chiefly anxious to beat all the ancient legend and lore out of their tender heads: the mid-summer bonfires, the midwinter Yule ceremonies, the beautiful stories of seal and trow and vanishing island; all of which (I am convinced) are necessary for the health and harmony of our rural society; boreal equivalent of the timeless classical myths.

No: Smellie will see to it that they stand commonsensical in the light of common day. Smellie is not transmuting knowledge into wisdom; he is dissecting it and reducing it to the bare bones of fact and statistic. I tremble at what the man does to a fine passage of prose, in English or in Latin. Instead of letting the beauty of the piece unbud and flower serenely in the minds of his pupils, he analyses it in the way that Dr Knox of Edinburgh dissected corpses. That is what the printed stories and poems have become for Mr Smellie and such: dead things.

This horrid perverse kind of 'education' is slowly taking effect. Now the young farm boy is beginning to be ashamed that he lives next door to cows and pigs, under the one sheltering roof. It is subtly impressed on him that the earth-worker is the basest of men, hardly higher than the ox he drives. To break out of this cycle of root and dung and broken earth, he must strive to master enough of the new knowledge – Mr Smellie's kind – to get a job at an office desk in Kirkwall or Hamnavoe; or perhaps open a shop there, be draper or grocer, dimple the cheek to buyer and seller, have a framed text on the parlour wall, go to the kirk with polished boots on the Sabbath, write black and red figures in a ledger.

Slowly, over the last decade, in the enlightenment brought by Mr Smellie, the young men are beginning to leave Njalsay, in order (as the modern phrase has it) to 'improve themselves' in the island towns. A few go south to Edinburgh. Some (I know) have sent for information about a possible emigration to Canada or New Zealand. Mr Smellie's numbers and facts have wrenched the frame of a whole community.

The very day after Gavin Forss and I saw the steamer sailing between Scandinavia and America, I walked along the coast.

There on a rock in the encroaching sea, sat a young golden-haired god. His only clothing was the brightness of the sea in which he had been swimming.

'Rob Stronsay,' said Lizzie Scar that evening, serving me supper on a tray beside the library fire, 'that would be Rob Stronsay. A lazy good-for-nothing boy, if ever one was. Straw-coloured hair did he have, all twists and curls? That was him, Rob. His poor father, Willum Stronsay. They could be doing with Rob in that boat, the *Sea Swift*, three old men rowing miles out west every dayspring, and them getting no younger, and one of them, Joe Harper, bad with the sea scabs. But no – the bold boy sleeps in three mornings in the week, or thereabouts. No wonder – up at the shebeen in the hills, he's out till beyond midnight, or in Ed Sinclair's ale-house in the village. And so he sleeps in, and spends the rest of the day down at the shore, till the boat comes in again, all weathers. Oh ay, but when it comes to eating the ling and the cod, there's nothing lazy about Rob's jaws, I can assure you. He'll eat more than the three old men of *Sea Swift* put together, he will – and then beg a sixpence from his old fool of a dad so he can wash the fish down in the shebeen after dark. A right parasite. Mind you, when the thing does go to the fishing, he kens what he's about – *Sea Swift* comes back smothered in big fish. I only hope, soon Rob'll take a tumble to himself and work hard. He will, I suppose; some fine day soon he'll meet in with some lass, and they'll want to get married, and that'll be his ale-house days finished, and his days of idleness at the shore, too, waiting there with his wife to gut the fish. I hope so. His mother, God be good to her, was a fine woman. So is old Willum too a fine man, but too easy-going. I'll tell you what Mr Smellie the teacher says about Rob Stronsay – he was simply the most obstinate pupil he ever put through his hands in the school of Njalsay, a lazy idle nuisance of a boy. Mr Smellie was never so glad as when Rob came to the age of leaving the school. *Salt and fish guts, that's all he's good for*, was Mr Smellie's verdict. *He'll never be other than he is*, says Mr Smellie . . . At the Gannet Beach was he, sitting on a rock in the sun? The limmer. And them three old men dragging fish out of the ocean, and not fit for it, to keep the creature in ale and idleness. You should have a word with him, sir. That might

bring him to his senses. Idle at the rock, a blot on a fine summer
day' . . .

That was what my housekeeper thought of the young golden-
haired hero I had seen . . . If only I dared have had a word with
him, as the old prattling woman had suggested! – I would
certainly not have urged him to mend his ways: to change ale-
froth for sea-spume, so that he would be a respected somewhat
lowly member of society in the island. If I could have spoken to
him, it would be to say: 'Be you, always, as you were that day in
the sun, true lord of the island' . . . A foolish plea it would have
been, for time changes every living thing, and upon perfection it
can work only darkness and deterioration. Apart from that, the
boy would not have understood the words. Most important of
all, between him and me there was a crystal barrier: on his side
utter indifference, on mine, awe and delight and most utter
mute wonderment. All the beauty I had ever garnered from the
classics, all I had imagined fine and pure and good, was
suddenly embodied in a young fisher lad. I had stood there,
shaken and tongue-tied.

Did he see me that golden morning, he sitting glistering on
his rock, I standing on the shallow cliff above, entranced? He
seemed totally absorbed in the movements of the incoming tide,
with the gentle sea sounds everywhere, on rock and sand and
cranny. He must soon be cut off by the bright encroaching
waters: then he would be like a young sea-god, a son of
Poseidon, on his rock throne. And (I presumed delightedly)
when the sea touched his knee, or his thigh, he would let himself
down from the rock and swim lazily ashore: he had left his
clothes on another rock, just under the cliff. Meantime he sat,
his finely-moulded white arms girdling his shins, his exquisite
head down on his knees, in idle contented contemplation of the
incoming sun-spangled sea.

Perhaps an emotion can communicate itself from one being
to another, without words. Once, and once only, as if he heard

music, he raised his gold-clustered head from his knees and turned his eyes towards me where I stood on the cliff above, not twenty yards away.

He looked, but he did not see me; or if he did, the sight of me – and I the chief man in the island – left him utterly indifferent. His lucent sea-gray eyes lingered about me for (I conjecture) a few seconds: but blankly; then he turned his head again, and was a part of the splendour and golden music of the inflowing Atlantic. A part of it? He was the essence of it, the embodiment, the pure beautiful god.

I must admit, the one indifferent look he put on me stabbed me to the heart, but the wound too was delicious, and set all my spirit trembling.

A wounded transported devotee, I might have remained at my station on the clifftop all morning, feasting my eyes and my soul. But ugliness, in the form of words, fell about me from the road above, and shattered my idyll. Mr Smellie said, 'Ah, Mr Ponsonby, I'm glad I've run into you. Did you not get the note I sent up to the Hall? What I was wanting is this – I would like to take some of my senior pupils up to your house, not one of them has ever darkened the door, I thought perhaps it might give them some insight into the history of the island – which in a real sense is theirs as well as yours. The tree, the tombs, the rare books in the library, the rooms that are no longer in use – do I have your permission?' . . .

I nodded, abruptly. The man is as impudent as he is ignorant.

'Perhaps on Friday afternoon – would that be suitable? . . . Dear me, is that a seal down there in the bay?' . . .

The seal with the golden pelt, the god, the truant fisherman, tore the blue silk apart, making for the sand.

'Do as you wish!' I said to the schoolmaster, and turned from him into the sun.

The incoming sea began then to make cave songs.

*   *   *

That bright happy summer passed slowly into autumn and harvest. I never remember the island to have been so bounteous in sheaves and stooks. The farm folk, with bronzed brows and arms, did their work contentedly and well in the ripe fields, and the work was so ancient that it had the grave inevitability of ritual. The children were freed from school for garnering and rabbit-chasing; and it did my heart good to hear their laughter all along the hillside and in the two valleys of Njalsay. It was a good time for us all – I felt, when the harvesters turned to smile at me, that there was no mockery in their faces: we were all God's creatures in an island saturated with fertility.

The few fishermen of Njalsay were not concerned with all this. Their harvests – if they reaped any at all – were swift and sudden, and had nothing to do with sun and seed and nurturing earth. I heard indeed that the fishermen were having a poor season out west; it was meagre catches, baskets half full of tarnished silver, that they were bringing ashore. The only thing I could do about that was to write to the lawyer in Hamnavoe; advising him that, this coming winter, he was to charge no rent for bothy or boats from William Stronsay, Neil Pegal, Magnus Breck, Thomas Fea, John Olafson: all fishermen about the shores and waters of Njalsay.

Occasionally I saw Rob Stronsay, but now it seemed he had turned over a new leaf (as Smellie would say) and was working hard at his trade. When I glimpsed him, there he was, at the end of his father's black hut, making creels or baiting lines; or bringing ashore the day's small silver harvest (while above, on the hillside, the golden oats and barley fell before the march of the scythemen). If he ever saw me, his eyes went over me with the old indifference. Hard he worked that late summer and early autumn; never again did I see him on the rock in his purity and comeliness. He was out at the niggardly west with the three elderly fishermen before the sun was up. Said Lizzie Scar, 'The thing's ta'en a tumble to himself'. Rob Stronsay, that is, sir. No more ale – I suppose there's no spare money in the shore houses. They're having a poor time of it, I hear. Well, thank goodness, the bad times are making him work, we should be thankful for that' . . .

Autumn merged into the first gales and sleet of winter. The last few leaves fell from the sycamore in the Hall garden. Harvest was crowned with a huge feast of meat and bannocks and cheese, ale and whisky, in the new enlarged barn of Pennybrae farm; and the fiddling and dancing, eating and drinking and kissing under the stars, went on till the sun got up. I called there briefly, before midnight, and was given, politely, a plate of cheese and oatcakes and a glass of whisky; but I felt that I somehow dampened the merriment. True, as soon as I left – as I was lingering in the yard outside, wondering whether to go home by the shore road or the hill road – the interior of the hushed barn erupted with fiddle-music, merriment, and festive fiddle-driven feet.

Half-way along the shore road, going home, I met a shadow coming slowly the other way: he emerged from a cluster of shadows. He was Rob Stronsay; he stood aside to let me pass.

Before shyness and panic could prevent me, I said, 'I hear, Rob, you fishermen are not doing too well at the fishing.'

He answered, 'We'll do better soon. We'll have a good winter in the boats.'

I had not heard him speak before. Reason tells me his voice was no different from the other islanders': a slow wondering lilt, a mingling of Celtic and Norse rhythms. But his speech seemed to me more beautiful than any song.

'If I can help in any way,' I said, 'I would be only too glad' . . .

'We'll manage,' he said. 'You've been kind enough, in the matter of the rents. Thank you.'

I lingered out our time together, under the first stars of winter. 'All the island,' I said, 'is at the Harvest Home in

Pennybrae barn. I wonder you aren't there. I've just drunk from the whisky jar myself.'

'I'm going there for an hour,' he said. 'No more. I have to be up early in the morning. We have creels set under Selskay.'

He smiled at me, shyly.

Perhaps I exaggerate if I say that that was the happiest moment in all my life. I managed to say, 'Goodnight' as on he walked, at once careless and unutterably graceful, towards the lighted barn door of Pennybrae half-a-mile off. The happiness had a tarnish: what country lass, once the flush of drink is on him, will he take out under the stars? It can't be – it's impossible – no woman is worthy of his kisses . . .

He turned back and shouted, 'Goodnight, Mr Ponsonby.' His voice rang under the stars.

I turned my tranced feet in the direction of the Hall. Under the cliff, where I had glimpsed the hero in high summer, the sea made sullen winter music among rocks and fissures.

Just before I fell asleep, in the early hours, a half-forgotten image, a first shred of dreaming, a fragment from my childhood, startled me awake. My grandmother, Annabel Guthrie-Somerville-Ponsonby, was speaking to a child. She said, 'The one I truly and only loved, little Toby, was the fisherman Thord in Njalsay. I stood under the tree. I was a girl. But that love could never be, poor Tobikins' . . . (The child, Tobikins, was myself. I expect she thought it was safe enough to say these words to the little ugly uncomprehending boy clinging there to her silken skirts.)

The winter was as rough and storm-ridden as the summer had been sun-drenched. The farmers' work was mostly done, except for the necessary ritual of the barns: threshing, winnowing, malting, milling (and now a fine new mill stood beside the tumults of the burn; and the miller's ducks drifted and quacked across the pond). With the few fishermen along the shore it was otherwise; whenever it was at all possible, between storms, the three boats were out. I had walked down to the shore, on a gray winter day, and there always was a cluster of shawled women, their eyes on the sea. I suppose it was a tableau that had gone on since the first boat had put out with nets; it would continue till the sea had no more fish to give.

The women waited for the boats to return out of the great swells westward. Among them stood Rob Stronsay's mother, a tall handsome dark woman. She was higher by a head than the other women, and seemed to be the leader of that mute chorus.

I must confess, I felt none of their anxiety. Since the end of harvest I had passed my days in a euphoria, as if my veins coursed always with an eager wine (and that in spite of the fact that the building of the mill had squeezed almost the last gold sovereign out of me). It seemed to me that nothing in the elements could touch that rare creature. I indulged foolish notions: the recent marvellous harvest was his doing, even though he had not cast one seed; the mere fact of his presence in the island was a pledge of fertility. If he was in such favour with the potent energies of earth, how could the sea harm him, which was his own element? I remembered, with joy, the confidence of the boy that night of the Harvest Home when I had met him on the darkling road: *We'll have a good winter in the boats*, he had said . . . Once or twice, so steeped I was in the infatuation, it seemed to me that not even time could touch him. He had somehow existed since the first boat-load of settlers from Lewis had set foot on the barrenness of Njalsay; that day Rob had been there too, strong and radiant, but with another name. Through the generations he had lived on, a young immortal among the teeming children and the witherings of age. No one had praised him; no one had paid particular regard to him. But because of his excellence and beauty the tree of generation continued to flourish and fade in the island: a rhythm good and acceptable to all. His benison reached out even to the laird and the tramp . . . These strange notions would go through my mind like music, sitting by the library fire after dinner, nodding over Theocritus or Sir Walter Scott. Once, I caught myself giving utterance to my thoughts. 'He is a fisherman, this timeless one, because the first people in Njalsay had to be fishermen until they had sweetened the primeval bog with shell sand; only then could the plough be put to it . . . And there will come a time when the earth of Njalsay will be drained and exhausted; and then the few remaining islanders will dredge the sea, as in the beginning, for fish' . . .

The wind was rising. The beginning of yet another storm rattled the library windows. I drank down the last of my toddy and crept upstairs to bed . . .

The weather, from the west, with sleet showers carried on trumpet blasts of wind, was wilder than ever next morning. After breakfast I shrugged into my greatcoat in the lobby, and pulled my hat down over my eyes; for I was not to be put off my walk on account of foul weather. I thought, as I leaned into the tumults of wind, going shoreward, 'There will be no fishing today – it is impossible. The shore houses will have to endure a day or two more of smoked sillocks and cods' heads, until their luck turns. And that won't be long: in spite of this harsh beginning, they'll have a good winter in the boats. But not today, not in hideous weather like this. The fishermen will be smoking their pipes beside the bothy fire' . . .

The wind almost choked and deafened me as I ventured down to the crag above the shore. This had been my place of vantage that day, the previous summer, when I had glimpsed the boy on a rock, a being that did not belong to sea-slime and roots, who was altogether beyond the net of Mr Smellie's numbers and parsings.

The little cove under the cliff was full of shatters of wind and of moving mists of spume. The tide was far out, which lent the scene an added desolation. My spectacles were opaque with the flung wet salt. I turned my back to the wind in order to wipe the lenses with my handkerchief. 'Now,' said I, 'I'll go home to the library fire, and a book, and a glass of sherry' . . . I turned my new-scoured vision for a farewell glance at the beach. Someone – a tall man – was standing at the rock, looking steadily out to sea. In his hand he held a broken lobster creel. He stood as if he had been there, alone, for a long time. It was Rob Stronsay. He must have been soaked through, and ice-cold, with the storm, but he did not move. I could not see his bright hair; he was wearing a sailor's cap and his collar was turned high. The storm threw me about on the sea-banks. He held up, for a few seconds, the broken creel: as if he were pleading with the unquiet elements. Then again he was a cold statue, a sea-watcher with an eye of stone. How long the boy stayed there I do not know. My spectacles salted over again; I turned for home, and now the wind scourged me on like a drunken runner all the way to the garden gate. Lizzie Scar 'tut-tutted' as she took my wet coat off. 'No weather for a dog to be out! Sit at the fire – I have some hot soup for you.'

That was the last storm before the snow came. As often happens, the onset of snow was preceded by a few days of halcyon calmness and light. The sky was clear, the low winter sun set a blazon on the mirror of the sea. I thought, on the second halcyon morning, 'Well, this is the weather for fishermen! It was a spell our Rob was putting on the sea, that stormy morning on the beach. Now the spell is working. They'll get basket-loads out west today' . . .

But I was wrong. The fishermen had gone out in the three boats indeed; they returned at sunset with empty baskets. I watched them. They dragged *Sea Swift* and *Emily* and *Hope* high on the beach. Wordlessly the women took the empty baskets out of the boats. The men looked as if they were ashamed; they were far more crestfallen than the cats and the waiting gulls.

I hastened down the shore road to the beach. They would not so much as look at me. 'If I can be of help . . .' I said to William Stronsay. The old man turned his back: as if to say, 'What does this creature know about the ways of the sea and of fish?' Indifference they offered me now, which is in a way harder than mockery.

Rob came out of the tarred shed. He said, 'The sea's like that. She'll be good to us soon.'

He spoke as if the sea was an ancient wise mother who knows better than her children what's good for them. He looked at me and smiled; that radiant recognition was better than a promise of a thousand shore rents.

The mirror of the sea began to brim with shadows. And there, on the north-west horizon, stood an enormous blue-black cloud, battlement and turret and embrasure.

William Stronsay said, 'It'll come on to snow soon.'

The snow came the very next afternoon, thick and blinding. It caught me in the middle of my afternoon walk. I was thawed out in the croft-house of Sneuk. It was the heaviest snow that Orkney had known for many years. In the farms they kept indoors, warmed by blazing fires, their cupboards full of last summer's plenitude. The blizzards came, heavy and unpredictable, day after day. From the library window I could see the great purplish-black wedges of snow between sky and sea, far out on the horizon, moving slowly. The page would dull and darken in my hand as I read; then on to the library window they drifted, immense gray moths, another host of snowflakes.

The fishing boats made one or two half-hearted attempts to fish, but in that weather it was too dangerous. Skerry or rock might reach out of the blindness and tear a hole in the side of a small boat: and none of the local fishermen could swim. (If the sea-mother claimed a life, that was her due: to strive unduly to save oneself, or others, was to insult her. The skill of swimming was all right, indeed admirable, in the minister's daughters, or the Smellies, or visitors from the south: they had entered into no pact with the sea.)

The thaw came after three weeks, clothed in filthy sodden tatters, like some old tramp that had slept all night in a ditch.

It was that afternoon when the snow had shrunk to fringes under high walls and across the hill fissures that, returning from my walk, I found the three fine haddocks on the table just inside the door: it was the first fruits of the fishermen's labours that winter, an earnest that the rent would be paid, a sea-tribute.

I did not care about these things. It was a shining gift from the young man who had made this island so precious to me. If I had been at home – if I had opened the door to him, standing there shy and proud, I do not think that (for excess of joy) I could have said a word to him. Perhaps, taking the fish from him, our fingers might have touched, as briefly and exquisitely as a snow crystal endures on a fire-warmed window.

They had caught a great haul in the west.

Nothing could touch him, for ever. Deep down the mind was imagining another thing – slowly shaping, questioning, assenting.

Two mornings later Lizzie Scar brought me my breakfast. There was an excited glitter in her eye, although she contrived to wear a mask of woe. 'I doubt there's bad news this morning,' she said, and paused, as if to make more dramatic the burden of her tidings. But I knew already: it was as if the old woman was reciting lines from a play that I had written and must now see performed and worked out to the last bitter syllable. 'The *Sea Swift*, she didn't come back from the west last night. The two other boats are in. Old Willum Stronsay was in her, and that boy of his. It seems they sailed further out to get one last big haul before the sun went down. I doubt something bad's happened. It was a stormy night. Just listen to that wind' . . .

On and on the old sibyl went, telling me her 'news', but after those first few words she was pouring out an ancient litany into ears of stone.

I wander sometimes down to the private yard where my predecessors lie in their marble carved with ornate obituaries. I think about them, and about what relation the words have to what was once flesh-and-blood-and-breath. Whatever we have been in life, we ache to bequeath fragrant memories to posterity, whether true or false. Not what a man says about himself, but what others say about him after death, comes nearer the truth, though it can never be the truth wholly; that final secret of a man's worth is known only to the encompassing wisdom of the universe that Shelley divined.

The islanders laugh at me still. As I grow older, and poorer, and more decrepit, their laughter is touched now and again with pity and kindness. I have not intruded into their lives too harshly; that is all that the last laird of Njalsay can say in favour of himself. (As soon as it is said, mockery comes back, touched with pity and contempt.)

The Somervilles, my ancestors, were choice spirits, according to their epitaphs. Some believe that there is a recording angel that notes down, as briefly and eloquently, the stark truth about every man's life. Which of us would be able to look unflinchingly on that adamantine page?

That I have not intruded too deeply into the life of the Njalsay islanders is scarcely good enough to be carved on my deathstone. My delight in one human being, for a short time, would perhaps be worth chiselling: but I am not Theocritus or Bion, and so I cannot share my secret joy with those unborn who might stop to read.

What does it matter whose dust lies beneath? A name is a small spelling of breath, meaningless to the generations coming after. I propose, therefore, that I will not even do myself the truncated posthumous honour that was cut in the stone for poor mad James Somerville a century ago: his name, simply.

Perhaps we come out of nothingness and go into nothingness, and we leave a small silence behind.

Yet the fact that a man has lived, and done such and such, and at last perished, means that he has caused some slight displacement in the cosmos: but for him, the vast equation that is being worked out in time or in eternity would be minutely otherwise, the collision of a speck of dust with a star. This is to look at our mortal affairs with the eye of Mr Smellie, perhaps. More rapt creatures see our lives as notes in a vast interlocking music: in our seventy years we perceive only discords and hints of things that might be, or will be, or ought to be.

Who is to say? I think it best, speaking for myself, to leave a silence. Let 'the wisdom and spirit of the universe' write in the number or the note; if such, or such, is deemed necessary.

The house was young, the stone, newly-hewn – built into the roots and dews of the hill. The sea sang around the island, many-voiced. I passed out of the house and through the garden – the little music of the burn, the thick-leaved whispering tree – and on down to the shore. The crofters stood at their doors watching the first brightness of harvest in their fields. They turned young tanned faces on me. (They were all young.) They said mildly, *It is our harvest now, man.* And I said, *It is the harvest now of all the island* . . . Down near the shore a girl with a string of new-washed fish in her fingers said, *We haven't lost him. The boy isn't drowned. He's living in another island in the west. Didn't you know that? He'll come back soon* . . . The girl touched my cheek with her fresh red mouth. I had not known such happiness. I lay down between the fields and the shore. I felt myself to be a part of everything – waves and clouds and heavy ripe earth. Then I heard, very far off, a small voice in the wind. It cried, *James is hurt. He tried to fly. He fell out of the tree.* There was no pain in the words, only wonderment. A bird sang, phrase after immaculate phrase, from a quivering branch. Two children laughed, hidden voices.

Golden whispers; a first scythe was at work in a cornfield.

It was a dream of the young earth.

I woke up starkly, in my withered room, and I was old Tobias, with the rack-screw in my shoulder and my mouth an apple slowly rotting. A winter wind shook the high pane . . . All I can ask is, now, that I have a few such dreams before the dreamless end.

11 TWEEDIE

There was a man who in the 1920s and early '30s tramped all over Caithness and Orkney and the west. He was called, simply, Tweedie. Nobody knew much about him. He was strong and healthy but he would do no work. If he was given, at a farm door, a fish or a bannock or a mug of tea, he took it cheerfully and thanklessly. He was expert at catching rabbits and eels. Sometimes he would be suspected of stealing a chicken or a cheese from this farm or that. He spent a few days in prison now and then for thieving and fighting. He stood often at the Hall gate, his hand out. Sometimes a coin or a leg of chicken was given him; or the dog was turned loose. (The Hall belonged now to a rich manufacturer of bolts and screw-nails, who only came north in summer to fish and shoot. The islanders had long owned their own farms.)

One night in August, in the Njalsay inn, Tweedie came and stood in a corner. He had no money to buy beer. Normally the young men would have rattled shillings on the counter to entertain Tweedie; especially as it was the night of the Agricultural Show, a free festive time. But the weekend before, there had been trouble in the village between the son of Pennybrae farm and the tramp, on account of some girl. It had come to blows, and Giles Garth had been taken home with a bloody nose. (More than Giles had fancied the girl, who was the island beauty that summer.) Tweedie stood ignored in his corner. Tweedie waited for charity and forgiveness – it didn't come – it seemed the men turned their backs on him and spoke louder than before. Suddenly – it happens once on a time in every pub, no one knows how – as if a dark angel was passing through – there was a silence between barrel and fire.

Tweedie spoke. 'You ought to look up to me, because I am the true laird of Njalsay. But I don't care about you any more. I drink my own drink' . . . He was holding in his hand a phial of evil-looking liquor. He uncorked it and tilted it to his mouth. He threw the empty phial down; it smashed on the flagstone floor. Then Tweedie bowed with mock ceremoniousness, and left the bar.

When the barman looked out of the window, Tweedie was a shadow in the gathering shadows of the late summer night.

That night, the stone kestrel over the lintel of the Hall was smashed by a granite rock. Someone had thrown it in the darkness.

The Wanderer's Tale

I was born in the island of Selskay in Orkney. My father kept a croft that he paid rent for. I never remember my mother. I had six brothers and five sisters. I was the youngest one.

So, when I was seven years of age, my father sent me to a farmer in another part of the island, to keep the cows out of the oatfield.

My wages were half-a-crown a summer.

The farmer's sister was spited against me. Once she beat me till my nose bled for breaking a cup. She would laugh at my patched shirt and trousers. I got the poorest food to eat. I shared thin milk with the cats.

I stayed at that farm five summers. I went home in the winter. Some of my brothers had gone to sea; one was Australia-bound in an emigrant ship; three of my sisters got married, one after the other, in distant crofts.

I cried – but against a hidden wall – when it was time to leave home and herd cattle. I cried for cruelty and for shame at myself.

But one summer the farmer's new wife came, and then the woman whose lip was always curling like a dog turned her face from me. This young woman was good to me. I think she had lost her first husband at sea when she was still not much beyond the whiteness of a bride, and before she could rock a cradle.

I felt like a young laird whenever Williamina showed kindness to me, such as making clothes out of the farmer's old suits, and putting thick cream on my porridge.

The old crow that had pecked at me so hard and so often

seemed to shrink and shrink, after Williamina came to be mistress. At last she kept to her room. I would hear moans in the darkness of night, and then I was sorry for her.

Williamina took me one day to the Hamnavoe Lammas fair, near harvest time. Never had I thought such crowds could exist in the world! Nor that there could be such noise, or such silken hectoring talk from the fairground folk. In the crowded street Williamina parted from me; she told me to wait at the shop door till she bought needles and ribbons.

I was carried from my place by the great tide of people. I was a small boy, and now am a small old man.

I was tossed and driven this way and that, crying out, 'Williamina', till a sailor took me by the arm and lifted me on to his shoulder and carried me into a public house. Many men, and one or two old wives, were drinking and smoking and arguing there. The sailor man said, 'Never mind Williamina. Put this in your mouth.'

It was my first taste of whisky. (I had drunk a mug of ale from time to time.) Slowly the public house and its folk began to move up and down about me, a faster and faster wheel, till I was in utter confusion. And when I woke up, there was confusion still in my head and in the house I found myself in; it plunged and wallowed and creaked.

Soon I was to know it was no house, it was a ship on the sea. 'Williamina!' I shouted. A brown face bent over me. 'You're a sailor now, boy. Brave days ahead of you, boy. You'll get used to the motion.'

I didn't get used to the ship's motion though, nor anything else concerning that ship and the sea. I thought I would die with the spasms in my belly and the retchings in my throat and the spew heaving up in my mouth and nostrils. I thought, once, I had died and gone to Hell; this would go on for ever and ever, for the ship's tossings did not lessen; and then I woke to another gray unquiet dawn.

It stopped at last. The sea and earth met each other in stillness. I did not run away from the ship so much as I was thrust forth out of it as a useless kind of a creature. The sailor that had blinded me with whisky at the Hamnavoe fair walked with me through streets busy as beehives, and he took me into another pub, and tried to give me more whisky, but I went out alone and dry as a fish on a rock.

I would like to tell the story of my days as a builder's labourer in New York. They were long and hard but in the end they were happy, for I met a young Irish woman called Kitty Brogan, and she was even kinder to me than Williamina had been. Kitty took me to live in her house, the finest place I was ever in up to that time, with a clock and a coal fire and a gas light at the wall. At first I didn't understand why Kitty had to be out all night. But when I did understand the reason, I felt such grief and rage that I broke five china cups against her wall, and out-cursed the sailors, and drank a whole bottle of whisky that was in the sideboard and struck Kitty, and left that house and that city for ever.

I had been told by the bircklayers there was war raging between the various states, and that soldiers had a fine time of it, always moving into different places, and got a smart blue uniform and good pay, and as much loot as they could stuff into haversacks and bellies.

There was not a word of truth in it, apart from the uniform. We soliders marched, thousands of us, keeping in step to the sound of fife and drums. Round the flank of a great hill we met on the other side the rage of cannons. Men in blue dropped near and far, a man had his arm shot away right in front of me, and the horses on in front reared in terror, and whinnied and screamed till foam flew from their black lips. We were ordered back to a defensive position. Next morning our own big guns were wheeled up, and there was smoke and din and flame, and death-cries from the half-hidden gray-clad enemy. The horse soldiers rode against them. Then we were ordered to advance.

The fine life of a soldier! – I saw little but death and mutilation and horror everywhere. I found myself standing astride a wounded enemy soldier. He looked up at me with such horror and fear as I raised my bayonet to despatch him, and then – could such a thing be? – a look of joy came on his face, as if Death had opened a welcoming door to him. I gave that red-headed boy a piece of tobacco in his hand, and raised him to his feet. I pointed to a wood and shouted, 'Run for the trees, you'll be safe there.' It was only a surface wound he had on his neck, that wind and salt and sun would cure.

For that dishonourable conduct on the field of battle I was arrested, and taken to a tent behind the lines to await court-martial. Two other men in the tent said they were deserters, and it was likely we would all be shot in the morning. One spent the night singing songs, the other wept until his sorrow and fear ended in a dreadful spasm of sleep.

Being small-boned and supple, I contrived in the darkness to slip the rope binding my wrists, and then freed my feet. I saw that the sentry was smoking his pipe beside the watchfire. Soon I was off and away and free as the wind.

I changed my uniform for the rags on the back of an old hobo – and I think of him from time to time, how pleased he was with the exchange – and I hope he wasn't shot by the rebels or the Union military, for the wheel of war is cruel and merciless. But he was old, old, and knew how to avoid such mischances.

I lived among Indians for a month. I will say nothing about that time. I came out of that camp with scars on my face. Look, here they are still, under the beard's stubble. There was a girl there called Water-Petal. What has become of that flower? Where are they now, the eagle-faced men who took knives and flames to me?

Two years I worked on the railroad, laying the track from east to west. Many a day in that burning desert I thought of the rain and mist of Orkney, and good Atlantic winds on the face. We earned high wages, and I learned soon to drink with the Irishmen. I was quick-tempered in drink, but if I spat at the feet of some big Irish labourer, the man would laugh and lift me by the collar into the air, I was that small and light. The Irish thought it great fun: the little Orkneyman hung up in the air betwixt sun and sand, and spitting and spluttering with the whisky-rage.

But mostly I got on fine with them. We gambled, and the tides of money either drowned us or left us dry.

One day a group of us were making tea in a kettle. I heard a labourer say to another, 'Yes, she's dead and gone, Kitty Brogan, and there's a star gone out of the sky' . . . I asked this man to describe Kitty Brogan, but he only covered his face with a fist like a stone. 'May the saints be good to her,' was all he would say . . . And whether it was my Kitty Brogan that had died, I never got to know. There must be hundreds of Kitty Brogans in Ireland and America.

Soon we were swinging our hammers up in the cold mountains, at other business than building the railroad.

It was a hard life. I was longing to be married to a decent woman, and building a log house and keeping cattle, and breaking bread at my own hearth.

And that did happen. I met and married a Quaker girl, and we built a log house and kept a few hogs and turkeys. I had to give up the bottle, and foul language too; for Charity my wife would have none of those abominations under her roof. And I did not love her, and she did not love me, but we both liked the little clearing we had made, and our fowls and crops. One day I went to the new town in the desert that didn't yet have a proper name, to get fencing stobs and wire and a new plough. As I came home in the evening driving the cart, I saw smoke ahead of me. My cabin was burnt out, there was no sight or sound of

Charity, and all the stock and poultry were scattered through the waste-land and scrub.

Stark among the ruins, the crib smouldered that was to have held our first child.

I rode back under the stars to the nameless town, and told the new sheriff what had happened. 'I can't do a thing about it,' he said. 'There's law out here and yet there's no law. It could have been any one of a hundred rascals and ne'er-do-wells. Sorry, partner. It could have been a spat-out coal. That's the way life is out here. That's what war and progress does to men.'

There was a new ranch ten miles to the south-west of my blackened house and acres. I worked for a year and a half among those great herds. I learned to wield the branding-iron and the lasso.

I said to a cowhand, eating our bacon and beans one evening, 'The skull of my wife was not found in the ashes. I ruined my fingers looking for it.'

'There's talk,' said this man, a Jew from Romania, 'that a woman was taken away from hereabouts, then the place was burned. The burner – who is he? It is his bacon and beans we're eating. We get drunk on his dollars every weekend.'

Later this cowhand said, 'More than one can make tar torches.'

In the saloon he said, 'Three of the men are taking his horses some night soon and riding north. Come with us.' We struck glasses of whisky together.

'We will get better work in the city.'

We opened a gate in the stockade and drove out hundreds of the burner's cattle one moonless midnight. I threw a torch at his window, but rain and wind beat the flame out. The torch hissed like a snake.

Then we rode north on the burner's horses, five of us in all.

The kind of work in prospect in the city was this: that I had to stand outside the door of a bank while the four robbers inside pointed guns at clerk and cashier and took thousands of dollars out of the vault. I stood in the street, keeping the horses. Then I heard two shots, inside the bank, and a woman screaming. I mounted my horse and rode north, leaving those four to their immense wealth, or to jail and gallows.

My father had a brother in Canada, at a fur post there of the Hudson's Bay Company. I rode north, into Canada. I got what food and shelter I could from lakes and forests.

I rode until the redness of fire and blood was forgotten in the grayness of ice.

Shall I tell of my dealings with the wolf-pack, or how I brought a caribou down by its antlers, and sucked the blood from its cut neck to keep me from starvation? I have told such stories a score or a hundred times, and there is a grain of truth in them. But stories, like whisky, improve with age.

The truth is, I never found my Uncle John – no man anywhere had heard of him – a likely thing was that he had long been bones in the ice, a forgotten man, like many a thousand more (but somewhere the good that is in every man born, even the worst, must be hoarded like jewels. Nor does a single sparrow die unrecorded).

I found among the gray wastes an Eskimo girl. In the thunders of spring the ice of a great river was breaking up. I leapt from floe to floe, to save her. That's the story I sometimes tell among the pipe-smoke on a winter night. Here's the truth: I woke up under a rock, and there a fat moon-face was smiling down at me. I struggled to get out of my blanket but she was up and off, shrieking with terror or laughter, I couldn't tell which. Then she stood in the centre of that waste of ice, waiting for me. She took me by the fingers a great distance to an ice-house with other ice-houses all around. The old man was her father. He joined both our hands together, and nodded twice or thrice. Many other Eskimos came into the fish-stinking ice-house, men and women and children. All laughed. All looked at me. All opened their arms in a gesture of welcome.

Then the old man turned and struck the girl on the face. All, one after the other, struck the girl, but lightly, as a skua wing brushes the skull. The girl wept, but no tears came, only a narrower smile. A man and a woman came behind her. They thrust her out under the stars, shouting threats and insults.

Then all their eyes were on me. Solemnly their faces turned to me. The old man pointed at me. He spat. And the old mouths and young mouths spat afterwards. Even the children had a wetness on their chins, driblets of mock rage.

The old man indicated that I must sit on the floor. One by one they came to me and wet their fingers and touched my face here and there with the spittle. They all, but the old man, passed out into the night. He and I were alone together. He quenched the lamp, and limped out himself. There in the darkness and bitter cold, I sat alone, like the earth's last man. I slept. I dreamed of a clover field and a burn.

When I woke there was a green ice light. I saw that the floor was strewn with bones: walrus, whale, skua, reindeer, fish, wolf; and there on a stone plate at my side the skull of a man. Against the wall stood a gun. Why not a harpoon or a fish-spear? It seemed to me as if I had created all the carnage and death; or as if I represented a race of deathdealers, murderers of an old simplicity and wholeness.

The gun was our sign.

In that one night I suffered the last hundred years, maybe, of our race: a horror of cold and darkness and increasing hunger and ghosts that came and went in the darkness but gave no comfort.

An old woman came in, and six young women with her. The old woman tied a blindfold of skin about my head. The silent women moved here and there carrying out – as I thought – the bones.

What would be done to me, after the first horror? I was aware of a coming and a going of many feet, whispers, little buds of laughter. Then the everlasting fish-stench was little by little replaced by such a fragrance that my tongue and gums ran with sweet expectant water. Soft fingers untied the knot at the back of my head. The house had been swept clean of charnel. On the stone plate had been set a little smoking loaf of bread, gold-crusted, and a flagon that even to smell made my senses reel, like a bagpipe on a lonely loch shore, or verses of the poet Burns recited between decanter and hearth-flames. They had ornamented a lamp in such a way that it had burnished rays all about it; the lamp was meant to represent the sun.

The old man was there again, with three young men and a young woman and a child. All smiled, as if their fat faces were made only for cheerfulness, whatever evil time and history had put on them. The old man indicated that I should eat and drink, I alone. The joy of corn was all about me. (I was in such a trance of fatigue and cold and hunger by this time that I did not stop to consider how the people of the ice had got hold of the corn that is the base of all civilizations but their own.) I crammed my mouth with warm texture of sun and wind and rain, and between every mouthful I took a gulp of whisky; the spirit, I thought, they could easily have got from the French or English trading posts. It seemed possible that this was only the remnant of a tribe that had been decimated by those destructive waters, as many of the Indians I had known had been reduced to infirmity and impotent rage. The ice-house and the smiling faces wavered about me, after the last crumb and the last drop; and the ice-dome disintegrated and the gray blocks fell in on me, and buried me in a long polar sleep.

How long? I lifted my face from the floor in utter wretchedness. Again, I was alone, and the green light from the ice-lands pierced me to the bones, worse than before. I tried to rise, but my hands and feet had been bound with hide thongs. I toppled over on to the floor, a parcel of the ultimate wretchedness, a bag of rotted chaff in a forgotten corner of a mill, that even the rats avoid.

After a debauch the mind, though stuffed with thorns, is true and steady as a compass needle afloat upon certainties and simplicities. I understood that those people hated me (or hated, through me, my tribe of despoilers and murderers), and meant that my death should counterbalance many innocent deaths.

Again they stooped in, the six that had watched my merriment among the corn, and the old man was as solemn now as a prophet.

Again, the blindfold.

There was a sound of slicing and tearing all round me, a series of quick slashes, from which I understood that my clothes were being cut off; a thing I would also have known from the intensifying cold. Fingers at nape, the unknotting; and my eyes saw that there were a dozen lamps all about me, but trimmed so low that they were only beads of light, a scattered constellation. A knife of pure ice was given into the ancient hands by the solemn child. The feeble shadow trembled over me. The knife passed into my body, and found the heart (that broke into flames) and went on through. Again, I was a prone man on the floor. So, in last ice and fire, the old Scandinavians believed that man shall perish from the earth.

I woke out of this death, and found that I had been carried outside, and was kneeling under the everlasting sun of their northern summer. My hands were still tied behind me. There, in front of me, stood the girl who had been driven away from me with blows and insults. She began to move in a kind of dance, and there was no music that I heard; and the movements she made were very strange: circlings, slow foldings and unfoldings of her fingers. She did not look at me, her face was as frozen as the landscape. She beat on the ice with her feet, slowly; she arched her body backwards as if to drink from the sun's cup.

She seemed to mime sometimes the flight of a bird, and sometimes the prowl and watchfulness of a hunting wolf. Or her hand wavering through the air was like a fish in a stream. It was the strangest sight I ever beheld, and I must tell you that meantime the sun in its endless unsetting wheel about the sky made flashings from a thousand ice facets far and near.

There was no one else to be seen in the village, near or far. But I sensed a hundred eyes watching. At last the girl's dance brought her within touching distance of me. She knelt in front of me, with offering hands, in my own posture of kneeling (though I had hands tied), as if each of us was a mirror that the other looked into, in silent wonderment. It was then, when the dance was over, that hidden music came from one of the huts. The music unfroze the masks of bird and fish and beast; she decided that she was, after all, a girl. She smiled, she cupped my head in hands as soft as roses.

The crude beautiful music continued.

The girl leant forward and kissed me.

Then from every house the people came; the old ones shuffling, the hunters and their women standing sturdily all about us, the children dancing here and there.

The village shared one great look of joy, as if the sun had entered into them.

Then the oldest man, my stern inquisitor (but now he too was smiling with his shrunken mouth), came and untied my hands. He put my numb hands into the pulsing hands of the girl.

I was told her name, but I will not set it down here, for fear of the laughter of the ignorant.

I told them my name.

They laughed much at the strange sounds, but in delight, not in mockery.

The hidden music went on.

A distant mountain flashed and flashed in the sun, and then was a bluish distant peak again.

The dogs barked their happiness.

That was how I came to have my Eskimo wife.

I tell you, we lived in our own hut for twelve years together, and I learned to hunt the caribou and the whale, and I learned their strange language, that is simple and complex at the same time.

Often, from this hut or that, I heard the mysterious music, at times of ceremony, like midsummer, or at midwinter when the only light comes from their lamps and faces, and at the time of the death of a great whale.

I was forbidden, all the time I lived among them, to take part in the greater mysteries that were so precious to them. (My people had put such suffering on them, I had to be kept out. Perhaps one day, when I was old and about to go into the great darkness, they might unfold the mysteries to me. They would lead me to the source of the music, that put a spell upon them at every birth and death and marriage.) I never saw a musical instrument in any hut or ice-house. Yet there was music, at the great stations of the year.

I lived with that woman for twelve years altogether and she bore me five children.

Among that people I never or rarely saw such passions as are deep-rooted, it seems, in the higher civilisations, such as jealousy, greed, anger, or pride. Only once in that time did a tincture of love-jealousy appear, and that was when the hunter Aak went away for three months with the French fur traders, to show them where the great fish were and how they were to be taken. When Aak returned from the river-mouths, he found that his wife Troda had been putting sun-looks on a bone-carver called Yanek. Indeed, though ashamed of her disloyalty, she still put sun-looks on Yanek and openly too. The carver of bones was terrified for his life, for Aak was a strong youth. The village people began to take sides, some saying that Troda had been given to Aak and had borne him a son; how would it be with the people if this wild passion went through the village and all the people of the Great Ice, like the Orkneymen's fire-water? The source must be choked, and quickly. Let the lewd woman go back to her true and only man.

But no, said others, love – if such a thing is, divorced from hunger and hunting and the making of lamps and fish-spears – love of itself, independent love, love that falls like a bird of fire upon the heart (who knows how?) – it happens but rarely – but when it does happen then it must not be thwarted or stamped upon, it must have its way, let it pass freely from heart to heart: it brings a blessing. Aak would grieve for a month perhaps; then he would forget and begin to smile and hunt again.

It went so ill in the village that summer that I feared murder would be the end of it.

The old man shook his head.

There was no such thing as love, he said. Love was grained into the texture of all things, it had to do with utter necessity, so that they would not starve, and that new ones would come into the world when the old ones began to fail and to turn their faces to the black sun. Threatened with hunger and extinction, any man and any woman could feel a kindling of care and keeping for each other at last, perhaps after many years. This was a bad business indeed, this of Aak and Troda and Yanek – he did not know what the end of it would be. The songs should be sung. The 'white bird' should be summoned.

In the end the dangerous affair was settled by the performance of a mime, or play, or dance – all those elements entered into it. I myself witnessed this extraordinary performance. At the end of it, the three smiled upon each other; indeed the whole village was lit with smiles. All our western arts, I believe, come from this simple healing of wounds; though in the great cities of the world that is unrecognised and forgotten. Music and literature and carving are treasured there as being entities in and for themselves, obeying their own laws, of no practical value whatsoever. I am sure now, that they are unguents and salves for the pain of mankind, whether they come in golden caskets or in crude-cut boxes of walrus-bone. Left to themselves and to an elite self-appointed priesthood of the arts, that alone understands and appreciates them, they wither from the lives of the great masses, there is nothing to staunch the wounds and the weariness, as they draw near (as draw they must, all men and women and children born) to the Stone of Death.

I set down this healing play as I remember it from the mouths of the performers.

It was enacted one night in early spring, when the as yet sparse sun was drawn up from the well of darkness, like a single bucket of light, only to be let down again. But the people knew that the well was filling up; their long winter was over. In darkness the poem began, there were words in the middle that had the spilled sun-lustre on them, the last words were spoken in the darkness on the other side. Drop by drop, light was stirring at the roots: circle by circle it was rising: soon all the village jars and buckets would be splashing over.

THE PLAY OF THREE LOVES

Girl

I did not expect this coming. (Sleep on.)
A sledge broke the horizon.
He is home with coins and French words.
I keep my face
Inside the house of walrus tusks.
Fat lips lately for me, at lamp-out.
(The lamp is lit. Sleep.)
I must travel far, alone. 'Grandmother,
I am to bide here awhile.
I will stir your pot.'
Dark shiftings of mouth and hand in that village.
(Sleep well, spear-maker.)
The hunter is home with fierce hungers – Aak.
Small sleep after tonight
In your house of sharp ivory.

Hunter

'Show us,' said the bread-eaters

'Where salmon are.

  We pay silver and tobacco.'

I led them north and west and north.

  Thunders and torrents of light!

I left their tents at the mouth of the Green River.

  I missed Troda, that girl.

  Now I am home

I wish I was with the weave-wearers,

Drinking rum and tea, explaining

  The circles of walrus, wolf, caribou.

Bone-Carver

I will say to Aak the hunter

  'You were away too long.'

I will sing

  'A flame of longing has been lit in the village.'

I will be wise –

  'Coins and kin don't mix.'

I will accuse

  'Old and young went hungry, you away.'

I will threaten

  'No sharpness like the sharpness of my ivory!'

I will thunder and sing and laugh.

Old Woman

I was prettier than Troda once.

Troda breaks ice,

A water face looks back at Troda.

I did not have to do that.

My man was not as strong as Aak.

He brought home sufficient ivory and oil.

My man surpassed the spearwright in all ways.

Yet Troda has left Aak.
She has stood white in the fires of Yanek.
I do not want to be young again –
Blushings, bodings, bleedings.
Troda has greased her hair.
She is to go north tonight on a sledge.

Troda's Child and Troda's Dog
   'Who is my father, Aak or Yanek?'
   'I gnawed a sweet summer bone.'

   'My mother is sent on to another village.'
   'I whine at twenty cold doors.'

   'Who'll give me milk now and kisses?'
   'Dare I return to the gray pack?'

   'Two fathers, no mother, is grief.'
   'I like now to sleep near embers.'

Poet
   One girl left five children to be with Indians.
   That was in my childhood.
   The pain was made pure in a poem.
   Another girl
   Whose man got a howe near the fur post
   Told a story of bears.
   She came back, that liar
   Smeared with bear blood, silver in a pouch,
      smelling of Orkneymen.
   That was made good in verses, later.
   Another left pot and needles,
   She went north
   Borne on a skua's wingbeats, they said.
   A whole month

Her man prowled near the ice verge.
Then he turned back
Bidden by a good harp-stroke.

To woman, a mixing of snow and fire
Goes the simple hunter.
His house is a circle of darkness!
Though our words and metres are coarse now,
I call on a white word to fall between two doors.
Troda may return.
Troda, come back: take the bird in your bright hands.

Fur traders came to the village, six of them, with sledges and dogs.

They had lost themselves in blizzards, their compass had frozen, they had veered too far north.

They spoke in crude mime to the ancients. The ancients smiled at them – nothing but smiles, smiles.

Women came to them with slices of raw fish. The Orkney-men ate with relish; for a week they had eaten two of their dogs – little flames among the blizzard, the terrible howling of the dogs at the smell of blood and roasting.

The ancients pointed north. There they should go, the hunters. Thousands of beasts, further north, tumultuous as a brown river in spate.

The traders were doubtful. They consulted with each other; an argument; shaking of heads; glints of greed in the blue eyes.

They bought a barrel of fish from the villagers, giving whisky and silver in payment. They pointed their sledges north.

I spoke, apart, to the trader that carried the gun: a few words only. He started as if I had struck him – then a slow calculating smile – then a whispering to the others.

The villagers had gone into the chief's house, every one, even the children, to divide the coins.

The men would drink the whisky, all five bottles, before morning. There would be ancient songs, shouting, sickness, perhaps a fight.

I alone waved farewell to the hunters.

Indeed there was a splash of blood in the snow before morning.

When they returned, nine or ten days later, one of the sledges was piled high with bundles of skins. They were in a merry mood, driving into the village. The village dogs and the dogs of the Company men snarled at each other.

More silver given. A barrel of fish requested. An armful of bottles of whisky, which one of the women accepted. Then she smashed them, bottle after bottle, against the ice. Marvellous barley fumes came on the wind, and lingered, and went again on the wind.

Some of the village men looked ashamed.

Then all went into the chief's house for the division of silver. My wife and my five children went in to gawp at the corrupting silver.

Room was made for me on a sledge, between the guns and a great bundle of skins.

So I came again among my own people. A week later the ship *Empress* left St John's for the Orkneys, with a score of young men whose sovereigns were sewn into their sarks.

I stepped ashore among blood of my blood. The young Orkneymen stepped into open arms or the kindly light of known faces. The gentle music of greeting was everywhere.

For me, nothing. No one nodded or smiled at me. Some of the faces looked familiar and strange. I recognised only the gunner who had lost a leg on the HMS *Victory*, gray-thatched and shrunken he stood. When I went to speak to him, I got a cold gray eye-glare.

What was I doing, a man past the best time of life, in this place of strangers?

Then a tall gaunt grim-jawed woman stepped out of the throng and stood in front of me.

So the wanderer told his story for glasses of malt and schooners of ale in the ale-house at Burntoon, a hundred nights a winter.

Every winter he would add a new piece to the story, to make it more entertaining. It was not, the men at the lamp and barrel were given to understand, that he was inventing new material; no such thing, he was simply putting a finish and a veneer on what had been rather rough-hewn, he was putting a carving or two on what had been plain before, to bring out the full depth and relish of an incident. Thus, the story of himself among the Eskimos had begun as a mere scrap of narrative, as brief as a crack or growl in the ice – 'I lived among Eskimos for a while, and got married in their fashion of marriage, and she bore five children to me. But in the end I began to yearn for Orkney, and so I went off with fur traders, who took me to an Orkney-bound ship' . . . That had been the original story. Over the winters he had elaborated it into the complex web printed above. This of the ice-people was the story he dwelt on with most enthusiasm, on it he lavished his best skill. I think by his last winter he had done what he wanted to with the ice-folk and their ceremonies; he was beginning that winter to fill out his rather bare story of the American Civil War and his part in it, and some thought he was beginning too to make the Irish-American girl Kitty Brogan more interesting, by a subtle stroke here and a shading there. There is no doubt that he had a large sketch-pad of experience in his mind to elaborate and work upon; till the time of gray hairs and silence.

One night she came into the ale-house, his Orkney wife, or at least the woman he lived with; for his true wife might have been a Red Indian or an Eskimo; and this Williamina was not in the sweetest of tempers. 'Is it here? Is that fool here? Where is it? You all look like red-faced ghosts in this tobacco smoke. Ugh! I swear, it's a wonder this island can exist at all, with all the drinking and smoking and swearing and spitting that goes on, in this den of iniquity! Think shame of yourself, inn-keeper! When did you last darken the door of the kirk, eh? You'll answer for it. Oh, there it is – I see it now – the famous adventurer trying to hide behind the ox-girth of Tam of Waithe farm. I see you. I see you sucking the last drops of whisky from your whiskers. Who stood him that glass of whisky, I wonder? And what story was it tonight – was he building the railroad across America? Or was it the famous bank raid? Or was it the Eskimos spitting and scratching at him, for kissing a blubber-mouth lass? Come from behind the barrel, you weed. What famous story was it tonight, you cadger of drink from ignorant farmers? (Come out from behind the barrel – I have a thing or two to say to the wanderer and the hero.) Who took the florin an hour ago out of the tea caddy, eh, a piece of silver from the funeral money? Coffined corpse or no, he was determined to have his share of funeral drink and funeral tobacco, let the mourners stand sober and long-faced about his open grave. Did any man here, in this decent ale-house, ever hear the like, that a man would try to cheat his own funeral guests of the drop of whisky and bogey roll that was their due? Landlord, has he spent every last ha'penny of the grave-money? Just take the thing by the scruff of his neck, landlord, and hand him over here, to me, for the bones of the thing are as light as a bird. Now it's off under the counter, among legs. I have something to say here tonight, but why I have to say it I don't know, for you know it already, and still you encourage the mouth of the thing to open and shut. The truth is, this hero and far wanderer has never once set foot outside this island. Not once, not even to go to the Lammas fair in Hamnavoe. Once, when Mr Ward his master was alive, I tried to entice the thing to the Hamnavoe Market. O no, it would rather bide at home. It yelled and kicked when I took its hand. 'Come,' said I, to encourage him, 'a sailor'll take thee, thu'll see all the good places and the famous places of the world.' It yelled and kicked my knee. So I went to the Hamna-voe Market on my own. No, he hasn't so much as set foot in a fishing boat to haul a codling out of the Sound. Oh! it was a bad day, the time my poor man that's dead and buried took pity on the motherless wisp of a thing and set him to keep the cow out of the corn. The thing sat blowing dandelion seeds while old Nell the cow ate half the green oats. Useless and worse than useless. Yet back he came here next summer again, and my man's maiden sister did right to clout the little lazy brute about the ears. I mind it well, that was the time he knocked over the jar of fish oil and left us darkling for a week, and that in the heart of winter – how the thing howled in his black corner till my poor man, his master John Ward, gave him a cup of hot ale to quiet him. Oh, she knew him all right, that bissom. Yes, thank you, inn-keeper, I *will* have a dram to calm me down. You might well ask, how was it I gave the creature house-room, yes and bed-room too, and kept the bite in his mouth all them years? My good sweet man, he was hardly cold in the ground when that thing says over the supper table, one night, 'Williamina, I'll tell a thing in thy ear alone, it's so wonderful I hardly believe it myself. Wait till that old black hag goes off to her bed. Well, there she goes, to nightmares I hope, the slut. Williamina, on the rocks of the shore this very morning I found a metal box. It was bound with brass. It was double-locked – oh, so heavy I could hardly drag it an inch. I took a stone to the lock. I battered and I battered. Inside, Williamina, I plunged my arms up to the elbows in gold, and again and again, as if I was washing my arms in purest streams of gold. Williamina, tell this to not a living soul, I closed the chest again, and I covered it up with the heaviest stones I could find. And I vowed there and then, 'This Indian gold is for Williamina, her alone, once she's wiped the sorrow of widowhood from her eyes and made me a little corner beside the fire, for care and keeping' . . .

'Inn-keeper, and all present, I tell you this, I listened to the little liar, and though my heart was like a stone inside me, I felt a laugh gathering in my throat, and gathering, till my mouth rang like a ship's bell, on account of the droll tongue of this liar and butterer-up. 'Williamina,' said I to myself, 'he might keep the grayness of the world out of your spirit for a year or two' . . .

'I sent him out for a bucket of water from the barrel, so that I could think it over; and of course, he stumbled on the doorstep and splashed the water all over the floor, and wet his feet, and made a right mess of smoke and steam and cinders about the hearth.

'And, men, I'm telling you, that's as far as he's ever been, to the well for water, and for an armful of seaweed to spread on the tattie-field, yes, and to slip off with his hoard of lies to this den of iniquity when I'm not looking.'

Then she set him down on the counter, and threw back her head, and vented great shouts of merriment; till the crofters laughed too, and all the ale-house was like an ark of joy, and in the midst of the folly sat the wanderer, with a look of stars and horizons on him.

I, Alexander Sweyn the laird, have written the above account. I have reasoned, 'The story, or anthology of stories, will be forgotten, if someone doesn't record them soon, somehow . . .'

So, one week of wild westerly gales, before Yule last year, I sat down in my library, between desk and fire, and wrote it out as best I could.

And how should I, the laird, know what stories are told in one of the island ale-houses? That the laird should visit such an establishment is out of the question.

I drink alone, sometimes with the minister or a neighbouring laird, or a passing naval officer or a magistrate from Kirkwall; whose stories, in general, are but self-important puffs of wind, likewise their opinions on the state of the nation and of the world.

No: it is Gilbert Seatter who farms my glebe so cheerfully and efficiently, who has been bringing me those stories over the past three or four years, ever since I came here from Lanarkshire in Scotland to take up my inheritance.

It is Gilbert who goes to the ale-house two or three nights in the week. Who shall blame him? He works hard in field and byre and barn. It is right that he should lay the dust of corn with the merry essences of corn. There is, to me, something peculiarly satisfying in the image of a company of farmers and crofters and earth-workers, drinking the fruit of their labours after a hard day's work in the fields, and meantime telling stories that have the richness of the earth grained into them. And the fishermen with their salty tales add a warp to the country weft, so that the whole island has a fabric woven for it; to give it an identity and to distinguish it from other villages and islands; and to keep its blood running rich and red in the cold of time and circumstances.

True, and good. But what I have written above are the stories of a man who, by laziness or contrivance or sheer handlessness, had never shed a drop of sweat to turn a single furrow, or to lower a creel. I have seen him lounging down at the shore, or at the gable-end of the village shop, and truly he was an insignificant fellow. But when he opened his mouth in the ale-house, he put some kind of awe and delight on all ears; and this though they knew that his tales were a tissue of lies from beginning to end.

This 'weed' (as some of the islanders called him) had laboured in the smithy of his imagination, amid flames and mighty ringing of iron and water hissings, to give shape and power to the idle fantasies of his brain.

The island men rewarded him with laughter and shoulder-clappings and glasses of whisky.

But, in the light of common day, he was the no-good, the parasite, the weed among the strong green cornstalks.

He took no offence, so long as Williamina gave him two hot meals a day and kept a coat on his back and boots on his feet; so long as there were earth-and-sea-weary men eager for the imagined treasures that lay beyond the horizon westward, to which only he had the keel and the key.

Gilbert Seatter and I met once a week at least, to go over the business of the farm. The business did not take long; Gilbert is as good a manager as any laird could desire, and I trust him utterly.

How we first came to discuss the little idle rascal and his stories, I cannot remember. But Gilbert, after our brief work with papers and ledger was over, must have told me one or two of the stories he had heard the night before in the alehouse, and immediately I was held by this ancient mariner's eye (though at second hand, for the eye was the delighted and gently mocking eye of Gilbert Seatter). Thereafter, every business session in the library ended with a new piece of narrative, or an old piece that had been worked on and reshaped and polished and carved in the interim.

I was assured, pouring whisky out of the decanter into two glasses, of one hearty feast of laughter in the week.

One Friday afternoon, late in November last year, Gilbert arrived for our weekly piece of business. It was done with despatch. I took the crystal stopper from the decanter, and lay back in my chair, and waited to know what saga stuff had enriched the ale-house in the course of that week.

Gilbert frowned, and bit his lip, and was silent. At last he said, 'I'm sorry. There were no stories. It seems he's sick. He's taken to his bed. No, I don't know what's wrong with him. Williamina says nothing. She stands there and glowers if anybody asks for him. "He's being taken care of," is all she'll say. So, it's been a barren place, the alehouse, all this week. Men drink their drink and look at each other and go away. He could be better by Monday. I hope so' . . .

The wanderer wasn't seen on Monday, or any day or night of the next week. I sent word privately to Williamina, by the mouth of Mrs MacKinnon the housekeeper, saying I had heard of the sickness in her house, and that I would be very willing to bring over a doctor from Kirkwall or Hamnavoe, to help in whatever way possible, at my own expense. To which Williamina replied, 'Tell him to mind his own business' . . . Then she added, as Mrs MacKinnon left her door, 'And you mind your business, too.'

However, at that week's end Williamina had business to transact with the minister, the undertaker, the grave-digger, and the registrar of deaths.

And the following Monday the story-teller, in a little light cheap coffin, was lowered into a grave by eight crofters and fishermen. There was but a meagre attendance of mourners. I stood at the back of the little group, my head bowed until I heard the sound of the first strewment of earth. Then I looked up, and was moved to see that gaunt mountain of a woman shaken with grief.

None – least of all I – dared to break in upon her sorrow. I invited the score of mourners up to the Hall for a valedictory dram: a viaticum.

We left Williamina alone among the tombstones.

I have seen the man, maybe a hundred fugitive glimpses of him. I have never heard a syllable out of his mouth.

And now he is dead, and his stories are already becoming echoes, growing ever fainter, going from mouth to mouth. The harp is broken.

What you have read above bears little resemblance to the stories as he must have told them in the ale-house. It is all echo and shadow. It is a veneer without substance.

Alas, I fear, it is worse. I have been in my youth to Edinburgh and Oxford for my education. Such a scheme of classical and liberal studies was mapped out for me from the day of my birth. I was by no means a brilliant student; all the same, the true ancient forms of literature were impressed on my tender mind and can never now be eradicated. Also I have read widely in what is called 'the best of modern fiction'. What you have read is a kind of echo-chamber filled with the voices of novelists who were fashionable in my youth; many, I have no doubt, faded and scentless as pressed flowers in a book.

The original was like the powerful curve of a plough.

How, for example, to reproduce the Eskimo play? Much of its effect lay, according to Gilbert Seatter, in the story-teller's mimicry, in the swift sequence of masks (as it were) he put on and took off like a puppeteer who both mocks and celebrates; so that it seemed a whole imaginary community spoke through him. Yet it may be possible to see those speeches as authentic utterances of any community anywhere on earth, faced with a like situation. My rendering of *The Play of Three Loves* hirples along on the crutch of third-rate literature.

There is, too, the passage in which our island story-teller pours scorn on all the arts of gallery and concert hall and publishing-house, as being exotic shallow-rooted flowerings, doomed – however brilliant they might seem to be to the society sophisticates who experience them – to certain extinction, because the strength of the elements is not in them. How the little story-teller uttered those sentiments was told me at the time by Gilbert Seatter, mostly by gestures and facial grimaces and snorts and grunts of distaste, impossible to reproduce. *You're tired. You stop. You listen. You wonder. You laugh. The world is made new. You are young again. You could dance.*

It is all over. He is dead. The world-wanderer who never set foot outside his island has put a coin into the hand of the dark ferryman; he has found another shore, where there is no need (as I believe) of song or story; for all who set foot there are enclosed within a horizon of pure silence; and are content that it should be so.

Paddy Crowsnest and the Elements

I WATER

There was a boy in an island. His name was Thord.

Thord Anderson lived with his parents in a stone house down by the shore. Thord's father was a fisherman.

Thord had one sister. She was older than him and worked at a big farm on the other side of the hill. Her name was Signy.

Thord went to the island school whenever he felt like it. He was often in trouble at the school for being absent. His hand was as red as a bruised apple some days after Mr Scott the schoolmaster had beaten him with a leather strap.

The other pupils' faces shone with delight. Thord bit his lip and uttered no cry.

One day a certain event happened. Thord's father went out fishing in his boat *Lightfoot*. That month they were lifting lobsters under the cliffs of Hoy, Thord's father and an old man from the farm of Saithers called Willo Ritch. Thord would have been in the boat that day, too, only his mother had ordered him to go to school.

'What!' she cried, 'do you want to end up as ignorant as your father and old Willo of Saithers – as ignorant as a peat and as poor? Get off with you to school. You'll learn grammar and spelling and geography and Latin. That way, you'll get a good job in an office in Hamnavoe or Kirkwall. And I'll have some comfort in my old age. There's your bag of books in the corner. Off with you!'

As Thord walked slow as a sea-slug to the school, he saw his father and old Willo Ritch turning the boat *Lightfoot* into the west.

It was a beautiful morning.

Thord had to bite his lip to keep from crying. His whole desire was to be sitting in the boat among the stacked baited creels, with the sea birds circling all around, and here and there the sleek head of a seal in the ebb.

The class was doing a history lesson in the middle of the afternoon – how King James the Third of Scotland was killed by a man pretending to be a priest after the Battle of Sauchieburn – when a witless wandering man called Paddy Crowsnest opened the door and half sang, 'Eh, sir, there's a terrible thing happened on the sea today.'

'Get away, you idiot!' cried Mr Scott. 'Never dare to interrupt the work of this school again in that manner.'

Paddy closed the door and went away.

'The poor-house, that's the place for a thing like that!' said Mr Scott.

Now the subject changed from history to arithmetic – long division – a thing dreaded by Thord and a few others besides.

There was suddenly a very small girl, Roberta, Mr Scott's daughter – too young for school – standing by the blackboard. She had entered as soundless as a butterfly.

When Roberta saw the children's eyes looking at her, forty eyes of all sizes and shapes and colours, she all but turned and fled out again.

'Roberta!' cried her father. 'What takes you into the class-room? You know it isn't allowed.'

'I was at the shore with my shells,' whispered Roberta. 'I looked up and there was a big wave and I saw two faces in the sea.'

'Now Roberta,' said Mr Scott, 'you know perfectly well you saw no such thing. I can see the sea from where I'm standing.

It's calm and blue. I know you see wonderful things in your mind, Roberta. She's always telling me the most wonderful stories, children. But you must never take your imaginings to me in the classroom, Roberta. Go home to your mother.'

Little Roberta gave one wild look at the ranks of pupils and she fled away into the blue and gold morning.

'I think,' said Mr Scott to his class, not entirely displeased, 'that little daughter of mine will grow up some day to be a novelist.'

The boys and girls heard Roberta shouting to the collie from the next farm, that barked all about her with even wilder delight.

'Enough of arithmetic for today,' said Mr Scott. 'Tomorrow, for arithmetic, we will proceed to decimal fractions. Now, geography. And I hope you've learned the exports and imports of Spain. I intend to ask a few questions on that subject.'

He cast a baleful look at Thord, who had vaguely heard of a land called Spain but that was all he knew about it.

Just then the door opened again and Mr MacVicar the minister came in gravely.

'Mr Scott,' he said, 'pardon my intrusion. Pardon my haste. Have you the boy Thord Anderson in your class? Also the girl Matilda Ritch from Saithers farm?'

'Stand up, Thord and Matilda,' cried Mr Scott.

'Have they been up to some devilment?' said Mr Scott to Mr MacVicar in his semi-jocular vein. 'Have they broken the Manse window? Have they stolen white roses from Mrs MacVicar's rose-bush? If they've done that, or any other mischief, they'll answer for it, I assure you, Mr MacVicar.'

'I wish,' said Mr MacVicar, 'that was the worst that had happened today. It is much, much worse.'

Thord felt his warm heart turn to stone inside him.

He stood up at his desk.

Matilda Ritch, at the other corner of the classroom, stood up, with frightened eyes.

'Thord and Matilda,' said Mr MacVicar, 'I want you to be as brave as you can. A dreadful thing has happened on the sea this morning. The fishing boat *Lightfoot* has been swamped by a big wave. The lifeboat is out. The shore is being searched thoroughly. It may be, of course, that your father, Thord, and your granduncle, Matilda, have come ashore somewhere, in Graemsay perhaps, or in Yesnaby. There was a strong ebb running. Alas, neither of them could swim, I understand. I think it best, Mr Scott, if Thord and Matilda are excused school today. Their place is to be home with their people.'

'This is terrible,' said Mr Scott, speaking as if the blackboard duster had been thrust half down his throat. 'Of course. Of course. They must go home.'

The boys and girls were as silent as a shoal of fish.

Thord bit his lip.

The silence was shattered by a wild howl from Matilda Ritch. (Matilda was old Willo's granddaughter). It was one long shriek broken only by pauses for intakes of breath.

As last Matilda stopped. She seemed to shrink into her desolation of misery like an animal.

Then suddenly she leapt at Mr MacVicar and kicked him hard on the shin and rushed out into the sunlight.

Thord stayed where he was and dropped his head. He still gnawed his lip. His eyes were like two blue stones whenever he glanced up.

'Come Thord,' said Mr MacVicar, 'I will take you home.'

The children had never seen Mr Scott looking so foolish and so useless.

'Leave me alone,' said Thord.

Then he left his desk and walked out slowly into the sun.

The lifeboat was out in the Sound, going in a wide circle.

Thord didn't go into the house. He sat on the stone step of the bothy where the fishing gear was stacked.

It was enough to deal with his own grief; to be caught up in his mother's was more than he could endure.

He slept there, in the sun of early summer. He dreamt he was on a great ship, in pursuit of a whale. The floes and the bergs were full of noises.

Thord woke. The sun had moved the shadows of peat-stack and bothy round a little.

The little house was full of voices – voices of wonderment, voices on the verge of laughter, one silent tongue that he understood well, because he had inherited it.

There he was, beside the fire, his father, wrapped in two blankets, sipping a cup of hot whisky. And the neighbours, men and women, on every chest and chair and even on the stone wall niche. A few men leaned against the wall, smoking.

Thord rushed at his father so violently that the cup of whisky fell and smashed on a blue flagstone of the floor.

His father ruffled Thord's hair, the only endearment he allowed himself, and that rarely – maybe at the Lammas fair or at New Year.

'Never mind!' cried his mother. 'There's more whisky, and I have a whole shelf of cups . . . Andrew, Tom, Sando, drink up. I've sent Paddy to the inn to get another bottle.'

'Well,' said Andrew from the croft of Gyre, 'I would rather drink the whisky this way than at your funeral, Jock, and we were near enough to doing that.'

Some of the women clucked and tutted at the way their men were swilling whisky about in the white-cracked cups.

'Thord, leave your father alone,' said the mother. 'He's had enough to contend with today. Ah, here's Paddy back with another bottle of Old Orkney . . . Remember this, you men, we must keep some of this bottle for poor Willo's funeral.'

There was a short silence in memory of old Willo Ritch's drowning.

'But the boat's safe,' said Tom Burray the blacksmith. 'The *Lightfoot*'s lying safe on the Sandside beach at Graemsay.'

A half-cup of whisky was poured for the messenger, Paddy. It had been a very good day for him.

Jessie Allan, who was standing at the door, pointed, then touched her finger to her mouth, then pointed outside again.

The people in the house, except the half-drowned fisherman, went to the door and window.

Some men were carrying a burden in a sail up from the shore across the coastguard's field.

Tom Burray shook the last drops of whisky out of his cup on to the floor. He looked longingly at the new bottle on the table.

'You've had too much to drink already, my lad!' cried Meg Burray. 'You'll drink not one drop more.'

II AIR

It was such a windy day it scoured the sun brighter than the copper pot at marmalade-making time.

It went through the hayfields and the cornfield of Saithers in long surges. The oats darkened as another gust hit them, then the long stalks lifted their radiance to the sun. They made corn songs, surge on surge on surge, all day long.

A small bird spurted out of the heather – it seemed such a frail thing must be blown down, a flutter of feathers, in the high wind. But no, it seemed to be mounting a ladder of bright air; occasionally you could hear a note or two of its song, then the wind scattered the music – time after time, until the lark was lost in the highest blue, but then its song in lulls of the wind rang out clearer than before.

A few women going to or returning from the village shop with their closed baskets were swept this way or that on the dusty road, and old Merran Kyle ended in the ditch in a flurry of skirts and petticoats, and the eggs she was taking to the village shop to barter for groceries rolled this way and that, and five of them were cracked or broken against stones. Paddy Crowsnest the island nuisance put four whole eggs into his pocket. Then Paddy saw Albert Weyland the postman approaching, hurrying his step when he saw the old woman lying wrecked in the ditch. Paddy cracked the stolen eggs, one after the other, and slid them down his throat. (He had turned his back so that Albert wouldn't see him.)

Paddy seemed to be a contented man, in spite of his rags and pennilessness. His one overpowering dread was that they would have him put in the poor-house in Kirkwall.

Paddy's Adam's-apple negotiated the fourth gut-seeking egg. Then, looking very concerned, he began to pull the old woman out of the ditch, and he had her on her feet before Albert Weyland appeared on the scene.

'Poor Mistress Kyle,' said Paddy.

'Don't touch her, man,' said Albert severely to the 'gaanaboot man'. 'Merran is a very particular woman. She doesn't want any of your fleas or beasts. Are you sure you didn't knock her into the ditch yourself? If you did, man, you'll be shipped to Kirkwall on the next boat. It's the Sheriff Court you'll end up in.'

'As God's my witness,' said Paddy, 'it was God's own wind threw the poor old soul into the ditch. My arms are out of their sockets, near, dragging her out!'

The wind blew Paddy's ragged coat like a dozen fluttering flags.

'You're the kind men to a poor old wife,' said Merran. 'I did a foolish thing coming out on such a stormy day. But when I looked through my window this morning, there was the sun like a brass trumpet over the hill. *Come out*, it cried, *on such a brave day.*'

A bucket trundled past them on the road, empty, but with every clanging wind-bluster, it let fall a few white drops in the dust.

'That's the Ritchs' bucket,' said Merran. 'I know the Ritchs' bucket. Matilda must have set it down on a loose stone after milking Bluebell. They'll have to spread margarine on their bannocks up at Saithers this weekend . . .'

The bucket, after a pause, danced and clanged along the road, a hundred yards further on.

'I'll take the lady home in safety,' said Paddy, his rags cracking like whips in the wind.

'You'll go on to your hovel,' said the postman. 'What's that yellow splash down your chin? I'll take Mistress Kyle with me as far as the village shop for her errands . . . I might have to report you to the poor inspector, you vagabond. I haven't decided yet.'

Paddy went as furtive as a rat along the ditch verge.

From the crest of the brae he saw Thord Anderson down on the shore, going here and there among the scattered boards of his father's boat, salvaging good timber to use for the new fishing boat he was building.

Already the keel was set up in the cave.

Paddy had heard that old William Burray was very angry that his boat *Lightfoot* was being broken up. But he could do nothing about it, being confined to his straw chair beside the fire with rheumatics.

Thord was a progressive young man.

His granduncle, an ill-natured old shepherd, had left him a hundred pounds in his will at the end of winter.

Thord intended to have a new fishing boat with an engine in it, the first of the kind on that shore: the *Zephyr*.

The wind took the boards of *Lightfoot* and threw them about, this way and that. Thord picked out the sound boards and took them into the cave of making, staggering now and again in the wild onsets and back-draughts of wind.

A board went trundling into the sea. 'Go then,' shouted Thord into the wind. 'Sink. Smash on the rock. That's what you were fated to do, the time you nearly drowned my father. You're rotten with worms!'

The words came clear on the wind to Paddy.

Paddy marked down half-a-dozen planks that would burn well enough in his fire. He would collect them later, after Thord had gone home.

'A strange man, that Thord,' thought Paddy, 'shouting out like that, as if dead wood could hear him!'

Another violent gust up-ended an old curved plank and set it down with a slurp among a heap of wet seaweed.

'You, too,' shouted Thord Anderson to the fugitive wood. 'A killer. Didn't you drown old Willo Ritch that same morning? It doesn't do – unlucky planks tied into the same boat with good sound soaring timber . . . Rot among the ware, you traitor Judas.'

'I suppose they were always a droll family,' said Paddy. 'But I never knew one of them to shout into the wind like that, such wild nonsense.'

When Thord had taken the last good curve of wood into the cave, Paddy turned for home.

Out of the shelter of the cliff, the wind took him and trundled him along – a man with a spy-glass on Norday island across the Sound would have thought Paddy was dancing to some mad music. He bent his head and butted into the gale that sometimes threw him a few steps backwards for every homeward step.

He sheltered in the lee of Saithers farm, on the sea edge.

There Paddy saw a young woman with a covered basket leaving the road and going down, one perilous foot after the other, holding tightly on to the basket, to the wave-lashed beach.

Paddy recognised Matilda Ritch.

What would a country lass like Matilda Ritch be wanting on the shore on such a day, carrying a flask and food – oatcakes hot from the griddle by the smell. (Paddy had very acute nostrils.) And Scotch broth in the thermos, for sure, well onioned and leeked.

Once on the sand, and out of sight, the last Paddy knew of Matilda that morning was a shout. And a young man's shout in answer. The wind took their joy and mingled the echoes, and the love song was one with the hills and the waters.

'Ah well,' thought Paddy to himself, 'let them be happy while they can. There'll be storm enough to thole.'

The wind urged Paddy on his way, with now and again a huge step and now and then a quick little trot, until he got to the shelter of the inn. In the inn old Cameron might give him a half-pint if he washed last night's beer glasses.

III FIRE

It had been an eventful year in the island.

The electrical engineers and the labourers had finished their work and now a line of electricity poles, strung with cables, strode across the island. Every house from the month of April on, had electric light. The tilley lamps and the paraffin lamps were either stored in attic or outhouse or thrown 'afore the face' (over the cliff) as useless.

Those who had felt a little reverence for their lamps and kept them were glad when the blizzard came the following winter and plunged them in ancient night. But this is to anticipate.

There was more to the great electrical revolution than light. Mrs Spence of Overlift got a cooker. The Camerons of the inn got two cookers and a water-heater, a washing machine and an electric iron and a freezer-refrigerator, and storage heaters in every room. The inn blazed like a battleship after the Easter sunsets.

Every farm, except for a very occasional canny farm here and there, had an electric fire. The old peat-burning grates were boarded up and neat shiny compact electric fires were put in. A finger flick and there the bar glowed! Another flick, and a second parallel bar glowed, sending out an immediate clean heat, with not a wisp of smoke or a speck of ash. A reflector at the back of each electric fire seemed to redouble the radiance and the intensity.

A farm wife might say, in an excess of joy, 'We won't need the poker either. Nor the tongs, nor the hearth-brush!' Those faithful instruments of service were banished too, flung on the muck-heap.

'Ah,' the young men and the lasses said, 'there'll be no peat-cutting either. Imagine that, we won't ever again have to go to the peat-hill with our tuskers, to dig winter fire!' . . . 'No more sweat and no more sore bones' . . .

Thord and Matilda's young brood said such things, a few mornings after the electricity had come to the shore farm of Saithers.

The day before, electricity had been installed in the byre. The cows were to be milked in a new way from now on.

Thord Anderson the father said nothing.

The whole island seemed to be in a trance of joy over this great marvel.

The big farm of Dale got an all-electric wireless. The old wireless, together with its two batteries – one wet and one dry – was thrown over the cliff. (The next winter, in the blizzard, the folk of Dale farm were to regret this rejection of a friend that had given them 'Children's Hour' and Henry Hall's orchestra and Raymond Gram Swing's 'Letter from America' for years, when the snow drew a silence of ancient ice about the island.)

'Daddo!' cried Andrew Anderson. 'We must get a mains wireless too.'

'We will,' said Mrs Matilda Anderson, 'when we can afford it. First things first. There's that Hoover thing coming – the one the salesman showed us – but of course we won't be able to use it till the new carpet for the parlour comes from Kirkwall. No point in having a Hoover unless you have one carpet at least. I

don't know how we can afford all this new electric parapher-
nalia as it is . . .'

Apart from such small frictions here and there in the island –
which happen whenever progress takes a big step forward – the
island was enchanted with electricity.

Cameron the inn-keeper told the men leaning on the bar
counter that there was an electric-driven gadget called television
that would soon be a part of every household. 'Imagine that!' he
said, 'a private picture-house in every farm-house . . .' A few of
the island men took leave to doubt that. A few of them had been
to the 'talkies' in Kirkwall or Hamnavoe, and seen Charlie
Chaplin, Matheson Lang and Pola Negri; but to think of such
magic in the corner of every farm kitchen passed all credulity.

'I assure you it'll come,' said Cameron. 'Of course it's only in
London and roundabout yet. Only rich people can afford it. But
we'll see it in Orkney in our time . . .'

'There's something far wrong,' said Thord to Matilda his wife
one day when they were alone, the four young ones having gone
to the mobile-cinema show in the Community Centre (this
innovation was of course thanks to electricity) – 'There's
something far wrong in this house.'

'It looks all right to me,' said Matilda.

'*You* feel it too,' said Thord. 'I know by the look of you. A
blue-gray look. It's the croft. The warmth has stopped flowing
through it.'

'It was never so warm in the days of that old hearth-fire,' said
Matilda. 'Never! When the three electric bars are on, on a very
cold night, you have to shift your stool back.'

'In the morning this house is as cold as a grave when I get up
to go down to the boat,' said Thord. 'That never happened
before. The fire stayed in all night, there were still glowing
embers in the morning. All right! The fire had been here in
Saithers for generations, never allowed to go out for centuries,
ever since your great-great-great-grandfather built the place two

hundred years ago and more. Once that electric fire is switched off, this house gets colder than the cave I keep the boat in.'

'You're a simple-minded man!' said Matilda. 'The truth is, you're getting old, man. Your blood is thinning. No wonder the young ones can't wait to get out of the house whenever you come in from the sea, grumbling. Do you want to drive them out of the island for ever? I assure you, the young folk of this island won't put up with the old ways of doing things. They're right too. Life on this island was hard and painful in the old days. The kirkyard's full of young bairns. My old granduncle Willo was twisted this way and that with rheumatics, and him only fifty-five when he drowned. Life's easier now. We should be thankful.'

Matilda went to heat the soup pot on the electric ring.

All night they didn't speak to each other. Matilda continued knitting her jumper. The two bars of the electric fire scorched their shins. The glare of the electric bulb shone on the white pages of Jack London's *White Fang*, which Thord was reading. The draught from the door cut into the side of his face.

These new events occurred in the island in the spring of that *annus mirabilis*.

At the end of April news was brought to the island that Major Douglas Lees, the young laird, had been killed in a flying accident. His monoplane had struck a hillside in East Lothian and burst into flames. He was the only son of old Sir James and Lady Lee, and he had not married, though he was rumoured to be engaged to the beautiful young woman he had taken for a holiday the previous summer to the big Hall, with the girl's wraith-like mother in attendance, as chaperone. The soldier and his fiancée had spent many happy afternoons on the hill, or down at the shore.

The island prepared for a funeral with all the Orkney gentry present. There was a subscription to buy flowers, out-of-season roses from the Kirkwall florist, apart from the daffodils that throned the island that month; the island women would bring along armfuls, for the boy had been well liked.

Of course the young laird would be buried among his ancestors at the private graveyard up at the Hall. The 'Pisky' (Episcopalian) minister from Kirkwall would perform the ceremony; the local minister, Mr Sauchie, being Presbyterian, had no jurisdiction. (Mr Mac Vicar, the old minister, was long dust.)

It turned out, there was no funeral at all.

Instead, the island councillor, Jock Scabra of Nessleigh, received a letter from an Edinburgh solicitor, stating that the remains of Major Douglas Lee would, in accordance with his own written wishes, be cast to the winds of the island, and it was sincerely hoped that none of the islanders would object to this simple natural ceremony.

Word was passed round the island. Nobody objected. Such a thing had never happened before. ('Well,' said the new school-master, Mr White, 'it would have happened here four or five thousand years ago, in this very island. They're still finding urns here and there with bits of charred bone in them.')

The beautiful young woman whom the laird had called Poppy the summer before arrived on the ferry-boat from Hamnavoe one morning at the beginning of May when the sky was threaded with lark song. She was carrying a small jar in her hand.

She greeted the village people cheerfully. She even remembered some of their names. A few women had slipped indoors when they saw her climbing out of the ship's boat onto the ebb; how could lowly folk the like of them ever think to offer condolences to the gentry? A few, observing Poppy from their curtain-fringes, and her cheerful arrival in the island, thought she must be a heartless young hussy after all.

And that jar she was carrying must be – ?

Poppy took the sheep track to the hill. Along the shore that day it was calm and warm, but on the summit a sea wind blew out the frail scarf round Poppy's head.

Poppy took a knife to the wax round the opening of the urn, till the cork came loose. She shook out the dust, six or seven times, and the wind was stained briefly and then it sifted out the grains, whisper after whisper. Some grains fell on the granite rocks, some blew down to the farm-land below, some went on swirls and eddies out to sea. A few grains settled in Poppy's bright hair, and she shook them out and away.

'*To the elements, and be thou free,*' said Poppy.

She looked across at the big house, the Hall, that would either be sold to a stranger, or inherited by some fourth or fifth cousin who had never seen it before, or be left to dry-rot and dampness.

Poppy threw the stone jar on to a granite outcrop, when it smashed to pieces.

'They have no reverence any more,' said Mrs Taylor of the post office. 'What's the world coming to?'

'There should have been somebody there to say the Lord's Prayer at least,' said Jock Scabra the island councillor.

When Poppy got back to the village, they saw that her face was stained with grief, and two new bright beads were gathering in her eyes.

The ferry-boat *Thule* was just about to leave, with a cargo of eggs, butter, cheese, lobsters and a dozen terrified sheep.

Poppy was rowed on board, and the island never saw her again.

This committal of dust to wind, next to the installation of electricity, was the most remarkable thing that happened in the island that spring.

The third, that had an element of scorn in it, was the sight of the Anderson family of Saithers – Thord and Matilda and the two eldest Alex and Maggie – trekking in the peat-hill in the last days of May, with tuskers for digging the peat, and one basket with oatcakes and cheese in it, and another basket heavy with bottles of Matilda's home-brewed ale.

The islanders could see how resentfully Alex and Maggie trailed behind. 'And little wonder,' the villagers said. 'Peats indeed! Forcing young folk to dig peats when peat will never be needed in this island again. Who would ever have believed it! They have electric fires in every room at Saithers, and the very latest kind of electric cooker. I heard they paid *fifty pounds* for it. And there they go, trudging to the peat-hill like slaves, the way the old folk used to do in the old days. There was always something a bit droll in that Anderson family. They never went the way that other folk took. It's the young ones I'm sorry for . . .'

'Alex! Maggie!' cried their father from the peat-hill. 'Hurry on with the tuskers. We don't have all day to waste. I've missed a good fishing day.'

The sun shone and a westerly blew for three early summer days, while the Anderson family of Saithers dug dark fire out of the droning hill, and left the wet squandered squares of turf to dry in sun and wind. A week more, and they were set up in little dolmens, till they were as dry as tinder, and eager for the winter flame.

And in August, Thord Anderson ignored another good fishing day. He yoked his horse to the cart, and he brought the peats home, and he built them into a neat blue-black stack against the end of the house, a thousand and more squares, each as light as a cork float. 'They'll moulder to dust, them peats,' said the island folk. 'You'd have thought Matilda at least to have had more wit.'

At harvest time the folly of the folk of Saithers was forgotten, as the golden round of labour and fruitfulness went on in this farm and that croft, and they all helped each other as well as they could. (Of course, there was not so much neighbourliness required now, since tractors and farm machinery were being increasingly housed in the stables from which the horses had been exiled, in farm after farm.)

The snow came early that year, in late November. It lay lightly, a chaste cover, over the island for a day or two, then the islanders woke one morning to find the fields sparkling with dew in the late dawn.

'The snow has a way of coming back, when it comes this early,' said the old man of Bu farm, smoking his pipe at the planticru wall. (It could be said that old Mansie had a hundred snows and sixty harvests grained into him. Nowadays nobody paid much attention to old men like him – they had their weather forecasts on the wireless.)

It could be said that the November snowfall was a single spy. The battalions came one day between Yule and the New Year. The snow fell for two nights and a day, thick incessant flake-showers driven on a north-easterly wind. When the islanders woke after the first night they could scarcely recognise their own hills and loch and houses: all were buried in a deep white dazzlement. The islanders went about looking transfigured. They called to each other across snow-loaded fields and their voices rang like bells, as if time had restored to them the tones of youth. The laughter of children, from field to field, was like thin delicate crystal, touching and tinkling. The farm collies barked in amazement. The old people whispered for a moment in their open doors, shook their heads, and went indoors to their double- or triple-barred electric fires. The swans on the loch were crowded together by the frozen water. The three burns that fed the loch lyrically all the year round and then flowed on to the sea were locked and silent.

Then, with mighty sighs and whispers and susurrations, the wind got up again and blew blinding snow over the island. That afternoon only Sam the shepherd stirred outside to see to his sheep; he dug three of them out of snow graves, and he just got to his door before the hill-road was drifted under. 'I was just in time,' said Sam.

The wind shifted north and blew a dark blizzard over Orkney, surge after surge.

About nine o'clock, when they were listening to the news, those who had wirelesses, the farms and crofts were plunged in darkness and cold. A voice on the battery wireless said, 'Heavy snowfalls have disrupted life to some extent all over the north of Scotland. In some places electricity poles have been blown down. As soon as the weather moderates, the engineers of the Electricity Board will assess the damage and attempt restoration work. Most roads are blocked. People are advised to stay indoors unless they have urgent business.' The progressive farms that had had mains radios installed heard nothing of this.

Meantime, the crofts and farms got very cold inside.

In the Bu farm, nothing was visible except when old Mansie struck a match to light his pipe. 'There might be a peat or two left, from the year before last . . .' he said. His son, Tommy the farmer, looked in the shed; there was only a clod or two and a drift of brown dust. 'There was a time,' said the old man, 'when we saved bits of wood from the ebb, they kept the fire going on a particular cold night . . .' His daughter-in-law Bella broke up two old worm-eaten chairs in the barn, but she had no sooner brought the firewood in than she saw the boarded hearth . . . 'My grandfather,' said Mansie, 'once built an igloo on the shore of Hudson's Bay. The Eskimos showed him. But he never passed on his knowledge to me.'

In the end the four generations who dwelt together at the ancient farm of the Bu went to bed to keep warm.

Through the sky-light windows they had never seen the stars flashing so bright.

Only one man was abroad in the island that night, Sam the shepherd. There were fifty sheep to be accounted for. He found forty-seven huddled in the lee of old byres and walls here and there. Sam was almost buried himself in the drifts, struggling home. In the morning he would, somehow, get the flock into shelter. It could be, the lost three were still alive, having made breathing-holes for themselves under the snow.

In the distance, a mile across the loch, Sam could see a frail light in the window of the farm of Saithers. He had heard indeed that Matilda Anderson had saved a paraffin lamp and a bottle of paraffin from the big clear-out in the springtime. And he knew that the folk of Saithers had cut peats in May, and had kept one hearth in reserve.

He knew, too, that Matilda brewed good ale.

Sam yearned towards Saithers. If he had been ten years younger, he would have chanced it. But tonight he was very tired, and even as he paused to look across at Saithers and speculate, the wind got up and another flurry of snow dimmed his sight.

He wasn't far from home, only down past the well and the smithy. That fool of a sister of his had filled their house with electrical gadgets, there was no hope of a mug of mulled ale beside the fire before bedtime.

In a desolate part of the island, unseen by anyone, Paddy Crowsnest the outcast sat in peace in his hovel. A candle burned in an empty bottle on the sill. The stone hearth blazed with bits of broken driftwood, and now and then sent out showers of salt sparks. Mr Cameron of the inn had employed Paddy on a few afternoons before Christmas to deliver bottles of whisky and sherry to a dozen of the more distant farms, and had paid him with a half-bottle of Barbados rum.

Paddy was warm and comfortable in his hovel. After the first dram or two of hot rum, it occurred to him that he liked blizzards and gales and wrecks very much indeed.

IV EARTH

A very old man sat in the chair beside the peat-fire. His name was Thord.

Sometimes he tore a strip off a page of *The Orcadian* and lighted it and put the flame to his pipe. A puff or two, with a chime and gargle of tobacco juices from inside the pipe, then the pipe went out and he set it down on the hearth again.

'I wonder,' he said to the chair on the opposite side of the fire, 'are the boats in yet? What time is it? I would have thought the boats would be in by now. Go to the sea-bank, see if *Zephyr*'s in with a catch of haddocks.

'Still nothing to say? You had plenty to say in years past. This house was full of words. I could hardly move for women's words. Gossip, tittle-tattle. I could hardly think. I was glad to be down at the shore among the sea birds, many a day, at the shore or out on the sea, in *Zephyr*.

'That was a bad thing to do, to turn me away from my own boat. How many years ago? I forget. *There's no fishing from this shore any longer. The Zephyr, she was sold the winter before last in Wick. You agreed to it, we have your signature on the paper. There's a bigger boat now, grand-da. We operate from the new pier at the village. A seine-netter, the* Lively Lass . . . I would never have thought a son of mine would have spoken to me like that. No, grandson. *You bide at home, grand-da. Your fishing days are done. Yes, I would take you with me, but I have the other boys to consider. There's new kinds of gear to operate, you have to know what you're doing. You wouldn't be at home in* Lively Lass, *old grand-da – a danger to us all.*

'That I should be forbid boat-room! I forget the name of that boy. I forget names now, all the time. I think he's Maggie's son.

'The mills grind slowly. The heavy stones turn, we are ground into dust, even while we draw breath. Every word. Every thought a grain of dust. The bairn whimpers, he turns a face to the sun. There is a hard road in front of you, man. The golden stone begins to turn. The quernstones of sun and earth.

'Fishermen? Men drown in time.

'Old wife – Matilda, is that the name? – old wife, you were up early this morning, there's a bonny shine on the blue stone beside the chair. And the plate and cup put by in the cupboard. But I don't remember eating your porridge. I don't remember getting out of bed. I remember a confusion of pains. A scarecrow of aches and tatters, like Paddy Crowsnest. If Paddy comes by this fine morning, give him – be sure now – a sup of milk and some oatmeal. Good luck, to give a bite to a wanderer. No millstones for Paddy, he's free dust on the wind. We might be poor as Paddy some day. Poorer. But I haven't seen Paddy this long while.

'The grass withereth. The flower fadeth. The bonny rose on a lass's cheek. Yours too, once, old wife. A pity. Flesh is ground to dust, shadows come and fill the hollows. The hollows of the face, the strong thews of the net-dragging arms. A withering down to skull and skeleton. But still . . .

'Sea in the eye-holes.

'The kirkyard, that's the place in all this island I like to visit, whatever the weather. Friends all foregathered. Silence better than any story, sweeter than the Yule fiddle.

'Well, if she gave me morning porridge, who puts the broth bowl in my hand, day after day? Not much hope of fish now, so late, the tide turned an hour ago, *Zephyr* at her mooring, the lads baiting the lines for next morning's sea work. No smell of salt. No smell of salt. No smell of haddocks with sea sklintering off them, and the knife in the guts, and the gulls abroad in a wild windy asylum.

'No, I haven't lost the sea smells. I won't forget the smell of crab or heaped rotting ware in the ebb, never till Sutherland hammers the last nail in my coffin.

'Wait a minute, Sutherland died in the first snow. Too much

snow, that year again, they had to carry Sutherland to the kirkyard on a sledge. Who sees to the dead now?

'You're the old fool, Thord. You might have known, this is the day they cut the harvest. This is the great day. Your nostrils ought to be brimming full with the smells of barley. The scythemen are out, the women are building stooks, the children are chasing rabbits and larks, the whole island's loaded with gold. We will eat and we will drink all next winter, whatever storms blow. But first, the harvest home, the ale going round, the drunken feet dancing, flash and soar of the hairst fiddle. What fiddler? I think, Tomison, but there was another fiddler another time, earlier I think, I forget his name. There was never a fiddler like that one, I forget him.

'Thord, old boneman, you are a fool of fools. Tomison died all of forty years ago, he went over the cliff – afore the face – going down after fulmar eggs. Smells. You've smelt nothing this while. You smelt oil fumes – boat and tar and tractor – then nothing.

'As for harvest and harvesters, the last one left the fields a while ago. There have been no oats or barley cut in this island this ten years and more. They grow foreign stuff that hurts the eye to look at.

'The harvesters are taking their rest under stone stooks.

'You will find their flails and querns and scythes in the country museums here and there, to show to the tourists.

'What would your old kirk elder father and councillor and progressive farmer have thought of that, Matilda? He might have been glad of it – I wouldn't put it past him – a great fool, his lass with the bright hair and a dowry coming with her, too good for the likes of Anderson the fisherman's son . . . Ah well, he'll know all about it now, he'll know if what he went to the kirk for Sunday after Sunday, is true.

'There he sits with wise island ones – the council chamber of silence, in the kirkyard.

'I wish him no ill, Matilda. He kept a fire going when I came in cold from the sea, many a day. And a dram in winter, when sea spume and snow were in my beard. He thought a lot in the end about the old man Willo that drowned, his uncle, the one who was no good on the glebe, and not a lot better at the fishing.

'The millstones, sun and earth, wore the man at Saithers to silence. If only we could say, the mill wears us to wisdom, that would be a fine thing but it wouldn't be true. I have more rage and bitterness in me now, I think, than when I first knew you, Matilda.

'And time didn't sweeten you either.

'Eaten up at last, quickly, by that trouble, as if a nest of rats was inside you, devouring. The cruelty.

'It's a shadow that sits opposite me in the chair. Of course I know that. Sometimes I know that. Who makes the oatcakes and the tea then? Who makes the blue stone shine? Who cuts my toe-nails?

'It must be the granddaughter. What's her name? I forget. There might be still a little goodness in the world. Can it be kept from going sour?

'When was it I visited the kirkyard? It must have been a summer day, last year. Bill drove me there in his car. I can't walk there, not now, not for six or seven years, that's sure.

' "You go and have a dram," I said to Bill (is he grandson? Son-in-law? Something like that). "Just leave me here for an hour with the farmers and the fishermen and the wives, and the bairns that only drew a few breaths. Just leave me here. I'll be all right. Maybe they have things to tell me."

'This fire could do with a few peats laid this way and that, to catch the draught. Not enough flame to light my pipe.

'Well, now, that was a good day, when we all met together in the kirkyard. Besides the few I knew, in my time, I suppose a hundred or more, there were a host from times past, thousands and thousands, a scattering of worn names, a crowd from earlier with no names at all.

'And the sun was warm that morning on my head, and there my boots were splashed with clover and buttercups and dew. There must have been half-a-dozen larks.

'And nobody in the kirkyard and alive that day but me.

'A wonderful thing! Somebody has taken a big stone out of the ebb and painted a name on it, Paddy. PATRICK CROWSNEST 1890–1964. A foolish thing, as the world sees it, a day of rain will wash the lettering away.

'What does a name or a few years matter, anyway?

'Matilda, are you there lass, in the shadows? I think the sun must be down. This room is a net of shadows, a thickening cluster. Light the lamp, Matilda.

'MATILDA ANDERSON. There you were, among the poor shore folk. Not – as here at Saithers farm they'd have wanted – among the prosperous hill folk who coin wealth between the ripening sun and the teeming earth, and have granite tombstones.

'You won't have that long to wait. Not that time means anything there, where you are – and only a little to me, a salting.

'I wanted to be this morning on the *Lightfoot*. The wind's rising. I hope our grandson knows what he's doing. Bill.'

What's this, man? The fire nearly out. This'll never do. Will I switch the light on? All right, it hurts your eyes, I'll just light the candle. I must see to put this fish in the pot. Yes, the Lively Lass *is in, a heavy catch, fish you never troubled with in your day, you'd have thrown them back. Monk-fish. You'll enjoy it all right with a scone and butter. Where have I been? You have a great-grandson I must see to, as well as you. I left him rocking in his cradle in the new house of Saithers like a peedie fisherman in a boat. Matilda? I don't know anybody of that name. Bill and the boys, they're having a drink at the inn. A long haul they've had since the weekend. They'll be back soon. If you're a good old man, and don't grouse, there might be a little in the heel of the bottle for you.*

Poet And Prince: A Fable

I

So, WHEN THE old poet died, the news came quite quickly to the towns and rather slowly to the hill farms. No one gets excited by the life and death of poets, especially a laureate who had lived most of his life up at the castle, unseen and unheard. Poets aren't generals or chancellors.

Six poets arrived one after the other at the prince's castle, summoned. They sat a long while on a hard bench outside the Office of Culture.

The poets were of different ages, sizes, complexions. Two of them were from the capital. Those two would have snarled and sneered at each other, had they been sitting in a tavern. Here, they looked at one another and curled their lips. Three poets came from the far end of the kingdom; two looked a bit frightened.

One poet was very young.

At last the door of the Office opened. A voice inside called a name. A poet from a mountain village rose up from the bench and went inside.

One of the city poets sneered silently after him – That such a yokel should put himself forward!

The chief clerk at the office desk asked questions and wrote down words on a form: six times.

Six times he said, 'The prince wants you to write an elegy for the dead poet. The poet who writes the best elegy will be the next court poet. He will be paid as follows: a barrel of red wine at midwinter, and a gold piece every new moon. You will have your elegy here tomorrow morning when the first cart comes in through the city gate with onions or cheese or strawberries.'

Five times the clerk was asked questions: what form was the elegy to take? Except for the two lip-curling city poets, none of them had seen the laureate: could the clerk give them a few facts, such as the late laureate's age, his way of life, his favourite flowers and music, how many children and grandchildren he had; so that they would have something to go on?

The clerk said, 'I hardly knew the poet: I do not like poetry. All I know is, you are to write an elegy.'

The poet who was little more than a boy asked no questions.

A soldier with a ceremonial lance led each of the poets to a separate cell in the castle.

It was a stone cell and there was no fire, no bottle of wine, no loaf. There was a small table and a chair and on the table a candle burned and there were sheets of paper, an inkpot and a pen.

The door was locked upon each of the six poets.

The prince had his breakfast of cold chicken, white bread, and wine of a pale golden colour . . .

A trumpet sounded. A colonel entered, bowed, laid a scroll on the linen table cloth beside the plate of small bones and crusts.

'I will not review the cavalry today,' said the prince.

The hound barked twice outside the door. The chancellor came in, unrolling a long scroll as he came. 'This is serious, Your Highness. An insurrection in the mountains. As you know, the seven villages have paid no taxes for three years. One of the taxmen has been found with a dagger between his shoulders. Higher up, the soldiers found a skeleton; the eagles had picked it clean, but they found on the wrist this chain with the taxman's name on it. That was the taxman who disappeared two years ago. Rocks were thrown down on the soldiers. This is a matter of great urgency. The first smoke of rebellion must be stamped out and that at once. I propose—'

'Why should I be troubled with nonsense like this?' said the prince. 'Send a column of the mountain troops up, those trained to fight in the snow passes. Let the goatherds see them, and they'll dig their money-boxes from under the beds, soon enough' . . .

Down at the harbour the guns thundered, thrice. A chamberlain bowed in at the open door. 'The Emperor's envoy, Your Highness,' he sang. 'The ship has dropped anchor. The following is a list of gifts: a monkey, a web of blue silk, three golden rings (one with a large diamond), a peacock. The ambassador is waiting outside with his retinue. The ambassador *demands* to see you. A matter of the greatest urgency. He has a personal letter from the Emperor himself.'

'I will see him later,' said the prince. 'Tomorrow, perhaps. I find it very exhausting to read bad poetry. That is what I must do today.'

In its silver cage the prince's bird began to sing. Sweet and blind it chortled, trilled, carolled. It had heard footsteps.

The prince made himself blind as the bird. He was aware of the scents, satins, cajolings, kisses fluttering about him. It was said, there had not been a more beautiful woman in the land, ever, than Rosalind.

'Leave me,' said the prince. 'And take that bird with you. I have an important business to attend to.'

Did she weep? There were a few lucent sounds. Then there was silence. The prince opened his eyes. He rang a little bell. A small door under the stairs opened, and a man dressed all in black stood there – a man with a gray gaunt face.

'I will see him now,' said the prince.

The prince followed the man in black along a silent echoing corridor. The man in black opened the door upon a small chapel with two tall candles burning. The morning sun came in, richly stained, through a rose window.

There, between the candles, lay a very old man, dead.

The man in black took a comb from his coat and put to rights a silver curl beside the poet's ear. The smile of the death-man echoed, corruptly, the pure smile of the old poet.

The prince wept.

II

When the first poet entered the music-room with his elegy in his hand, next morning, there at a table was sitting the clerk who didn't like poetry and a young man in a plain gray suit.

'What are you waiting for?' said the clerk. 'Begin.'

The city poet, who had spent much of his life in libraries and taverns, had learned well the structures of Bion and Theocritus. A shepherd had died. A wolf had torn him where he stood faithfully keeping the fold. Now about his gore-splashed body came the shepherdesses and they strewed their dead shepherd with the sweetest flowers of the springtime. And they kissed the cold mouth, one after another. And they came away, weeping. And under the stars country folk gathered branches for the shepherd's funeral pyre: for him who had played so sweetly on his pipe at their dances.

The man in the gray suit nodded. The clerk said to the poet, 'You may go.'

'When,' said the city poet, 'will I come to the palace and take up my duties?'

'The man at the gate,' said the clerk, 'will give you a shilling for a drink' . . .

*   *   *

The second poet came in. He glanced shyly at the great mural behind the table depicting the nine muses round a fountain. His paper shook in his hand.

'Begin,' said the clerk.

The poet belonged to a distant part of the principality, a land of crags and waterfalls and farms and quiet villages.

What is death? went the quiet tenor of his verse. What is it, to die? It is not such a fearful thing. It is nothing to make the cheek blanch. It is simply to be dispersed among the elements, to become one with the dust and the wind and the waters. Dust of the sun, dust of the stars. For the man had been wind, water, fire, dust, before the music of birth summoned him. The flesh grieves and rejoices upon the bone for a few years, then it is free. Come soon, good music of death . . .

The man in the gray coat smiled and nodded. 'Thank you,' said the clerk. 'At the gate you will see a man in a wooden booth. He will pay you three shillings for your fare home, and any lodging you may require.'

'I have written better poems,' said the poet, 'in a cave at home. That cell was too cold.'

The third poet was a ruddy thick-set man with red-and-purple tattoo marks on his wrist. He spoke in the rough accent of the seaports. 'I had a cold night of it,' he said, 'but I've had one or two colder watches up in the crow's-nest.'

'The poem,' said the clerk. 'Begin.'

The poet is the one who has knowledge of trees. The mystery and beauty of the trees were with him from the beginning. A child, he knows what the crib is that is rocking him into sleep, and out beyond sleep to a new day.

He is the friend of birch, alder, willow, ash, oak, rowan, hazel, poplar, fir, yew, pine, blackthorn.

First green leaves whisper overhead. He wears masks of stag, wild boar, bird, hound, hunter. Laughter, mime, song, among the trees! The same sap rises in the child. His little tree arrows pursue the gentleness of the faun.

Leave them. Leave the parents. Leave the breadbaker and the old scarred hunter. Leave the young brother and sister. The hut has become a prison. The song of the trees is calling the young man away.

One morning between branches he glimpsed a face. Such loveliness bird never had, nor wild rose, nor dew on the stone.

She was gone as quickly.

The trees said gravely, 'She is to be your wife.' And the trees shouted in the wind, 'Beware – she is princess and witch and mother and keeper-of-the-dead-and-of-the-unborn and muse. She is torturer and bringer of solace. She is hard as rock, as fleeting as foam.'

The trees sang, 'Make a house for her.'

And they cried, 'Hunt! Tear, now, blood from the animals.'

They murmured, 'Lead the sweetheart through the new door to the fire of logs.'

The poet put an axe to the trees. And the trees cried out in pain, and they fell. And he built the house in a secret part of the forest.

Then his arrows sang through the air and ended in a bitter cry, as the gazelle or the pigeon became a sudden fountain of blood, and fell, and soon after began to rot.

And his jaws gleamed with the fat of wild boar and wood pigeon.

And the great stag fell with a bitter cry like a trumpet under a branch of the oak tree.

When he dragged the great beast home, there outside the door stood the girl. And she kissed him so that the wild honey had never tasted so sweet. And he led her in to his fire.

Because of the beauty of her voice, he did not listen to the tree-language so often. 'You will become an animal like the beasts you kill. Make a clearing about the hut, ten or twelve acres. Turn the trees to things of peace, plough and harrows and sickle and flail. There shall be no more blood.'

But first he made a cradle. The song of the child was more mysterious than the songs and spells of the mother.

The trees spoke less and less. They surged from their roots in the tempest! The branches whispered in the first wind of morning. But they no longer had words for the man.

But the earth sang. The little field in front of his hut sang. Especially in summer his cornfield was one continuous surge of singing, from the time of the first tender stalks to the bronze waves of harvest. The lucency of rain, the shouts of wind, the silence of the sun and stars, were gathered into the earth-song and the earth-promise, *You shall eat in peace next winter, you and your wife and children.*

Now three children sat at his table, and there was a new cry in the cradle.

In winter, beside the fire, the poet-farmer made corn songs. One tree had given him a most precious thing, a fiddle.

The king sent a taxman once a year with a cart and a scroll with names and figures. And that was a bleak day in the glebe. The taxman rode off with his sack of corn, one out of twenty.

'What would we be without the king?' said the woman. 'It is the king who keeps us in safety. Without the king, the foreign soldiers would destroy everything, forest and

cornfield, and burn our thatch. Pay the tax gladly' . . .
Another time she would say, 'That king! He's grinding us
into the dust with his taxes. Build a secret barn in the
forest. Hide half your grain in it' . . .

That was the way of the woman always. She had two
tongues. She had many tongues. She would say to him
bitterly, 'The ox trampled the barley this morning. Why
can't you keep the fence in repair?' . . . The beauty of her
voice when she spoke to the children! Then, an hour later,
'Another child, a sixth! When will there be an end to those
burdens and bitternesses and anxieties. I am broken with
too many children!'

He looked at her. There was a streak of gray in her hair.
Her mouth was sometimes a thin bitter line.

He made a poem in the depths of winter for the new
child. The woman cried – pure joy – lifting the burden
from crib to firelight. The poem rang from her tongue like
a sweet bell for days. Then she was more beautiful than on
the day of that first glimpsing between the branches.

Then, a few days later, 'What will become of us! Life is
stale and barren in this place' . . . (That was the day the
second son had gone to the city to look for work. Three
years before, the firstborn had gone, and no letter or word
had come from him. He might be dead of consumption in
some garret – he might be among the mountains, in the
king's army . . . And the sweet good daughter, she was
coming home under the moon from visiting the
falconer . . .)

She spoke another language, the woman, that he hardly
understood sometimes: the same words as himself, but
they seemed to be dredged out of some deep ancient well
that he knew nothing about, from where water and roots
mingle, deep down in the darkness; and whose meaning
frightened him. More than once he had struck her,

because of her riddling nagging talk. Patiently she had
covered her bleeding mouth, and gone out, and come
back again after an hour as though nothing had happened
– quiet, going about her tasks with eager hands, making
the many tumults of the children into a single disordered
happy chorus.

Then he felt himself a stranger in his own household.

One morning he went for water to the burn for his ox.
Before he plunged in the bucket, he looked into the still
pool. The face that flashed back at him was a stranger's,
old and gaunt and silver-bearded. No: it was his own!
Time was working its will on him. Time was wearing him
to a skeleton. His story would soon be told.

That night he had a dream. His dream was one single
cold image, a shell . . . How can this be, he thought, when
he woke, I have never seen the sea – all my life has been
spent in the forest – and I have dreamt of a shell, a thing I
have never seen and hardly imagined?

He told his wife about the shell-dream. 'Don't trouble
me with your dreams,' she said. 'I have other things to
think about, such as, the pain is in my shoulder now – I'm
nothing but a sack of rheumatics. Dreams, indeed! That
slut of a girl has gone to be a servant, a floor-scrubber, in a
big house, just at the very time I needed her help here,
with the hens and the goats and the young ones.'

The pure clean image throbbed in his mind all morning; by late afternoon it had faded.

He was selecting a branch to make a new flail when the
wind that stirs sometimes at sunset went through the
trees. The trees spoke to him for the first time since he had
put spade to tilth. 'You don't think, man, that you're to
stay here for ever. This is only a station on the way. Your
next place is far from here. Did you not know that? You've
been preparing for it all your life. Once we were friends,

man. You have largely forgotten us, except when you want firewood or a door or a new flail. But we will never forget you. We are to do a beautiful thing together, you and the trees. The work is three-quarters finished, man.'

It was because he was so tired that he was hearing the voice of the forest. (Now, as year followed year, he was more and more tired at the day's end.)

He cut down a branch and took it to his barn where he had a work-bench and tools.

That night, he dreamed of a bird, a white-breasted bird with gray plumage. It was an ocean wanderer. In his dream he smelt the sea air wafted from its wings. It drifted, the bird, between gray sky and gray sea.

He woke. His wife was turning in pain beside him.

He did not tell her at breakfast-time his dream of the sea bird. She had other to do than listen to dreams. She was scolding the youngest child for his lateness. 'You haven't even washed your face. What will the school-master say? Do you want to grow up to be like your father, eh, an old poor cottar? Hurry along with you.'

And she had to sit down, the old one, because the words and the worry and the work of cooking the porridge had all but exhausted her.

He put his hand on her shoulder. The kissing times were long past. 'Get into the field,' she said. 'Do what you can with the crop, such as it is. The king will be wanting his tax.'

Another night he dreamed of a fish.

It was one of those thin harvests, unnourished by rain, burnt by the sun's face day after day.

The window darkened. The man had hardly gone over the door with his sickle when the rain came, a silver teeming out of a dark cloud, that lasted all morning. He could hear the earth drinking this cold sweet refreshment.

Still the rain fell. He stood at the edge of his field. He glanced back. The face of his wife was looking through the window at the violets growing among the corn and at the rainbow between the hill and the forest. She looked as she had done that first morning, among the apple-blossom: all the eagerness, sweetness, promise.

He left his sickle against a stone and went back to the house.

'First the sun!' she cried. 'Now the rain – if this rain goes on there'll be nothing but mush out there. I'm tired of it all! You should be cutting – the taxman will be here at the end of the month.'

The corn sang under his sickle all next day. Dying under the circling edge, the stalks uttered in golden syllables the great song of the earth.

The man, tired as he was, made a corn-song on his fiddle after supper.

The woman didn't say whether the song was good or bad. She sat in her chair at the other side of the fire, and seemed to be utterly taken up with the gaunt inscape of her life.

(And the chairs had been given by the trees, and the table, and the bed, and the door and the window frames and rafters – and the tumbling flames in the hearth – and the fiddle trembling now into silence. Yet the trees promised something beyond . . .)

The old man smoked his pipe. He sat, alone, with his pipe made of briar, smoking and thinking, long after the woman had gone to bed.

In his dream that night, he was troubled by grayness, coldness, a bitterness on his lips, a huge perilous trackless unquiet waste, and mingling with the menace that girdled him a lucent murmurous many-voiced bell-brimming congregation of sounds, near and far. He was afraid.

Then came on the wind the multifoliate whispering of the forest – 'It is the west. We will meet you there. We will be your friends still when it is time for you to set out.'

Now there was no one on the little farm in the forest clearing but his wife and himself. The youngest son had gone away – how long ago? – and was working in the new iron-works in the town higher up the river where they paid him in silver coins every Friday. At first he had sent a few occasional letters, but for more than a year there had been silence.

One night in early winter he threshed corn in the barn by candle-light.

When he got back to the house he found her lying on the floor, cold. The face that had once seemed to him so beautiful was wrenched all to one side, as though she had fought hard against Death.

He put on the pot to heat his supper ale; he put bread and cheese on a plate. After he had eaten and drunk he closed her eyes and tied her jaw, and composed her hands.

Then he went back to the barn and made a coffin of boards. He worked all night. 'Thank you, tree,' he said. When he carried the coffin back to the house the winter sun was rising. He had to set the coffin at all angles before he got it in through the door at last. When he lifted her to put her into the coffin she was as light as a sack of twigs.

'There might be visitors,' he said. 'I won't nail the lid down yet.'

A bird came and looked in through the window. This was the bird she had fed on crumbs and milk all winter. Then the bird flew onto the edge of the coffin and looked at the dead face. Then the bird flew out and away among the trees.

The man dug a grave under a tree.

When he came back to nail down the coffin lid he saw that the bitterness and pain had melted from her face. She

looked remote and serene as a star. There seemed to be
the beginnings of a smile on her face. Hurriedly he drove
the twelve nails in, one after the other. He lit two candles,
one at the head and one at the feet.

Five men came next day at noon from the hill and the
forest. They buried her and covered her over with earth.

Afterwards they sat round the fire and drank for a
while. A few words were spoken: praise of the dead.

One by one the mourners went away.

The first snowflake of winter clung to the pane, a gray
glimmering moth, then melted to a drop of water.

The old poet took down his fiddle:

> 'How long is it with you, fiddle?'
> A short dance.
> My songs go into the silence.
>
> 'How long, first blossom of snow?'
> Not long.
> I seek down to the roots, a drop.
>
> 'Do you feel time in you, stone?'
> A slow throb,
> I am dust and corn again.
>
> 'Candle, your flame is out.'
> Gone back to the sun.
> I have done what the night begged of me.
>
> 'How late is it with you, star?'
> I spill out.
> Like stone and flower and crystal of snow.
>
> 'The lass didn't stay long.'
> Long enough
> For taste of honey, then salt and cinder.

'*Forest, be still my friend.*'
Dying
We give the fiddle, the fire, the ship.

Then the old poet drank another cup of ale, and went to his bed.

He slept. He dreamed.

A young man had been building a little ship above the tide-mark, among rocks studded with shells and tasselled with seaweed.

The work had been going on for a long time, and now it was almost finished. The dream was filled with sea sounds: the shifting murmurous bell-like thunderous chorus, shell-echoes, cry of sea-mew, silent fish-songs. But now the sounds came purer and richer with the clustering of the first shadows. The man was putting his tools into an oak box. He brushed a wood shaving from his sleeve. There lay the little ship, all ready for launching, the sail furled at the mast, the name *Hesper* cut into the stern. A few men were on their way to push her down the slipway. They should hurry, the launchers – the sun was touching the western horizon. The builder-skipper was urgent to be sea-borne . . . As he waited among the rocks, an image drifted across his mind: black trees in a wintry forest, a hut with no smoke from the chimney, a grave with a little wooden cross – strange, what fancies come! – the dweller by the sea had never seen a forest in his life, but the snow on the black branches put a shiver through his soul . . . Soon he heard voices on the shore, approaching. The sun was down. The first star was in the sky. The launchers approached, laughing shadows.

'Is this all?' said the clerk, mocking. 'You haven't finished already?'

Gravely the poet put his manuscript on the table, and bowed.

The man in the gray coat rose and gravely shook the poet by the hand.

'In the first place,' said the clerk, 'this is not a poem at all. Where are the rhymes? I was not aware of any of the usual rhythms. The thing had no strict stanza-form, that I could see.'

The man in gray leaned across and whispered to the clerk.

The clerk signed his name on a form. 'The treasury clerk will pay you a sovereign on production of this chit. Your manuscript will be retained.'

'I haven't got the job, then?' said the sailor-poet.

The clerk shook his head.

The fourth poet came from the college in the city.

He breathed on his spectacles, polished them, adjusted his floppy necktie and the sleeve of his velvet jacket, united a silken string from his manuscript and unrolled it, made a flourish with it as if he was presenting a white rose. He cleared his throat. He chanted, *Elegy*.

> 'When are you coming, Cleotas
> To drink wine with me: to sit
>> Either in my garden
>> Between the sundial
>
> And the stone boy at the fountain, while bees
> Go tipsily among the white roses
>> Or in the study, where
>> Virgil in marble smiles
>
> Upon my scrolls and manuscripts?'
> This letter from a friend
>> I read this morning, happy.
>> And then the postscript

'The old laureate, master-singer, is dead.'
'Dear Sylvanus,' I answered,
      'I cannot come to your villa ·
      Nor wash nor eat nor sleep

Until at the palace I have
Stanched with elegy the great
      Golden grief of the prince
      And after, linger perhaps

Stayed by a golden gratitude.
Sylvanus, dear friend, next month
      You will drink from my crystal cup,
      Augustus having bestowed
      Prudently the golden laurel.'

The man in the gray coat looked for a long time at his fingers' ends.

The clerk said, 'I think you can go now.'

The poet said, 'Should I not stay? Or should I go to my room at the university and wait for the official summons? My books and papers are already packed. I have written my letter of resignation.'

'The paymaster's clerk will give you a fee for your trouble,' said the clerk. 'Please leave the poem on the table.'

There was a brief silence.

'It is unfortunate,' said the poet, 'that my elegy had to be cast before a pig and a gray bureaucrat. It was for the prince's ear.'

He made as if to tear his poem in pieces. Then he paused, rolled up the paper and tied it again with the white frayed ribbon, and put it inside his coat. He curled his lip at them, and left.

'I am a poet from the mountains. I come from a simple good people, now (it so happens) in distress. I keep goats and a falcon.'

'Never mind that,' said the clerk. 'Read your elegy.'

The mountain poet read his elegy. It was uttered in an outlandish dialect, so that the man in gray had to lean forward, furrowing his brows; and the clerk kept shaking his head at the crudity of language and delivery.

The soul of the dead laureate lingered in the palace. Nobody recognised it. The prince looked through the crystal of the soul of his laureate and saw nothing.

'Well,' said the old dead singer, 'now I will have what I have always longed for, the freedom to go where I want. I have long been tired of dukes and ladies and flunkeys.'

The dead poet lingered long in the heart of the city. He longed to drink wine in the wineshops and eat plain bread.

The people looked cunning and cruel to him, and beautiful, as if they were corrupt angels, or animals burdened with knowledge of forbidden things.

No one looked at him.

He heard sounds of great beauty. It must be the organ in the cathedral. The silver soul flowed in under the arch. A man was playing on an organ but no sound issued from it. Later, at the foot of a steep alley he saw a poor man playing on a tin whistle. Four or five children danced about him, laughing. But no sound came from the tin whistle. The poet cried, 'I'm a music-maker too!' But neither the musician nor the dancers paid any attention to him.

The poet wandered out through one of the five gates of the city. Normally, citizens leaving or entering had to show their passes, but the spirit went through unchallenged.

Beyond the city, he heard the music again. Sometimes

he lost the music but never for long. Always it went before him.

He passed through villages and little woods, beside rivers, over hills, through cornfields and vineyards. The people of the land seemed to move to this mysterious music. Milkmaids, swineherds, farmers, blacksmiths, horsemen, children, inn-keepers: all their actions were governed by the universal song.

Why was this music so much more beautiful than the music of the court musicians: who had often honoured him by setting his poems to their lutes and oboes?

The music drew the crystal desolate soul among hill farms and among little villages high up, near the snow-line, and there the music lingered, and never had it sounded so pure and sweet and enchanting.

But there was something wrong. The mountain people seemed not to hear the music. Their movements were halt and maimed. The soul of the poet came among them and looked closely into the faces of those good people. He saw suffering and hunger and oppression.

A young man said, 'Tomorrow the taxmen are coming again.'

And a woman said, 'The barns are empty.'

A child said, 'Why do the birds have plenty to eat and we go hungry?'

An old man said, 'I curse this bad prince in his castle.'

A beautiful girl said, 'We have sent down complaints. They never get to the city. They are torn up before the prince gets a chance to read the petitions. Now our poet has gone down. Perhaps a pure word can touch the heart of the prince.'

The mountain was vested in song. The people in their misery did not hear it. It had been taken from them. They went here and there with broken bewildered mutinous steps.

The soul of the famous laureate understood then that his life and his works had been a lie. The odes and sonnets and rondels he had made to please the prince's ear were poor rags compared to the great fabric of song that is the breath and soul of a nation: except here and there, from time to time, when by fraud or malice or negligence a flaw and a shredding appears in the fabric: as now, in this loyal mountain village, when usurers and politicians had come between prince and people, and their blades had gone through warp and weft, till the loom was all tatters.

The soul of the dead poet grieved. He longed to tell the crippled folk that the prince was a good man, and would listen to the poet they had sent, and soon afterwards they would be part of the great music again.

But to them, in their misery, the laureate's soul was only a gleam in the snow, the sound of the fall of a waterdrop from an icicle's tip.

But he thought he ought to stay with them until their poet – who was falconer and goatherd also – returned from the court.

The mountain poet set his poem, with a kind of rough courtesy, on the table where the man in the gray coat and the clerk sat.

The man in the gray coat looked as if he had been struck across the face.

'I hardly understood a word of the rigmarole,' said the clerk.

The gray man tugged at the clerk's sleeve and whispered urgently to him.

'Five hundred sovereigns!' cried the clerk.

The poet from the mountains was standing there as though he expected fetters and rack.

'Listen,' said the clerk, 'you have not got the job. The treasurer at the gate is to give you a wallet with five hundred sovereigns in it. The money is not for you, it is for the village. (Well, you can have one gold piece, for expenses.) Tell your people the prince is coming to see them. He will come tomorrow. He will come alone, and you are to guide him.'

Now it was the mountain poet who looked as if he had been struck: but with a branch of apple-blossom.

The sixth poet entered.

'Begin,' said the clerk. 'I hope it is a short lyric. There have been one or two would-be epic poets here today.'

The man in gray looked into the still face of the young man with the cluster of golden curls about head and chin. The lips lay light on one another – the upper lip fringed with slight golden feathers that curled away on either side – a sensuous eager lightly-latched seal it was, that mouth.

'I said, begin,' said the clerk.

The young poet laid a blank sheet of paper on the table.

'This is nothing,' said the clerk.

'Perhaps the poet can't write,' said the man in gray. 'Many of the greatest poets who ever lived couldn't write. I expect Homer couldn't write. The ballad-singers were illiterate. Can you write, man?'

The poet nodded. He could write; he knew letters and scripts. He smiled: but too well he knew how to write.

'Perhaps you are dumb?'

A slow shake of the head, so that a corn-coloured ringlet of hair over his ear was displaced. He could speak (the implication was) when there was something worthwhile to say: when there was somebody worthwhile to listen.

'You impudent scoundrel!' cried the clerk.

The man in gray said, 'Pass me the file the Ministry of Arts sent concerning this man' . . . He read the file while the clerk muttered to himself and glared from the poet to the file that the man in gray was turning, sheet after sheet, and back again.

'There is a covering letter from the minister – "This young poet is considered to be the most brilliant of a group of young poets whose work is read and admired in the cafés and salons of the avant-garde. For a year and more he has written nothing and published nothing. He has, as the enclosed letter of application shows, dedicated the rest of his life to silence. Yet he has asked to be considered for the post of laureate. Because of his great renown, I have in a sense been forced to place his name on the list. If Your Highness cannot unlock his lips, no one can. I enclose herewith his mysterious letter"' . . .

The papers rustled. The clerk scowled and muttered. The golden-haired poet stifled a yawn.

'This is the letter that the applicant wrote: "Why should I not have written poems, hundreds of poems? I have been in love. I have seen the birds and daffodils returning after winter. (And the snow was beautiful, too, and the stars.) I have looked into an old dead face. All these things struck poetry from me, as if I was the legendary harp hung in the branches to make beautiful the changing winds of time. They were considered by the young intelligent critics to be excellent poems, the like of which (in form and texture) had not existed before. My pulses raced with joy and pride at having made such lyrics. Not for long. After a day or a month, or a year, always I was disappointed. In the silence that followed a poem dead echoes came back, again and again: I was angry, I was hurt, I was afraid. The praisings went on, louder than before. Prizes and honours were put into my hands. I tore up the new manuscripts, I stained the wind with ruins of verse. But they have existed and so in a sense they cannot be lost, those bits of imperfection. All they have done is sully the crystal of silence. I am sorry for that crime. I carry a weight of words with me always, like a prisoner forever shifting stones in a quarry. I will be summoned to the palace. I will be asked to make a poem for a prince – an elegy perhaps for the old poet that he loved so much. I will sit all night in a cold cell with a candle at the wall and a sheet of paper and a pot of ink and a pen. In the morning I will bring a work of great beauty to the prince, a blank paper, silence. After the perfect poem – which no poet ever will write – the second-best poem is silence. That I will offer to the prince. The poem will be in every way better than the scribblings of the other candidates – so unmistakably superior that the prince, who has thought long and hard about the mystery of verse, will name me as his laureate: of this I have small doubt. He will give orders at once for the laureate's room with its tapestries and engravings and clavichord to be made ready for me. I request that I be returned to the cell where I wrote the second-best poem on the night of my examination, that all-but-seamless splendour, a nothingness on a sheet of parchment. Perhaps I could have a small fire of coals on a winter night. A little bread and wine will keep me alive for a year or two, with a fish or a few apples on a feast day. There should be a window where I can see the stars. And there, if fate wills it, I will at last come to some kind of accommodation with word and world"' . . .

The clerk's face had gone a kind of magenta colour with rage. His tongue could hardly break through his clenched teeth. At last he managed, 'You shameless scoundrel! . . . You will answer for this . . . And that before the sun goes down' . . .

'It will be cold in his cell by the time the sun goes down,' said the man in gray. 'See that a fire is lit for the new laureate. Give him a jug of wine and a lamp. There must be two chairs – I expect the prince will want to come and sit with his poet sometimes. They will be sessions of sweet silent thought; a chessboard might be a good idea.'

The man in gray stood up and held out his hand. The poet kissed it.

The clerk looked as if he had just awakened from a crazy dream.

Rosalind said, 'So there's a new laureate!' . . . How do I know? I met him in the garden an hour ago – at least, I was in the garden and he was leaning out of that narrow window, three storeys up. Young and very handsome. Of course I called up to him. And got no answer? . . . How should I get no answer? – he has a mouth. He threw a kiss down to me. *Poet*, I called up to him, *I'm expecting a few sonnets and rondeaux from you soon* . . . He has a grave beautiful voice, your new poet. *I will make you a poem, but it may take some time*, he called down to me from that cell.

'Just our two voices in the garden. The birds lodged in the branches like little stones.'

III

The prince was sent into exile, to a small island in a northern sea, and left there to fend for himself.

The island was bare, storm-beaten, inhospitable; well away from sea routes.

The barest necessities of life were set ashore with him: cooking pots, a few cups and plates, steel and tinder to make a fire, saw and hammer and bag of nails, hooks to catch fish, seeds of potato, turnip, carrot, a few blankets, a few jars, chessboard, a blank notebook.

The boat pushed off. The prince was left alone on the shore.

The country had been heavily defeated two years previously by the armies of the Emperor. A peace was dictated and signed, and the imperial armies withdrew, except for a garrison here and there on the frontier.

The prince, after the defeat, lived very much as before. But in the cities especially there was hunger, discontent, disease, a wild uncontrollable inflation. Men with burning eyes and incantatory speeches harangued the shabby mobs in city square and seaport. The people suddenly turned and surged, wave after wave, against the palace walls. Guardsmen fired into the yelling crowds. Men and women and children fell and were trampled on by the horses.

Then the cavalry rode out, splendid in scarlet and gold, and their sabres herded those lawless hordes back to their factories, work-benches, bread-queues, garrets, cellars.

Clever minds, cold intellects were, all this bitter while, turning the shapeless violence into an organised machine. In the various trades and professions little cells of activists were implanted, and the rage and helplessness cohered about these nuclei, and the nuclei were organised by one subtle incisive pellucid mind into a blueprint of revolution. Even the most backward conservative classes of the nation were encouraged to graft cells within the new revolutionary organism. Thus there were peasants' communes, and a commune of mountain foresters, and even a hawkers' commune. The writers' representative was the poet who had written the Horatian elegy. Now he wrote marching songs for the new tatterdemalion army.

The turning of the tide came when the soldiers and sailors formed their own communes. They spat at the colonels. They turned their guns on the commodores and captains. They marched, singing, to join the mobs. And the girls wreathed their rifles with flowers.

The next day the prince and the poet played chess in the little music-room in the palace. But four soldiers stood at the door, two outside and two inside. A fifth soldier thumped on the magnificent piano and sang barrack-room songs.

'I expect,' said the prince, 'we will be shot. It is a pity. What if the perfect poem were to come to you in the time between the bullet's leaving the gun and striking your heart?' . . . And he laughed.

Down below, soldiers had broken into the cellar. Nearly all the soldiers in the courtyard were drunk. One brought an armful of bottles to the music-room.

'There are glasses,' said the prince, 'in the cupboard over there.'

The cut crystal glasses were filled and they all drank, the prince and the poet too.

The soldier pianist came over to the chess table. He raised his glass. 'You were a prince,' said he, 'and I was a clerk before they took me for a soldier. But we're all men, and we must all die.'

'That's true,' said the prince, rising and pledging the soldiers. 'Some of us will die sooner than others.'

'There ought to be a poem in this,' said the prince after his third glass. 'All this rage and confusion could be distilled to a pageful of words more vivid than a hundred books of history.'

'Open another bottle,' yelled a soldier at the door.

At that very moment, a dozen sober men with intelligent faces and cold eyes were discussing the prince's fate in a bare cold schoolroom that was the powerhouse of the revolution for the time being.

Ought he to be tried before a people's tribunal? Ought he to be shot out of hand? – most of the committee inclined to such a quick clean end. One man with a great black beard and a laughing face was of opinion that the prince ought to be kept alive, 'let live as a citizen among the three million other citizens of the state', only he would have to work to earn his bread. 'I suggest,' said the jovial revolutionary, 'that he work as a labourer in the iron mines in the north' . . . There was laughter round the table, but the Father of the Revolution (who had been an eminent lawyer in the old state) raised a cold palm, and the laughter ceased. 'There will be a time for merriment – and for music and dancing too – but not today.'

They were discussing which soldier to put in charge of the execution party, when one of the committee who had been silent hitherto spoke. He represented the mountain people; in his youth he had been a well-known poet, until the sufferings of his people had diverted his energies into politics and revolution. He urged mitigation – exile on a lonely inaccessible island rather than death.

The committee listened with cold attentive faces.

A team of geologists was set down on a remote island, a century later, to take away some rocks. It was known that the island was rich in uranium.

They gathered their samples quickly. Then they had an hour to spare before the launch returned for them.

One of the geologists, in an autobiography published when he was a distinguished old man, wrote a brief account of the visit to the island.

'I discovered signs of habitation, viz., the remains of a wooden hut above the shore. The door hung on a single hinge. Inside I discovered: (a) a rough-hewn table and two benches; (b) a wooden recess that might have been a bed; (c) a cupboard with a few empty stone jars; (d) a black hearthstone and a chimney-piece, much dilapidated; (e) a hammer, a saw, a bag with a few nails, an iron pot, all badly rusted; (f) an oil lamp; (g) on the table a chessboard with the pieces still on it; (h) a notebook under the bed, much eaten by mildew and salt.

'Outside the hut I found a midden composed mainly of fish-bones, wood-ash, broken shells of mussel, limpet, winkle, lobster and crab. There were no animal remains.

'On the summit of the hill was a mouldering cairn. Near the cairn, a bone knife with scratchings here and there on the hilt.

'The island is a rough circle of cliffs three kilometres or so in diameter, except for the break made by the beach. Where the cliff ends abruptly above the sand there is a cave. Here too there were signs of habitation: fish-bones and shells and a crude pipe made of whalebone.

'Very likely the island was used by fishermen as an occasional shelter from storms.

'I took the notebook back with me; I doubt if anyone will be able to decipher it. It is lodged now in the university library' . . .

NOTEBOOK

I must have been in the island for six weeks or so before I was aware of his presence.

A month before, a young whale had stranded on a reef – it died. Quickly it began to putrefy. When there was west in the wind, a medley of stenches wafted into my hut, and I had to go outside, away from the stream of worsening stink, to breathe pure air. But soon hide and flesh and blubber withered from it, and the skeleton began to show through.

I did not see what I could do with this amazing articulation of bones.

I looked out over the sea-banks one morning. The tide had ebbed far out. A young man, up to his knees in water, was working inside the framework of the whale. He plucked out bone after bone and examined it.

I called down to him. He paid no attention.

It had been made very clear to me that I was to be alone – utterly alone – on the island.

He gouged at one long hollow bone with some kind of gimlet, making holes, it seemed.

I went down the sea path to meet him. It was as much a matter of curiosity as of comfort to me, to know that I was to have at least one companion.

When I got nearer, I saw that it was my poet! I ran to greet him – I slithered and all but fell in the swathes of seaweed. 'Welcome!' I cried. 'Oh, how glad I am to see you! I did not know. Where have you been all this time? A hundred welcomes, dear friend.'

He turned; he blew a harsh note at me from his whalebone pipe. The dotterels on the shore scattered, running this way and that, from the bruise he made in the air with that sound.

I invited him up to the all-but-finished hut above the shore. It was a cold morning. He could share the fire and a little food with me. No: he shook his head. He gestured towards the cave under the crag. The entrance was festooned with a piece of net. The door was piled with driftwood. He pointed it out to me – this was his house – but he did not invite me inside. He did not, in fact, seem pleased to see me in the least.

(But how could this be? I had passed the cave many times, and there had been no sign of habitation. Where had he been for half a year? He had not, to my knowledge, been set ashore with me. Yet that voyage into exile is confused – like a dream – I must have been heavily drugged for days on the sea. I woke – and in the dregs of the dream discovered that I was in process of constructing a wooden hut, and that I had learned how to light a fire and cook a hare and a pigeon . . . I woke. And a well of joy opened in me. I was man the maker, man the hunter . . . I discovered too that I had broken out a square of soil beside the hut and planted vegetables: there were a few ordered ranks of green. I would not die of starvation after all. I remembered, further back in the dream, a few vague timorous attempts to catch fish from the rock – no luck with that . . . The poet must have been set ashore on a cove at the far end of the island.)

He blew a few ugly notes, like an insult, and went into the cave.

In the next week or so, I plundered the whale for bones that have been of great use to me ever since.

I knew then from the start that he did not want me down at the tide-line. That was his territory.

His pipe screeched and moaned, seven or eight times a day.

I made a spade of whalebone, and a hoe and other passable implements.

Presently an easterly storm broke and scattered what was left of the whale.

All this was in the early days of our exile. I met him once or twice after that first encounter, near the rockpools. 'I hope you are remembering my poem,' I would say lightly in passing.

He actually waved to me one morning. He was rifling the pool for whelks. Then he remembered – the shore was his – he gave me a brusque dismissal, from afar, with his hand.

And I, who had come to gather whelks too, went up to my hut with an empty basket.

My garden promises well. The cabbages and potatoes will be good, I think. Onions doubtful. I think some kind of worm has got into the carrots.

Now I know just how much seaweed to nourish the garden with, though the seaweed is grudged me.

There are rabbits in plenty, and pigeons. How long did it take me to learn snaring and neck-breaking? I remember how I retched and retched, to begin, gutting the creatures.

I never learned to fish. I watch from my door. Silver arcs from the offshore rock. The poet is catching trout or mackerel. He keeps that treasure to himself.

Those screechings – they set the teeth on edge . . .

He has a pipe made of a hollow bone. I think he is trying to imitate bird calls.

It did not take him long to climb up and down the perilous stone cliff-ladders, to the bird ledges.

He has a good living in the summer: fish and eggs.

Some night in early winter – an easterly blowing – I'll hear his knock at the door. He has come for broth or stew, hot from the pot and fire.

I have not been to his cave. I am sure he eats his fish and eggs raw. Earth and fire are mine.

Silence between us. I set the pieces on the chessboard. We play for an hour.

He tilts his head. Ah, the wind is less in the chimney – it has moved into the north or west.

He ties his coat round him and goes. Thanklessly, like a dog.

The lucent stillness of a winter morning in the north.

There, breaking it, his bird-shrills. The birds fall silent, then make louder outcry than before.

I have made things out of bone too – knives, and a spade for the garden and a heavier spade for the peat-bog. I have mentioned the whale that blundered ashore, that first summer. I plundered the skeleton. I was allowed to do that, after the poet had discovered his musical instrument in it. The skeleton was left to me, grudgingly. There is one knife I am still working on; I think it will be used for nothing; I think of it as ceremonial, a sign of my lordship of an island – I reproduce as well as I can the ancient heraldry – sun and ship and eagle – on the hilt. How Rosalind would have laughed at those scratchings of mine, compared with the original richly-dyed quarterings on tapestry and chapel window, and the grave considered carvings on sundial, lintel, tomb: the work of master craftsmen over generations.

I take down the ceremonial knife at the solstices and the equinoxes. I put it in my belt then, climbing up with a few pieces of driftwood and peat to the beacon on the hill.

Up here, one can see the whole round ocean. The fire will blaze, some day. The passing ship will turn, will anchor off the stacks. We will be free.

'Listen,' I say to the poet, 'the next ship that comes, we are free' . . . He smiles, shakes his head, points to the chess-board on the shelf.

'When are you going to give me my poem?' I say. 'Soon?'

No ship will pass, in such a tempest as howled about the hut all night.

For the first time, he slept at my fire. He was gone in the morning, when I woke.

When did the drought come: the seventh or the eighth summer? It was unexpected; there is a plenitude of rain all the year round in this latitude. Most summers, rain and sun apportion the time so well between them – if capriciously, now and then – that the crop roots, and water comes sparkling from the rock fissure. One takes it for granted that sun and cloud will always conspire together for one's good. That year the sun came up day after day, the gold chariot went up the blue field of sky, higher every day, and went down into the western ocean, in a vacant red glow.

It was pleasant, the first rainless month.

Then, as I saw the wilting cabbage leaves, and water came reluctantly from the spring, I began to be uneasy.

I climbed to the hilltop. There was not a cloud to be seen.

It would have been a comfort to talk to my fellow-islander, even if I got no answer. He was not to be seen. But I heard his pipe from here and there: now he was learning to make passable imitations of tern and lapwing and fulmar.

I might glimpse him on a cliff ledge with birds all about him, putting eggs into his bag.

The rabbits seemed to be scarcer that summer too.

Forty days beyond the solstice, I began to be afraid. I went to the rock spring one morning – it had dried up.

I put my ear to the rock. The spring was still there, I could hear the water songs deep down, but the spring sang to itself alone. There was only a slight moisture at the fissure – I wet my mouth.

Certainly, if the rain didn't come soon, I would die in the

winter. The vegetables in my planticru were like a troop of diseased outcasts, beggars, gangrels.

No, I would die, long before winter, of thirst.

Two nights later – the sun now a yellow scab in the sky – I went down to the cave, carrying my empty bucket. I called – he wasn't inside. I ventured in – never since the first days had I dared do this; I wasn't welcome, he drew his brows against me if I so much as strayed to that part of the shore.

That plundering of the whale's skeleton, years since – that still rankles with him, deeply. For many weeks afterwards, he had made wide circles about me. The sea and the things of the sea were his. But the bones – at last that had been permitted, I could take what bones I wanted. He shrugged. But still, he wasn't pleased. I will not yield to him in this – the whole island, including *the shore,* is mine . . .

A runnel of fresh water issued from the roof of the cave and ran down one darkling wall.

I put my bucket to it.

A new shadow was added to the shadows of the cave. I turned. There he stood at the entrance, carrying fish on a string.

He gestured to me to get out – to leave my bucket and get out! I obeyed.

I waited on the sand outside. Presently he came out with my bucket three-quarters full of water.

I put out my hand for it.

He slowly tilted the bucket, water splashed out, he upended it, he squandered that treasury of crystal and opals and pearls at my feet.

Then he handed me the empty bucket.

I swung the bucket at his head. He avoided it – he is lither and stronger than I am, much – and he leaned against the cliff laughing.

But if I had had my knife in my belt, I would have made an end of him.

Disloyalty! Ingratitude! Hatred! I had never in my life, back in the hut, spent such a bitter night. At last I must have slept, though my heart was a limbeck of poisonous thoughts and desires. I woke to hear a steady rhythm, a low drumming, on the roof. I heard, under it, the earth drinking. I went to the door and was blinded and soaked by a cold wet drench of rain.

I went back to bed. *The rain is my friend, at least. She might delay but she always comes at last. Welcome, rain.*

But it may be too late for the vegetables in my yard. Hunger might see me off yet . . .

When I woke in the morning, it was raining still, though not so heavily. The hill through the window was like a ghost.

I opened the door. There on the step lay two fat haddocks. Bird notes came from the far side of the island.

In the rain, now gently falling, I went to look at my vegetable patch. That wretched fairground of tramps and outcasts looked doubly wretched.

The clouds thinned and shredded; the sun came out. I would have run to the spring but for the pain in my haunchbone that had troubled me since the end of last winter. Ah! The spring was gushing with cold sweet streams, and the rock throbbed with water music . . .

After three or four days of sun and rain, my plantation was a green fertile fairground. My cabbages hid in their curls water-drops like pearls.

(Two autumns ago, I had taken the precaution of sheltering the beacon on the hilltop under a piece of canvas sail I had found on the shore.)

That drought was many summers ago: how long?

Since then age and privation and sickness have woven gray harsh threads through me. Often the pain in my legs is so bad that I can only hirple here and there on a stick. My beard is more silver-gray than black now.

Then explain this to me. How is it that the poet is not a day older than when we were set down on this shore? The fearsome crags on the west side of the island are nothing to him – he has the complete freedom of that chaos of broken steps and ladders. And the sea – he will stand up to his waist in the sea like some young god, and the sea-glitter makes even more beautiful the bronze of his beard and hair. And I swear the bird notes he takes out of that bone pipe grow purer with time.

No one would guess that we were born in the same year, the poet and I.

Yet he must live in misery in that cave, compared to the crude comfort of my hut.

The east winds in winter, they scour him out of his cave. I know, roughly, the times he will be here, shivering in the door, blue with cold, his nostrils stretching with the incense coming from the pot of rabbit stew over the hearth.

Afterwards, always, the game of chess.

In the mornings, having lain before the fire all night, if the storm continues, he will be gone – if not back to his cave, to some other more sheltered fissure along the shore.

If I wake to find him buttoning his coat, on one of those rare mornings, I say, 'I hope you haven't forgotten my poem. You owe me a poem. I hope you are working hard at it.'

Then he is gone, my silent Ariel, and old Prospero puts on pain and age and wretchedness with his clothes.

At least Prospero had his Miranda to comfort him and give him sweet anxieties. One day I saw a girl on the shore. I looked again – she was gone.

My eyesight is going too, possibly. Or there are blurrings in my mind . . .

There is a small loch at the far end of the island. It is fed by a burn that flows down from the hills. A few swans drift among the reeds and the green islets. On summer evenings I try to catch trout in the loch.

I often see the poet at the loch. He sees me coming, he edges round to be if possible on the far shore.

I think the swans attract him. He looks at them among the glittering water. One winter, ice covered most of the loch. The swans were closed in an ever-narrowing circle of cold blue water, like too many princesses in a crystal prison. Then a thaw came, ugly and wet, and unlocked them.

He cannot learn any songs from a swan.

It is dangerous to go near a swan's nest. With a blow of the wing it can break a man's arm. There he squatted one day in spring, his arm about the neck of a swan, silence in silence wound.

I turned and climbed up to the beacon on the hill, carrying a fardel of dry heather to add to it.

For the rest of that summer, I had only a glimpse of him.

I know he caught many fish that summer. Apart from the one and only offering, long ago, he keeps all the fish he catches.

I have small success with the trout in the loch.

The mysterious, lovely, and painful year of the women: when was that?

It was later than the year of the drought, I know, because in my body I was much feebler.

Was it the year that the poet began to build a boat? It was a thing to laugh at, that boat, a cluster of boards and bits of fish-box of different sizes, held together with lengths of tarred string.

At first I thought he had built it for escape – one big wave would have scattered the thing.

A part of me wished it would happen: that he would drown and I would be free of him.

In the end he had to dismantle the crazy thing and reassemble it in the shape of a raft. It wasn't for escape, it was to catch lobsters and crabs further out in the bay. On summer evenings, in the calm gray waters, he drifted here and there, along the reef, sinking his creels or hauling them. Even so, the raft looked dangerous enough.

If anything happened to him, would I miss the bird calls? Would I miss the occasional winter game of chess?

The name Miranda, never spoken, lingered in some chamber of the mind . . .

And there, one morning, she was, on the far side of the beach, half-a-mile away. A young woman was kneeling at a rockpool, her arms up to the elbows in water, swilling and gathering. What was she after? Either it was shellfish, or she was washing clothes.

That morning I had come down to the shore to look for driftwood. Strictly speaking, this was the poet's territory. He was far from pleased if he caught me gathering 'his' driftwood. Let me burn my peat!

I dropped the sea-bleached board I had found, and went as fast as I could across the stretch of sand. I couldn't go fast, one of my legs was weak and withered after years of arthritis. Miranda was still there, about her task.

I laboured on, the breath harsh in my mouth.

A piercing bird note was blown from the far end of the island.

Once, when I paused for breath, I saw the white oval of her face. She had seen me coming. She pushed back her long black hair, and bent over the rockpool again.

It was a fine summer morning. The sun had thrown a silver sparkling net over the sea, it looked with blazing face into one or other of the many rockpools, as on I hurried.

Now I was near enough to see this Miranda plain. I stopped, to get my breath. Another fifty yards and I would be at her side. She looked straight at me, and she was Rosalind.

I called to her. She pushed back her dark clusters of hair, and smiled. Slowly she got to her feet.

At that moment the sun fell straight into the triangular pool she had been working at. Flashes of intolerable brightness! – among which she vanished, a ghost or a vision.

When I got to the rockpool she wasn't there. *Someone* had been there, there was no doubt about it. Among a cluster of lucent rockpools, it was the only disturbed one. Small ripples washed still over the stone. And there were wet footprints on the rocks.

'Rosalind!' I called, three or four times.

There was no answer.

What was I to make of this? I do not believe in ghosts. Rosalind was dead, most likely – shot in the hunting-lodge I had bought for her at the edge of the forest. Or if she wasn't dead, arrived at some accommodation with the revolutionaries, she might be doing quite well for herself in some communal farm or branch of the bureaucracy. (She was no fool, my Rosalind, she was an expert at turning new seemingly inauspicious circumstances to her advantage.)

Supposing she *was* a ghost, an island like this would be the last place she would seek out! I realised, it was not for love of me she had enchanted three of my last four years in the palace.

A few nights later, surprisingly, the poet visited me. He rarely comes in summer.

He even brought the gift of a lobster.

After supper, while I was setting out the pieces on the chessboard, I said casually, 'I thought I saw a young woman on the shore the other morning' . . .

He raised his eyebrows. He nodded. He smiled.

Then the game began.

It might have been two weeks later. I was coming down from the beacon, having set a few more peats into it. It had rained all night, and I was anxious lest the pyre had got wet. I needn't have feared. The piece of old sail, jetsam, that I covered the pyre with was still weather-proof. I wove the new peats in with dry heather, and spread the sail over all, and turned for home.

Half-way down, I saw that the pigeons near the hut door were agitated. There was a fluttering gray column, then arms shook them off, and a very young girl stood there, breaking pieces from a small loaf and scattering it. The loaf was finished – there were no more white fragments – gently the doves protested, they flew about her, they settled on her arms and shoulders and head.

I stumbled down the last slope. It was Rosalind, gone back in time, into childhood beside her peasant cottage! I huried across the stones and yellow iris to greet the dove-coated visitor.

I might have known. When I got to my feet, after a stumble, there was no one there, only doves hopping and pecking at the few last crusts.

An old man, whose faculties are deserting him, falls into drowsings and dreaming. So it must have been with me, on two occasions lately.

But I cannot explain this. There has never been any corn sowed or reaped in this island. That day I held in my hand a fragment of bread, a crust. The pigeons pleaded for it. I denied them.

Three-quarters of a year passed. The sun weakened, until at the solstice it made a brief silver arc between south-east and south-west. The great storms went shouting over the island, days-long, with rain or hail or snow. Then after sunset the sky would clear, and the great hemisphere above was thick with stars. The moon, a girl or a queen or a crone, would linger in the sky, looking into the waters. Day after day was held in a crystalline peace.

At sunset on the darkest day, I laid the ceremonial peat on the pyre: the best peat in the stack, a thick blue-black square.

Miraculously, it seemed, year after year, the sick sun began to renew its strength. But then the worst storms would come – such gales as scoured the poet out of his cave and brought him, blue and spittled with spindrift, to my door.

We would eat hot stew beside the fire. (Every winter saw me well stocked.)

I set out the chessmen.

I said, 'I had a strange dream since I saw you last – how long ago, four months, can it be as long as that? It was a beautiful dream, and yet it was like a knife in my heart. I dreamt I saw a dark-haired girl, no more than ten years old, feeding pigeons outside this hut. She was breaking a loaf of bread among them. The birds rose about her and covered her like a coat.'

He nodded, as much as to say that that was a nice dream to have dreamed.

'Rosalind,' I said. 'You remember Rosalind. The child in this dream was the lady Rosalind.'

He nodded again, curtly. So be it. Enough of dreams. Let the game begin . . .

That wild beautiful winter passed, and now it was spring. Time to turn over the earth in my planticru and sow the vegetables. This April, I noticed, the delving was more difficult for me.

A few weeks on, and a harder task lay ahead, the digging of the peats: the spade turns up great black wet heavy slabs out of the bog, the digger heaves them onto the heather. Then the wet peats have to be set up in a hundred or so little dolmens for wind and sun to dry.

The bird-pipe was everywhere that day, as if the poet was welcoming the birds back to the island.

I drove the spade into the moss again. It struck the edge of a stone. I scraped off the seeping bog, and found that the stone was one upright of a long stone box with a cracked lid. Inside, mummified, lay the body of a very old woman with a tow of gray hair, and with the remnants of a woollen coat about her. The hands were like leaves. The face was a gnarled shrunken nut. The eyelids, black-lashed still, lay light on the blackness beneath. *Rosalind*, I said aloud. This was her, caught in the web and sucked dry by death. I put the stone back carefully, and covered up the grave. I looked for a place fifty yards away to put my spade into.

Yet there is no sign that anyone has ever lived in the island. There would surely have been signs of habitation: burnt stones, artefacts, shards of pottery, arrow-heads.

A queen or an enchantress had been brought here for isolate sepulchre, removed from the comings and goings of men.

I have convinced myself that it was another drowse and dream among the peat-banks on an afternoon in May.

But I will not put my spade into that particular bank again.

That year, the early summer was fragrant with wind and sun. The peats dried quickly, among drifts of bog cotton.

I did not mention the tomb on the hillside to the poet. All summer, he did not visit me. I saw him often, out in his raft fishing, or here and there on the broken stone ladders of the cliff face, putting eggs in a bag.

I listened, enchanted, to the bird notes.

On that very strange day, there he was on the cliff face, moving here and there like a clumsy spider. He had the bag over his shoulder for collecting eggs.

I moved along the beach looking for driftwood.

It was a warm bright afternoon in late summer. Drifting here and there on the shore, finding little, for doubtless he had carried off any driftwood there had been, I was suddenly aware of a silvering in the air, a grayness, a dankness. A bank of fog had moved in suddenly and silently. I was enclosed in a shifting caul, that sometimes thinned out like a web and sometimes was a wet thick fleece. The island seemed either a ghost or a complete blank. My hand was cold and dewed with dampness.

I delighted in those days of sea-haar. Everything was mysterious and surprising. Sounds changed – or does one only imagine that they are more distinct? The visible world becomes

a phantasmagoria. Common features of the natural surround-
ings loom immense and menacing: a rock, a passing cormorant.
The sea and the great crag faces are completely blotted out at
times. Only at times – the sea fog is an inconstant shifting
element. It shredded out – there was the gray heave of ocean,
now the huge crag face loomed more immense than ever, before
the haar wove itself about them once more. It was like the
passing of a multitude of ghosts, legion after legion, endlessly.

The fog thinned. There he was on the cliff, a bewildered
spectre, uncertain which way to move, for one false step would
drop him to his death. He must have made a hesitant step, and
dislodged a stone; it clattered, unnaturally loud, among the
stones at the base; the echoes went on longer than usual. A
frond of fog hid the cragsman from me.

The thought that he was afraid pleased me.

The line of cliffs itself was in constant change and movement
as the mist washed silently among the fissures and outthrusts,
sometimes obliterating, sometimes making strong definitions.

I became gradually aware of the immense face of a woman
sculpted in the crag. The sea-haar spilled across her brow and
nose and jaw, deleting and defining. There she was, looking
calmly out over the blind murmurous sea.

I took a few steps forward. Her profile was lost in a hundred
other blurred perpendiculars. Only from where I happened to
be standing, by accident, was it possible to see this powerful
hewn spirit of the island (for so, in long retrospect, I like to
think of her).

It occurred to me that of course I had see that particular line
of cliff a thousand times. By the light of common day it was
impossible to see her; sun mingled her among the multitude of
perpendiculars: it was the soft hands of haar that had hewn her
out of the rock.

As the fog fingers continued to work on her, the face kept
changing: forbidding, benign, compassionate, mocking. The

haar heightened a cheek-bone, momentarily, and there was the undoubted face of Rosalind. My old heart fluttered inside me! It did not last. A huntress gazed superbly from the cliff – a patient fish-woman – the first girl to step ashore after the ice's retreat, a strong swift delicate assessor of this island and its possibilities . . . Sometimes a silent heave of fog washed out the profile, then once more it defined itself still more powerfully. Time and again, out of those changing densities of wetness, glanced the face of Rosalind.

It amused me, meantime, to watch the struggles of my fellow-islander. He was obviously in difficulties up there. His normal movements along the cliff were fluent and graceful. Today he was like a spider in a broken web. It must have been cold for him up there, too. He moved along a ledge, tentatively, in the direction of The Woman.

From his situation, it was impossible for him to see what I was seeing. He edged closer to the serene powerful face. His fingers were clawing at her stone hair . . .

The fog went, as quickly as it had come. I was aware of points of light in the rockpool, there was a kindling in my hand. I looked behind. The sun had split the fog like a sword; it blazed on the sea. The great fog-bank was a few rags and tendrils. Swiftly the island reassembled itself, it was what it had always been. A few last ghosts, a troop, dwindled round the headland.

On the horizon lay the huge mass of silver-gray that had covered the island for an hour.

The Spirit of the Island was gone too, vanished into a multitude of uneven crannies and perpendiculars. The crags-man sprawled across where her mouth might have been.

The sun had freed him. In the time of a dozen wave-falls he was standing on the shore again, smiling, a young bronze hero in the light. And yet there was still a shadow of terror in his eyes.

He went so far as to give me two eggs. On a normal day this would not have happened.

'Well,' said I, 'that was a near thing, eh? This could have been your last day. One false step in the fog, and down you'd have come, head first, humpty-dumpty. Thank you for the eggs. But I didn't employ you to get eggs, man. I employed you to write poems. Now, supposing you give me a date – a rough estimate – as to when a poem will be ready' . . .

He smiled, sharing the mockery with me. He half-turned. His cave was only yards away, round a cliff buttress.

'She's here,' I said. 'The woman is here, in the island. I've seen her a lot lately. I saw her this morning, hewn out of stone.'

He looked at me gravely. Then he shook his head and left me.

It gladdened me, to think that I had seen her and he had not.

It touched me, with a slow smoulder of rage and envy, that perhaps he had touched her mouth with his mouth, while an old cripple man watched from the shore . . .

One morning, a few weeks later, I saw the poet walking across the hill with a woman.

It was the morning of the autumn equinox.

I had been up to my beacon on the hilltop with the quarterly offering. (I had found a few sea-bleached boards that morning on the shore. I sloped them over my shoulder and made up the shore path to my hut. There he stood in the cave-opening, not at all pleased. What came out of the sea was his . . .)

I had a rest outside the hut; then I put the heraldic cere-monial knife into my belt; then I made for the hill with the kindling. The way up became more and more wearisome. I had to stop often for breath and to rest my leg.

Ah, but the beacon was a formidable thing now – a young god of fire waiting for the torch to be touched to it! And it would be greater yet.

I turned from binding in my boards with thongs of dry heather, and saw that pair crossing the shoulder of the hill, lower down. The young woman was doing all the talking, and once, to emphasise a point, she made a gesture with both hands that I could not possibly mistake.

Rosalind! – It was Rosalind.

I sat down at the base of the pyre. It was impossible. It was utterly impossible . . .

It occurred to me, 'This is the beginning of madness. The delusions have been stealing over you all summer – at first they were sweet and beautiful. This is anguish. It is the loneliness that is making you crazy! It is the presence in the island of one who hates you.'

Three mornings later, I dreamed that someone was singing in the palace garden. I woke. The voice went on, outside the hut door, a conspiratorial urging. 'Too long!' Rosalind was saying. 'The game has gone on too long. You must finish it soon . . . Think, we'll have the island to ourselves – young for ever!' . . . Then, after a pause, 'I do feel a pity for him, wearing out so slowly. It's cruel . . . Finish it soon, for his sake as well as ours' . . .

I heard a clash of stones – the poet moving down from the hut to the shore.

If a man goes mad, in a lonely island, what will the end be? I would have prayed, if I had known how to pray. The time had come, perhaps, to sift through the fragments of ancient wisdom I had hoarded from my youth. Particularly I remembered a long prose-poem about trees and a peasant and a ship. The thing to do, for a man in my desolate ebb-time, was to build a ship out of the wisdom I had learned from my tutors, and discovered for myself in the great library of the palace. Be patient – construct – caulk and fashion and freight – have the keel ready for the rising of the terrible dark waters.

I passed quite a pleasant week, writing down the pensées and poems I remembered, in the intervals between bringing home the peats in a basket and taking the potatoes out of the earth before the autumn rain got to them.

I went down to his cave. There was a word of a poem that I couldn't remember. Memory supplied a word – it did not seem to be the right word. I would ask him. He would say nothing; but he might nod, or shake his head, or (beyond belief) write the actual word with a stick on the sand.

He was standing at the cave entrance as if he half-expected me.

I forgot about the poem and the lost word.

I said, 'You have been stealing things from me, peats and turnips – I know it. Worse, you're robbing me of my youth. You've brought the evil days on me before my time. *This island is mine.* I forbid you to play on that pipe. From now on you are not welcome any more in my hut. What have you done with the years you have taken from me? See to it.'

He put on me one of those grave looks that is the nearest he can get to concern and kindness.

As I climbed up to my hut, I was aware of desolate cries. I paused. It was out of myself that the sorrow was streaming, without let or stint. Tears like dewdrops hung in my beard.

How many years since the year Rosalind was in the island? A dozen, maybe. She has never appeared again.

The bone pipe sounds, sweet and pure, from the skerry. A score of seal faces turn to the music.

Reading over my journal, this strikes me: a reader might think I had quite an exciting time on the island. What ought to have been chiefly recorded is the unutterable dreariness of this exile, day after day of futility and nothingness, the incessant struggle to keep warm, especially at the end of winter and the beginning of spring, when snow lingers and my store of vegetables and salted meat is nearly done, and the peat-stack is down almost to its brown-black mouldering base.

Simultaneously, though, the light is returning. The bright springs begin to well earlier, the sun goes down further to the north each day – I could have notched the point of its setting for a week to come, on this outcrop or that declivity on the hill-line in the west. 'And when it sets over the beacon on the summit, it will be the equinox' . . .

One spring morning I went down to the ebb for food. My store of vegetables was exhausted.

The poet had strung a line of drying fish athwart his cave entrance.

He was that day on the far side of the island – I could hear, faintly, from time to time, a curlew call.

Hunger was a dull clench in my guts. Why should I not take a couple of fish and cook them over my fire? It was my island – everything on it belonged to me – he was my servant.

In the end, I simmered pieces of seaweed in my pot.

Increasingly, the monotony was hard to bear. In the first year or two, there had been a zest and a delight in doing and making things: the hut, the garden, the peat-stack; in close consultation with *The Handyman's Cyclopaedia*, the only book I had been allowed – and how much better it has served me than if I had taken some book of my choice – *The Greek Anthology*, for example. The mere fact that I could nail boards together – who had never done a single thing for myself, life-long – filled me with happiness. That water I drew myself from a rock spring, and was not brought heated in a pitcher by a valet each morning – that was a surprise, a leaping delight. And the low wet slope of the hill – it was full of dark fire that might keep a man warm for a thousand years, if he was willing to work at it. The planticru was a miracle: that a few seeds should, at summer's end, produce pale globes of potatoes by the hundred, and round firm green cabbages with water-drops in the outer curls, and carrots like a torrent of red daggers aimed at earth's centre . . . I had shot deer and grouse ceremonially – but to kill a bird or an animal to keep myself alive, this was to enter upon a kind of bond with the creatures – a blood treaty, in which they forgave me time after time for the cruelty I was forced to inflict on them. Not forgiveness: their innocence knew no such thing. They, in 'their fifth day of creation', had torn the hearts and throats of other creatures. Many a morning, I watched the kestrel pivoting slowly above the hill.

There was something to be said for those early years when I strove to master a few crafts, like some fifth-rate Robinson Crusoe. I think at times I was happier then than I had ever been in a palace or a royal forest. But even then there were long spells, especially in winter, of boredom, futility, regret, longing, wretchedness.

Ah! that was a rustle in the thatch, a wind from the north-east was getting up. Tonight it might be uncomfortable in the cave.

By the time the low knock came to the door, the broth pot was bubbling over the fire, and the chessmen were set out in order. 'Don't knock. Just come in.' And in he came, blue with cold, my silent guest.

But always he knocked first.

Every year the steel-wire meshes thicker in my beard. The palms of my hands are like horn – the backs are slack and blue-veined, but shiny as washed stones when I clench a fist.

Surely he – who hasn't aged by an hour or a year since we were set ashore here – will give me decent burial when he finds me dead, in my garden perhaps, or down among the rockpools . . .

I woke this morning to hear a lark singing. Bitter thought: might it not be the poet pitting himself against the ethereal purity? (So dull my hearing has become.) No – that sifting and spilling, that scattering of the March necklace over the sea and the hill, there was no mistaking the pure song of the lark 'in excelsis' . . .

I knew that, that same evening, the sun would set directly over my beacon: the spring equinox. It did: the interstices of the beacon brimmed with lingering red-gold fire.

I laboured up the hill, slowly, to lay a celebratory peat on the pyre. I wore the knife in my belt.

Summer lay before us – another summer – whatever it would bring.

The bone pipe had been urgent all day with many cries, as if he was summoning back the birds, one after another, to their summer bourne.

There it was suddenly, a mile or so offshore, in the lingering summer twilight – a yacht!

There was no time to lose. The sails were furled in the light airs – the sea as far as the horizon was one luminous darkling gleam – engine power was taking the yacht northwards slowly; I could hear the gentle pulse of the engine.

I lit the heather torch at my fire and set off, a wavering rag of flame, for the hilltop. The moths were amazed, a few accompanied me all the way.

I had to go carefully. The sun had just gone down in the north-west. The path I knew well in broad daylight had become eerie and perilous in twilight, 'the two lights', dying sun and first brilliant star.

From time to time I looked back. The yacht was lit from stem to stern. Perhaps she would drop anchor in the bay. No: through the still darkling air came the leisurely 'chug-chug' of engines.

Then, against the ridge of the hill, climbing too, but far more lithely than me, was the poet. He had seen the yacht. There he was going up, urgent to signal from the beacon. No doubt he was right – he would get to the summit far sooner than me, with my withered leg and bruised lungs. But I felt a resentment. I had spent years – how many? – building and tending the pyre, nourishing it, keeping it from rain and snow. Surely I alone had the right to summon the yacht.

I had to sit down on an outcrop, now and again, to get my breath. The yacht still drifted north on her gentle heart-beat. Then I heard it, a thin ghost of music from the vessel. A violin? No, there was a weave of instruments. Someone had put a wax disc in the phonograph, and the horn was sending forth the music on the waters.

Climbing up, I saw that the poet had arrived at the summit. The pyre stood black still against the roseate sky.

I limped and slithered up the last scree, a man of smoke and flames. I summoned the utmost of my breath to shout at him, 'Why aren't you doing something? Wave your coat, man! They'll see you against the sunset. We must hurry!' And I thrust my torch into the heart of the beacon. It hissed like a nest of snakes, and went out.

I saw what my enemy had done – he had emptied a bucket of sea water over the beacon. More: he had festooned it with wet seaweed, a whole sackful. The empty sack lay at his feet beside the bucket.

He laughed.

I struck him with the bone knife. I struck him again and again. I felt the tremor of the knife going into soft flesh, the jar of it striking against bone.

And again – into where, in that darkness, I guessed his heart might be . . .

He made no move to defend himself.

A fleck of his blood came on my lips, salty.

(He could easily have kicked the knife out of my hand. He could have lifted me and flung me against the beacon, to cool off among his sea-tangles. He had done nothing to defend himself.)

The sound that came from him, lying there on the scree, was the black death cry. It sounded little different from his mockery.

I didn't wait. I stumbled over something – his body or the bucket – in the darkness.

Very slowly, now, because there was no moon, I groped my way down the path.

The yacht was still there, but far off now, a line of glow-worms on the horizon.

I fell to thinking about the sailors and passengers. Were they dancing still to the music of the phonograph? It was late: they were probably sitting down to their supper at a long table – a wealthy host and hostess and their guests, men and women of birth and wealth, drawn north by the enchantment of mid-summer, that is nowhere so beautiful as at sea. Light talk and laughter over the wine. A young man and a girl exchanging secret looks – love is born of the rhythms of sea and light; 'the two lights', dawn and the last star.

Suppose they had seen our fire on the island, would they have done anything about it? If a small boat had rowed from yacht to island, what could they have done with two crazy-looking creatures, one broken with sickness and twenty-five winters, the other a young sea-god with the throat of a bird?

My poet was right.

Here we were. Here we had been fated to bide till time shore our threads. It was good, so. There was no place on earth for us, but here alone.

Ah, here we were. But the young immortal was dead. The old done man, the murderer, was alone on the island!

I broke some peats into the half-dead fire in the hut.

I lit the lamp.

I would bury him in the morning – it was the least I could do.

I thought of dragging him down and burying him in the sand, deep. The sea would cover him twice a day. That was his element, water.

There had never been room for two princes in the island. The wonder is, we had existed together so long.

The island was mine, the waters about it and the sky above it, all the way up to the burning centre, the sun. The revolutionary government, mockingly, had given it to me, a crust of my country, all that was left after the royal banquet I had lingered at so long, so arrogantly, so thoughtlessly and thanklessly – as the Congress of Vienna had thrown Elba to Napoleon.

But that another prince should have been set ashore: one who truly 'saw into the life of things', and had lordship and governance of a realm where I could never set foot . . . That he too, the silent one, was a prince: I only understood that now, when he was dead.

And not dead, either, according to the acceptable ordering of nature, but *murdered*. And here I stood, trembling, between the lamp and the fire at midnight, judge and murderer, both.

And executioner also.

I would yield that function to time. I lacked the courage and the will to be 'an antique Roman'. Time was fretting my thread fast, fast. It could not be long.

I felt in my girdle for the knife. And I touched the bone pipe of the poet . . .

I looked out of the window. The yacht, with its cargo of music and jewels, was under the horizon.

I did not bury him in the morning. Either the weather was too bad, or I shrank from the task.

Days passed. I didn't go near the hilltop.

I justified myself, as more and more days passed without the living performing its duty to the dead.

It was justice that he should lie and rot beside the pyre he had ruined.

I was the man of earth and fire. He had had keeping of air and water. Let the rain wash the festerings from his bones. Let the birds – let the birds he had mocked so long with his pipe – let the birds pick him clean.

Ariel was dead. I had dismissed him, given him his quitance. 'To the elements, and be thou free' . . .

It was well.

Time soon to break the rod, bury the book.

I spent a day or two idling by the shore, if it can be called idling when a man must hobble from rock to rock, painfully, on a stick. I looked into his cave – that a man could have existed so long in such desolation, and kept his youth until the end!

I knew myself to be much feebler. The thread was fraying fast. The quicker the better! And yet the terror of the last thin strand going – no, not so much that as that there would then be no web of senses to respond to the endless beauty of earth and sky and sea, all that treasury squandered, no mind to note solstice and equinox, the year's quarterings.

How went it now with the dead man on the summit? Unweavings, unravellings, tearings. Would a cheek-bone be showing?

Sometimes, as I stood watching the waves breaking, I thought of the blows I had struck – and then I felt again the surge of power in my arm. Ah, that was the greatest thing I had ever done! – never had I experienced such joy and beauty! Little wonder that soldiers are the world's darlings, who have filled history with such horror, hunger, and desolation. To kill is the greatest of joys. To acquiesce and to be the victim: that too is to drink deep. The killer and the killed lean towards each other, give and take the kiss of utter fulfilment. 'Each man kills the thing he loves' . . .

Shuttling such nonsense through my mind, I was aware of a flash of silver in a gathering wave. The wave broke. A live cod thrashed at my feet.

A gift of the sea.

It writhed strenuously in my hands, slipped through, fell back on the sand, that dulled its splendour, put sackcloth of sand on it. Then I carried it, still alive but the sea life ebbing out of it, up the sea path to my hut. It gave a last gulp and the air choked it.

'I do not need the fisherman. The sea will give me what I need' . . .

The fish simmered in the pot. To pass the time, I began to arrange the chessmen on the board for a game that would not be played.

I found that I was setting two plates and two forks.

There was a knock at the door. The door opened and the poet stood there.

Quietly he took his place at the table.

It was I who felt like the ghost – such vacancy, such ice at the heart – as I divided the fish into two portions, and filled the plates and sat down opposite him.

We ate in silence. Having managed to swallow a first barbed-wire gobbet, I took a covert look at him. There was no change. Where was the pattern of wounds in his head and throat and chest? Nothing: only the one long transverse silver scar on the forearm, where a hook had cut him fifteen years since.

I managed to say when we were scraping the bones, 'Ah, you didn't know that I could fish' . . . A slow shaking of the head. And again, just before the game of chess began, 'Now then, it is really time that the poem was ready! I give you notice, I want it before the winter solstice. Agreed?'

He nodded.

We fought the game to a draw.

I said, putting the pieces away, 'I found your bone pipe. I think you must have left it on the table, last time you visited. Here, take it.'

He held up his hand. He shook his head. He wouldn't be needing his pipe again.

I did not feel like Macbeth when Banquo comes to the feast, a ghost. At least, not after that first quake of terror, when I dropped the fork into the simmering fish pot.

This meeting turned out to be as pedestrian as all our other meetings.

I gave him a turnip and some onions to take home with him.

Leaving, he took my hand in the doorway. This had never happened before.

The thought that he is back again and living in the island: as I went to bed, that realisation put surge after surge of joy through me.

And yet, everything is not as it was. For one thing, the bird notes are no longer heard from this part of the island or that. Only the natural bird cries, and they are beautiful enough. Yet there is the desolate feeling that between us and them a gulf is fixed: there should be a man with a bird-mask and a bird-whistle trying forever to tie up this thread in the broken web of nature.

Ah, the rush of blood to my head one morning when I was carrying full water buckets from the spring! Sky and earth and sea reeled round me. I came to, sitting in the heather. A surfeit – I had eaten too much for breakfast, I ought to have known better, an old man like me – the tide of the blood obstacled and held back, momentarily, by a block of food. But when I tried to lift the water buckets, one in each hand, there was no power in my left arm. The face that looked back at me from the trembling water mirror seemed to be wrenched to one side.

'He won't bury you either,' I thought to myself, as I accepted this new intimation of mortality. 'It will never occur to him.'

I dragged home. I slept the afternoon out. When I woke I felt stronger. I had to make two journeys for the water bucket, my left arm being still weak.

By the end of that week, I seemed to have most of my strength back. But not all. Another invisible fine filament is gone. The thread shears and frays.

If this wretchedness happens again, it might be difficult next spring to delve my garden and dig the dark fire out of the hill.

The wearing-out of the mind, that is more to be dreaded. A

strange thing happened. I do not know whether it was dream or actuality.

Since the passing-by of the yacht and its music, I no longer bother with the beacon on the hill. I carried one evening a few bits of driftwood from the shore. When I opened the hut door, a bird flew at me! – I was aware only of a storm of curves, talons, beak and wings, that enveloped my face, and then was out and away on the wind. The sea-bleached boards lay about the floor. I sat – how long? – in the deep chair, then I got up and looked outside. A kestrel was drifting on the wind, high up: my assailant. But how had it got into the hut? – I always, leaving it even briefly, close the door against rats. (The island from end to end is scrawled over with rats.)

The talons had gone into my cheek and brow – the sensation of the eager curves entering was so vivid. Yet when I took my hand from my face, there was no blood.

I had dreamed it. I had drowsed off in the chair and dreamed all that of the kestrel.

When, later, I stooped to gather my pieces of driftwood, there was a kestrel feather on the floor.

But it could easily have fallen from the poet's coat. He comes from the cliff often, or from the hill, mottled with feathers.

Last summer he had tamed a kestrel. I would meet him among the rocks with the fierce blood-drinker sitting tranquil on his wrist . . . And I had said to him, mild and mocking, 'You know, you have no right to that bird. It belongs to the hill, it is mine. You should have asked my permission' . . .

Another image: dream or reality? I am standing on top of the sea-bank. There, below me, the poet is making marks on the sand with a stick. I bend forward. No random markings – he is forming letters, words. The wild idea storms into my mind, *The poem!* He is writing the poem. There, on the tide's brimming edge, at last, the poem. A foolish nineteenth-century jingle comes: 'Lives of great men all remind us / We may make our lives sublime / And departing leave behind us / Footprints on the sands of time' . . . I am hurrying down the shore path. The poet is there still, writing. But the sea is flowing, the tide is coming in fast, the tide is lipping the poem, a new wave washes the side of it away. I hurry and stumble over a ridge of rock, as fast as my poor leg will allow me. The poet throws his stick into the sea – he turns to me and shakes his head – then he walks away swiftly, he begins to run, he leaps from rock to rock. By the time I get to the poem, the sea has erased it, except for two words, *end* and *again*: the last words of two disparate lines. Another wave, and even the ruins of the poem is cancelled.

This was a dream – no doubt about that. I woke in my chair, the images throbbing in my mind. I thought angrily, 'That foolish Victorian rhymester, he took no account of the sea.'

Yet the dream had roots in actuality. Some earlier morning, a month since, perhaps, I had indeed seen the poet making idle marks on the sand with a stick.

And what were the knocking and chipping sounds I had been hearing frequently from the cliffs lately?

Let him be about his business.

His bird notes no longer imitated curlew and kittiwake and fulmar and red-throated diver.

I missed that.

The birds had withdrawn into their own realm. Between 'the fifth and sixth days' a bridge was down.

His pipe lay on a ledge in my hut, gathering dust.

More and more often I slept during the day, in my chair. It might be that I will be eased so, gently, into oblivion.

Dreams, dreams – my day is fretted with dreams. At night I hardly sleep at all, because of the wanderings of my mind into past and future, like a prisoner in a treadmill, round and round, an endless futile trampling.

The poet came, one fine summer evening: an unusual thing. I offered him food, a vegetable soup. (I am no longer so skilful in the trapping of birds and rabbits.) No. A shake of the head. He has eaten. He will play a game of chess.

We play. By this time we have gotten so accustomed to each other's style of play, that most of the games are boring – we foresee each other's moves, from a distance. White against red, they lock and clinch, time after time: a stasis, after a few blind blunderings across a tilt-yard.

Occasionally, still, a surprising thing happens, like a trumpet blast. Then the chessmen hover and pounce, the game moves swiftly to its end.

A hand opens, acknowledges defeat, offers a truce.

Tonight there are no surprises. We have been this way often before.

I had seen a few chess masters in the palace in my youth, and their games had kindled a wonderment in me. The board had seemed like a mirror of life – a contention of opposites: ice and fire; animal and angel; past and future; sword and plough; palace and sty; wheel and axe; stone and spring; crib and coffin; loom and moth; machine and flower – all held in this slow dance of red counters and white counters on a board of sixty-four squares.

I used to pride myself on the general neatness of my cabin. Once a week everything – shelves, fireplace, floor – was swept and washed. Lately, a sun-shaft discovers a layer of dust, wherever it strikes.

He raised his hand. The game was drawn.

I nodded.

Then with his forefinger he wrote on the dust of the table:

THE POEM IS MADE.

'This is good news,' I said. (My heart was a stone.)

He looked at me. I ought to be making further enquiries. I said nothing.

He rose from the chair and gestured me to follow.

The sun was down, but the evening was still bright, and as sometimes happens then a sea-haar had crept in silently. He gestured me down to the beach. Well, the tide had ebbed. The poem, if it was written on the sand, would still be there.

The sand had only a few shells and strands of seaweed.

I followed him, very cripple.

He waited, patient and courteous, till I came up with him. He pointed to the cliff, half-way up. The poem was there! He had cut it into the rockface. Like a deaf-mute he pointed and gestured: cliff, poet, prince, poem.

There and nowhere else was the poem, my poem, his life's work.

It was time now for the poem to be read. I was to go with him, at once, now, before it got dark.

I said, 'I'm very glad you've been able to make the poem, at last. I'm glad that it exists here, on our island. But it must be obvious to you that I can't get up there to read it. It has taken all my strength to walk down to the beach.'

He looked at me as if I was a pig who had turned away from an offered jewel.

The shadow was on his face. Once more he pointed. The poem was there, up there, carved. We were to go up and read it together. There was no other way. He took me by the elbow, beseechingly. I was to come at once. He would help me.

'Listen, man,' I said. (I had forgotten his name.) 'Write it on the sand – I'll memorise it – I'm good at that.'

It would not do. Once more he threw up his hand at the cliff face.

From where we stood it was impossible – even if I had the eyes of a hawk – to read any markings on the cliff. It would have been impossible, even at noon. And now, shadows and a gray bloom of sea-haar were investing the interstices.

It struck me that the poem was carved in the region of the

crag where, one summer day long ago, the fog had sculpted the woman's face.

'The simplest thing of all,' I said, 'would be for you to write the poem in my notebook. There is a page or two left. My last pencil is worn down to a stump.'

I was talking to vacancy. He had left me, he had gone into his cave. I was conscious of a seething rage in the air.

Ah, but this must have been a dream, too. I woke up in my chair, cold, for the fire was out. The window was a script of stars. I got into bed, but I did not sleep until the dawn dappled one wall with wavering golden sea-lights.

It had been a strange cruel dream, yet somewhere in it was a promise.

The chess pieces stood on the board as we had left them the night before.

The writing THE POEM IS MADE was there, on the dust of the table.

I put on my coat.

The best thing, from now on, is to ignore him, I think: neither to give him house-room nor to accept the fish he brings me from time to time. He is generous as never before with fish. Twice or thrice a week he lays them on my doorstep, the quicksilver still on them.

I took my bucket and went slowly to the spring for water. The water was slow in dribbling into the bucket that morning. When it was half full, I turned. He was standing nearby. He held out his hand – he would carry home my bucket for me.

I saw, with utter amazement, that he had been weeping.

Sorrow had cleansed him. He stood like Tithonus in the dawn: not on that first morning in the music-room, presenting his blank sheet of paper, had he looked so powerful, so pitiful, or so pure.

He carried the water bucket to the hut. He carried in peats from the stack and filled the hearth-side box.

The fire he lit blazed up at once. He put a fish in the pot.

Then this happened, more staggering to me than a blow from his fist. He bent over me and kissed me on the cheek.

He took his pipe from the shelf and left the hut.

Now it was no more bird cries; it was like the song of Adam giving names to the birds and all creatures. Never had I heard such beautiful sounds.

I know this now: all that has happened to me in this island has been a dream, such as might come between bullets leaving the guns of executioners and entering the chambers of a condemned man's heart.